FOUR YEARS GONE

ALSO BY DALLAS GORHAM

The Carlos McCrary PI Mystery Thriller Series

Six Murders Too Many

Double Fake, Double Murder

Quarterback Trap

Dangerous Friends

Day of the Tiger

McCrary's Justice

Yesterday's Trouble

Four Years Gone

Debt of Honor

Sometimes You Lose

FOUR YEARS GONE

CARLOS MCCRARY PI
BOOK 8

DALLAS GORHAM

Book and cover design by eBook Prep
www.ebookprep.com

August 2023
ISBN: 978-1-64457-649-6

ePublishing Works!
644 Shrewsbury Commons Ave
Ste 249
Shrewsbury PA 17361
United States of America
www.epublishingworks.com
Phone: 866-846-5123

ONE

Carlos McCrary

M y cellphone played *The Eyes of Texas* as my crazy Aunt Carrie's picture flashed on the screen.

Oh, Christ, I thought. *Aunt Carrie: That's all I need to ruin a perfectly promising day.*

Aunt Carrie wore reindeer antlers on a gold headband; her hair colored red and green. A Santa Claus earring hung from one ear, a tiny tree ornament from the other. I had snapped that picture when I visited Adams Creek, Texas for Christmas. A relic from a happier time, almost ancient history.

It was a week after Labor Day. In Port City, Florida, where I live, the temperature was in the low eighties and the sun had climbed halfway up the eastern sky. The sea breeze chased scattered puffy clouds across the heavens. After working at home all morning, I planned to spend the afternoon with friends, fishing in the Gulf Stream on my boat, *The Gator Raider Too.*

Aunt Carrie's call changed that. Forcing a smile, I accepted the video call.

"Aunt Carrie, how nice to see you."

Her hair was salon blonde to mask the encroaching gray of middle age. Faint crow's-feet traced the corners of her red-rimmed eyes. "Is this a bad time, Chuck?"

Anytime was a bad time for crazy Aunt Carrie to call, but I was much too polite to say that. Aunt Carrie can talk the ears off an elephant. At best, she jibber-jabbers trivia for a half hour until I pretend I have an appointment. At worst, she ruins my day.

I edged the wireless keyboard to one side. No more work for me for a while.

"I always make time for family, Aunt Carrie."

"It's about Emily."

The name sent a shot of adrenaline coursing through my veins. Ghosts of old memories wrenched at my gut.

Out of habit, I swiveled my desk chair to the framed, original 1936 *Dick Tracy* Sunday comic displayed on my wall. Another relic.

Too late, I realized Aunt Carrie could see the wall in the background on our video call. "You spun around to look at Dick Tracy, didn't you, Chuck?"

Whenever I walk in my home office and see that comic, it reminds me of Emily. That's a good thing, even though it hurts. Like this whole conversation with Carrie hurt, pulling scabs off the unhealed wounds to my conscience.

Acid rose from the back of my throat. Did Aunt Carrie intend to resurrect that heartache? "You have news about Emily?"

"Yes and no."

"Aunt Carrie, even the world's greatest private investigator can't solve a riddle from a clue like *yes and no*. Tell me what happened."

"I heard from Emily."

"That's great news. Where has she been the last four-and-a-half years?"

"I can't tell. She approached me in a vision."

Oh, geez. Every time I wedge myself into an economy seat for the three-hour flight from Florida to Austin to visit my aunt and uncle, I know Carrie will recite my horoscope from the newspaper each day I'm there.

While I love her sincerely, it's hard to fathom how a college graduate can believe in auras and astrology. Now visions? Just one more reason my cousins and I think of her as our crazy aunt. Of course, it didn't help when Carrie *McCrary* married Frank *Crazinski* and became Carrie *Crazinski*. It was only a baby step to calling her Crazy Aunt Carrie.

On the other hand, she and Uncle Frank figure I committed treason against the Great State of Texas when I earned my criminology degree from the University of Florida rather than the University of Texas. Nobody's perfect.

"A vision? Emily approached you in a vision?"

"My horoscope predicted it. It said to be receptive to new approaches. Last night, Emily stood at the foot of my bed and said, 'Mom, I need you. Please, come find me.' I saw and heard Emily clear as a bell. As unmistakably as I see you right now. It happened around midnight."

"And you were asleep?"

"It was midnight; of course, I was asleep. Emily woke me. I was drenched in a cold sweat."

"I see." Next, would come the favor that would suck me into the gravitational field of my crazy aunt's Black Hole. Despite her good intentions, Aunt Carrie's favors always affected me that way. Maybe this once, I should decline. But I knew I wouldn't. She's family.

"I know what you're thinking, nephew, but I didn't imagine this. I've dreamed thousands of dreams, good and bad, but never like this. It was like Emily in the flesh. Well, sort of..."

"That's why you called it a vision instead of a dream?"

"Yes." She straightened her shoulders. "Emily is alive and she communicated with me...spiritually or telepathically. I'm not sure how she did it."

When Aunt Carrie goes into mystic mode, it's better to go with the flow. "In the vision, did she say anything else? Maybe give you a clue where she is?"

Carrie shook her head. "Only what I told you, 'Mom, I need you. Please, come find me.'"

"Did you tell Uncle Frank?"

"Of course. He was asleep beside me. The vision woke me and I woke Frank." She waved a hand. "You know Frank. He pooh-poohed it. He said her ghost wants me to find her…" She stopped, then shook her head. "Find her body and give it a Christian burial."

"Do you think that's what Emily meant?"

Carrie pursed her lips. "I don't know whether Emily is alive or not. Maybe Frank's right. Maybe it was her spirit asking me to find her body." Carrie's image on the phone jumped as she waved her hands. "But she could be alive and being held captive in some lunatic's basement."

"For more than four years?" That thought jerked at my insides again. If that were true, my failure to find Emily four years before was even worse.

Carrie's eyes flashed. "It's happened to other girls. I looked it up on the internet. Remember those girls in Detroit or Cleveland or someplace? The kidnapper held them captive for ten years before they escaped. Emily's been gone less than that."

She was right. It was possible. Stranger things had happened. Still…Up to now, this conversation had been the windup. Now she was about to deliver the pitch. No sense delaying the inevitable.

"Carrie, I'm glad you heard from Emily. I'm always glad when you call, but you didn't call just to tell me about your vision, did you?" It felt almost dishonest to call it a vision, but I didn't feel like fighting over terminology.

"I want you to find Emily."

Bang. She had dropped the other shoe. This was no favor; it was a commitment of monumental proportions.

"How does Frank feel about it?"

Carrie made a sour face.

"You know Frank. He thinks Carrie's…" She hesitated. "He thinks she's gone for good. He says we should get on with our lives without Emily. He wants to adopt an older child, for goodness sakes."

"Did you tell Detective Ortega about your dream?"

Carrie's lips tightened into a hard line. "Don't call it a *dream*. I saw Emily clear as day, standing right there at the end of the bed."

Oops. That slip of my tongue hadn't made either of us feel any better. "Sorry, Aunt Carrie. Did you tell the detective about your *vision*?"

"I made Frank call him first thing this morning. Lord knows, *I* couldn't handle that arrogant, know-it-all SOB again. His aura is dark purple. He refuses to do anything to find Emily."

"Forgetting his aura for the moment, what did Ortega *say?*"

Carrie blinked away tears. "Detective Ortega said he can't investigate a *dream*. He called it a *dream* too instead of a *vision*, but what can you expect from that prick?"

I pictured Ortega on the phone, scowling as Frank told him about Carrie's *vision*. It was not a pretty picture.

"Carrie, with no new leads or new clues, Ortega has nothing to investigate. When Emily disappeared, I rechecked everything the police had done. They made a good, by-the-book investigation."

"But they didn't *find* her, for God's sake. They didn't *find* her."

Carrie seemed about to cry.

Me too, because I hadn't found her either. Every day that passed I saw something to remind me of my missing cousin.

"Emily's out there, Chuck, I *feel* it. I don't expect you to work for free. Please, try again, one more time. What could it hurt?"

"Carrie, with no new evidence and no new leads, it's a waste of everyone's time."

"I'll pay you, Chuck."

"I love you dearly, Aunt Carrie, but I have other responsibilities. There are clients here in Port City who need me. I reconciled with my girlfriend Terry Kovacs and we're working to rebuild our relationship. Reopening Emily's case could swallow days, even weeks. And with no new evidence…"

"I said I'll pay you."

"Damn it, Carrie, it's not the money. You know that. If I come to Austin, it's because you all are family. I don't charge my family. But it's pointless. Uncle Frank is right; you need to get on with your lives. We all do."

You hypocrite! Every time I noticed the Dick Tracy comic, I resolved to put Emily's disappearance behind me and move on with my life, but the hole in my heart was still there. It was far easier to give advice than accept it, even the advice you give yourself.

Carrie's lips compressed into a thin crease. "Nephew, I'll tell you what I told your Uncle Frank: While there's breath in my body, I will never give up hope of finding Emily. Never."

She sighed. "Promise me you'll think about it. Discuss it with Dad. Your Grandpa Magnus is a wise man. Talk to Michael too. Your father would never steer you wrong."

In ending the call, I promised Aunt Carrie I would think about it. That was a lie. The whole idea was ridiculous. The whole family knew it. The whole Austin Police Department knew it.

Letting my previous online research slide, I scrolled my phone's pictures until I located the one from Emily's driver's license. Sun-lightened, shoulder-length hair curled at the ends and wavy on top, tucked behind her ears; cornflower-blue eyes; and a wide innocent smile that knew no fear and anticipated no evil. I'd downloaded it when I traveled to Austin the first time to search for Emily. I'd showed that picture to hundreds of people at James Bonham High School, in her neighborhood, and in neighborhood shops and stores. People knew Emily and recognized her picture, but nobody had seen her since she disappeared.

I kept the picture to remind me I had failed. It kept me humble. The ache in my heart receded sometimes, buried under other concerns, but it always surfaced again, like when I worked the case of that Nebraska girl who vanished in Port City. She and Emily looked enough alike to be sisters.

I have other pictures, including a family photo taken the Christmas after Emily's sixteenth birthday. Proud of her new driver's license, she showed it to anyone who would look. She had driven her parents to Adams Creek in the Ford Fiesta they gave her for her birthday. I snapped her picture in front of our grandparents' house in her new Bonham Bobcats letter jacket, standing beside the red Ford, her arm draped across the car's shiny roof. She grinned like a cat in a fish market.

Later, she drove me to the Dairy Queen and asked about my time in the army. Emily planned to follow my example and join the army after graduation, then enroll in the University of Florida after her enlistment was up. She felt the time away from home would help her develop as an independent adult, away from sticky family pressure. She swore me to secrecy because she worried that her parents would be against both the army and the University of Florida. Carrie and Frank were diehard Longhorns.

Emily was a sophomore, so she might change her plans three or four times before she graduated. Still, it gave me a tug of pride that she wanted to follow me into serving our country and as a Florida Gator, but she didn't know the real story. Since I was the closest thing she had to an older brother, I had to tell her the truth.

I had slurped a spoonful of my chocolate shake while I considered how to share my deep, dark secret. "Cuz, I didn't join the army to serve my country. I joined to escape a broken heart. The patriotism came later."

"A broken heart? Tough guy Chuck?"

"I never told you about Liz Johannes, my first love?"

"No, you didn't. I would remember that, because I have my own first love." She smiled—shyly, I thought.

"Anyone I know?"

"You tell me first. Then I'll tell you."

"Fair enough. Liz and I met when we were sophomores at Teddy Roosevelt High. I had just won the starting tight end position and the Rough Riders went to the playoffs. Liz was in my homeroom and flirted with me all through football season, but I was terrified of girls."

"You? Afraid of girls? You got a medal for shooting it out with a dozen Taliban. You're not afraid of anything."

Emily was exaggerating about my medal, but then was not the time to tell her about the member of my Triple Seven squad we lost in Afghanistan.

"You better believe it, Cuz. Not only was I afraid of girls, I still am somewhat. Here's the first humiliating fact: I never asked a girl out on a first date; they always asked me first."

Emily's eyes narrowed. "Mags never told me that." Mags—Margarita —is my younger sister.

"There are some things I can tell you that I couldn't tell my own sister."

Emily scoffed.

I raised my right hand. "Hand to God, I have never asked any woman for a first date without her approaching me first. I can converse with any adult, man or woman, on regular social topics: weather, sports, the economy. Even religion and politics. But you girls terrify me. The spring semester of our sophomore year, Liz cornered me walking back to class after a school assembly. She grabbed my hand, pulled me into a janitor's closet, and kissed me so hard I thought she would suck my tongue out of my head. Startled the heck out of me."

"No kidding?"

"No kidding."

"That was your first French kiss?"

I nodded. "Next excruciating secret: I said the stupidest thing anybody could say."

"What was that?"

"I said, 'What did you do that for?'"

Emily giggled. When she giggled, she looked about six years old and as cute as a basket of puppies.

I raised my hand again. "Hand to God. And Liz answered, 'Because I want you to be my boyfriend.' I said okay, and she said I should learn to kiss better. She promised to teach me after school, because we shouldn't be late to class."

"That's incredible. I never knew that."

"I never told anyone. After school, Liz took me back to the janitor's closet and gave me kissing lessons." I grinned. "She was a good, enthusiastic teacher."

"Did, uh…did you…?"

Despite our familiarity, Emily couldn't bring herself to ask if Liz and I had had sex.

"Not then. That started a few days later and went on all through the rest of high school."

"How long were y'all together?"

"Over two years. By the time we were in the spring semester of our senior year, I was in love. I planned to propose at our Senior All-Night Party."

"You're kidding," she said. "You would ask her to marry you when you had never dated another girl?"

"It sounds improbable, but I was as romantic as any teenage girl. I confused sex with love. While I thought we were making love, Liz was just having sex, if you see the distinction."

"What happened? How did she break your heart?"

"The night of the Senior All-Night Party, she told me she had been accepted at Northwestern University and intended to start summer school in Chicago after graduation. We had never discussed our plans after high school. She never asked my plans before she made hers. That's when I realized I was irrelevant to her decision."

Emily stirred her shake. "Why didn't you go to Northwestern to be with her?"

"Because she didn't encourage, even me a little bit. In hindsight, I realized I was a high school romance to Liz—her training wheels for real love."

"How did it end?"

"After graduation, we had one last date. She banged my brains out in the hayloft of our barn one last time, then she announced she was driving to Chicago the next morning."

"Bummer. Did it hurt?"

I shrugged. "I survived. I always survive. It helped that Dad told me three different girls broke his heart before he met Mom. I told myself, 'That's heartbreak number one,' and joined the army the next week."

I stuffed my used napkin in the empty cup. "No patriotism involved. I didn't join to serve my country; I joined to get away from painful memories."

Emily twisted a paper napkin in her hands. She studied that wrinkled napkin as if it held the secrets to the Universe. I could tell she wanted to tell me her first love story, but was hesitant.

"Cuz, I just shared my most embarrassing secret with you. I know you won't tell anyone." Touching her hand for a second, I said, "What do you want to tell me?"

She set the napkin down but didn't look at me. "I have a first love too."

"That's good news. Anyone I know?"

She hesitated for a moment. "No, and that's all I'll say right now. I'm not even sure it's real love. I want to see where it goes. Maybe I'll tell you about it when I see you at Easter."

Of course, Easter never came for Emily. That Christmas was the last time I saw her.

I thought I had lied to Carrie when I promised to think about taking the case, but it seemed I hadn't. Just because I was considering Emily's case didn't mean I would reopen it. Terry and I had reunited less than a week before. We were working out the kinks in her schedule as a police detective and mine as a private investigator so we could spend more time together.

My client responsibilities were real. A large insurance company had hired me to investigate a policyholder who claimed a car accident had totally disabled him. The insurance company smelled a rat. If the case worked out, it would generate a stream of lucrative investigations. I was developing background on the policyholder's personal life when Carrie called.

But, dammit, I felt guilty that I hadn't found Emily. I was a rookie detective then—green as they come. Since then I had developed much useful, but painful, experience.

When I called my father, Michael McCrary, he answered on the first ring.

"Hello, son. Did Carrie call you?"

"Yeah. What did she tell you?"

"That Emily appeared in a vision last night. She asked Carrie to come find her. I'm sure she told you."

"Yeah. It was a vivid dream. She called it a vision. Why did she call you, Dad?"

"If I know my sister, I bet she called everyone in the family. Carrie believes Emily sent her a message. She called it an 'approach' since that's what her horoscope said. She believes it means Emily is alive."

"Do you think she's alive?"

Dad smiled dolefully. "I think Carrie is my sister and I love her."

"But do you believe Emily communicated to Carrie in a dream?"

"Your Aunt Carrie is your Aunt Carrie. She believes Emily contacted her, or approached her, or whatever she chooses to call it. That event is real to her. Who am I to say? Your grandpa had a vivid dream in Vietnam when

14

his grandfather—my great grandfather—died. Dad already knew his grandpa had died before he received word through the Army."

"I never heard that story."

"Things happen that no one can explain. The odds are overwhelming that Emily is dead. You and I know that, and Carrie does too. She knows it in her head, but she can't accept it in her heart. Unless and until someone finds Emily's body, Carrie won't give up hope, and she shouldn't. That hope makes her life worthwhile. Between us, I believe the hope keeps her sane. If she loses hope, God knows what she'll do."

"She asked me to reopen the case. She offered to pay me."

"I know. She asked me if she could call you. I told her she didn't need my permission."

"Should I do it? Should I reopen the case?"

"Not my decision, son."

"I have to run McCrary Investigations, you know."

"That's why what I think is not important. It's your business, your life, your time, and your decision."

"A new insurance company client hired me last week on a disability fraud case. They can send me more business and I hate to make them wait."

"Can Snoop or some of your other operatives handle the insurance case?"

"Yeah, but for new clients, I want them to know the boss is involved."

Dad and I stared at each other over the phone. As I rocked in my chair, the creak of leather and springs filled the silence.

"Son, why don't you call your grandfather and discuss this with him?"

———

"Hi, Grandpa."

My Grandpa Magnus's expression creased into a wide grin. "I figured you'd call. Did Carrie ring you?"

Grandpa Magnus knew that phones don't ring anymore, but he still said that occasionally.

"She wants me to reopen Emily's case."

"Figured as much. You going to do it?"

"I haven't decided. I called about something else. Dad told me that when you served in Vietnam, you knew your grandfather died before the Army notified you. Is that right?"

"Pretty much. Is that what you called about?"

"Yes. That story sounds, uh, magical. If it happened, what was it? A dream, a vision, a premonition? It sounds like more than a coincidence."

"It happened and it was no coincidence. I was in 'Nam, asleep in a tent. Middle of the night, my grandfather comes to me. I had visited him three or four times in Northern Ireland where he lived. He didn't speak to me in my dream like Emily did to Carrie. He smiled and waved, and I knew it was goodbye. Two days later the Army notified me that he had passed away in his sleep, but I already knew."

"Do you believe Emily communicated with Carrie like your grandfather did with you?"

"I believe it's possible. I also believe it's possible that Carrie misses Emily so much that she conjured a vision from an emotional craving. Your Aunt Carrie, when it comes to thinking, her foundation ain't built exactly on the level."

"So much is happening in my life and my business that my first inclination was to tell her 'no.' But then I remembered a case I worked earlier this year—a missing Nebraska teenager who was a sex slave. We were able to find her, eventually. What if Emily is alive somewhere, forced into prostitution. Maybe we could find her too."

"You'd feel like the lowest scumbag on earth if you discovered later she was alive, but you had refused to hunt for her? Right?"

Grandpa had read my mind.

"The odds that I'll find Emily alive are slim, Grandpa, almost nonexistent."

"People joke about there being two chances of something happening, slim and none, but a 'slim' chance doesn't mean 'no' chance."

"Grandpa, that slim chance is gnawing on me like a termite in the walls. The odds are statistically better than the odds of winning the lottery, but I could spend years on the search and come up empty-handed. When Emily disappeared, Carrie put her entire life on hold."

Grandpa's eyebrows knitted.

"I understand how someone would put their life on hold for their only child, but not for a cousin. You have to draw the line somewhere. You love all your cousins, both in the U.S. and Mexico, but you can't put your life on hold for a missing cousin like you would for a missing daughter. Even Frank thinks it's time to accept defeat. Carrie put her life on pause, but you don't have to."

"Yes, I love my cousins, but Emily and I were particularly close. That's why her disappearance hit me so hard. Like I said, I haven't decided yet."

"When I face an important decision, I consider it from three points of view. Did I ever mention that?"

"Only about a thousand times. Listen to your head, your heart, and your gut."

"And what does your head tell you, Son?"

"Analyzing this like it's happening to someone else, keeping my emotions out of it, and evaluating the pros and cons dispassionately, my head says to pass."

"And your heart? What does it say?"

"Drop everything and go balls to the wall until I find her."

"And if you never find her? What then? How long do you search? How long is too long? And how would Carrie and Frank feel if you discover that Emily died a terrible death? Would they be better off not knowing?"

"Grandpa, you're arguing both sides. That makes this decision more complicated."

"The hell I am. *I* didn't make it complicated; it's the universe that's complicated. Son, life and death are complicated."

"My head and my heart disagree."

"Maybe your gut can break the tie. What does your gut say?"

"My gut is torn in two directions. I haven't told Terry about Carrie's call yet. What do I say if she wants me to stay home and my family wants me to try again? I love my family, but I could easily fall in love with Terry."

"Don't borrow trouble. Maybe Terry will want you to take the case and try again. It's pretty silly of you to assume that she'll be opposed when you haven't asked her opinion yet."

"What do I do if my head, my heart, and my gut disagree?"

Grandpa grinned. "Constance always says to pray on it. Of course, she's more religious than I am." Constance McCrary is Magnus's wife and my American grandmother.

Oh, great, now I had four points of view to consider, not three.

TWO

"The King Ranch casserole was delightful, and the tiramisu was to die for."

"Thank you, Terry." I waved the bottle. "More wine?"

Teresa Kovacs winked. "I'd be a fool to say no."

I tipped Pinot Noir into her goblet.

She lifted hers.

"To us," we said together.

Terry sipped and threw me a mysterious smile.

"Okay, lover, you have me in a great mood. What touchy subject are you broaching tonight?"

"You sure we've been back together less than two weeks? You read my mind."

"I don't need to be Port City's finest police detective to figure you out. You served my favorite meal from three years ago: King Ranch casserole, Pinot Noir, and tiramisu. Served on your balcony overlooking a sunset on Seeti Bay, and it's not my birthday. What gives?"

"Last year, I worked the case of a missing teenager, Liz Jenkins. Literally, a corn-fed farmer's daughter from Nebraska."

"I read about her in the *Press-Journal*, and a local TV station interviewed you after the rescue." Terry squeezed my arm. "You looked handsome on television."

"Thanks. Anyway, emotionally, that case was my second toughest case ever. Snoop and I hunted for Liz day after day and came up empty. The quest ground me down like a file scraping a brick. I was degenerating into a pile of gritty dust before we caught a break in the case."

"But you did it. You found her."

"One reason that case distressed me was the Nebraska girl reminded me of this girl." Scrolling to Emily's picture on my phone, I handed it to Terry.

She zoomed the image. "It's an expired Texas driver's license. Emily Constance Crazinski. A street address in Austin. This girl on your phone reminds you of the girl you rescued?"

"Could have been her sister."

Terry looked down at the screen. "She's a lovely girl. Who is she?"

"Emily is my cousin—or *was* my cousin. She disappeared four-and-a-half years ago."

"Isn't your grandmother's name Constance?"

"Yes. Emily is named after both grandmothers."

Terry examined the picture before returning my phone. "Tell me about her."

"The last time I saw Emily was the Christmas she turned sixteen. I had recently been promoted to homicide detective. She found an original 1936 *Dick Tracy* Sunday comic strip for sale on the internet. She framed it and gave it to me for Christmas. It hangs on the wall in my home office."

"I noticed that cartoon. I figured it was an example of your weird sense of humor."

"Nope. That was one hundred percent Emily."

"You and Emily must have been close."

"Emily didn't have any siblings. I was ten years older and she looked at me like an older brother. The Crazinskis lived in Austin and I lived in Adams Creek. Growing up, we saw each other at Christmas and Thanksgiving and weddings and funerals. In the summer, a couple weekends a year, we would visit them in Austin or they would come to Adams Creek, two hundred miles away in the Piney Woods. She lived in the big city and I lived on a farm, but we developed a link closer than our DNA."

"And she thought to give you *Dick Tracy*."

"She was a remarkable girl."

"What happened to her?"

"It was St. Patrick's Day. She didn't come home from school. Aunt Carrie and Uncle Frank called all her friends and nobody had seen her after school let out. The cops found her car in the school parking lot."

Terry set her wine glass down and touched my hand. "Why did you get involved?"

"She was family, and I was proud of my shiny new detective's shield, and I took a week's vacation to fly to Austin to find Emily. I was an arrogant know-it-all, full of piss and vinegar, who believed he would do a better job than the Austin cops."

I squeezed her hand. "One week stretched to four, so I used vacation days and took a leave of absence. I figured I was smarter than the Austin cops. It was inevitable that I would find her. Hubris, thy name is Carlos McCrary. Finally, I ran out of ideas and gave up the search. It was either that or lose my job."

I didn't admit to Terry how devastated I felt when I failed to find Emily. For three years, the wound didn't heal. Instead, it grew a protective scab. Eventually, the pain eased until the Liz Jenkins case knocked off the scab and resurrected the old injury.

The Liz Jenkins case had a happy ending. Now, I risked failing to find Emily a second time. "I felt guilty when I didn't find Emily or her body. I still do."

"Of course. You hold yourself to a higher standard than other people. Why tell me now?"

"There's been a development in Emily's case. Sort of."

"What kind of development?"

"Aunt Carrie had a dream. She called it a *vision*."

I told Terry about Aunt Carrie's dream and Grandpa Magnus's dream of his dying grandfather. By the time I finished, our wineglasses were empty.

"Wow," she said. "That's quite a story."

"Aunt Carrie called yesterday and wants me to reopen the case."

"Based on her dream?"

"Pretty much, yeah."

"Is there a new lead you didn't mention?"

"No."

"Any new clues?"

"Nope."

"Your aunt's dream? That's it?" Terry seemed skeptical.

"You'd have to know Aunt Carrie to understand. She's...eccentric. My cousins all call her Crazy Aunt Carrie. Not to her face, of course. To you and me, a dream isn't a clue; it's a dream. Or a hallucination. Carrie's been torn up over this ever since Emily disappeared. She was never the Rock of Gibraltar emotionally anyway, and since Emily's disappearance, she's even more fragile. She put her life on hold when Emily disappeared. My Grandma Connie, the one Emily's named after, says it's placed a strain on Aunt Carrie and Uncle Frank's marriage."

"That's too bad, but what does their marriage have to do with whether there are fresh leads on the case?"

I tilted my glass. Empty. I hate it when that happens. Holding the bottle to the light, I said. "An inch for each of us."

Terry gave a go-ahead gesture and I poured the rest.

Terry waited with a smile.

When I set the glass on the glass-topped table, it broke the silence with a soft *tink*. "There is no new evidence to pursue. If I go to Austin, it could require days, weeks maybe, to reinvestigate the old case. Statistically, the odds are a hundred to one she's dead. Even if I locate her body...that might just reopen old wounds."

"You gave me reasons you shouldn't accept the case," Terry said. "Here are three you didn't mention: me, Clint, and your business. I can't go with you, either to help or give emotional support; I don't have enough accrued vacation. You and I said we were serious this time around. With you in Texas and me in Florida, that could be dangerous for our relationship. Then there's Clint. He's in Gainesville, but when I was a freshman there, I drove home on weekends when I didn't have other plans."

Clint Watkins had been a teenage runaway from an abusive foster home. We met when Clint witnessed a murder that one of my friends was arrested for. Clint helped me solve the murder and we developed an unlikely friendship. I offered to take him off the streets of Port City and into my home to mentor him and provide a semblance of normal life that he had never known.

"Knowing you, Terry, I bet you didn't visit home often, even living near the Georgia border."

She grinned. "I studied like a monk in a monastery four nights a week, and I partied like a rock star on the weekends. I didn't drive home until Thanksgiving, and then I didn't visit again until the semester was over before Christmas. Okay, forget Clint. He's not a reason to refuse the case. But consider McCrary Investigations. Your PI business won't run itself."

"That's why I often hire Snoop and Gunner and Angelina as operatives. With email, Facetime, and cellphones, clients don't know I'm gone."

"Unless they ask to meet in your office."

"Unless that."

Terry frowned. It didn't take the World's Greatest Private Eye to deduce how she felt.

"Are there any good reasons to reopen the case? Any shred of new evidence that doesn't rely on visions, spirits, or ghosts?"

"Not really, no."

"Perhaps your aunt and uncle are better off not knowing. How will they feel if you raise their hopes and then come up empty-handed? I'm guessing it would destroy them."

Terry put her hand on mine. "Lover, you may be the world's greatest private eye, but this isn't Hollywood; this is real life. If you reopen this case, you'll bust your ass four or five weeks and annoy the hell out of the Austin cops. Don't tell me you won't because I know how single-minded you are when you're on a case. This is a fool's errand."

She smiled, but it was sympathy rather than amusement. "It isn't your fault Emily's gone. You spent four weeks and uncovered nothing. Don't throw away your life chasing ghosts and goblins."

"You're right. You and I are getting reacquainted. For me to go away for weeks to focus on a case involving my family…This thing would snag my attention like a mammoth in a tarpit."

"That's right. If a real clue pops up, that's different. But until someone uncovers a real clue, I say take a pass."

Of course, she's right, I thought. *Then why did I toss and turn all night? Why couldn't I sleep?* Maybe there was a clue out there, but it was waiting for me to uncover it in Texas.

———

At three a.m. I decided. But how to tell her?

Grandpa said: If you know you must pay an emotional price in the end, pay it now so you can stop dreading it.

At breakfast, I bit the bullet.

"Sweetie, three years ago, I neglected you when I moved Clint into my home and let him dominate my attention. I believe that decision, combined with my arrest for murder, was the last straw for our relationship. You say you're okay now to share my attention with Clint. Frankly, I wonder if our relationship is too new to strain it by accepting Emily's case again."

"That's why I want you to pass on this." She put down her fork and locked eyes with me.

Damn. This was as bad as I thought it would be. "I have to take the case. It's family."

Terry frowned, then her forehead smoothed. Her face became as expressionless as an empty plate. I wondered how bad this would be.

"Regarding Clint, I know you see yourself in him. Without you, God knows what would have become of him, so I'm okay with that. Besides, I know that you always have a project, and Clint is a worthwhile one. I know you saved his life. But I can't live like a nun while you're a thousand miles away. You and I agreed to an exclusive relationship a week ago, and now you plan to leave on a wild goose chase that could absorb you for weeks— even months. It's not fair."

My breath caught. I realized I was on the brink of losing her again.

"Sweetie, I'm never on a case 24/7. There's always slack time. I'll fly home every few days, or you can fly to Austin. Heck, it would give you a good excuse to meet my family."

She pushed the scraps of her omelet around on her plate. Did she buy the promise?

"Sometimes it's best to let sleeping dogs lie."

"This dog isn't sleeping; it's barking in my head like a hound from hell. I keep asking: What if Emily is alive? Imagine what she experiences every day, day after day. Who cares if the odds are a hundred to one or a thousand to one? That dog keeps howling in my ear."

"Why must you play the damned hero?"

I saw where this was headed—where *she* was headed.

"Last night I mentioned that Snoop and I were stumped on the Nebraska teenager's case until we caught a break."

"I believe you said the case was 'grinding you into dust.'"

"That's right. The reason we caught a break in the case was because we didn't give up. We kept searching until we found a clue. I have four more years' experience now—four more years of tricks and techniques that I didn't know then. If I'd known then what I know now, maybe I would have found a clue in Emily's case. A clue that might still be out there."

She pushed her plate aside.

"You'll take the case against all the odds, aren't you?"

"Like I said, she's family."

She dropped her napkin on the table and rose to her feet.

This was about to end badly.

"Go play the hero, Superman. Throw away another month. Throw away the rest of the year. Throw away your whole damned life for all I care."

She seized her purse. Her eyes glistened. "Don't bother to see me out."

THREE

G randpa stood near the bottom of the baggage claim escalator among the chauffeurs. Most drivers held signs with passengers' names on them. Grandpa's sign said Carlos McCrary—World's Greatest Detective.

I couldn't help but smile. "Are you trying to embarrass me, Grandpa?"

"Wouldn't dream of it, son."

He lowered the sign and seized me in a bear hug.

"It pays to advertise. Besides, I want everyone to know how proud I am."

"Austin is fifteen hundred miles from Port City."

"You think I care? You can't stop me from bragging." He stuffed the sign in a trash can we passed. "How many bags did you check?"

"Two. Why are you here? We're supposed to meet at Carrie and Frank's house. I reserved a rent car."

"I cancelled it. Airport rentals cost a small fortune, and there's no rich client to pay the expenses. Austin charges local fees and taxes on car rentals."

"I appreciate you meeting me, but we can't share one car. We'll need to split up during the investigation."

"I know, son. I rented you a Jeep Grand Cherokee at an off-airport location. It's the same price as that sedan you reserved at the airport. Four-wheel drive and it will ford a creek almost two feet deep."

"You think we'll drive cross country?"

"You never know how much capability you'll need. Consider it a variation on Rule Nine: *You can never carry too much firepower.* Quit bellyaching and fetch your bags. I'll drop you at the rental, then follow you to the house."

———

I parked my Jeep under the basketball goal beside Carrie's SUV. Grandpa parked at the curb.

Frank Crazinski hustled out the front door.

"We just got home from work. I'll get your luggage, Pop."

"No need, Frank. I'm staying with George and Melissa."

"In that case, maybe I can help Chuck."

We shook hands.

"Thanks, Frank." I popped the trunk. "I'll get this one; it's heavier. Did the crate I shipped arrive?"

"Saturday. What made it so heavy?"

"It's a foot locker with super-detective secret equipment stuff. Odds and ends I couldn't bring on an airplane. Boring stuff, if you're not a PI."

"Such as?"

"Weapons and ammo and spy gear, a lot of which is illegal, if you must know."

Frank's face reddened. "Okay then."

I hoped I hadn't embarrassed him, but he hadn't taken my hint not to ask.

He grabbed a suitcase. "Carrie is in the kitchen. She started dinner after you called."

Carrie shifted a pan from one burner to another and wiped her hands on her apron. She hugged Grandpa and me. "Thank you for coming. I feel better already."

"I haven't done anything yet," I said.

"Dinner in twenty minutes," Frank said. "What do y'all want to drink?"

"Shiner, if you have it, or Lone Star. Texas beers are scarce as snowballs in South Florida."

"Same for me," Grandpa said.

"Lone Star. Let's go to the den."

After dinner, I edged my plate aside. "Frank, it's time to examine Emily's room."

Frank scooted his chair back. "I'll do the dishes, honey. You go with Chuck."

Grandpa stood. "I'll help with the dishes, then I'm off to George and Melissa's. I'd like to get there before Rebecca's bedtime. I haven't seen my great-granddaughter in three weeks. Chuck doesn't need my help to search a room."

"I'll do the dishes, Pops," Frank said. "You go and kiss Rebecca for me."

Grandpa grinned. "You don't need to offer twice. I'll see you all tomorrow." He left.

Carrie stacked her dishes. "You remember where Emily's room is?"

"Of course." I led the way across the house.

"We left her room like it was before she...before she...disappeared. When we reported her missing, the police searched her car, her room, her school locker—everyplace we could think of. They suggested we not touch anything until they finished their investigation."

She opened the door and stepped into the bedroom. "I figure the investigation isn't finished until they find her."

Emily's room was a time capsule. Bed made, chest of drawers and dresser dusted, mirror freshly polished. The pristine vacuum cleaner tracks on the carpet indicated that no one had sullied this shrine to the missing daughter.

A Bonham High School pennant in bright red and white hung on a wall to the left. A basketball team picture hung on the right. A photo of Emily making a jump shot hung beside it, along with a portrait of her in a Bonham Bobcats letter jacket.

A sanctuary for souvenirs.

"We didn't even wash the sheets." She gestured. "Do your thing. I'll stay here in case you have questions."

I commenced with the chest of drawers. I slid the top drawer out and set it on the bed.

"The police searched the room. Come to think of it, so did you."

"I have more experience now. I might have missed something. I'll search it again." *Maybe the cops missed something too*, I thought, but kept my doubts to myself.

The drawer was filled with panties and bras. It felt as awkward to poke through her underwear now as it had the first time. I removed each item and placed it on the bed, ensuring nothing was hidden in the folds. I emptied the drawer and flipped it over and examined the back, bottom, and sides.

"What are you doing?" Carrie asked.

"Sometimes people tape things to the back or bottom of drawers. I intend to search the room exhaustively." I refolded a pair of panties to return the underwear to the drawer.

"I'll do that," Carrie said. "You start the next drawer."

I slid out the second drawer.

Carrie refolded Emily's undies and arranged them in the drawer like she was tucking her daughter in bed. She finished and started to return the drawer to its place.

"Leave the drawers on the bed. After I finish them, I'll flip the chest and look behind it and underneath. I can't do that with the drawers in."

The third drawer held an address book underneath the folded shorts. Carrie picked it up. "I remember that." She opened it. "I recognize the names. They're Emily's friends."

"Let's set it aside," I said. "I'll review the entries later."

The fourth drawer was unexceptional.

I removed the bottom drawer. Three red, blue, and green volumes lay on the wood bottom beneath the drawer slots. Four years earlier, I had opened the bottom drawer but I had not removed it. A pang of guilt plucked at my mind. What else had I missed?

I picked up the red journal. "Are these diaries?"

Carrie lifted the green one. "Emily didn't keep a diary."

"It might belong to a girlfriend. After you review them, set them aside for me to study."

Carrie opened the volume and quickly closed it. "It's Emily's handwriting." She set the book on the bed like it burned her hands. "Oh, no, it wouldn't feel right to read Emily's journal. If she wanted me to know she had one, she would have told me."

I stacked the other two books on the first one. "You know I need to read them, right?"

"I know. It's just…Frank and I value Emily's privacy. She is never in trouble at school, and she makes good grades. We give her freedom." She stared at the three books. "Go ahead. If there's anything you think I should know after you finish, you'll tell me."

Carrie still spoke of Emily in the present tense, as if she might walk in the door any moment. "Count on it." I squeezed Carrie's shoulder. "It might be easier for me to do this alone. I won't finish her room tonight. I'll need a couple hours in the morning too. I'll search under the bed. I'll strip the bed. I'll examine her clothes, books, shoes, magazines. You'd be amazed how thorough I am. You do whatever you and Frank do after dinner. I'll work another hour."

Carrie surveyed Emily's room. "You know where your room is. I'll leave you to your work. What time would you like breakfast?"

"I'm still on Florida time. I'll wake at five o'clock. You and Frank sleep late. I'll make coffee and wait to eat breakfast with you all."

———

That night, I dreamed of the three journals I had found, but they were giant red, blue, and green doors. In my dream, I tried to open the doors and pulled on the handles until my arms ached, but they wouldn't open. I woke with my pillow damp from sweat. Thank goodness, the real journals would open more easily than those doors.

Carrie found me at the kitchen table, drinking coffee as I read the journals.

"Good morning, Chuck. How did you sleep? Is the mattress okay? If it's too hard or too soft, we'll buy another one. I ought to replace that mattress anyway. It's ten years old if it's a minute."

Jibber-jabber, I thought.

"The mattress is fine. I slept like a log." No sense telling Carrie that I'd tossed and turned. That wasn't the fault of the mattress.

"Now that you're on the case, I slept the best I have since that vision from Emily. My horoscope yesterday told me a new person would bring changes to my environment. That's you. You'll find Emily now since she's helping in the hunt. I know she'll contact me again, maybe with a clue."

And the Florida Gators will win national championships in football, basketball, softball, volleyball, and baseball in the same year. Don't engage her on that. "Stranger things have happened, Aunt Carrie."

"What do you want for breakfast?"

"Whatever you eat. I love all food without discrimination. Except okra."

Carrie smiled. Like everyone else in the family, she knew my aversion to okra.

"Frank will want waffles when he gets up. How about waffles?"

"That's fine."

She stirred around the kitchen. "Learn anything useful?"

"Emily's handwriting is hard to make out."

Carrie opened a waffle mix and poured a portion into a stainless-steel bowl.

"That's because they don't teach the kids how to write cursive in school. Too many keyboards in their lives."

She jibber-jabbered while she plugged in the waffle iron and applied a non-stick spray to the cooking surface. She poured the batter and closed the lid. "Your first waffle will be ready in a minute."

I closed the journal I was reading; no sense trying to concentrate with Aunt Carrie in the room.

Carrie sat at the table and opened the newspaper. "My horoscope says: *Be in tune with what others need. Give of yourself and be available and sensitive to certain people.* That means I'm supposed to help you today. I'll try to decipher Emily's journal if you're stumped."

"Thanks for the offer, Aunt Carrie. You've been a big help and I know I'll call on you for more help soon."

Carrie beamed.

"Your horoscope says: *There is a difference between taking risks and going overboard, both of which you do. A friend might irritate you since you could be tired. Listen to this person's ideas while weighing the pros and cons."*

She set the newspaper aside and poured coffee.

"In grade school, they taught us to write cursive in the third grade and made us practice until we wrote legibly. I taught cursive to Emily, but I didn't make her practice. If there's something you can't make out, let me know."

"I've deciphered it all so far, but thanks. Was Emily having difficulties at school?"

"She never gets into trouble and always makes As and Bs."

"I don't mean academic difficulty. I mean a personality conflict, a feud, or a physical threat. Was she bullied?"

"No. What makes you think she was in trouble?"

I opened the red journal. "Listen to this: *'LL' looks at me sort of creepy, like he sees through my clothes. He did it again before class today.*" I flipped a few pages. "Here's another mention: *'LL' almost said something after class today, but Pattie walked over before he could say anything. He practically ran away. I wish I didn't have to see him every day.* Did she mention a classmate whose initials are 'LL'?"

Carrie's eyes lost focus like she was scanning the inside of her skull. "Nope. Nobody comes to mind. But the school will give you a list of her classmates."

"Maybe not. There are privacy laws involved. I'll ask Detective Ortega to grease those skids if needed."

The waffle iron clicked. Carrie glanced at it. "Your waffle is ready."

"What about her teachers? Any have the initials 'LL'?"

"What a horrible notion that 'LL' could be a teacher. But you see bad stuff on the news every day. You never know…" Carrie shuddered. "Emily would tell me if a teacher behaved inappropriately, wouldn't she? Wouldn't she?"

Carrie dumped the waffle on a plate and carried it and a butter dish to the table.

"Thanks," I said, buttering the waffle. "Teenagers are funny. Sometimes they don't know what's appropriate and what's not. Remember that doctor who abused those girl gymnasts with their parents in the examining room."

"I heard about it. Crap like that makes my skin crawl."

"He got away with it because kids don't have enough real-world experience to spot warning signs an adult knows."

"God, I hope not. Anyway, no one named 'LL' comes to mind. The school should help you with that."

"I haven't studied the other two journals. I hope she identifies him in one of those. I haven't finished searching her room either. I read this journal while I drank my coffee. After breakfast, I'll finish her room, then I'll study the three journals cover to cover."

Carrie claimed she didn't want to read Emily's journals. Maybe that was so she could cling to the belief that her daughter fit her mother's stereotypes.

Before I agreed to reopen Emily's case, Grandpa told me about Carrie's own shenanigans when she was a teenager. Tomfooleries my aunt thought her parents didn't known about. Grandpa said they affected her emotional stability and her feelings about the disappearance. She felt guilty somehow.

———

I finished examining Emily's room. For a popular, active teenager—that's what her parents claimed—her bedroom revealed no insight into her personal life, not even the boyfriend she told me she was in love with. I had promised not to tell anyone about that, so I wouldn't mention it to her parents unless I had no choice. Emily left no love notes, no pressed flowers, no concert ticket stubs, no prom photos. Either Emily had no social life with boys—which she told me was not true—or she was secretive about her romantic activities. Or maybe she was gay and had lied to me about being in love. Now that I thought about it, I remembered she hadn't said she had a *boyfriend*—she said she had a *first love*. Was Emily gay? She would have hesitated to come out with Frank and Carrie.

I tucked that question into the back corner of my mind in case it became relevant to the disappearance.

Frank stuck his head in the door while I worked, wished me good luck, and left for his office.

When I returned to the kitchen, Carrie was rinsing the dishes. "You missed Frank. He had to eat and run while you were in Emily's room. I'm going to work as soon as I get these dishes in the dishwasher."

"He came in and wished me luck before he left."

I poured another coffee and opened the green journal on the table. The handwriting wasn't Emily's. I set it aside for Carrie to read. This one, she could read with no reluctance. The dates in the blue journal were older than the red one.

I settled back to do some serious detecting. Perhaps the journals would reveal the secret identity of "LL." Her handwriting made deciphering the entries like slogging through ankle-deep mud.

A half-hour later, I found it.

Lizard Lips. "LL" was short for *Lizard Lips.* In the blue journal, Emily said she took English Literature with Lizard Lips. I wrote that in my case notebook on the page for questions to ask at the high school.

I hoped Emily's car revealed something useful.

———

The double-wide garage door rattled open when I punched the button. Emily's Ford Fiesta sat on four flat tires, alone in the two-car garage. Outside on the triple-wide driveway, oil specks marked where Carrie parked her SUV beside my rental car. A smudge of tire marks indicated where Frank parked his car. It seemed strange that they didn't park one of their cars in the garage with Emily's Fiesta. Perhaps the garage was another shrine to Emily.

Flipping on the overhead lights, I saw that dust filmed the Fiesta's fire-engine red paint job.

Christmas four years earlier Emily had flaunted her shiny, new car—a combination present for her sixteenth birthday and Christmas. She drove her parents in it to Adams Creek for the holiday. She was so proud when she drove me to the Dairy Queen where we shared the secrets of our first loves. Well, at least I shared mine.

I tugged on a pair of crime scene gloves. The dashboard didn't light when I opened the driver's door, nor did the interior lights come on. No surprise there, the battery was long dead. No sense cranking the engine. A faded oil-change sticker said the car was serviced the week before Emily's disappearance.

I opened the other three doors.

After removing the floor mats, I flipped them on the garage floor. Nothing fastened to the underneath sides. A discarded gum wrapper lay on the floor of the back seat. It had been under the mat. I photographed it in place and slipped it into a paper evidence bag I'd shipped to Austin from Port City, noting the date and time. It might have a fingerprint. I replaced the mats.

After sliding the front seats forward, I removed the rear seat cushion and laid it on the concrete floor. Two gum wrappers and a quarter lay beneath the seat. The quarter might have a fingerprint. I photographed the scene and slipped the items into evidence bags.

I remounted the seat cushion and shined a Maglite under the front seats. Nothing but dust bunnies lurking there. The pocket on the back of the passenger seat held a folding umbrella, which I removed. I stuck my hand in the pocket and felt around. What was that? I hauled out a foil-wrapped condom.

Emily told me she was in love. Had she been knocking knees with her boyfriend in that tiny backseat? She hadn't even hinted at it in her diary. If she hadn't told me in the Dairy Queen, I would never have known.

I recalled my high school trysts with Liz Johannes. I hadn't told Emily, but Liz and I had used back seats, haylofts, even a horse blanket in the back of a pickup once. I was embarrassed to buy condoms and drove thirty miles to the vending machine at a truck stop on Interstate 45. This condom was the same brand. Liz and I used two or three condoms a week. I paid truck stop prices to avoid the embarrassment of buying condoms in Adams Creek, where someone in the drug store might recognize me. Remembering Liz Johannes made me smile. The last time I saw her at our tenth anniversary high school reunion, she was married with two children and co-owned a local hardware store. If she hadn't dumped me, I might have been the one running the hardware store with Liz.

I photographed the condom and stuck it in another evidence bag. The foil wrapping might have a fingerprint.

Maybe Emily had been embarrassed too. I wondered where she had bought the condom.

The garage had to be relatively dark to test the car for blood and semen, so I lowered the garage door and waited the required four minutes for the motion-sensitive light on the garage-door-opener to click off. After dragging the back seat onto the garage floor again, I took a spray bottle luminol and an ultra-violet light from my equipment trunk.

I examined the entire interior of the car and rear seat lying on the floor under UV light. No sign of semen or other body fluids. That made sense: Emily had owned the car for four months before she disappeared. That didn't mean she hadn't had sex in the car, but if she had, she and her sex partner had been neat. I sprayed luminol on both front seats and the rear seat-back to test for blood. Nothing. I checked the trunk too. Nothing.

The glove compartment held maps of the Austin metro area and four Hill Country counties to the west. Stuffed beneath the maps was the Ford's owner's manual that looked like it had never been opened. An expired insurance card was stuck loose in the plastic wallet with the manual. I reviewed a wrinkled receipt for the oil change one week before her disappearance and removed the glove box. Nothing was hidden behind but the fuse panel.

I popped the trunk and poked under the floor mat. Nothing. The compact spare tire had never been used. I looked under the hood. Nothing unusual.

The important discovery was the condom. Who hid it in the seat pocket? And who was supposed to wear it? And which girl was it supposed to protect, Emily or a friend?

———

"Burgers are ready," Frank called from the back deck. He slid open the screen door and carried in a platter with eight hamburger patties topped with melted cheese. "How'd it go today, Chuck?"

I debated whether to tell Emily's parents about the condom. I decided to wait until I discussed it with Detective Ortega and sent it for fingerprints. Maybe it was intended for one of Emily's girlfriends. Maybe the leaves wouldn't fall this winter.

"That green journal hidden under Emily's chest of drawers wasn't hers. It belonged to another girl."

"Was there a name in it?" Carrie asked.

"No name in the front or back. I haven't studied the contents yet. The handwriting isn't Emily's."

"How do you know it's a girl's?"

"Ninety-eight percent of diaries kept by high school students are kept by girls."

Carrie's eyes widened. "I never knew that. Where did you learn that statistic?"

I grinned. "Ninety-four percent of statistics quoted in social conversations are invented on the spot."

She laughed. "Your figure is bogus but, come to think of it, I never knew a boy to keep a diary."

"I can't imagine a teenage girl leaving her diary at another girl's house and not reclaiming it," Frank said.

"My thought too. Why did she abandon it?"

Carrie set a stack of three plates on the island.

"It's too nice a day to stay inside. Let's eat on the deck. After dinner, I'll review the journal and look for clues. I'll be your assistant detective."

After we ate, Frank and I cleared the dishes while Carrie read the green journal.

I brought a glass of iced tea out to the deck and sat across from her. "Uncover any clues, assistant detective?"

"This is Ling Cheng's diary. She played basketball with Emily."

"Spell it."

Carrie spelled both names and I recorded them in my notebook.

"Was she close to Emily? I interviewed all Emily's friends during my first investigation, and I don't recall her."

"Ling was two grades ahead of Emily. They weren't close, but they played basketball together. Ling was born in China. Her parents immigrated to Austin when she was a baby. Frank, you knew Ling's parents."

"Yeah, we sat with them at Emily's basketball games. Emily made the Bobcat varsity basketball team her sophomore year. Ling was a senior varsity player."

"I want to talk to her."

"Too late," Carrie said. "She and her parents transferred back to China in May after Ling graduated. That was two months after Emily disappeared. Ling said she was upset about the relocation. She had visited her grandparents in China, but she didn't speak the language well. It was February when we talked. I remember because basketball season was nearly over. Her parents worked for a high-tech Korean-owned fabrication facility in Austin. A Chinese company acquired the Korean company, and Ling said that the new owner was transferring them to Shanghai."

"That explains her entry three weeks before she disappeared. It reads 'LC is PO'd her parents are leaving.' Do either of you know who they worked for?"

"It was Trans-something-or-other. Frank, do you remember?"

"Trans-Pacific Circuits."

"If Ling didn't leave the country until May, she had two months to get her diary," I said. "Why didn't she?"

"Maybe it wasn't important to her," Carrie said. "From reviewing it, it was a casual hobby. She made entries once a week or so. After the season was over, Emily invited the basketball girls for a sleepover. That would be when Ling brought her journal. The girls wrote farewell messages in back. Other than the sleepover, Ling and Emily didn't hang out together."

"The sleepover could be when Emily hid the journals," I said.

"Why hide them?" Frank asked.

Carrie scoffed. "Typical teenage drama, like swearing an oath to meet in twenty years on top of the Empire State Building. Nobody takes these things seriously. I did sillier things when I was a girl."

"Farewell messages?"

Carrie flipped toward the middle of the blue journal. "Here they are." She scooted the open journal across.

I studied the two facing pages. The chicken scratches were hard to decipher, and it took discussions with Carrie to discern the meanings.

"These farewell messages say 'I enjoyed playing basketball with you and good luck and stay in touch. Go Bobcats!' They don't say 'have a nice life in China and we're sorry we'll never see you again.' I don't believe Ling planned to return to China. If interpret the well-wishes from another viewpoint, Ling intended to stay in America and attend college. If I decode this scribble rightly, this message mentions MIT. See that?" I pointed to a scrawled note. "Does that say MIT?"

Carrie studied the message again.

"Now that you mention it, it does. Her parents were both engineers. It makes sense Ling would apply to MIT. Her mother bragged that Ling was near the top of her class, grade-wise. But what difference does that make? That has nothing to do with Emily's disappearance. The sleepover was the only time Emily and Ling hung out together. They weren't *friend*-friends. They were teammates."

"It might be nothing," I said, "but it's a loose end, and it places Ling here two weeks before Emily's disappearance. I want to ask Ling about the sleepover and why she left her journal. If she did plan to retrieve it, why didn't she?"

———

Carrie Crazinski

"Sweetie, we can't preserve Emily's room for a shrine," Frank said. "It's not healthy. We have to accept the truth: Our daughter's not coming back. It's time we move on with our lives. Heck, we're young enough—we could adopt an older child."

Carrie gazed in Frank's direction, but she didn't see him. He wouldn't let it go, she fumed. He wanted a home office, or a TV room, or even a nursery, for God's sakes—anything that wouldn't remind him of Emily. He kept bringing it up, bringing it up, bringing it up, never letting it rest. Carrie squeezed her hands into fists, then realized she had dug her nails into her palms.

"If we had made Emily's room into a home office, we wouldn't have discovered those journals."

"Or we'd have found them a long time ago, when we gave Emily's furniture to charity."

Carrie had tried and tried, but Frank wouldn't acknowledge how important it was to them—okay, to *her*—to keep Emily's room ready for her return. Her room symbolized the hope Carrie would never give up. Never…

"Frank, while there is breath in my body, I will believe Emily is alive. Not unless I see her body. If that's too much for you to handle, I'm sorry, but that's the way it is. Emily's room isn't a shrine, for goodness sake, it's her *room*. It's where she *lives*."

Where she will always live, Carrie thought. *Always.*

FOUR

Carlos McCrary

D etective Rodrigo Ortega glared from his desk and waved me to a seat while he continued a telephone call. He spun his chair to face the wall behind him. As the World's Greatest Private Eye, I deduced that he wasn't glad to see me.

Setting my briefcase on the floor, I took the visitor's chair.

Ortega continued his personal call another five minutes. Not a great example of Texas hospitality.

He finished the phone call and pivoted to me. He didn't stand or offer his hand. "Carlos McCrary, right?"

I responded in Spanish. Perhaps reminding him I'm half Mexican would warm him up. "Good morning, Rodrigo. Yeah, I'm back."

Ortega stayed with English. "I figured you'd show up again—what's that saying—like a bad penny. It's been what...four years?" That Rodrigo Ortega, what a funny guy.

"Four years last St. Patrick's Day. I presume Aunt Carrie or Uncle Frank told you why I came back to Austin."

Ortega gave me a sad shake of the head. "Carrie Crazinski is single-minded when it comes to her daughter."

"Aunt Carrie and Uncle Frank asked me to reopen Emily's case. I'm a private investigator now."

"A hotshot PI like you ought to solve the case in no time. Let me know when you find Emily, and if she's alive. And tell me who kidnapped her and we'll arrest him. Or her."

Ortega jerked to his feet, his chair rolling back to the wall. He clenched his fists.

"There's nothing to investigate, McCrary. We exhausted all leads; you know that."

"Yes, you did." Wouldn't hurt to agree with him where I could.

"You looked over our shoulder every damned step of the way."

Ortega made a face and sat.

"We followed every lead, which was easy to do since there *were* no leads other than a nut who claimed he saw her in the Hill Country. We sent dozens of volunteers up every creek and cranny in Gillespie County after a screwball said he saw a blonde teenager picking bluebonnets in the hills."

"I remember."

Ortega scowled.

"It was like sending them on a snipe hunt. Then we sent dozens more to search a thousand acres of wilderness near Dripping Springs."

"I spent three days on the Dripping Springs hunt myself," I said. "I never knew there were so many boondocks so close to civilization. The one thing we discovered was a thousand-year-old Indian campsite in a cave." *And briars*, I recalled. *Lots of briars with lots of thorns.*

Ortega leaned forward. "Nothing new has popped up. Believe me, I would reopen the frigging case in a heartbeat if I had something to investigate, but there's no new evidence. How the hell do I investigate a nightmare?"

It helps to have a crazy aunt, I thought.

I kept my face impassive and counted five seconds silently. Best not to meet anger with anger.

"Then I guess you'll be glad to know there is something new to investigate. I discovered new evidence."

The detective's eyebrows rose. "Yeah?"

"I found a brand-new condom in its foil package, a quarter, and three gum wrappers in Emily's car. They might have latent prints or DNA." I hoisted my briefcase. "Can we give the evidence to your forensics lab?"

"Where did you find them?"

"In Emily's car."

"Can't be. We processed the car. We collected what evidence there was, which was *none*."

I placed the briefcase on my lap and didn't say what I thought.

Ortega scoffed. "You think my guys missed something?"

"You're the Missing Persons Division, not Homicide or Human Trafficking. I was a homicide detective. Homicide detectives view things with different eyes than your guys."

"Then why didn't you find this so-called evidence four years ago?"

I showed my palms. "Inexperience? Your guys processed Emily's car in the high school parking lot before I arrived in Austin, then Frank drove it home. I didn't examine it. I'd made detective three months before. I've learned better in the last four years. I suggest you investigate this like a homicide or a kidnapping instead of a missing person."

"Where's the homicide evidence, McCrary? You find blood?"

I shook my head.

"You found a condom—no—an *unused* condom, so there's no DNA—a coin, and a gum wrapper. Forgive me if I'm not impressed. It's still a missing person. No evidence of foul play. Our Missing Persons detectives know how to conduct a proper investigation."

Sure they do, I thought. *That's why I didn't find any new evidence in Emily's car. Oh, wait. I did.*

"It is what it is, detective. I found it in Emily's car yesterday."

"How do I know your so-called evidence wasn't left in the car after Emily disappeared? Maybe her parents used the car or loaned it to a friend whose car was in the shop."

"Her parents have left the car in their garage since they drove it home on the day your criminalists finished processing it. The tires are flat, the battery is dead as an anvil, and the car is coated in enough dust that it looks brown instead of red."

"You trying to make me and my department look bad, McCrary?"

I don't need to do that, smartass. You do that well enough by yourself. But I kept my opinion to myself.

With Ortega's attitude, I decided not to reveal the three journals in my briefcase. He might confiscate them for evidence and I hadn't finished them. "What I can say is there were five pieces of evidence in her car. Why not process it and see if it turns up anything?" I hefted the briefcase. "Can we take this to your crime lab?"

———

Detective Ortega drove to the Austin Police Forensic Science Division building three miles east of downtown and I followed in my car. Ortega would never admit it, of course, but he had to be embarrassed that his detectives had overlooked evidence in processing Emily's car.

By the time we arrived, I had decided to stay in the background at the crime lab. He could present my findings anyway he wanted, even if it meant he took credit for finding new evidence after four years.

Wordlessly, we climbed the stairs to the second floor. Ortega handed the paper evidence bags to a Latent Print Examiner. "This is new evidence in a missing persons case. Try to get prints off these, then send them to Trace Evidence. Maybe they can find DNA."

The technician affixed a reference number to the evidence bags and logged them into her computer. She swiveled to Ortega. "What's the case number?"

He gave her the case number.

She tapped a few keys. "From the case number, the person has been missing four years."

Ortega cut his eyes to me before he replied. "What's your point?"

"You just now uncovered new evidence?"

Ortega tugged at his collar. "Yeah. How long to process it?"

The technician glanced at the case bins lined up on the shelves. "Old case like this, I can't jump it ahead of the queue. It'll be a couple of days before we even get to it, let alone process it. After that, it depends on how backed up Trace is."

Ortega started to object, but I lifted a hand. "A few days is fine. I have other leads to handle."

The technician glanced at my left hand before she smiled at me. "I don't believe we've met. I'm Ruby Voight. Are you new to Missing Persons?"

So much for staying in the background.

"No. I'm the missing person's cousin and, incidentally, a private investigator and a former homicide detective. I reopened the old case with cooperation from Detective Ortega."

With Ortega's animosity toward me, it might be good to have a friend in the crime lab. I laid a business card on her desk and returned her smile. "I'm Carlos McCrary. My friends call me Chuck."

Ortega snatched my card as she reached to pick it up.

"Ruby won't need to call you, McCrary. This is still my case, not yours."

He jammed the card in my shirt pocket and glared at the technician. "Any communication about this case goes to me, not pretty boy. Legally, he's not law enforcement in Texas; he's a civilian. You got that?"

Leaning across her desk, Ruby stuck two fingers in my shirt pocket. "Ooh, muscles too. I like a man who works out." She smiled at me for Ortega's benefit. "I'll bet you have a lot of stamina."

She retrieved my card and glared at Ortega. "Maybe I'll call Chuck on a personal matter. I don't work for you."

Ortega's face reddened.

She set the paper bags in a plastic bin and made a space on the shelf. "Whatever. I'll let you know when I have results, *Rodrigo*." She said his name like it was another word for "asshole."

FIVE

A unt Carrie lifted the bottle. "More wine, Chuck?"

"No thanks. I'll switch to iced tea." I blotted my lips with a napkin, scooted the chair back, and started to get up.

Carrie jumped to her feet. "I'll get it."

She carried my empty wine glass to the kitchen and left Frank and me alone.

"How was Detective Ortega?" Frank asked. "Still an arrogant, hard-nosed, SOB know-it-all?"

"Pretty much. He acts like it was my fault his investigators missed the, uh…the evidence in Emily's car."

"You can say it, Chuck. It's a condom. It's the twenty-first century, and teenagers do have sex. Hell, Carrie and I lived together before we were married, so we can't point fingers." Frank grimaced. "How did Ortega's guys miss it?"

"Missing persons detectives see cases from a different perspective than detectives for sex crimes, homicide, or human trafficking and vice. Ortega and his team are the Missing Persons division. Their cases involve runaways, people with dementia who wander off, or an estranged parent who snatches a child they don't have custody of. A case like that, the cops know what happened and who did it. Their cases are search operations, not who-done-it or how-done-it. Homicide division cases are different."

Carrie returned with a glass of iced tea. "What will you do next?"

"Interview Emily's friends—of both genders—and ask who the condom was meant for."

"Didn't you interview her friends before?"

"To tell the God's honest truth, Carrie, I had been a Port City patrol cop for two years and spent most of that in a police cruiser. I was promoted to detective the December before Emily disappeared. I had three months' detective experience. I was so green I would give a two-bit answer to a two-dollar question. I missed stuff. For example, I should have examined Emily's car after the cops finished it. If I had discovered that condom, the whole case would have developed from a different angle. This time, I'm treating this like a new case, like I never investigated it before. I'll give you my old list of Emily's friends and you can update it for new information."

"I'll look through my address book," Carrie said. "I have the names and phone numbers of her friends' parents. A couple have moved, but I keep up my Christmas card list."

That night I dreamed of Emily buying condoms in the Adams Creek pharmacy. The cashier was pointing at Emily and laughing at her. Emily shouted at the cashier, "They're not for me. They're for my girlfriend. I swear. I'm still a virgin."

I knew she was lying—at least in my dream.

———

I ran through the list of friends from my first investigation and compared it to Emily's address book.

Riley Sorrento had been in Emily's homeroom class and played junior varsity basketball with her when they were freshmen. Carrie gave me contact info for her parents. Her mother said she was at Texas State University in San Marcos, working toward a Bachelor of Fine Arts in Musical Theatre. It was an hour's drive south of Austin.

I didn't know a BFA in Musical Theatre was a real thing, but I'm a cultural caveman. My idea of fine art is a new *Star Wars* movie.

Riley's mom said Riley was a sophomore. I was shocked to realize Emily would be a college sophomore too if she hadn't disappeared. Intellectually, I knew that, but the last four years I had pictured a sweet high school sophomore frozen in time like her driver's license photo.

After reaching Riley's voicemail, I also texted her to call me.

Next was Debbie ("only my mother calls me Deborah") Sane. Debbie had the same cellphone number as four years before. She worked as a paralegal downtown. She was busy the rest of the week but agreed to meet me for lunch on Saturday. I offered to text her my picture so she would recognize me at the restaurant.

"That's not necessary unless you grew a beard or something."

"No, I look the same."

"I remember you. Six-foot-two, brown hair and eyes, lots of muscles, and a killer smile. See you Saturday at 12:30."

Kenneth Hoar's parents said he was on a basketball scholarship at Davy Crockett State University in Huntsville, a three-hour drive to the east. Hoar was the only boy on Emily's friends list. Perhaps the condom was for him. Did Emily and Kenneth practice slam dunks in her car?

The Austin PD Forensics Science Division hadn't yet processed the evidence I gave them. I hoped to hear a report from Detective Ortega before I met Kenneth Hoar.

If Kenneth got lucky with Emily, I might get lucky and catch his prints on the condom wrapper. I could use that when I interviewed him.

Kenneth's parents gave me his new phone number, and I left a voicemail and a text. I figured he would come home soon and I could arrange a meeting.

Sandy Lynch was a sophomore at the University of Texas at Austin. I reached her while she was at lunch and she agreed to meet me after her one o'clock class at her sorority house.

———

I hadn't eaten a thing since breakfast. I stopped for lunch on the way to Kappa Alpha Kappa sorority. It's always a good time for barbecue, and

Austin has the best in fifty-seven states. Of course, every town in Texas claims they have the best barbecue. And they are all telling the truth.

The KAK house was three stories of red brick Georgian architectural splendor. Neatly trimmed azaleas framed the building in the midst of a lush carpet of St. Augustine grass. I was amazed how well these college women kept their landscaping. Maybe the unlimited budget helped.

I parked in the rear lot in one of eight slots marked Visitors Only Please.

A discreet brass sign on the back door asked visitors to enter without knocking, so I did.

A muted chime dinged when I opened the back door. I waited in the vestibule for a tuxedoed butler from the Earl of Foggy Bottom's centuries-old manse. Maybe he would be bringing a silver tea service.

No butler showed, so after a few minutes, I followed the central hallway toward the front of the house. My rubber-soled Rockport dress shoes squeaked on the parquet floor, echoing in the tomblike silence.

The soft click of heels resonated down the hall, followed by a matronly woman of a certain age who introduced herself as Mrs. Hampton, the KAK housemother.

"Good afternoon, Mrs. Hampton. I'm Carlos McCrary. Sandy Lynch agreed to meet me after class."

We shook hands. She appraised my suit, dress shirt, and tie. I was glad I had shined my shoes.

She smiled warmly. I must have passed inspection.

"Pleased to make your acquaintance, Mr. McCrary."

She led me to a seating area near the window of a front parlor just off the hallway. "Why don't we sit, Mr. McCrary."

"Please, call me Chuck."

As if on cue, a large black woman wearing a gray housedress and an apron in KAK colors materialized behind the housemother, carrying service for three, on a silver platter, of course.

"So, Chuck, I don't believe we've met. How long have you known Sandy?"

"I interviewed her four years ago. I don't expect her to remember me."

I handed the house mother a business card. There was no company crest in the McCrary Investigations colors to print on my card. If McCrary Investigations had company colors, they would be the black and blue of my occupational bruises. My company crest could be the Port City Police shield I once wore. Or maybe a set of brass knuckles.

"May I ask the nature of your interest in Sandy?"

"I'm investigating the disappearance of Emily Constance Crazinski, a friend of Sandy's."

Mrs. Hampton perused my card. "And the family retained a private investigator from Port City, Florida to search for her?"

"Emily is my cousin. Or was. We don't know whether she's alive or dead. Emily's parents are my aunt and uncle and I'm conducting the investigation without charge. Sandy is, or was, Emily's close friend. I hope she'll give me some insight into Emily's situation at the time she disappeared."

"Do you suspect foul play rather than a voluntary runaway?"

I told Mrs. Hampton what I knew of Emily's disappearance. It couldn't hurt.

She listened and her questions demonstrated keen interest. She made an excellent role model to teach young ladies how to carry on a conversation on any subject. Before I knew it, she had charmed me into telling my life story.

I would still be talking if Sandy hadn't shown up.

Sandy paraded into the room like a fashion model on a runway, dressed in an outfit appropriate for an audition for Floozy of the Week on reality TV. Her makeup and hair looked like she had come from a beauty salon instead of her one o'clock class.

Mrs. Hampton excused herself.

Sandy poured herself a coffee and sat like a proper lady, knees together and ankles crossed, contradicting her aggressive apparel. I suspected her posture reflected Mrs. Hampton's influence.

"I appreciate you meeting me. I interviewed you when Emily disappeared, but you wouldn't remember me."

"I remember you, Mr. McCrary."

"Please, call me Chuck." I handed her a business card. "To refresh your memory, I'm a private investigator and Emily's cousin. The family has reopened the case. If Emily is alive, we obviously hope to find her and bring her home. If she's dead, we hope to recover her body and give her a decent burial."

"Of course. How can I help?"

"We discovered that Emily kept a diary. Did you know that?"

Sandy nearly spilled her coffee.

"A diary?" She peered at the chandelier.

Most people can't stand silence in a conversation. They feel an irresistible urge to fill the gap. Nature abhors a vacuum.

I waited.

She cut her gaze my way, then to an ill-defined space over my shoulder.

"What about her diary?"

"It's more journal than diary. She didn't make an entry every day, just when something significant happened."

I began with something easy. If she told me the truth on the easy one, it would be harder to lie about the big one I was saving for later.

"Emily mentioned a boy named Lizard Lips in her English Lit class. Who is Lizard Lips?"

"That's Mr. Drucker, the teacher. We called him Lizard Lips behind his back. He is certified, genuine creepy. He looked at me like he was undressing me in his mind. Made me want to take a shower every time I finished his class."

"Did he say or do anything he shouldn't have? Any inappropriate touching of you or another student?"

Sandy shook her head. "No. He was just...creepy, you know? There was nothing you could take to the principal or complain about, but it was there, lurking at the edge of your awareness."

"Did he behave inappropriately around another student that you witnessed or heard about?"

"No, but he flicked his tongue in and out like a lizard when he looked at me or one of the other girls."

"But not the boys?"

"No. Just the girls."

"Emily refers to 'SL' in her journal. Far as I know, you are her only friend with the initials 'SL'."

I don't trust the "left brain, right brain" theory, or the notion that a person who tells a lie looks up and to the left to access the creative side of their brain to construct a believable lie. Or maybe the left side is creative. Or do they look down and to the right? Whichever side it's supposed to be, I assign little value to those theories.

Instead, Sandy flashed more reliable signals. She blinked her mascaraed eyes twice and jerked her head, then delayed before she replied. She flared her perfectly made-up nostrils and covered her mouth with a manicured hand before she spoke. "What…what did she say about me?"

I tugged out my notebook for effect. I had memorized the entry. "Emily wrote 'Helped SL get rid of an unwanted visitor last weekend.'"

I lowered my notebook and waited until she faced me. "Emily explained about the unwanted visitor." That was a bald-faced lie, which I let dangle in the silence of the sitting room like an unidentified stink.

Sandy's gaze darted around the room like she wanted to escape.

I sat statue-like so I wouldn't spook her more than I already had. "Don't worry, your secret is safe. Emily's mother hasn't read the journal and she won't…unless I tell her she ought to." That was my next lie.

Closing the notebook, I slipped it into my inside jacket pocket, symbolically hiding her secret. I patted my jacket over the pocket, a signal that no one could pry her secret from my cold, dead fingers.

"Was your unwanted visitor connected with Emily's disappearance?" I sipped my coffee. *Good old harmless Chuck. C'mon, Sandy, you can tell good old Chuck anything.*

"No way. For God's sake, we did it two weeks before she disappeared. And it was in Las Cruces, of course."

"New Mexico?"

"Of course. They have less restrictive laws there. I was a minor, so I had no choice. You know how conservative Texas is. Parental notification and all that crap. And Las Cruces is over 600 miles on I-10—a ten-hour drive, for God's sake. I couldn't drive ten hours all night alone, do it, then flip around and drive ten hours back. Emily is the best friend in the whole world."

Sandy clasped her hands and rubbed the palms together. "After it was over, I…I was upset and I couldn't stop crying. Emily stopped in El Paso at a Dairy Queen while I pulled my shit together."

Relaxing my posture, I said, "Ice cream helps, doesn't it?" When I relax, sometimes the person I'm interviewing relaxes.

Sandy smiled without humor but didn't look my way. She raised her cup and it rattled on the saucer. She drank coffee, then held the cup and saucer on her lap.

"Whose car did you drive?"

"Mine. That was fair. It was my problem, so we burned my gas." She fidgeted. "Besides, my car is—was—a BMW. More comfortable for a road trip than her Ford."

"I found an unused condom in Emily's car."

Sandy blushed. "After the other girls learned about my…my *accident*, most of us began to carry condoms. For emergencies."

"Who was Emily's condom intended for?"

Sandy hesitated.

"Knowing who her boyfriend was might help me find her."

"Kenny Hoar. Emily and him hooked up after homecoming dance. October, I think it was. Emily told me everything. They'd been, uh, sleeping together for five months when she disappeared."

"Do you have a picture of Kenny?"

"I have one in my phone's contact list." She found Kenny's portrait and showed it to me.

"Would you send that to my phone? I'll need to talk to him." I already had Hoar's contact info from Carrie, but his number might have changed.

"Sure." In a few seconds my phone dinged with the incoming contact page.

Sandy glanced at me. "Could Emily have been pregnant?"

"If she were, what would Kenny do?"

Sandy held her cup without drinking. She peered over her shoulder at the door where Mrs. Hampton had been. "Will you keep what I tell you confidential? I mean so secret you won't tell anyone ever?"

"Yes," I lied.

"Not Mrs. Hampton, not my parents, not Emily's parents, not *anyone*. And for God's sake, not Emily, if she ever comes home."

"Okay."

"If Emily was pregnant, Kenny would make her get an abortion." She stared at the coffee cup held on her lap and muttered, "That's what he did when he got me pregnant."

"Did Emily know Kenny was the father of your baby?"

"Oh, God no. I could never tell her. She would never speak to me again if she learned I had banged her boyfriend."

SIX

A neat brass Mr. Fisher sign sat in the precise center of the principal's clean desk. No first name, no middle initial. Mr. Fisher, like he couldn't risk someone calling him by his first name. He didn't seem happy to see me.

The principal stood when I entered his office but didn't come around the desk or offer his hand. Button-down white shirt, three-piece pinstriped navy-blue suit, tie in Bonham's signature red and silver colors. Thinning gray hair, closely cropped. The image of a career bureaucrat. I bet he wore wingtips.

"Come in, Mr. McCrary. Please, make yourself comfortable." He gestured to an institutional wooden chair that made comfort impossible.

I stopped at the edge of his desk and extended a business card.

He accepted it and sat, gestured again to the chair. "Detective Ortega said you would drop by. I'm sorry to report that—absent a subpoena—our student records are confidential."

Funny, he didn't look sorry. If anything, Fisher appeared smug as he lined up my business card with his nameplate.

"That's okay, Mr. Fisher. I don't need your student records right now. I am here to arrange interviews with Eleanor Feinstein and Emily's English Literature teacher, Mr. Drucker."

"Ms. Feinstein retired two years ago. We have a new Student Counselor. I'll arrange an interview with her."

"That won't be necessary."

I had interviewed Eleanor Feinstein during my first investigation, but I didn't keep her contact info. Another rookie mistake made before I learned Rule Five: *You can never have too much information.* "May I have Ms. Feinstein's phone number?"

"We can't give out personal information on our employees, current or former. I'm sure you understand the security risks."

I didn't mind. I would locate her on the internet. "What about Mr. Drucker?"

"Mr. Drucker has sixth period free. I can text him to meet you in the teachers' lounge in one hour."

"Great." I stood up. "In the interim, I'll poke around and refresh my memory of the school's layout."

"That's quite impossible. Security was tightened after the, uh, the shootings, you know. We don't allow unaccompanied members of the public to wander the halls unsupervised. Our School Resource Officer would be quite distressed. You understand, I'm sure. If you'll wait in the reception, a student guide will escort you to the teachers' lounge."

I had met the SRO, patrolwoman Darla Yates, when I arrived at the school's reception desk. Officer Yates signed me in, relieved me of my sidearm, and issued me the optic yellow visitor's pass. She clipped it to my jacket lapel to warn everyone I encountered that I was a potential mass murderer. That was a new development in the last four years too. Couldn't say that I blamed them; we had the same rules in Florida schools for the same reason.

"We wouldn't want to distress Officer Yates." I stood. "I'll wait in reception."

While I waited for my student guide, I located Eleanor Feinstein on a social media page and sent her a private message. The internet has made private investigating almost too easy. She called a minute later. "Hello, Chuck. I got your message."

"Thanks for calling back," I said. "I'm in Austin. I reopened Emily's case."

"Has there been a development in her disappearance?"

"*Uh-huh.* That's why I reopened the case. Can we get together?"

"Of course. Since I retired, I write a cooking and decorating blog. I spend most days in my home office. I'll text you the address. Come now if you like."

"I have an appointment with Mr. Drucker in an hour. Can I come after that?"

"Mr. Drucker? Desmond Drucker?"

"He was Emily's English Lit teacher."

"Mr. Drucker is *everybody's* English Lit teacher. English Lit is all he teaches. But why interview him? Did he have something to do with Emily's disappearance?"

During an investigation, I keep my hole cards close to my chest. If you give people information they don't need, they can adjust their answers based on what they think you want to hear. They can also shade their answers to throw you off course, depending on whether they're a good guy or a bad guy. I figured Eleanor was a good guy, but I wanted her mind and memories unbiased when I interviewed her again.

I glanced around the reception area to see if anyone was paying any attention to me. They weren't.

"Why do you ask?" I lowered my voice. "Do you think Drucker was involved?"

"I don't know. It's just…" she paused and I waited for more.

"Desmond Drucker is…*off*. There's something mentally off kilter. I can't articulate it, but he's a weird duck, that's all."

While Eleanor and I talked, my phone signaled a text. The student guide walked in, a perky five-foot-nothing girl dressed in school colors and sporting a Bonham Red and Silver sash emblazoned Student Ambassador Jennifer.

I smiled and lifted a finger to signal her to wait while I finished with Eleanor. I made my goodbyes and hung up.

"Okay if I check this text?"

"Sure thing. It's important to reply to a text."

Kenneth Hoar had texted.

Coming home for the weekend. Let's meet at my

house Sunday afternoon at two o'clock, after I get back from church.

I hit *reply* and confirmed the appointment.

"Okay, Madam Ambassador, take me to your teachers' lounge."

———

Jennifer and I reached the teachers' lounge as fourth period ended. The perky Student Ambassador held the door for me. I had an hour to kill.

"Thanks, Madam Ambassador. After I finish, do you trust me to find my way out to the front door or should I call for another guided escort?"

Jennifer grinned. "Don't take this security shit too seriously. The Student Ambassador gig earns brownie points and pads my resume for college applications. You don't look like a nutso school shooter to me. You're on your own as far as I'm concerned." She flounced out and disappeared down the hall.

A beverage station with coffee, decaf, and a hot water dispenser stood against the wall, a refrigerator at one end. A teacher offered me a coffee before she left for her fifth period class. I thanked her and stuck a dollar in the honor jar before I poured. I sat at a small round table with four chairs.

I called Terry. Straight to voicemail. I sent her a text:

Miss you like crazy. Making progress on the case. Hope to see you soon. Chuck

It had been a week since I left Port City. Terry had ignored my messages since that awful breakfast when she walked out.

To kill time, I scanned the news on my phone. Murder, accidents, wars, and disasters. Maybe I'm a cynic, but if the world were as dangerous as the news media portray it, no one could afford insurance.

Sixth period bell rang. Drucker would arrive soon.

Near the end of the passing period, three teachers entered the lounge. Two were women. Each stuffed a bill in the honor jar, removed a soft drink from the refrigerator, and sat at another table. The third person had to be Drucker. He stood in the door and surveyed the room.

Eleanor was right. Drucker looked the part of a weird duck.

He wore a Union Jack bow tie. His dress shirt sported French cuffs.

William Shakespeare portraits on the cufflinks peeked from the sleeves of his gray wool jacket. He stood three inches taller than me and lanky. I outweighed him twenty pounds. His jacket was two inches wider than his shoulders. Maybe he bought it at a Big-and-Tall shop and didn't bother to alter it for his slender build. He had the body of a long-distance runner or basketball player. Maybe a high-jumper.

"You are Carlos McCrary, are you not?" His lips were thin as a razor slash. Lizard lips.

My research told me he was thirty-eight, but he dressed older. His bald head and tidy gray mustache reminded me of a portrait I had seen of Clement Atlee, the UK's Prime Minister after World War II. He needed a pipe to complete the effect. Come to think of it, in the portrait, Clement Atlee wore a similar suit.

I stood as Drucker marched across the tile floor to the beverage station.

"Yes, sir. Mr. Fisher arranged our appointment."

"I know that, McCrary. I know that. Fisher sent me a text, did he not?"

With precise movements, he selected a saucer and tea cup from a shelf and drew a cup of hot water. He slid a teabag from a jacket pocket and lowered it into the cup. He pivoted toward me like he was marching in a drill team and stood ramrod straight while he rhythmically hoisted and lowered the teabag to brew his tea.

"How may I be of assistance?" He stood at attention next to the counter.

I sat. "Tell me about Emily Crazinski."

His lips parted a split-second before they pressed into a thin line again. "Who?"

"The girl who disappeared four years ago last St. Patrick's Day. She was in your English Lit class."

"I have had thousands of students over the years." Drucker gazed at his cup while he bobbed the teabag. "It is hard to keep them straight, is it not?" He turned to me and stretched his lips into something that resembled a smile. A bluish vein throbbed under the porcelain skin of his temple.

"If you'd care to sit while we talk, I'll show you her picture. Perhaps that will refresh your memory."

"Yes, of course we can sit, can we not?"

He marched across the floor and positioned his saucer exactly opposite my coffee. He removed his jacket, folded it, and draped it across the chair on my right. Yellow perspiration stains marked the shirt's armpits. Red, white and blue suspenders held up his woolen pants, which gapped at the waist. I figured the suspenders honored the Union Jack rather than the good old USA.

Drucker sat across from me, ramrod straight.

I found Emily's picture on my phone and handed it to him.

"Oh, yes. She seems familiar." Drucker's tongue flicked in and out while he regarded the picture.

"Portraits are useful, are they not? A picture is worth a thousand words. Many people think Shakespeare said that, but he did not. The quotation originated in the early twentieth century to explain the importance of including product images in magazine advertisements."

He handed the phone back.

He dipped the teabag again and held it above the cup while it dripped. He laid it on the saucer. The label on the string had a picture of a raspberry.

Raising his cup with pinky extended, he held it under his nose. "I bring my own raspberry tea. I fancy the bouquet and the medicinal benefits. All the school provides," he gestured toward the beverage station, "is generic mass-market tea. It is rather *plebeian*."

Drucker probably thought I didn't know that plebeian meant *common*. "There's nothing like a good cup of tea."

"You said her name is Emily, did you not?"

"Emily Crazinski. Tell me about her."

He sipped, smiled his approval, and deposited the cup on the saucer. "I don't recall Emily. Was she a good student?"

"She disappeared before the semester was over. She never received a grade."

"*Hmm.* That's unfortunate. What would you like to know?"

"Did Emily have trouble with another student? A boy who may have harassed her?"

"I don't recall anything other than that she was a student. Did she tell anyone she was harassed?"

"Yes."

"Ask the person she told. They would know who the culprit was, would they not?"

"She wrote the complaint in a journal. She called him Lizard Lips."

Drucker's nostrils flared and he took a quick breath. It lasted a split-second, but there it was.

"Who was Lizard Lips?"

"Sorry. As I said, I recall only that she was in my class." He held up his phone. "If you will excuse me, McCrary, I have to return a phone call before seventh period."

I stayed put.

Drucker held his phone like a picket sign that said, Go Away.

"You will excuse me, will you not?"

"Sure. Don't mind me." I sipped my coffee and stared at him.

"It's a private call."

"As I said, don't mind me."

Drucker glared at me. He glanced at his watch, then back at me.

"McCrary, our meeting is at an end, and you have no further right to use the teachers' lounge. I demand you leave at once, or I shall call the School Resource Officer and report you as trespassing."

I drained my coffee and stood. I laid a business card on the table in front of Drucker. "If you remember anything about Emily, please call me. Good day."

I pitched my cup in the trash and walked out. Stopping at the next turn in the corridor, I observed the door to the teachers' lounge. Drucker exited and I snapped his picture with my phone and slipped around the corner.

Drucker was hiding something.

———

Eleanor Feinstein lived in a high-rise condo west of downtown. I braked on the parking garage ramp and punched in the access code she'd texted me. The steel gate rattled up, and I rolled into the garage. I slid into a visitor's spot on the third level up. I texted her I had arrived.

Eleanor looked the same. A touch more gray in her curly chestnut hair, but she flashed the familiar jovial smile when she met me at the elevator.

"I'm glad you caught a break in the case, Chuck. Come in, come in." She led me into her eighth-floor apartment.

She sported khaki Bermuda shorts, a Texas Women's University tee-shirt, and bare feet.

After the how-you-beens and the what-can-I-get-yous, we carried our wine to her balcony overlooking Lady Bird Lake.

"It's 4:30 in Austin, but it's after five o'clock in Port City," Eleanor said, toasting her Chardonnay toward me. "*L'Chaim.*"

"*L'Chaim,*" I repeated, clinking glasses. I sipped a drop to be polite. I was working, not socializing.

"What did you think of Desmond Drucker?"

"He is a weird duck."

"Why did you interview him?"

"I hoped he might provide some insight into Emily. I didn't interview him before."

Smiling at me over the rim of her glass, Eleanor took another slow sip.

"Pardon my French, young man, but that's BS. Tell me what's really happening."

"Do you know anyone called Lizard Lips?"

Eleanor laughed. "Of course. Where did you hear it?"

"Earlier this week I found three journals hidden in Emily's bedroom. She wrote that 'LL' gave her the creeps when he stared at her like she was naked. She mentioned it more than once. In another journal I learned that 'LL' was Lizard Lips."

Eleanor chuckled. "The students call Desmond Drucker Lizard Lips. He's known for years, but, of course, he pretends he doesn't."

That confirmed what Sandy Lynch had told me. Rule Twelve: *People lie. If they don't lie, they can be mistaken.*

"Did anyone file a complaint against Drucker while you worked at the school? Like for an inappropriate relationship with a student? Inappropriate touching, texting, or conversations?"

A large truck roared past on the street below, shifting gears to climb the steep hill. We stopped talking until it reached the top.

"I never heard any rumors, and complaints wouldn't be on the public record unless he was charged or arrested. Did you run a background check?"

"Not yet. I drove here straight from interviewing him. I'll contact Detective Ortega and ask him to run Drucker's criminal record."

"Could he have done something to Emily?"

"Do you think he has it in him to be a predator?"

Eleanor pursed her lips. "Hard to say. Like I said, there is something not normal about him. He wouldn't be the first teacher to do something terrible to a student. What was your impression?"

"He's on my radar now. Do you still have Drucker's phone or cellphone numbers?"

"I never purge my phone's address book." She held her cellphone and scrolled down the screen. "Here."

She laid the phone on the table. I added the number to my contact list.

"What's his landline number?"

"Try the white pages, either online or an old one in the library. Why do you want his numbers?"

"Because I don't have them. Rule Five: *You can never have too much information.*"

"What's rule five?"

"A rule I follow that helps in investigations."

We carried our wine glasses to the rail and admired Lady Bird Lake. The sun had dropped far enough to shimmer on the water. "Your view is magnificent."

"That view was the big selling point for this condo when I retired. After my husband died, I figured I would spend plenty of time here with my blog and all. My guestroom/office overlooks the lake. Pretty nice, huh?"

"Nice doesn't begin to describe it."

I returned to the glass-topped table.

"I have another subject to discuss. Another student."

"Who?"

"Ling Cheng. Do you remember her?"

Eleanor elevated her glass in a toast. "To Ling Cheng, a guidance counselor's dream."

"What do you remember about her?"

"She's smart, ranking about eighth or ninth in a class of five hundred. She worked hard so she could play sports. Basketball and volleyball. She didn't have a talent for either game, but she figured sports improved her resume for college applications. She wanted to be well-rounded with diverse interests. She made the debate team too. She didn't want to be another stereotypical Asian nerd. It worked. She was accepted at MIT, Stanford, and Rice."

"Which one did she choose?"

"MIT. One of her parents is an MIT grad."

"How do I contact her? Do you keep in touch?"

"I was a guidance counselor for thirty years. If I kept in touch with former students, I wouldn't have time to do anything else. Why the interest in Ling Cheng? I wasn't aware she was involved in Emily's case. As far as I know, they weren't even friends. Ling was two years ahead of Emily. Oh, I get it. Basketball?"

"Emily hosted a sleepover of the basketball team two weeks before she disappeared. Ling Cheng brought her diary and all the girls signed farewell messages to her. She hid the diary in Emily's bedroom. Why didn't she come back for it?"

Eleanor set her glass on a coaster.

"You can't call MIT and ask for Ling's contact information. They wouldn't give that to anyone without a court order, then they'd drag their feet just because they can. Did you Google her?"

"Yeah. She made the last entry on her social media accounts two months after Emily disappeared. The entry was her graduation pictures. Emily's parents told me that Ling moved to China with her parents after graduation."

Eleanor shook her head. "No. She planned to attend MIT. She received her American citizenship when she was eighteen, the month before graduation. I gave her an American flag to honor her new citizenship. She was one of two students at the Bonham awards ceremony who received a scholarship to MIT."

"Who was the other student?"

"I don't recall. Oh, I get it. The other student might have kept in touch with her. If you locate him, he may know her contact info."

"You remember that it was a boy?"

She smiled. "Another Asian. From the southeast—Vietnam, Thailand, maybe Cambodia. You want me to find out?"

"Yes please."

"I'll call a buddy at the high school on Monday. She'll look it up and she won't tell the old fussbudget Mr. Fisher."

She sipped her wine, then stared at the glass.

"If that doesn't work, I met someone in the MIT admissions department at a guidance counselors' convention." She glanced at her watch. "Too late to call now. I'll ring him Monday and ask how to contact Ling. One of those leads might pan out."

SEVEN

Carrie made enchiladas and served dinner on the deck. The sun dropped behind the oak trees.

"Pass the salsa, please," Grandpa said.

He slathered the spicy sauce across his enchiladas. "How's the investigation going?"

"I interviewed Sandy Lynch yesterday at her sorority house."

"How is Sandy?" Carrie asked. "She and Emily were close friends. A nice girl from a lovely family. Didn't we often say so, Frank?"

Jibber-jabber, I thought.

Frank shoveled another bite of enchilada into his mouth without comment. He knew Carrie could carry both sides of a conversation. *More jibber-jabber.*

"Sandy seemed in good health," I said, "but she's not the girl you think."

"Why do you say that?"

"A few weeks before her disappearance, Emily and Sandy drove to Las Cruces in Sandy's BMW."

Frank jerked his gaze up from his food. "Las Cruces, New Mexico?"

"Yes."

"Why did they drive to..." Carrie raised her hand to her face. "Oh my God. That's where girls go for abortions. Was Emily pregnant?"

"No. It was Sandy."

Frank's face clouded.

"Did she say who the father was?"

"Kenny Hoar."

"He used to come see Emily sometimes," Carrie said. "The kids call it 'hanging out.'"

"I know. Sandy said Kenny began seeing Emily after the homecoming dance. Emily considered him her boyfriend. To Kenny, Emily was just another hookup."

"They studied together," Carrie said, "in Emily's room. Oh, Christ. That nice-looking boy was diddling my daughter. In our house. Under our noses."

"Water under the bridge, honey," Frank said. He glanced my way. "Did Emily know Kenny and Sandy were, uh, intimate?"

"Sandy never told her. She was afraid Emily would never speak to her again."

"I'll bet," Carrie said.

Grandpa cleared his throat. "Did Kenny Hoar get Emily pregnant? Could that be why she disappeared?"

"I intend to ask him. If Emily were pregnant, Sandy didn't know about it. I asked her how Kenny would react if Emily got pregnant. When Sandy told Kenny she was pregnant, he made her get the abortion. She said he would have demanded an abortion if Emily were pregnant."

Grandpa gestured with his fork. "You know what that means. If Emily were pregnant and confronted Kenny..."

"Emily would gladly hop in Kenny's car after school," Carrie said. "They'd go someplace to talk—"

"Or do other things," Frank interrupted.

"She tells him she's pregnant, and he makes her disappear," she finished.

"I didn't find any evidence of blood or semen in Emily's car," I said. "That doesn't prove she *wasn't* pregnant, and they could have been having sex elsewhere."

Frank glanced at me. "You heard from Detective Ortega about the condom?"

"He texted me this afternoon. The only fingerprints were Emily's." *Another dead end,* I thought but didn't say.

Carrie laid her hand on Frank's forearm. "Your horoscope said you might receive shocking news today, honey."

He jerked his arm away. "But this news shocked us *all.* The damned horoscope didn't say that about you or Pops or Chuck, did it? That crap is superstitious mumbo-jumbo. I get bloody tired when you bring it up constantly like it's the Holy Bible."

He threw his napkin on the table and stalked into the house, slamming the back door.

Carrie's face reddened.

"You'll have to forgive Frank. He's under a lot of pressure. He pretends he's okay, but he's torn up over Emily to this very day." She started to stand.

Grandpa raised his hands. "Sweetie, you'd best let Frank simmer down."

Carrie returned to her seat.

"If Emily were pregnant, that changes the whole investigation," Grandpa said. "It becomes a murder instead of a kidnapping."

I pivoted to Carrie. "We have no evidence Emily was pregnant, but I'll ask her friends if they knew whether she was." I laid a hand on hers. "I know that idea is hard to contemplate, but I have no choice."

Carrie blotted her tears with a napkin.

"We can't worry about her reputation. That would handicap your investigation. Do what you have to do."

"What else you got, son?" Grandpa said.

"I met Mr. Fisher, the principal, this afternoon. He arranged a meeting with Desmond Drucker, Emily's English Lit teacher. He's the 'Lizard Lips' Emily mentioned in her diary."

"You forget," Carrie said, "I haven't read Emily's diary."

"I believe you should. Since we learned about Sandy Lynch's abortion and Emily's relationship with Kenny Hoar—which you and Frank knew nothing about—I want you two to read every word. An item I wouldn't notice might leap at you like a skunk in a perfume boutique."

"What about this Lizard Lips nickname?" Grandpa said, "Is that why you had me follow him this afternoon?"

"Yes. What did you learn?"

Grandpa slipped a small notebook from his pocket.

"Drucker departed school at 2:35 p.m. and drove to an H-E-B supermarket. He drives a twelve-year-old Hyundai Sonata." He recited the license plate number and glanced up from his notes. "The tires are bald and it hasn't been washed since the Obama administration."

He reviewed the notes again.

"He wheeled out a basket of groceries that included a twelve-bottle case of cabernet and drove home, where he arrived at 4:02 p.m. He lives in Hyde Park." He read the address. "He unloaded the groceries, changed clothes, and came out at 4:35. I followed him to Brentwood Park, where he parked his car and walked to the playground. He watched the soccer field from fifty yards away. A bunch of teenage girls were at practice. He stood under a big oak tree where nobody would notice him."

Grandpa looked at me deadpan. "He took pictures, maybe videos, of the girls. He used a telephoto lens."

"Where were you?"

"I stayed in my van seventy-five yards away. I zoomed my phone and videoed him. He didn't notice me. He made the videos with one hand and stuck his other hand in his raincoat pocket."

Grandpa and I eyeballed each other.

"I don't get it," Carrie said. "What's the significance of the raincoat?"

"Does your video show what I think it does?" I asked.

"It looks like it." Grandpa handed me his phone.

I played the video and sighed.

"Okay, guys, enough with the cryptic clues. What are you two talking about?"

I handed her Grandpa's phone.

"Play it yourself. Tell me what you think."

She watched the video twice.

"I don't understand this. Yesterday was a sunny day. Tell me what the hell the raincoat means."

Grandpa touched Carrie's hand.

"It means Drucker cut a hole inside his raincoat pocket so he could reach inside without anyone seeing his hand."

"I don't get it. Why did he reach inside his raincoat? He..." Her eyes grew big. "Oh my God. He was..."

She played the video again. After she finished, she thrust the phone away.

Grandpa squeezed her hand. "He has a thing for young girls."

That night, I dreamed that Kenny Hoar picked up Emily after school in a shiny black Jaguar. He told her they were driving to Las Cruces. There are hundreds of square miles of trackless desert in West Texas and around Las Cruces. Lots of places to hide a body. I woke up in a sweat again.

———

Debbie Sane met me at *Tres Hermanos* Mexican restaurant on South Congress Avenue in an older area that had gentrified after decades of decline. Parking lots were not on anyone's development plans when the century-old neighborhood was built.

I wrangled a table near the entrance. Debbie walked in and I stood and waved her over.

"Sorry I'm late, Chuck. All the Uber drivers were busy. This area is too popular."

"Reminds me of what Yogi Berra said about a popular restaurant in New York City. Yogi said, 'Nobody goes there anymore. It's too crowded.'"

"Who's Yogi Berra?"

I was astonished. Who hasn't heard of Yogi Berra? Debbie was a high school graduate and a paralegal for a big law firm, but her education was severely lacking.

"Yogi Berra was the New York Yankees catcher back in the Stone Age."

"The New York Yankees? Is that baseball?"

I let it pass. Poor girl. "No problem. I parked a block away myself."

"That's why I Uber. Well, that and because I love their margaritas a little more than I should. They don't ask for my ID either. Don't tell anyone."

"You're Emily's age, aren't you?"

"I'll be twenty-one next February, so I'm virtually legal to drink." She gave me bedroom eyes. "I'm already legal for other things."

I smiled at her. Fellow conspirators. I made a zipper motion across my lips. "What do you recommend?"

"The margaritas. *Sobre las rocas.*" *On the rocks.*

"I mean for an entrée."

We both ordered *chile relleno*. Debbie ordered a margarita *sobre las rocas*. I ordered a Dos Equis beer.

Debbie hoisted her margarita. "To Emily and to happier times."

Had I contributed to the delinquency of a minor? *Nah.* Debbie was already delinquent.

I clinked my bottle against her glass and a few grains of salt dropped from the rim.

She wiped the salt off the table with a napkin and swigged her margarita, downing half. "Oh my, that's good for what ails you. So, about Emily's case, how can I help?"

I pulled out a notebook.

"What can you tell me about Kenneth Hoar?"

"Why the interest in Kenny? Was he involved in Emily's disappearance?"

"He and Emily had dated since the homecoming dance the semester before she vanished."

Debbie winked.

"Emily *thought* they were dating, but Kenny treated her like another hookup. Emily wanted more, but Kenny wasn't into relationships. For example, sometimes he waited a whole day to reply to Emily's texts, and he forgot her sixteenth birthday after they'd been getting hot and sweaty together for two whole months. Can you believe it? Kenny was the first boy in her pants, and he forgets her birthday. She was royally pissed. He's a jerk about stuff like that. He won't even carry condoms. Expects the girls to provide them." She drank another mouthful.

"Did Emily carry condoms?"

"We all did. You never know when you'll get lucky." She finished her margarita and smiled like we were discussing the weather.

I was ten or eleven years older than Debbie and Emily, and she made me feel like I was from another generation. Perhaps it was my rural upbringing in Adams Creek—country mouse versus city mouse. Lots of my fellow students at Theodore Roosevelt High School were sexually active, but at least we felt a little guilty and didn't flaunt it.

"If Emily was sexually active, why didn't she use birth control pills?"

"Same reason I didn't. My parents might see them in the medicine cabinet. Birth control pills are too 'in your face' for parents to handle. Condoms I could hide in my purse. Once I reached eighteen, I started on the pill." She winked again. "Like I said: You never know when you'll get lucky."

She pressed her knee against mine.

I edged my leg away.

"What else can you tell me about Kenny?"

Debbie laughed. "Kenny is Peter Pan with a dark side. He's the bad boy who never grew up. He's gotten into legal trouble like since forever. His parents trail along behind with a checkbook and a pack of lawyers."

She signaled the server for another margarita.

"He's had trouble with the law?"

"Oh, nothing you'd uncover by running a criminal background investigation. As a juvenile, his records were sealed. His parents bought off people so they wouldn't press charges. Once he enrolled in Davy Crockett State, he toned down. Either that or he's learned how not to get caught."

"What kind of trouble was he in?"

"His bad temper gets away from him sometimes. He beat up a few boys and one or two girls. His parents kept everything out of the papers and off the court records."

Her second margarita arrived and she winked at the server as she drank another long pull.

I made notes while Debbie talked.

"He was barely smart enough to stay academically eligible in high school. His parents spent a small fortune on private tutors. His dad is a high-tech multimillionaire, and his mom's family owns half the oil wells in Oklahoma."

She leaned forward. "Can you keep a secret?"

"Try me." I figured she would appreciate the *double entendre.*

"Kenny and his parents tell people he received a basketball scholarship to Davy Crockett State, but he didn't. He's a walk-on and he doesn't play much. His parents spend a bloody fortune on tutors so he won't flunk out."

"Why haven't they gotten fed up with him?"

"Kenny is dumb as a day-old donut, but he's an only child. His folks have invested everything in him. He's their legacy, warts, farts, and all."

"Sounds like you know him well."

"I know him *intimately.*" She winked. "He was the first boy to get in my pants too. That was in the eighth grade, and he was already over six feet tall. We stopped fooling around after we started high school. I guess we each wanted to...*experience* other people. I wanted to broaden my horizons." She winked. "I still do." She nudged my knee again and chugged more margarita.

"Let's see...The one thing he's serious about is basketball, and, ironically, he's not that good at it. He's merely tall. Really tall."

"What would Kenny do if Emily got pregnant?"

"Holy crap! Was Emily pregnant?" She drained her glass.

"That's what I want to find out. Would she tell you if she were?"

Debbie waggled her empty class and signaled for another margarita.

"She would tell me if she needed an abortion. She would need me to go with her. It's a ten-hour drive to New Mexico, and that's one way. Then you gotta drive back. Can't do that alone. An abortion is stressful. Or so I hear." She rapped her knuckles on the table. "Knock on wood that I don't get knocked up." She giggled at her own joke. The margarita had loosened her tongue and her inhibitions.

"Would she get pregnant intentionally to force Kenny into a relationship?"

"If she did, it wasn't for the family money. Honest to God, she thought she loved him. I told her Kenny was not the long-term type. When things don't go his way, his vicious streak comes out. He's not marriage material, though he's great in bed. Love is blind, I guess."

"Did Emily discuss Kenny with you?"

Debbie smirked. "Yes. After Emily disappeared, Kenny and I hooked up again. We still do when he comes home for the weekend. He's coming to my place tonight. He's not a clever conversationalist, but he knows how to please a girl. He's had lots of practice."

Debbie's third margarita came and she drank half. I switched to coffee.

Our *chiles rellenos* came and we discussed the food and our favorite Mexican restaurants, hers in Austin and mine in Port City. Debbie polished off her third margarita and ordered a fourth. I hoped I could finish the interview before she became incoherent.

Debbie had scarcely touched her food. I wondered why she hadn't passed out in her plate. Maybe she had built up an immunity to tequila.

I scooted my empty plate aside. "Getting back to Emily, let's suppose for the sake of discussion that Kenny got Emily pregnant. Doesn't matter whether it was an accident or not. What would he do when she told him?"

"He would freak out and insist she have an abortion. He's totally irresponsible. One thing for sure: He would blame Emily, never himself. He thinks anything that goes wrong is someone else's fault."

Debbie's fourth margarita arrived. She smiled at the male server and signaled him to remove her plate. She patted him on the butt as he walked away.

"You never know when you'll get lucky."

I had lost track of the times Debbie had tossed that remark at me. Apparently, getting lucky was her goal in life. I felt like she wanted to add my scalp to her collection. Or maybe it was another part of my body.

She swallowed a generous portion of the new margarita.

"What would happen if Emily didn't want an abortion? What if she expected Kenny to marry her?"

"I wouldn't want to com— to *con*template that." Debbie focused on pronouncing the words. "No. You wouldn't want to be in Kenny's vincin...*near* him when he's crossed."

"Okay. Changing the subject: Did Lizard Lips ever behave inappropriately toward you?"

"Where did you learn about Lizard Lips Drucker?"

"I'm a private eye. Learning things is what I do. Was Mr. Drucker ever inappropriate around you or another student?"

"No. He flicks his tongue in and out when he talks to girl students. Looks like a lizard. Or a snake. He's weird and spooky, and he looked like he fantasized whenever he looked at me. He never *did* anything that I know about, but he made all the girls feel *yucky*. We used to talk about him all the time, about how weird he was."

"Who do you think kidnapped Emily?"

"I wish I knew, but I don't have a clue. Do you think Mr. Drucker did it?"

"I don't know. Yet."

The bill came and I dropped my credit card in the tray.

Debbie finished her fourth margarita. She gave me bedroom eyes while she licked the salt off her lips. Or maybe she was about to pass out. "Would you like to take me home, Chuck? I'm not a schoolgirl anymore." She winked. "You never know when you'll get lucky."

Even if she had been in any condition to consent to sex—which she wasn't—I didn't feel like being another notch on her bedpost. I told a white lie.

"I appreciate the offer, but I have another appointment. I'll wait outside with you until your Uber comes."

———

Kenneth Hoar dressed more like a choir boy than a bad boy. Pressed khaki pants, Davy Crockett State University sport shirt, and bright white DCSU basketball shoes. Perhaps he was still in his church clothes. A typical clean-cut All-American boy, except the typical twenty-year-old boy wasn't six-foot-seven. And a typical clean-cut All-American boy's eyes didn't look like ball bearings.

"Kenny, how about I buy you a cup of coffee? Let's go to Starbucks."

We were sitting in the second-floor media room in his parents' three-story mansion on a mountaintop in West Lake Hills, an affluent suburb for the rich and/or hugely-indebted.

"We have coffee. To tell you the truth, dude, there's a Cowboys game on at three o'clock. They're playing the Texans. To get to Starbucks, you gotta drive down the mountain, then you gotta drive back. I don't want to miss the kickoff. I don't like to watch sports on a DVR. I prefer to watch live."

Jeffrey Hoar, Kenny's father, sat on a custom-made sofa that curved its way across the huge room. It provided 50-yardline seats fronting a television screen fit for a movie theatre. Jeffrey had softened the audio on the Patriots-Dolphins game, but he was still concentrating on it. I figured he wanted to be polite, but he didn't want to miss the game between two undefeated teams either.

Like a twenty-first-century English manor house, the garages, servants' quarters, utility rooms, and storage rooms were on the ground floor. Those rooms had no view because of the trees on the wooded lot. The second-floor window wall looked out over Lake Austin with a million-dollar vista of Austin's skyline on the horizon. The Travis County Property Tax Appraiser valued the house at over $19,000,000. I checked it out after Kenny Hoar texted me his address. Know your enemy. Or at least, know your suspect.

"Where can we talk that won't disturb your father watching the game?"

Kenny smirked to prove how cool he was.

"What's so sensitive, man? You want to talk about Emily's disappearance, right? I don't know anything about that, so this will be a short conversation."

Glancing at his father before I responded, I pitched my voice for Kenny's ears only. "Let's talk about Sandy Lynch and Debbie Sane."

The smirk disappeared. Kenny cocked his head to one side. His eyes seemed even deader, if possible.

I lowered my voice to a whisper. "And let's chat about Sandy and Emily's road trip. You know, the one they made to Las Cruces."

Kenny's gaze flicked like a snake's tongue as if he planned to make a break for freedom. Or was contemplating where he could hide my body.

He spun to his father. "Excuse us, Dad?"

Jeffrey Hoar waved his approval without his attention leaving the game. "Sure, whatever." He reached for the remote.

"Okay, dude, let's go to my room."

As we left the media room, the sound rose again.

We skipped the elevator and climbed the curved mahogany staircase that spiraled from the ground floor to the third. The stairs wrapped around the chandelier hung from the foyer's forty-foot ceiling. The chandelier could have been looted from Buckingham Palace.

Kenny's third-floor "room" was a suite with a squash-court-sized bedroom. Through an arch I saw a sitting room with an office-sized desk and a computer with double monitors. Probably had a walk-in closet the size of Kentucky. He opened the eight-foot-tall sliders and led me onto a terrace big enough to park an eighteen-wheeler. The panoramic view was even better from the third floor.

It must be nice to have parents with enough money to buy a small country.

Hoar sprawled across a chaise. His skateboard-sized feet hung over the end. He waved me to another chaise. "Did you want coffee, dude, or was that a trick to talk to me privately?"

I gave him my hundred-watt smile.

"I wanted privacy. We need to discuss things you don't want your parents to know."

One of Hoar's eyes fluttered. He waved a hand. *Get on with it*, it seemed to say.

"Tell me about Emily."

"Not much to tell, man. We both played basketball. I went to her games; she went to mine. We hung out a couple times and sometimes we studied together. Then she disappeared. Now you see her, now you don't, y'know? Like *poof*."

"Did you get her pregnant?"

He blinked. "*Uh...umm...*What do you mean, man."

"It's a simple question. Did you get Emily pregnant?"

"No. Of course not. We never got together...that way. We hung out a couple times. We weren't banging each other, if that's what you mean. I swear."

"And I'll bet you never banged Sandy Lynch or Debbie Sane either."

He sat up on the chaise and swung his feet onto the deck.

"Okay, I mean, me and Sandy…the whole thing was Sandy's idea. She came onto me. What would you do, turn her down? No way, man. She was hot, hot, hot."

"Until she got pregnant."

"Okay, we hooked up a couple times, and she wasn't careful and she got pregnant. Shit happens, y'know? But she got rid of it. Her and Emily, they drove to Las Cruces and that was that. I gave her two thousand dollars to pay for it." He shrugged. Mr. Personal Responsibility.

"That's all, man. She didn't tell Emily I was the father, or Emily would kill me."

"If you weren't Emily's boyfriend, why would she have been angry at you for knocking up Sandy?"

Hoar froze like a deer in the headlights. Clearly, not the sharpest knife in the drawer.

"Same thing with Debbie Sane? She came onto you?"

"Me and Debbie been hooking up off and on since middle school. I mean, she banged my brains out last night."

"Kenny, Emily kept a diary."

I waited for that to sink in.

"I know every detail of what you and Emily did."

"No way, man. The bitch was lying, writing her fantasies or something. I swear I never touched her. Never."

I hauled a condom in a plastic sandwich bag from my pocket. "I found this in Emily's car. Her diary said you refused to carry condoms, so she had to."

Hoar stared at the condom like it was a ticking bomb.

"When the cops examine this for fingerprints, whose fingerprints will they find?"

Hoar gazed at the condom, hypnotized. His lips moved, but no sound came out.

"Tell me the truth. Did you get Emily pregnant?"

Hoar leaned his elbows on his knees and held his head. He stared at the deck. "Honest to God, dude, I don't know."

He peered at me with red eyes.

"I sure as hell hope not."

EIGHT

M y phone signaled a call from a number I didn't recognize—a 737 number, one of the Austin area codes.

"This is Chuck McCrary."

"Hello, Chuck. This is Ruby Voight. Remember me? From the Austin PD crime lab."

"Yes, Ruby. I remember you. How are you?"

"I'm fine, thanks. Listen, I've finished processing the evidence you found."

Mentally, I replayed our conversation when Ortega had given her the evidence. He had not mentioned who found it. Neither had I.

"What makes you think I found it instead of Detective Ortega?"

She laughed. "I'm a trained forensic scientist. The first clue was the evidence bags; they're not the brand that we use. I bet you brought them from Port City. Am I right?"

Busted. "Right. That's the brand we used at the Port City Police Department. I still use them—an old habit."

"The next clue was that this is the first addition to the case file in over four years. Ortega let that case get cold as a coffin. The case wouldn't heat up with no one working it. And right when you show up? Give me a break."

You, of course, the missing girl's handsome cousin. You breathed life into a dead-end case."

"Detective Ortega said you should report to him, not me. I don't want you to get in trouble."

"Ortega's a jerk. Screw him. Meet me for lunch and I'll give you a sneak peek at the evidence report. Or meet me for dinner, and I'll give you more than that."

I knew what Ruby had in mind when she offered "more than that," but I hadn't given up on Terry yet. "Lunch would be fine. Where shall I meet you?"

"Bernard's American Bistro. I'll text you the address. Twelve-thirty good for you?"

I was born hungry and I've been hungry ever since, but I didn't say that. "You're the one with the work schedule. I'll be there."

———

Bernard's American Bistro was an upscale French restaurant on east Sixth Street. You know it's upscale when they have a valet to park your car.

As usual, I was fifteen minutes early. "Reservation for two for Carlos McCrary. I'm a little early."

"No problem, Mr. McCrary." The host led me to a table with a view of the entrance. A server brought a loaf of warm French bread and a saucer of olive oil and a pepper grinder.

A half-hour later I had gobbled all the French bread in the first basket and ordered another loaf. Ruby Voight was still AWOL.

At one o'clock, she rushed to the host stand. She saw me and waved. "There's my date," she told the host and breezed past him.

She called me a *date*. Did she intend for me to hear that remark? Having spent my formative years in a small town, I still didn't understand the assertiveness of most city women toward men and relationships, although I had benefited from it. I was a country mouse in the big city and always had been. In every relationship I had ever had, the girl or woman had approached me first.

"I'm so sorry I'm late, Chuck."

She set her tote bag on one side of the table. The bag was a practical heavy-duty canvas with handles and a shoulder strap. The color scheme matched her khaki pants and navy-blue shirt. Good choice: stylish and practical for a criminalist.

"I got tied up with a forensic test that took longer than I planned. I hope I don't smell like a bunch of funky chemicals."

I held her chair. "You smell lovely, much better than a bunch of funky chemicals."

Ruby had called the meeting, so I let her set the pace. Handing me the evidence report would take a few seconds, and I looked forward to an untroubled meal with an attractive woman for the first time in over a week.

She didn't open her menu. "The *salade niçoise* is to die for, but most men go for something heartier."

I had devoured two loaves of homemade French bread with olive oil and ground pepper, so the *salade niçoise* would keep me from starving until I could get some real food later. "I'll have what you're having." Always a safe choice.

Ruby burst out laughing as her light brown face turned a bright red. She grabbed her water glass and took a swallow, then blushed again. "You must think I'm crazy, but you reminded me of that line from *When Harry Met Sally*. You know: I'll have what she's having."

I smiled. "No problem. Lots of women laugh when they see me."

This time she laughed normally and we continued through a pleasant meal that appeared like a normal, social get-together between a man and a woman. But beneath the veneer of first-date conversation, there was a subtext of separate agendas: Ruby was angling for a real date; I was waiting for the evidence report. Well, mainly the evidence report; Ruby seemed like a nice person also. Thoughts of Terry whispered at the edges of my mind. *Has she already moved on? Should I? If we're still a couple, why doesn't she answer my voicemails or texts?*

After coffee, Ruby pulled a small sheaf of papers from her tote and gave them to me. "You can keep this copy. I don't think there's anything here to help you. The only print I could raise was from the condom, and it was your cousin's. No DNA on anything."

"That's helpful, Ruby. It tells me she was the one using the condom and not one of her girlfriends. It's evidence that she was sexually active."

She blushed again. Not easy to see because of her dark skin.

I called for the check and stuck the report in my jacket pocket.

Ruby laid her hand on my arm. "I'd love to hear more about Port City Beach sometime. Maybe you could come to my place for dinner some night. That is, if you don't have a girlfriend in Port City."

"I don't know if I have a girlfriend any more. Before I came to Austin, I was in a relationship. My girlfriend didn't want me to take my cousin's case and she walked out on me. She hasn't answered any of my texts, emails, or voicemails."

"Look, Chuck, I'm normally not this forward, but our paths may not cross again and if I don't say this now, I'll regret it later. I'd like to see you again." She blushed, her mocha skin turning a dusty rose. "How can I make that happen?"

"Ruby, you are talented, smart, attractive, and smell lots better than a room full of testing chemicals." This elicited a smile. "There must be many men who would jump at the chance to have dinner with you; you just haven't met the right one. As for me, I'm not ready to give up on Terry." I placed my hand on hers. "This lunch has been great fun, and I wish you the best."

"You have my number in your phone. Call me if you change your mind."

I get peckish in the afternoon, especially after eating only a *salade niçoise* for lunch. The two loaves of French bread don't count. Driving to Detective Ortega's office, I bought an assortment of *pan dulces* and two cups of coffee from a Mexican bakery. The aroma of the pastry attempted to seduce me on the drive, but I exercised more self-control than normal and managed not to eat them on the way.

If anything would soften a hostile Mexican-American cop's heart, *pan dulce* was a good gamble. So far, my youthful charm hadn't worked. Ruby was right: Ortega was a jerk.

I set the box of deliciousness on his desk.

He inhaled and his lips twitched. Was that a smile? So far, so good.

I retrieved the coffees from a sack and handed one to the detective. "There are napkins, sugar, and creamer in the sack."

"Thanks." Ortega opened the box and inhaled a lungful of aroma. "I was just about to call you. I got the evidence report on the items you found in Emily's car." He shoved the report across the desk.

I read it as if I hadn't seen it before. "This at least proves that Emily was sexually active. She's the one who handled the condom."

"Yeah. Anyway, is that why you came here? For the evidence report?"

"No, I have something else."

"What's on your mind?"

He selected a *pan dulce* and edged the box an inch toward me.

"I have clues."

"Whoopee. What did you find?"

I told Ortega about the three journals. I told him I had leads in the volumes.

"Are you saying that my guys missed those journals when they processed Emily's bedroom?"

"All I'm saying is that I found them when I examined her room, and her parents swear the room is the way she left it."

I expected another tirade that I was making his department look bad.

"My detectives made a reasonable search under the circumstances."

Okay, so Ortega was getting defensive. It's never a good sign when a detective makes excuses for incompetence.

I wasn't sure how to respond to that so I followed Rule Twenty-three: *If you don't know what to say, don't say it.* I seldom get in trouble when I keep my mouth shut.

I chewed my *pan dulce* and waited.

Ortega rocked his head from side to side a couple of degrees. "What else did they miss?"

"So far, that's all."

"You gonna bring the journals in for evidence?"

"For now, I'd rather keep them. I want her parents to review them for leads I might have missed."

"They haven't read them? I'm surprised."

I gave him a half-shrug. "Something about trusting their daughter and respecting her privacy."

I told Ortega about Emily's concerns with Lizard Lips. "Lizard Lips is Desmond Drucker, the English Literature teacher at Bonham High. I had him followed after school last Friday."

"Why?"

"Two former female students told me he acted *creepy* around them." I made air quotes. "One girl said he stared at them like he could see through their clothes. Another told me she felt like he was undressing her in his mind. He made all the girls feel *yucky*." More air quotes. "Another teacher said Drucker was weird in a way she couldn't articulate. I interviewed him at school Friday. This guy is stranger than a witch doctor at a medical convention. After I finished the interview, I called an operative to follow him when he left school."

I cued the video Grandpa recorded at Brentwood Park and handed Ortega my phone. "Watch this."

Ortega played the video.

I munched another pastry while he played it again.

He waggled my phone. "Not bad work."

That was front page news, but it was too much to expect an actual "attaboy" from the caustic detective. For now, I had to be satisfied with a "not bad." I was tempted to tell him my operative was my grandfather. *Nah*, better not.

"Okay if I send the video to my phone?" he asked.

"Feel free."

Ortega fiddled on my phone until his cellphone signaled.

"I'll make sure I got it." He viewed the video a second time on his phone.

"That's disgusting, but it's circumstantial evidence. I'll give this to the DA's office and see what they can do. Child porn cases belong to the Child Abuse division, but this isn't child porn. Those girls are older teenagers, maybe college students. If he had exposed himself, that would be another matter."

My phone rang.

Ortega looked annoyed, like I should have turned my phone off in his office. I figured that if our positions were reversed, he wouldn't turn his phone off. Screw you, Ortega.

It was Eleanor Feinstein. I told the phone to signal her I was in a meeting and would call back.

"Emily's guidance counselor. I'll call her later."

I stuck the phone in my pocket.

"About Drucker's raincoat. At the least, he's a suspect for child porn or public lewdness. Who knows? If you get a search warrant for child porn, we might discover Emily held captive in his attic the last four years. Stranger things have happened."

Until I said it, I hadn't entertained Carrie's fantasy that Emily might be alive. The odds were too long. When children go missing more than a few days, they are either never heard from again, or their skeletal remains are found years later in a forest or some other seldom-visited place—like the New Mexico desert. But, like Grandpa had said: A *slim* chance doesn't mean *no* chance.

It was worth a shot.

"Child porn is the purview of Child Abuse. I'll see what I can do with them or the DA's office. In the meantime, can you keep the tail on him? If your operative videos him exposing himself, we can act on that in a heartbeat."

"I can't tail him every day, but, yeah, I'll have him picked up after school and on weekends for a few days. I told my guy to follow him after school today and stay on him until he got home."

"What if Drucker leaves again after dinner?"

"I'm doing this case on the cuff. To tell you the truth, my operative is Emily's and my grandfather. He wants to help."

Ortega gave me an expression I couldn't decipher. "I still have the question: 'What if Drucker leaves the house after dinner?'"

"Grandpa doesn't drive at night."

The detective regarded me.

"My grandfather doesn't either."

So, Ortega had a grandfather? He might be human after all.

"Without probable cause, I can't do shit. The ACLU would kill me and eat my liver if they learned the police tailed him without more evidence."

He wiped his fingers on a napkin and selected another pastry.

"What if I got a former student to file a complaint?"

"About what? That Drucker made her feel *yucky*?"

"You saw the video of Drucker playing pocket pool. Shouldn't you at least give Child Abuse a heads-up on Drucker as a potential child molester?"

"I'll see what I can do. I'll show them the video, but I can't promise anything."

I handed Ortega my phone again. "Here's a picture of Drucker's house that Grandpa took."

The house was a Queen Anne beauty built in 1905; I looked it up. With Drucker's fascination with all things British, the Queen Anne house made perfect sense.

"Note the round tower, the large second floor with high ceilings, and the steep roof above the half-story has room to hide a kidnap victim in the attic."

Ortega perused the photo and grunted noncommittally. He handed my phone back. "You have something in mind?"

"This situation poses an ethical question: Since there is a possibility that Emily is in Drucker's house...?" I left the idea unfinished.

Ortega leaned back in his desk chair and contemplated his coffee cup.

"You say he teaches English at Bonham High during the day?"

"English Literature, but, yeah, he's at school all day."

"Anybody else live in the house? Wife, girlfriend, kids, roommates, whatever?"

"Grandpa saw one car at the place, and that was Drucker's. I can crosscheck the address and determine whether anybody else lives there."

"Hang on a sec."

Ortega set his coffee aside. He punched his keyboard and studied the monitor. He repeated the process twice.

"House belongs to him. No criminal record. No marriage license. No one else lives there or receives mail there."

"What did you do there?"

Ortega smirked. "Special cop magic software. I could tell you, but..." he waved a hand.

"...you'd have to kill me," I finished.

"Just so we're clear, McCrary. Your grandfather is a private citizen who made a video in a public place with no expectation of privacy, like any citizen with a cellphone who videos a cop making an arrest. If the video is sufficient to show probable cause—which I doubt— we could get a warrant."

He waved a finger in my face. "But anything obtained by anyone—cop or private citizen—who illegally entered his home might not be admissible."

"You mean if a burglar stole Drucker's computer and found child porn on it and sent it anonymously to the cops..."

"We couldn't use it to justify a search warrant. We would have no proof it was his computer. We would need the burglar to corroborate where they got the computer."

"Thereby admitting to breaking and entering."

"But no District Attorney in the State of Texas would prosecute the burglar. Just saying."

"Of course," I said, "but if a burglar found someone held captive inside..."

The detective and I considered each other.

He nodded.

I selected another *pan dulce*.

"That's not all I learned. Emily was sleeping with Kenneth Hoar, a Bonham High School basketball player. That's why she hid the condom in her car. He had already knocked up another student at Bonham and made her get an abortion in Las Cruces. Emily knew about the pregnancy, but didn't know that Kenny was the father."

I related the whole story to Ortega, omitting Sandy Lynch's name. No point in involving her. I left out Debbie Sane's role too. Ortega made notes.

"Kenny Hoar was in serious juvenile trouble more than once, but my source tells me the records are sealed. His parents are loaded and they've shielded him from accountability his whole life. They bail him out of trouble with a checkbook and a bevy of lawyers. Combine that with his bad temper, a sense of entitlement, and a short fuse. That makes him a murder suspect if he believed Emily was pregnant."

"I'll see what I can pry out of his juvie files."

———

Eleanor Feinstein answered on the first ring. "I found the other student's name—the one at MIT. It's Bannak Pang. I'll text you his contact info."

"How about the guy in admissions at MIT?"

"He's moved to Stanford. Sorry."

"Thanks for the lead. I'll try to trace this Pang guy. I owe you one."

"No, you don't. Go catch Emily's killer."

Eleanor sent me Bannak Pang's email address, his cellphone number, and his parents' home address and phone number, all from four years before. I emailed Pang and texted him that I needed to locate Ling Cheng. I discovered two social media accounts in his name and left messages. If I didn't hear from him in a day or two, I would contact his parents.

———

Grandpa was chomping at the bit to assist on the case. Tailing Drucker on Monday while I met Detective Ortega whetted his appetite for sleuthing. After dinner with Carrie and Frank, he drew me aside. "I don't have to pick up that pervert Drucker's tail until school lets out tomorrow. I'll have all day with time to kill. What can I do?"

"Tomorrow morning, I'll have an important assignment for you."

"What is it?"

I told him.

"Hot damn. Count me in."

———

I waited half a block down the street. Desmond Drucker backed his old Hyundai from his driveway and beat his way north, trailing a faint cloud of oily smoke. The Hyundai needed a ring job.

Drucker's Hyde Park neighborhood was built before people needed two-car garages and off-street parking. My Jeep was one of a dozen cars parked on the street. A pebble in a gravel pile.

A half-hour later, Grandpa texted me:

Subject arrived.

I lugged a toolbox and clipboard from the Jeep and walked to Drucker's house. I wore generic gray coveralls. Carry a clipboard and you can go anywhere and people think you belong. Why else would anyone carry a clipboard but because they must? It's the next best thing to Harry Potter's Cloak of Invisibility.

The windows in the half-story of the Queen Anne house were covered with opaque material like butcher paper.

I mounted the six wooden steps, a worker at the beginning of a long day. The neighborhood was so quiet I could hear the *squish* of my rubber-soled shoes as I approached the century-old door. The clear window in the middle was accented by stained-glass border panes in various colors. The foyer beyond the window was lit dimly by outside light. I removed my woolen work glove to rap on the front door. Wearing translucent crime-scene gloves, my knuckles made a knock audible in the house but left no fingerprints, or maybe they would be knuckleprints. Was knuckleprints even a thing? I twisted the old-style doorbell.

While I waited, I pivoted to the street and surveyed the block for locals out for a walk. The coast was clear.

The odds were good that Drucker hid a key outside the house in case he lost his or locked it inside. I peeked under the welcome mat first. It's a cliché, but you would be surprised how naïve people are. No such luck.

Moving to the next common places, I ran my fingers along the door lintel, the bay windows in front and the side windows that looked onto the wraparound porch. The windows had no curtains and the rooms inside were also dark. No key.

I hoisted two flower pots tucked in the corner of the porch. Nope.

The key was under the seat cushion of a chair in the patio dining set on the porch.

Now that I had the key, was my visit still breaking and entering?

My police detective training said, "Absolutely—entering a residence without authorization." My private investigator training said, "Who cares? You're going in, regardless."

I knocked again and opened the door.

The entryway floor, woodwork, and stairs were all cut from longleaf pine. Six-panel pine doors opened to the dining room.

I mounted the steps two at a time to the half-story. *Squish, squish, squish.*

The huge room spanned the house's entire width. Dormer windows on opposite sides bumped their way through the sloped ceiling. Outside light filtered through the papered windows. A ping pong table perched in the middle under a long fluorescent light fixture. If not for the film of dust on the table and the two paddles lying on top, the players could have been on a break.

My heart fell. Emily wasn't there. Nobody had been there for years.

I lifted the paddle. The ball trapped under it rolled off the table and bounced across the wooden floor with crisp *clicks* that echoed around the otherwise empty room. It came to rest against the baseboard. A dark-green silhouette of the paddle's outline marked the table where the paddle had lain. I blew on the paddle. Dust fluttered in the beam of sunlight peeking through a rip in the butcher paper.

At the far end of the room was a wooden door, but the floor between me and it was dust-covered. Emily couldn't be behind that door, but I had to look. Never mind that I would leave footprints. It was unlikely that Drucker had been up here in years.

I tried the door. It was unlocked.

A round window in the rear gable admitted an oval of sunlight through the dusty panes. I yanked the cord of a bare bulb hanging from the ridge beam. Generations-old steamer trunks, suitcases, cardboard boxes full of old clothes—now moth-eaten—filled the attic, abandoned by previous owners and undisturbed for decades. Emily wasn't there either.

That was it for the top floor. I'd struck out. I felt so low I could have walked under a snake without removing my hat.

I descended to the second floor.

The master bedroom and bathroom required twenty minutes to search. The master closet had an M16 and the nightstand drawer held a revolver.

Pretty standard for Texas. The first guestroom took five minutes. Drucker had converted the second guest room into a man cave. A large-screen HDTV hung on the wall. An HDMI cable connected it to a laptop computer on a rolltop desk shoved against another wall. Perhaps the antique desk came with the century-old house.

A recliner in the middle fronted the screen. A side table held a wireless keyboard handy to the recliner. Another table on the recliner's other side held a dirty teacup and saucer and a used napkin.

The latest high-def entertainment setup for child porn aficionados.

I opened the laptop and pressed the power button. An idyllic landscape filled the screen behind Drucker's name and picture. A blank window beneath waited for me to enter Drucker's PIN. Four digits. Ten thousand possible combinations.

I tried Drucker's birth year, his birthday in month-day order, his birthday in day-month order, his street address, and the last four digits of his cellphone and landline numbers. After the seventh error message, the computer told me I had entered too many bad PINs. I rebooted the computer to start over.

This wouldn't be easy, but it seldom is.

Most people have more usernames and passwords than they can remember: banks, email accounts, credit cards, social media, etc. It's one reason Grandpa isn't fond of the twenty-first century.

I track over two hundred passwords. No, I won't tell you how I do it. As Grandpa says: My momma didn't raise no stupid children.

Drucker might keep his usernames and passwords in an encrypted computer file. If so, he had to remember the PIN on his welcome screen and the encrypted file's name and password. That's three pieces of information. A Barbie doll could memorize three pieces of information. If he did that, I was screwed. Ergo, use the favorable assumption that he wrote his passwords on paper.

I refer to my password list all the time. If Drucker had similar needs, he hid his list someplace handy.

If it existed, it was crucial to find it.

It wasn't taped to the bottom of the computer or his keyboard. That would be too easy. Nor was it in a cubbyhole or drawer in his desk. I stared at the oak desk. What had I missed?

I spotted the thin oak slide-out signature boards set into the top of each pedestal.

Bingo.

His password list covered two pages. He had taped one sheet to each board.

I photographed each list. Rule Six: *You never know what you'll need to know.* The list was alphabetized by website. Credit cards, social media, teachers' union, and...and...and...I didn't notice anything that looked like a computer PIN. The PIN might be so simple that he didn't write it down. Could have been his parents' wedding anniversary or another one easy for him—one I had no way to know. Four digits. Ten thousand possible combinations.

At the bottom of the list were several Deep Web sites whose names were a random letter string with ".onion" at the end.

There are legitimate uses for the Deep Web. Political dissidents in authoritarian countries, government defense researchers, internal networks used by banks and insurance companies, and medical records.

The Dark Web is also used by sellers of illegal goods and services like terrorists and child pornographers.

But I couldn't access Drucker's sites if I couldn't open his damned computer. The PIN number was on the list; it *had* to be. Ten thousand possible combinations. I had to figure it out.

I scrutinized both pages again.

This time through, I noticed that one entry wasn't in alphabetical order. "Hastings" and it was wedged between "Bank of the Hill Country" and "Best Buy." Why did Drucker slide "Hastings" into the "B" section?

I logged into Wikipedia and searched "Hastings." It's a town in East Sussex, England where the Battle of Hastings was fought in 1066 AD. "Battle" fit between "Bank" and "Best."

I tapped the mouse and woke Drucker's computer. I entered "1066."

Bingo! I was in.

Sliding an external hard drive from my toolbox, I plugged it into the USB port. Before copying the hard drive, I took a quick peek at three random jpeg files. There was child porn all right. I began to copy Drucker's hard drive while I finished searching the downstairs. Fortunately, his hard drive contained just 400 gigs of data. That would require two hours.

I finished the house with a half hour remaining before my hard drive copy finished. I moved to the frame garage behind the house. It was added sometime after World War II. It contained Drucker's lawn mower, hedge clippers, fertilize spreader, a workbench and a toolbox. Scrap lumber was stored in the rafters above the cracked concrete floor.

I did a final walk-through. Everything was like I found it except the footprints I left in the dust on the attic floor. Drucker had not been on that floor for years. Even if he noticed my footprints, he wouldn't know who made them or when.

At the front door, I watched through the glass and waited until a UPS van passed before I exited.

NINE

G randpa met me for lunch at a hole-in-the-wall Mexican restaurant near the UT campus. He smiled from a table with two menus and two iced teas on it. Students filled the surrounding tables.

"I ordered us iced tea."

"Thanks, Grandpa."

I consulted the menu while a server approached. We ordered and the server left.

Grandpa lowered his voice. "How did it go?"

"The bad news is Emily wasn't there. The good news is I copied his computer's hard drive and his usernames and passwords to give the cops."

"Is it bad as we figured?"

"I accessed three random jpeg files. They were child porn. Has a big-screen TV in front of a recliner in his man cave upstairs." I filled him in on my entire search.

"What will you do with your evidence?"

"Send it to Rodrigo Ortega anonymously and hope he can use it. On a more pleasant subject, did you visit Rebecca after Drucker arrived at school?"

Grandpa beamed. "She's cute as a spotted puppy. I forgot to tell you, I'm teaching her to play checkers. She yells 'Leap frog' every time she jumps a piece. George and Melissa send their love, and they invited you to dinner tonight."

"Melissa said that? Or George?"

Grandpa waggled a hand. "Your sister-in-law isn't your biggest fan, but she'll come around."

"It's been five years. Last time I saw her, she acted like I had bad breath, body odor, and had assassinated Santa Claus."

"So, Melissa got crossways with you. You can't let that stop you from visiting your brother and niece. At breakfast this morning, George said to invite you to dinner tonight."

"What about Melissa?"

"*Humph.*"

"Grandpa, I take Melissa best in small doses with other people around."

"You'll like this: Carrie and Frank invited the three of them for a cook-out this weekend. Ought to be a high old time with seven of us. I'll ask Grandma to drive over from Adams Creek and make it eight. You can lose yourself in the crowd."

"I planned to fly home this weekend to see Terry."

"Did you decide that before or after I said Melissa was invited this weekend?"

"I already made flight reservations."

"Grandma will miss you, but she'll be glad to hear that you and Terry patched things up."

He noticed my frown. "Y'all *did* patch things up, right?"

"Not yet. Terry hasn't returned my calls or texts in over a week."

"She's ghosting you?"

"I'm surprised you know what ghosting is, Grandpa."

"I may be old, youngster, but I'm no dinosaur. I even use some of the apps that came with my smartphone, like that video I made. Since you two haven't made up, what is your plan for this weekend?"

"I figured I'd show up at her place, drop to my knees, and beg her to open the door. That is, if she hasn't relocated to East Muleshoe without telling me."

"Fertilize the field before you plant. If she were my girl, I'd send a dozen roses and a card saying 'I'm sorry' first. I'd have them delivered to the squad room. That way, the other cops would see the flowers on her desk and ask about them. And of course, they would all read the card. That applies peer pressure."

"*Hmm.* You know, that's a damned good idea."

"You think I fell off the cotton wagon yesterday? Grandma and I've been married over fifty years. I've lost count of the times I landed in the dog house. A dozen roses does the trick for me. Of course, a sincere apology accompanies the flowers. Incidentally, it's useful to apologize even if you've done nothing wrong. Take the hint."

"Thanks. It couldn't hurt."

———

Bannak Pang had not contacted me since I left messages for him two days earlier. In his defense, he didn't know me from a timeshare peddler, and he did attend a tough school with a brutal engineering curriculum that kept him as busy as a Daytona 500 pit crew.

Since Massachusetts is on Eastern Time, I called at 8:00 a.m., which was 9:00 a.m. in Cambridge. I called instead of texting. Seven rings and it went to voicemail. The system message was generic—it gave the phone number without a name, so I couldn't tell whether Pang had kept the Austin cell number or it had been reassigned. He might have taken a Cambridge number. More prestige than Austin if you live in the Boston area.

"Mr. Pang, I need to speak to Ling Cheng, a student you knew in high school. She planned to attend MIT, but she is missing. Can you help me contact her? This is literally a matter of life and death."

If I hadn't heard from him by dinner, I would visit his parents' house.

After breakfast, Grandpa arrived at Carrie and Frank's with his laptop and helped me research their neighbors on the block, plus the block behind their house. We would locate someone's contact info and I would call for an appointment. Research, contact, appointment, interview. All day long.

I compared the list of neighbors' phone numbers to a plat map I downloaded from the Travis County Central Appraisal District.

Harry Nelson's address was listed, but not his phone. I penciled a note to ask Carrie and Frank for his number.

At two o'clock, Grandpa resumed his tail on Desmond Drucker. I was pretty sure nothing would come from following him, but we had nothing to lose; Grandpa had the time and the inclination. Perhaps he would catch Drucker flashing a teenage girl. Ortega could get Child Abuse to act on that.

I continued the neighbors' interviews alone.

At dinner, I asked about Harry Nelson.

"He lives across the street," Frank said. "He's out of town a lot. Half the time when I look over there at night, there aren't any lights. I think he camps, or hikes, or something outdoorsy. I see him when we mow our lawns. He keeps a fine lawn and nice flower beds. He likes to garden. Most of the time, he's working in the yard. You know, fertilizing, weeding, trimming, that sort of thing. I wish my lawn looked half as nice."

"He doesn't work?"

"I don't think so. He told me at a basketball game that he inherited money and manages his portfolio. Seems very intelligent."

"College graduate?"

"I don't think so," Frank said. "He never mentions one when we talk about football."

"Does he have a girl friend?"

"Not that I know of. I've never noticed him with a woman and I don't think he dates anyone."

"How about a boyfriend?"

"No, I don't think so," Frank said. "I never got that vibe from him. Not that there's anything wrong with that." Frank grinned at the *Seinfeld* meme.

"The poor man must get lonely, living alone," Carrie said. "He jogs every day. It's probably as much to see other people as to stay in shape. Could be that's why he attends Bonham High basketball games. I mean, why else does a childless bachelor go to high school games?"

Why indeed?

I considered getting a credit report, but privacy laws made that risky. I filed the idea in a corner of my mind under "Desperate."

My first investigation four years earlier revealed that Nelson and his wife bought the house twenty years before and divorced four years later. Carrie told me the neighborhood rumor was that Nelson had abused his wife, but I was skeptical. If that were true, why didn't the ex-wife get the house?

"You have his phone number?" I asked.

"I've never spoken to Harry on the phone," Frank said. "We used to see him at Emily's games and still do at Christmas parties in the neighborhood, but he never called us. Do you have his number, honey?"

Carrie blotted her mouth. "I did a March of Dimes fundraiser last year and I called everyone on the block. Let me check my contact list."

She fetched her purse from the kitchen counter and woke her phone. She scrolled through it. "Harry Nelson is not in my contacts list."

She stuck the phone in her purse. "Funny, he's the one person on the block I don't have."

"No matter," I said, "I'll trot over there after dinner and knock on his door."

After coffee, I crossed the street in the twilight.

Nelson lived in a large two-story brick house with a lawn like a putting green. A hedge of roses filled the flower bed between the side wall and the driveway. The driveway led to the two-car garage in the rear. A bright red-and-white Bonham Bobcat Booster sign was stuck in the grass in the center of his circular driveway. Beside the steps, another sign warned that Travis Security Systems guarded the premises and listed an emergency telephone number.

The signs were there four years before.

Two sabal palm trees in the front were larger, but everything else in the front yard was unchanged. I know, you think palm trees wouldn't grow in Austin, but sabal palms do well.

The windows in Nelson's house were as dark as the inside of a black trunk. I rapped on his door.

Nobody home.

I drove to Bannak Pang's parents' house. An Asian man in a golf shirt and Bermuda shorts came to the door. "May I help you?"

"Are you Mr. Pang?"

"Yes. And you are...?"

"My name is Carlos McCrary. I'm trying to locate Ling Cheng." I handed him a business card.

Mr. Pang flipped his reading glasses off his head and studied my card. "Who are you looking for?" Pang had a slight accent. If he hadn't looked Asian, I wouldn't have noticed it.

"Ling Cheng. She was in Bannak's class at Bonham High School."

"I remember. She was the one born in China." He smiled. "The last time I saw her was at the Bonham graduation."

He handed my card back. "As a matter of curiosity, what made you think I knew Ling Cheng's whereabouts?"

"She and Bannak were the only students from their class accepted at MIT. The school guidance counselor, Ms. Eleanor Feinstein, suggested that Bannak might have stayed in touch with Ms. Cheng in Cambridge. I sent text messages and emails to Bannak, but he hasn't responded, so I came here. The cellphone number and email address Ms. Feinstein had for Bannak were four years old. Has he changed them since graduation?"

Mr. Pang regarded me.

I gave him my honest, sincere, and trustworthy face. Works every time.

"Please come in, Mr. McCrary."

The living room was furnished with attractive wooden furniture of an unfamiliar style. I presumed it was Thai. I don't get out much.

"This is my wife, Som Chai Suttirat." He smiled at an attractive Asian woman wearing a colorful outfit, again of a style I was not familiar with. Like I said, I don't get out often.

"Please call me Chuck."

"How do you do, Chuck? I am Som, spelled S-O-M." She had a heavier accent than her husband. She didn't extend her hand, so I didn't either.

Pang gestured me to a carved teak chair. "Please."

"Would you care for tea?" Som asked.

"No, thank you. I can't stay long, and I won't impose on your hospitality."

"What cell number do you have for Bannak?" Pang asked.

I handed him my paper with his son's contact information.

"This information is obsolete. Bannak has this old email, but he seldom checks it. He uses his MIT student email, and he has a Cambridge phone number. Give me your cell number, I will send you his contact info."

"It's on my card." I handed my business card to him again.

Fifteen seconds later, I had Bannak Pang's cellphone number and email address in my phone's contacts.

After making my goodbyes, I returned to my car and called his new cell number.

"Hello?"

"Mr. Pang, your father gave me your cellphone number. My name is Carlos McCrary. I'm trying to reach Ling Cheng."

"Ling? You want to talk to Ling Cheng?"

"Yes, sir. Do you know how to reach her?"

"I haven't seen her since graduation. I wondered what happened to her."

"Everyone in Austin thought she attended MIT."

"She was supposed to. That's what she told me at graduation, but she never showed when classes began in August. I figured she changed her mind and chose Rice or Stanford instead."

"You never saw her at MIT?"

"I haven't seen her since we met outside the arena after graduation for family pictures."

———

I called Eleanor Feinstein.

"I hope it's not too late to call."

"No, it's fine, Chuck. What's happened?"

"Ling Cheng never made it to MIT."

"Then where is she?"

"Bannak Pang said she was accepted at Rice and Stanford also. Could she be at one of those?"

"My contact who moved from MIT to Stanford might know. It's seven p.m. in California. I'll call him."

"What about Rice? You know anyone there?"

"No problem. I'll call Rice admissions in the morning. I'll ring my guy at Stanford right now and get back to you."

"It's after office hours in California."

"He can access the university's records from his home computer. No problem. Stand by. I'll get back to you."

As I arrived at Carrie and Frank's, Eleanor called.

"Ling Cheng didn't enroll at Stanford either."

———

Thursday morning, Eleanor called at 9:30. "Ling Cheng never enrolled at Rice University. I don't get it. How can she be missing four years and nobody notices? Wouldn't her parents report her missing after she didn't call them?"

"Could she have changed her mind and relocated to China with them?"

"No. She was adamant about that. She stayed in America. She was an American citizen for God's sake. I'm worried about the poor girl. Do you suppose she disappeared like Emily?"

I promised to investigate it and called Detective Ortega. "We may have another missing girl." I filled him in on Ling Cheng.

"Where are her parents?"

"They worked for Trans-Pacific Circuits here in Austin. My aunt and uncle said they were transferred to Shanghai. If I were you, I'd check with Trans-Pacific Circuits personnel department at their Austin facility."

"You know my caseload. If she disappeared four years ago and nobody noticed, what are the chances we'll clear the case? Near zero, that's what. She was legally an adult when she disappeared, not a kid. Can you do it?"

"I'm not a cop. Trans-Pacific doesn't need to give me so much as a smile and a handshake."

"You have my business card?"

"Yes. What should I do with it? Impersonate a police officer?"

"Tell Trans-Pacific you work with me, hand them my card, and ask them to call me. I'll vouch for you."

"Will do."

"Keep me in the loop."

"Sure."

"With a four-year-old case, I'm glad you can work it. I won't make a file on it unless you find something. Let me know what you learn."

"Count on it."

———

Trans-Pacific Circuits sprawled across five wooded hills six miles southwest of downtown Austin. TPC's fabrication facility had eight low-rise buildings spread across seventy acres of prime Hill Country commercial land. A private boulevard named Trans-Pacific Way climbed the first hill between manicured lawns and stately live oak trees. Too bad someone hadn't built a golf course on the grounds. Maybe that was scheduled for next year.

The front of Building 01 was a hundred-yard wall, thirty feet high, of stainless steel with forty feet of smoked glass entrance jammed in the middle. On the left side, the company name was displayed in gold leaf in English. Below it were two lines of gold leaf in Korean and Chinese, also the company name if I was betting.

The reception desk was staffed by two Asian women and an Anglo man.

"I'm looking for the Human Resources Department."

"That's in Building 17. Do you need a map?"

"Yes, please."

She used an orange highlighter to mark the map. "Have a nice day."

TPC had eight buildings and I was sent to Building 17? A company of engineers didn't know how to count.

At Building 17, the receptionist scanned my driver's license, took my photo and my fingerprint, and printed out a visitor's badge. Cautioning me to be sure my badge was always visible, she directed me to Charlene Wilkinson in Room 172.

Despite her name, Charlene Wilkinson was Asian. Welcome to the melting pot that is America.

"Four or five years ago, you employed two engineers named Kuo Jiang Cheng and Ning Mu Wang. They are husband and wife." I handed her a sheet with the names on it. "I need to get in touch with them."

"Is this company business, Mr. McCrary?"

"No. Their daughter Ling Cheng, who stayed in Austin after they transferred to Shanghai, is missing. I need to notify them. They're Ling Cheng's next of kin."

"Are you with the police?"

"I'm a private investigator." I handed her a business card. "I am working with Austin Police Detective Rodrigo Ortega on this case. Here's his business card if you care to call him."

She accepted Ortega's card and placed it beside mine.

"Please sit down."

I listened to her end of the conversation with Ortega. She finished and glanced at me as she disconnected. "Detective Ortega said she disappeared four years ago."

"That's right. She was accepted at MIT and never registered for class."

"And the police have just now learned about this? That's…peculiar."

"This whole situation is peculiar. That's why I need to talk to her parents. When they didn't hear from their daughter, even if they were in China, they should have notified the authorities in the United States."

"Let me email Shanghai and get their contact information."

"Isn't it nighttime in Shanghai?"

Wilkinson's eyes twinkled. "All Trans-Pacific facilities are open 24/7." She thumped her keyboard. "…and *send*. This won't take long. Our personnel files are computerized."

Ten seconds later, she checked her email.

"Here it is."

As she read it, she opened her mouth to speak, then stopped. "This doesn't make sense. I'll call them."

She slipped a headset on and punched her desk phone keyboard. She spoke in rapid Chinese to someone at the other end. To me, she sounded fluent even though she spoke English with a Texas accent. She gesticulated with both hands, though it wasn't a video call.

She smiled. "I'm on hold." She stared into the distance and drummed her fingers.

Wilkinson straightened in her chair. Her voice became conversational, then sounded like she had asked a favor. She said something like *shay-shay*. I knew that meant "thank you."

She removed her headset. "The People's Liberation Army arrested Kuo Jiang Cheng and Ning Mu Wang."

"Arrested? When? For what?"

"My friend didn't know and it doesn't matter anyway; not in the Chinese workers' paradise. Six soldiers waving guns raided our plant in Weidong one week after they arrived in China. They hauled them off in an army truck."

"Where are they now?"

She shrugged.

"They haven't been seen since. Kuo Cheng's parents came to the plant three years ago searching for them."

She made an explosion gesture with her fingers. "*Poof!* He parents have disappeared too. Welcome to the workers' paradise."

TEN

The rest of Thursday and Friday, Grandpa and I cleaned up loose ends researching anyone who had a nodding acquaintance with the Crazinskis, thirty-two families in all.

Harry Nelson was still not available.

I had collected thick files. *Whoopee*. My consolation was that four years earlier, I worked as hard for longer and accomplished doodly-squat. This time, I had uncovered two bad guys in less than two weeks. Even if neither of them kidnapped Emily, Kenny Hoar and Desmond Drucker were guilty of *something*.

Friday afternoon, I parked the rental Jeep at the airport since I was flying home for the weekend. When I checked in for the flight to Port City, I was so tired that I sprang for a first-class seat. I lost an hour on the time change and hit my condo at 12:30 Saturday morning. I was asleep before my head hit the pillow.

———

It was time to play detective. I drove to Terry's apartment. Her reserved parking spot was empty.

I halfway expected my key to her apartment wouldn't work, but she hadn't changed her lock. Was that a good sign? Her toothbrush's spot in the holder was empty, but my toothbrush was there. My drawer in her bedroom held my extra underwear and two clean shirts. A good sign.

I dropped by the North Shore Precinct, my old duty station before I started McCrary Investigations.

Detectives Bigs Bigelow and Kelly Contreras had weekend duty. Kelly hugged me. "Look who the cat dragged in, Bigs."

Bigs bear-hugged me like a six-foot-seven-inch, three-hundred-pound Sumo wrestler. He pounded me on the back hard enough to loosen my fillings. "It's my turn to get the coffee. Kelly, you want some?"

"I'm good."

Bigs left for the coffee station.

Kelly glanced at the roses across the squad room. "Nice roses. How come you never sent me roses?"

"We never dated."

"That wasn't my fault; you never asked."

"If Terry doesn't come back, maybe I will ask."

"You'd be glad you did, big guy." Kelly glanced to make sure Bigs was out of earshot. "If you like it kinky, I could even put you in handcuffs again."

Kelly and Bigs had arrested me for murder a million years before.

"I didn't like it then, Kel, and I wouldn't like it now."

Bigs came back carrying coffee. "You looking for Terry?"

"Wow. You must be a detective or something. I drove by her place. Her car's not there and her toothbrush is gone."

"That's what we detectives call a clue," Bigs said. "From that evidence, I deduce that she's out of town."

"She's ghosting you, big guy," Kelly said.

"You sure?"

"Hell, yeah. She told me after those flowers arrived. She figured you'd come this weekend, so she drove to Georgia to visit her parents. She owed them a visit since she hadn't seen them since July Fourth."

Kelly patted her own shoulder. "Here's a shoulder to cry on. I'm between boyfriends."

"I haven't given up on Terry. She hasn't changed her locks and my clean underwear and shirts are in my drawer in her bedroom."

"Your loss, big guy."

———

After lunch I slipped into a swimsuit and carried a six-pack in a cooler to the pool. I flopped on a chaise in a corner of the deck where I wouldn't be overheard. I opened my first Port City Amber and called Vicky Ramirez.

"Terry won't return my calls or answer my texts. I sent her a dozen roses from Texas a couple of days ago. I flew back to Port City and went to her apartment, but she wasn't home. Kelly Contreras told me she's visiting her parents in Georgia. She's avoiding me."

"And you told me this because…?"

"I need advice."

"Legal advice?" Victoria Ramirez was a name partner in a boutique Port City family law firm. She sent me clients, mainly divorces and custody cases.

"Relationship advice," I said.

"You're out of luck. Relationship advice is beyond my expertise. That's one reason I'm single."

Vicky was my friend with benefits when we were each between relationships. In most ways, she was the perfect woman: smart, sympathetic, loyal, and ambitious. Practically a Boy Scout, except female. She would make a great mother except for an insurmountable problem: She didn't want children. Her career came first and she'd made that clear from the get-go.

Terry was smart, sympathetic, and intelligent. I wasn't sure about the "loyal." She wasn't as ambitious as Vicky either, but few people are. A big plus: Terry wanted children someday. Hopefully someday soon, and hopefully with me.

"You're a woman," I said. "You know more about women than I do."

"Everyone in the universe, male and female, knows more about women than you do. Furthermore, as an authentic, dyed-in-the-wool feminist, I am required to be offended by that remark. What makes you think that because

I'm a woman, I know what another woman thinks? Terry is unique, like everyone else."

"Guilty as charged. Sorry I called."

"That's okay. Give me a foot massage next time I see you and I'll forgive you. Tell me your troubles with Terry, sad guy."

And I did. I poured my heart out.

Grandpa said: Everybody has a story to tell and sometimes the best thing you can do is listen to it. Vicky listened like she always did. Listening helped.

"I'd invite you to spend the night, but I'm in New York City this weekend."

"I haven't capitulated on Terry. My toothbrush and bedroom drawer stuff were there, and my key worked."

"The toothbrush and your clean clothes may be relics from a failed relationship that she hasn't bothered to throw out. Your key working means she didn't re-key the door. She knows you're not the type to steal something. Truth is, Terry's not there for you, Chuck. That's what you spent the last twenty minutes telling me. If you ask me, you're back to square one with no girlfriend."

Oh, great.

The afternoon wore on and our high-rise building's shadow swept across the lounger. I glugged my way through the six-pack and fell asleep. Or passed out. Sunburn makes me sleepy. So does beer. Not sure which was the culprit. Not that it mattered. I was not the happiest person on Port City Beach.

It was a bye week for Florida Gators football, and I watched the Longhorns get the snot beat out of them by the TCU Horned Frogs while I ate take-out pizza in front of my TV and fell asleep on the couch. Alone.

It had not been a good day.

ELEVEN

Grandpa met me Sunday night at Carrie and Frank's. "What are we doing tomorrow? You want me to tail Drucker?"

"No. Drucker is guilty of child porn and being a general all-round creep, but he didn't kidnap Emily. I sent his computer files and passwords anonymously to Ortega. The ball is in his court, or maybe the Child Abuse division if he sends it to them. Tomorrow I visit the county sheriffs in the Hill Country."

"What for?"

"To review their missing persons reports for other girls who vanished."

"You believe a serial killer snatched Emily?" Grandpa asked.

"And Emily's friend, Ling Cheng. Both female, both teenagers, and both attended Bonham High. Most serial criminals, whether killers or rapists, follow a pattern. The pattern might be the location where the crimes occur, or the types of victims, or the *modus operandi* or something else. If I uncover the pattern, maybe I can anticipate his next move. Or use the pattern to uncover clues to his identity."

"You said 'his.' Do you know it's a man?"

"No, but women commit seventeen percent of serial murders, and most serial killings involve sexual gratification."

Grandpa frowned.

"I know that's hard to think about, Grandpa, but that's a fact. I'll keep an open mind about the kidnapper's gender, but it's convenient to think about him as a man."

"Why the Hill Country? Why not draw a circle around Austin? She could be in Bastrop, Lee, or Fayette County. Even Milam County, although why anyone visits Milam County is beyond me."

"Emily and her friends spent time in the Hill Country. Like you said, why would anyone visit other counties for fun when the Hill Country is next door? Someone she met on a Hill Country excursion could have kidnapped her."

"Her car was in the high school parking lot. He snatched her from school."

"I have to start somewhere. If I don't find a clue in the Hill Country, I'll pivot eastward. Now I'm hunting for more than Emily. I want to locate Ling Cheng and maybe other girls the killer murdered."

What I didn't say was that there is no shortage of places to search when you don't have a clue where to begin.

Austin is the county seat of Travis County, which, with Williamson County to the north, marks the Hill Country's eastern edge. Emily kept maps of Blanco, Burnet, Hays, and Williamson counties in her car.

The Williamson County Sheriff's Office headquarters was a modern brick building in the heart of beautiful downtown Georgetown. Deputy Bucky Cody welcomed me to his office. "Rod Ortega in Austin emailed me and said you have a missing persons case?"

I briefed Cody on Emily's case. "I'm visiting Hill Country cities and counties to see whether she was the victim of a serial killer. Do you have any similar missing persons or unsolved murders?"

"Similar how? You can't determine a pattern from one case. If there is a serial killer, is the common victim profile based on gender, race, age, economic status, place of disappearance, time of day? The criteria can be anything. How far back you want? Your cousin disappeared over four years ago. Is she the first of the pattern, the middle, or the end?"

"Bucky, I have two missing teenage girls from Austin, and I'm desperate for answers. Try missing or murdered teenage girls, any race, in the last ten years."

Cody punched his computer and input the parameters. "Seventeen missing girls meet your criteria. You want me to print the cases?"

"Yes, please."

After I left the sheriff's office, I visited the Georgetown police department and collected twelve more files.

While I met with the police chief in the Georgetown PD building, I had received a text from Detective Ortega.

Hoar's juvie files are not available. Sorry.

I called Ortega from my car.

"What does 'not available' mean?"

"It means I can't get the records unsealed. You're on your own, Chuck."

"Thanks for trying."

"Wait, don't hang up. I have news on 'Lizard Lips' Drucker. I showed the guys in the Child Abuse Unit the video of Drucker whacking off while he watched the girls in the park. I told them about your interviews with Drucker's former students. They said they'll alert their detectives about Drucker's proclivities."

"That's good news."

"I gave them your copy—excuse me—the *anonymous* copy of Drucker's hard drive and passwords that some publicly-spirited citizen sent me in the mail. They took one look at some of the files on the hard drive and opened a forensic investigation. They'll work backwards from the Dark Web links on Drucker's computer. Since they don't have a search warrant, they will start on the Dark Web sites and try to trace backwards to Drucker's computer IP address. If they can identify his IP address that way, they can get a search warrant without involving you."

"And if they can't tie the computer to him that way?"

"Then they'll ask you to swear that you made the hard drive copy. They can get a search warrant from that."

"I would have to admit I entered his house without his permission.

That's the definition of breaking and entering. That's a felony in Florida; I assume it's also against Texas law."

"Yeah, there is that, but I already told you that no DA in Texas would prosecute you. Look, Chuck, you and I have had our issues in the past; I'll admit that. But you're on the side of the angels here. This Drucker creep may have nothing to do with Emily's disappearance, but he's a bad actor and we need to get him off the street before he hurts somebody."

I couldn't resist making the pun. "At least from now on, the Eyes of Texas will be on Desmond Drucker."

———

Over the next four days, I made the rounds of the sheriffs of Blanco, Burnet, Hays, and Gillespie counties. If the county had a city large enough for a police department, I visited it. I told my story and gave a business card to anyone who might be able to help. Everyone was sympathetic and professional and didn't know squat.

I collected files each day and studied them each night.

After I finished that day's files, I stewed about Harry Nelson. What would I do if he didn't return to town soon? Break into his house?

By the weekend, I had 112 missing persons cases printed in a nice, tidy stack ten inches tall. I had studied each case on the day I collected it.

Saturday, I reviewed them again, hunting for patterns.

Eight victims were abducted after seeing a movie, one from inside the theatre. Thirteen were last seen at various discount stores, three at a mall. Twenty-two disappeared after grocery shopping. One after she visited a girlfriend. Six were not seen after they left high school or college. I gave those cases extra attention.

The rest were miscellaneous. That was the largest pile.

I reviewed every case until my head was swimming with facts. I was moving, or at least going through the motions, but I wasn't *progressing*.

My efforts were worthless unless I got a break in the case.

If that first group of counties didn't yield a lead, I would add Llano County out west and more counties to the east after I finished my interviews in Austin. That would take a bazillion years.

By Saturday afternoon, I was exhausted and my head was overstuffed with data.

At sunset Saturday, Hurricane Stefano made landfall and surged Matagorda Bay like a tsunami and dumped it on Point Comfort, Texas with a twenty-foot storm surge. After the storm wiped out Point Comfort, it set its sights on Central Texas. Austin was in the center of its projected path.

Sunday was a hunker-down day with alternating rain squalls and sunshine. Hurricane Stefano slowed to a tropical storm and blustered his way inland. It rained so hard the animals began to pair up. It dumped a foot of rain across the Hill Country. The weather soured so bad that my aunt and uncle didn't go to church.

Sunday afternoon late, I consulted Carrie and Frank to develop a list of additional people who knew Emily and saw her on a regular basis.

Those were my next interviews.

———

As fast as Tropical Storm Stefano came through, it dissipated faster. Monday morning, Stefano deflated to a low-pressure system over southwestern Oklahoma with heavy rain, but milder winds.

The City of Austin had already cleared the fallen trees that blocked traffic. Life returned to normal except for folks whose roofs were damaged.

Jerry O'Doul lived in a hilly district with mature trees. The front lawns had limbs and debris scattered about, but the storm had done little structural damage in the neighborhood. It was a sturdy, traditional neighborhood that hadn't changed in decades.

O'Doul's driveway ran from the street to the alley with a turning strip into the two-car garage behind the house. Two steps in the sidewalk accommodated the slope that rose from the curb to the house. Metal handrails stood on both sides of the steps.

Mrs. O'Doul lived with her son Jerry and used a walker to get around. I couldn't recall the mother's name. Something biblical that began with a J. Jezebel? No, it couldn't be that.

A ramp sloping to the driveway had been added on the side of the porch. I figured Mrs. O'Doul had switched to a wheelchair from her walker. People do grow older and she was in bad shape before.

I kicked broken limbs off the sidewalk as I ascended from the curb to the house. I mounted the concrete steps and tapped the bell beside the glass-paneled door. The first four bars of *The Star-Spangled Banner* played faintly.

Seconds later, the white curtain on the door fingered back an inch and a dim face peeked out. "Just a minute," someone said from inside.

I raised my voice. "No problem, Jerry. No hurry."

The doorknob rattled, a deadbolt clicked, and the door swung open. Jerry O'Doul stood in the doorway.

"Mr. McCrary?"

His hair was thinner, his waistline thicker, but he remained a bulky, muscular figure. He had played halfback at Texas A & M University in Commerce while he earned his degree in education. He still looked hard to tackle.

"Call me Chuck."

"Come in, Chuck. You came here a few years ago, after Emily disappeared. You're staying with Frank and Carrie Crazinski, right?"

"Yes. They're my aunt and uncle."

O'Doul's brown pants had a subtle design like tree bark. His tan golf shirt was lighter and reminded me of the pecan tree in the front yard whose leaves had turned. He wore brown socks and brown leather sandals. Maybe he was disguised as a tree stump. A very big stump.

The foyer had bare hardwood floors. The lighter wood indicated where an entry carpet had been. O'Doul must have removed it to make his mother's wheelchair easier to roll. Double pocket doors faced each other from either side. A television weather forecast boomed from behind one set of doors. An unpleasant odor filled the air. *Was it B.O.? No, something different, but familiar.*

"Did Frank and Carrie come through the storm okay?" he asked.

"Lost a limb or two off an oak tree. One fell on the barbecue grill. Frank wanted a new grill anyway, so no harm done. How about you? I noticed a blue tarp on your neighbor's roof."

"My roof has weathered worse storms than Stefano. I replaced it five years ago with one rated for hurricane-force winds, thank God."

O'Doul slid one door open. The weather forecast became earsplitting as he led me into the sitting room. The unpleasant smell intensified.

An old woman in a wheelchair slumped in front of a large-screen television across the room. A weather map shifted on the screen. Tropical Storm Stefano's remnants had crossed the Kansas border.

Mrs. O'Doul had an Afghan draped over her lap and a heavy shawl over her shoulders. A glowing electric space heater beside the fireplace blew heated air into the room. Sauna, old lady style.

Black-and-white family photos from decades before cluttered the walls.

Over the fireplace hung a painting of a sturdy old ranch house nestled among live oak trees. The picturesque house sat in a bluebonnet field nestled in a valley, a nineteenth-century pioneer monument. It was a typical Texas Hill Country scene. Every art fest in Texas has a dozen artists who sell similar paintings. Carrie and Frank had one in their den.

The drapes were drawn over the windows. The sole light came from the television screen. An old-fashioned TV tray straight from the 1950s sat beside the wheelchair, holding an insulated plastic glass with a plastic straw stuck through the top. A box of tissues sat beside it. A wastebasket beside the table was half full of used tissues. More tissues littered the floor around the trashcan, a lava flow from the trash volcano.

O'Doul raised his voice. "You'll want to say hello to Mother." He lifted the remote from the old woman's lap and softened the sound. He touched her on the arm. "Mother, do you remember Chuck McCrary? Chuck, you remember my mother, Jerusha O'Doul."

The old woman gaped in my direction. "Are you a doctor?"

"No, ma'am. I'm a private investigator."

As I stepped closer, I recognized the smell. A soiled diaper. I stopped midstride and wondered whether O'Doul would be offended if I backed toward the door. I stood my ground and didn't breathe. Courage under fire.

Jerusha snatched a tissue and blew her nose like a trumpet.

"You were supposed to call the doctor." She dropped the used tissue over the wastebasket. It missed and joined the other tissues on the floor. Air ball.

"No, Mom. Your doctor's appointment is next week, and it's in the doctor's office."

O'Doul raked the used tissues into a pile with his fingers, scooped them up in his hands, and tossed them into the wastebasket.

I had shaken O'Doul's hand. I hoped neither one had communicable diseases. *Too late*, I thought.

O'Doul smiled. "Mom has seasonal allergies, but the doctor's appointment is a routine physical. Sometimes Mom gets confused."

Now that I saw Jerusha, I remembered that the old woman was dotty the first time we met. After his father died, O'Doul moved into his mother's home to care for her. He was an only child. Carrie told me O'Doul's maternal grandfather came from a wealthy pioneer Texas family. Jerry's grandfather left his daughter and grandson well-fixed. Small consolation to Jerry that a disabled, demented mother devoured his life, but there you are. The old woman had no one else, and Jerry assumed responsibility. Kudos to him.

"That blinking storm blew through for three days," Mrs. O'Doul said. "Practically blew our house away, like Dorothy in *The Wizard of Oz*. 'Course, Dorothy was caught in a tornado, not a blinking hurricane." She snorted. "Did you see *The Wizard of Oz*?"

"No ma'am, I didn't," I said.

"Blinking good movie." She blew her nose again. This time her used tissue hit the can. Bull's-eye.

O'Doul placed the remote back in his mother's hand and kissed her on the cheek. "Chuck and I will be in the living room, Mom."

Thankful to escape, I edged to the door.

"It was nice to see you again, Mrs. O'Doul."

Jerusha snatched another tissue from the box. She pointed the remote at the television and cranked the volume.

O'Doul patted her shoulder. Boosting his voice, he said. "Mom's a little deaf nowadays, but she loves the Weather Channel. Let's talk in the living room."

We escaped the sitting room. He slid the double pocket doors closed. "This way."

O'Doul slid the opposite doors open. "This will be more comfortable."

The living room copied the sitting room but with a mirror hanging over the fireplace and a coffee table fronting the burgundy couch. Additional ancient family photos covered the walls beside autographed team photos of Bonham High boys' and girls' sports teams from past years. O'Doul closed the doors behind us, which further damped the sound from Jerusha O'Doul's television.

How did O'Doul live like that? The guy was a saint. Or deaf.

"When Carrie called, she said you wanted to talk about Emily. You reopened her case?"

"Yes. Carrie wants me to take a fresh look at the disappearance."

"Have you discovered new evidence? It would be wonderful if you did."

"You were Emily's Sunday School teacher?"

"Yes. I taught the high school students for a few years. As I remember, Emily was a sophomore."

"Yes."

"High schoolers are at an awkward in-between age. They're not kids but they're not young adults either."

"Tell me about that."

"You sure you want to get me started?" He chuckled. "I can moralize for hours on what's wrong with our culture and how the churches can fix it. How does my pontificating help you find Emily?"

"I want background on Emily, her friends, her school, her family. She was raised in Austin and I was raised in Adams Creek. That, and me being ten years older, meant I didn't know her as well as I wanted to. Fill me in on what it was like to be Emily. Pontificate all you like."

"You asked for it. Sunday School for younger children aims to develop a firm faith foundation. The teachers focus on the kids learning Bible stories and having fun. Teachers lead the kids in games—educational games, but fun, age-appropriate games. They also teach biblical history. The young adults are different. By the time they're old enough to vote, the young adults use the church for matchmaking."

"Matchmaking? Like a singles bar?"

What a concept: A Christian singles bar. *Nah.* More like church as Cupid, I figured.

O'Doul laughed. "Not quite a singles bar, but our college-age members want serious relationships that might develop into life-long commitments. You'd be surprised how many twenty-somethings join our young adult Sunday School to meet a future husband or wife."

"And Emily was in the high school class."

O'Doul nodded as he rubbed his hands together. He was warming to the subject.

"The high schoolers already know their Bible. They're fairly secure in their faith. They must learn to function as adults and handle adult challenges like sex, drugs, smoking, and gangs. In that order."

"Sunday School lessons about sex would be awkward." To say the least.

O'Doul emitted a frustrated grunt. "Awkward is an understatement for a single guy like me. After the couple teaching the class moved out of town, we didn't have another couple to step up to the plate."

"How did you come to teach the class?" I asked.

"I taught physics at Bonham High at the time." He gestured at the team photos on the wall. "Some of those kids attended my physics class. Since I taught at the high school and knew the kids, the church elders asked me to teach the class. It was supposed to be short-term, but it lasted three long, awkward years." He chuckled again.

"What happened? Did the elders convince a young married couple to replace you?"

O'Doul spread his fingers and waggled his hand in a *so-so* gesture. "Mom's health deteriorated until I couldn't leave her alone. Her dementia got worse until she couldn't care for herself. I quit teaching high school three years ago."

His eyes filled with tears. I felt uncomfortable watching.

"I told the elders I couldn't do it anymore. They convinced another couple to step up."

"You don't teach that class anymore?"

"No. I teach the adult men. The over-thirty crowd. Your Uncle Frank is in my class. If you'll be in town a while, come on Sunday morning. We meet at 9:30. You can ride with Frank."

"Thanks. I'll keep it in mind." *No, I won't,* I thought. *Easter and Christmas are more my speed.*

"If Mrs. O'Doul can't be left alone, how do you find time to teach the adult men?"

O'Doul beamed. "Believe it or not, the church's child care program takes Mom each Sunday during church. You saw Mom. She watches the Weather Channel sixteen hours a day. Has for the last ten years. I don't have a life. Sunday at church is my one time for adult conversation. That and the cashier at Walmart."

Now they were phasing in self-checkout. What would Jerry do? Shop at Whole Foods?

I nodded. "I can't imagine what that's like."

"Twenty-four seven. Except on Sunday."

O'Doul gave me an apathetic smile. "You didn't come to listen to my troubles. Let's talk about Emily."

"Okay. Tell me about teaching the high school Sunday School class. What was it like?"

"It's a tough class to handle. Teenagers are inundated with relentless media messages promoting promiscuous sex, recreational drugs, and the feeling that it's okay to have children outside of marriage. The media push the narrative that the nuclear family vanished with the twentieth century. The church has one hour a week to combat that, plus two or three weekends a year they hold teenage retreats. Sometimes I feel like we're bailing a sinking boat using a spaghetti strainer."

I wondered what Jerry would think if he knew about the condom I found.

TWELVE

Blanco County Sheriff Joe Bob Bowie called. "Two boys went dove hunting on the Perkins Ranch near Round Mountain. They stumbled across a body. It's been there a long time. There's not much left but bones and raggedy clothes, according to the boys."

"Could it be Emily?"

"The boys called it in twenty minutes ago. I haven't seen the body, but you asked me to call if anything turned up that might be your missing cousin. I'm driving to the site to meet an evidence team from Austin."

"You use the Austin CSI techs?"

"Chuck, 11,000 people live in Blanco County. Austin has over a million. Thank goodness we don't have enough local crime to need a heavyweight department to handle technical stuff. We handle car thefts and burglaries and assaults, but we send fingerprints and DNA to Austin for analysis."

"That makes sense. Text me the GPS coordinates for the crime scene, and I'll meet you there."

"I'll send them after we hang up."

"But it could be Emily."

Bowie paused.

"Those boys, they were torn up something awful. They could hardly talk on the phone. They ain't seen a dead body before. From what the boys said, they couldn't tell whether the body was a man or a woman. I think they saw part of one foot sticking out. I doubt they looked very hard. A body that old, it must've spooked them real bad. It had been buried in a creek bed and Hurricane Stefano washed it out."

I didn't call Carrie and Frank. The body could be anybody. I would wait until I had information, one way or the other.

———

Round Mountain makes a wide spot in US Highway 281 between Marble Falls and Johnson City. A few dozen homes and small businesses crowd either side of the intersection with Ranch Road 962. Three miles south of beautiful downtown Round Mountain, my GPS led me west on a two-lane highway into the rural stretches. It was cattle country. Yippee-ki-yay.

Trees dotted the countryside. Live oaks, junipers (which Texans call *cedar*), mesquite, and other varieties I can't name because I'm a city boy now. Wild grass, wildflowers, and cactus covered the ground beside the road and behind the barbed-wire fences.

Heading west, human habitation fell behind. Gates in the fences accessed gravel tracks that trailed out of sight on both sides of the highway. The absence of houses and barns made it feel like the Zombie Apocalypse had struck.

All the landscape needed was the soundtrack from an old Clint Eastwood western. Giddyap.

"In one-half mile, turn right on road." Even the GPS didn't know the name of the road. I eyed the rearview mirror. No one had been behind me for several miles. Pausing in the road, I consulted the GPS. The screen showed a gray minor road curving northward a short way, then stopping. Most of the screen was blank. I was Columbus, about to sail over the ocean's edge, but in a Jeep Cherokee.

Slipping the Jeep into gear, I pressed on.

"Turn right on road."

The two-lane road narrowed until it didn't have a center stripe.

A handmade sign at the intersection said Perkins Ranch Road. Somebody ought to tell the GPS.

A doe with a fawn grazed beside the road. They raised their heads as my Cherokee approached, then returned to their brunch until I was ten yards away. They jumped the fence and joined a small herd foraging the pasture. If you're a doe or a fawn, bravery is not a survival trait.

On the right, I passed a double-wide with a lean-to garage built against it. The storm had shoved the garage a few yards from the house. A faded red barn slouched behind it. An old pickup peeked through an open door. Their neighbor across the road lived in a single-wide with its carport peeled away. The neighborhood literally gone with the wind.

The driveway next to the single-wide passed through a sturdy limestone arch that framed two ornate steel gates with Lone Stars imbedded in the design on each side. A Texas flag flanked the private road on one side and Old Glory matched it on the other. Both flags were tattered. Sheep and goats grazed behind the fence.

Did the local cattlemen give the sheepherders trouble in this century? Apparently not. Perhaps that whole cliché was a Hollywood myth to create false drama in western movies.

The road narrowed to one lane.

"In one-half mile, navigate off road," the GPS said.

The pavement ended at a sign: County Maintenance Ends. The gravel track continued to a cattleguard. A neat sign hung on the fence: Perkins Ranch; private property. Another sign announced A baby calf and a soft rain are always welcome. A red sign with bright yellow letters warned Absolutely No Hunting. This Means You!

Calves and rain were welcome, but not hunters. How about the two boys who were hunting doves? And how did the rancher feel about tropical storms?

I bumped across the cattleguard and slowed to a crawl. The gravel disappeared, leaving twin ruts churned into the rocky earth. Puddles pooled in the low spots and disguised the potholes.

I was glad Grandpa had changed my rental to a Jeep.

An ancient pickup truck crested the hill ahead.

I angled halfway off the rutted tracks and stopped beside a sycamore to let them pass.

A gun rack in the rear window held two shotguns. Pretty standard in rural Texas.

The kid in the driver's seat clutched the steering wheel with both hands to control the truck as it bounded across the rough ground. He hoisted two fingers off the wheel in greeting as he inched past. *Howdy, partner.*

I waved back. I figured he and his buddy were the boys who discovered the body. They would remember this day.

Following the muddy tracks the boys had made, I mounted a hill. Red and blue lights flashed in the distance at the base of a mesa rearing sixty feet above the prairie.

The Jeep bounded and bobbled and dived and splashed along a rutted trail that had never felt a road grader or bulldozer. To call it a road would be an unearned compliment to a pair of grooves worn by four-wheel-drive vehicles. Dodging baseball-sized rocks, I closed the distance.

It looked like a good place to dispose of a body.

A white van with "Austin Crime Scene Unit" painted on it waited beside an SUV police cruiser marked "Blanco County Sheriff."

The twin ruts continued past the police vehicles and zigzagged up the mesa, disappearing over the top.

The official vehicles sat between the ersatz road and an overflowing stock tank. Stock tanks attract doves. Doves attract hunters. The boys had either ignored the "no-hunting" sign, or they were friends of the Perkins family.

The lights of the CSI van and the Blanco Sheriff's SUV flashed, but no one was visible.

Where was everybody?

The Jeep's instrument panel indicated the outside temperature at ninety degrees, not unusual for early autumn in Central Texas. I popped the door. The humidity felt like the nineties also. Puddles remaining from Hurricane Stefano dotted the prairie. I shrugged out of my suit coat, tossed it onto the passenger's seat, and loosened my tie.

I surveyed the area. The deserted site in the back of beyond was spooky. Where was the crime scene?

"Hey, Chuck. Over here."

Sheriff Bowie's ten-gallon hat emerged as he climbed from a depression in the ground. "I heard your vehicle and came up to fetch you. The CSIs are up this creek bed, near a swimming hole. Mind the barbed wire when you climb through the fence. Don't snag your clothes."

The years had chiseled Sheriff Bowie's craggy visage into an angular sculpture of muscle overlaid with weathered skin that could have come from an old boot. His Stetson hat shaded pale blue eyes which looked out of place with his tan face. Shaggy gray hair hung over his ears, balanced by a salt-and-pepper mustache to make Pancho Villa jealous. His khaki uniform was mud-streaked and sweat-soaked, though he couldn't have beat me to the site by more than twenty-five minutes.

I tugged off my tie and pitched it on my coat. I didn't lock the Jeep. I doubted the deer would steal it.

Bowie set his boot on a barbed-wire strand and leaned his weight as he tugged the higher wire for me to duck under. "Careful."

"Thanks, Joe Bob."

Bowie led me to the gully's edge. "This is the best place to climb down for a hundred yards in either direction."

"You had time to scout the surroundings?"

"*Nah.* I know this place. You'll see."

I followed in his footsteps down the limestone bank, seizing a scrub oak to steady myself on the slippery rocks. At the bottom, the creek curved out of sight twenty yards in each direction.

"Up this way seventy-five yards." Bowie led, stepping carefully on the creek bank. His left boot and pant cuff were muddy where he must have slipped into the swollen creek earlier.

"On my way here, I passed two boys in an old pickup. They the ones who found the body?"

"Yeah. Once we had their contact info and they led us to the body, we didn't need 'em anymore, so I cut 'em loose." He chuckled. "They wanted to stay."

"I thought the body freaked them out."

"They must have got used to it while they were waiting for us. After they led our guys to the body, they wanted to stick around. Got in the way. Nice boys, though; I know their parents."

"What brought them to this back-of-beyond place? I would expect them to hunt at the stock tank."

"There's a swimming hole up the creek a ways. The school kids know it. Hell, I came here when I was a kid. We all did. Doves, turkeys, deer, lots of wildlife around it from time to time. You'll see." He picked his way from one soggy foothold to another.

"Around this curve."

He stopped and gestured with both hands. "Ain't that a place you'd set a spell when you were a kid? Maybe go skinny dipping with your girl?"

A fault in the limestone bedrock had created a shaded oasis surrounded by flat stone shelves on either side of a pool of clear water twenty feet wide and forty feet long. On the sides and top of the gully, oaks and junipers hung over the water.

"Hot day like today, why aren't there kids swimming?"

"School day," Bowie replied.

"How about the two boys who were dove hunting?" I said. "They weren't in school."

"They're home schooled."

Forty yards upstream the rich black dirt on the gully's west side was marked by yellow crime scene tape stretched between the trees. Two technicians were processing the scene. Their gloves and pants were blackened by mud.

As I approached the yellow tape, I took care where I set my feet. It was too easy to slip into the creek. Stopping fifteen feet from the shallow grave, I watched the crime scene technicians.

I had met old death in Afghanistan. Our unit, the Triple Seven, cleared a village we had supposedly driven the Taliban from. We searched house to house—more accurately from hovel to ruin—to ensure the settlement was safe for displaced villagers to return. The Taliban were not good sports after they lost a battle. They weren't good sports after they won either. Win or lose, they booby-trapped buildings.

After hunting for tripwires, I thrust aside the dislodged door to the ruined house and discovered four long-dead family members that had been killed and left inside. A man and woman, and two girls, eight or ten years old. Throats cut. I won't tell you what the killers did to the woman and her daughters.

The Afghan scenario could have been a well-made horror movie, complete with decomposed bodies, dried blood, and old wounds, but it was real life. Or real death. The best-made movie doesn't prepare you for the reek of death. The stench, added to the vision I could never un-see, drove me back into the street, where I tossed my cookies. It wasn't the first time and it wouldn't be the last.

That Afghan house was a tableau of strangers' corpses—people I never knew from a culture I didn't identify with. Recalling those images and smells disturbs me to this day.

Now I prepared to confront an old death that might be my cousin, a girl I knew her whole life. What would her body look like? What would it smell like? What had the killer done to her?

My stomach growled a warning.

I took a deep breath and smelled nothing but raw earth and vegetation. The body was past smelling. Thank God for little things.

A crime scene technician photographed an article of clothing half-buried in the muddy bank. Covered by dirt and mud, it was hard to make out, but it was red. The technician photographed it from several angles, then set her camera aside. She teased mud off the garment with her gloved hand as she processed the ground for trace evidence. Finding none, she grasped the garment in two hands and eased it from the muck.

Yes, it was red. A shirt?

The technician exhibited the garment to Sheriff Bowie. "This was draped over the remains. Looks to be mostly a skeleton and rags of clothing buried in the creek bank. One foot was exposed when the boys found it. Whoever buried the victim laid this over the corpse before they filled in the grave."

The mud-caked garment had been buried for years, but it looked like a high school letter jacket. Enough of the mud dropped away to reveal Bonham Bobcats lettered across the back.

My heart juddered. I recognized the jacket from a picture hung on Emily's bedroom wall.

"That's Emily's basketball letter jacket," I said, "or its twin."

A sensation I couldn't identify flickered down my spine. This was a clue where there had been none before. It was good to have a clue—any clue. It was depressing that the clue proved I was too late to find Emily alive.

Emily's disappearance wasn't a kidnapping after all. She was murdered.

My stomach rebelled, and I leaned over the creek and vomited. Some tough guy.

I dipped my hands in the cool water and washed my face. I drew three long breaths while I regained my composure.

"Check inside the collar at the back," I said. "Look for the initials 'ECC' embroidered there."

The technician held the jacket at arms' length. "Too much mud to read. 'ECC'?" she repeated.

"Emily Constance Crazinski. She was my cousin."

She stood, flipped the jacket around, and opened the collar. "Don't see any embroidery."

"Her mother said it was on the collar. Look under the back of the collar. Maybe the mud didn't get under there."

The technician reversed the jacket and lifted the collar. She stared at it. From her expression I knew what she discovered.

"ECC. I'm sorry about your cousin."

I knew better than to reach for the jacket. It was evidence in a murder case.

The technician bagged the jacket.

It felt like the bottom had fallen out of an elevator and I was plummeting down the shaft of the tallest building in the world. It was hard to speak. I cleared my throat. "There was a locket around her neck with her initials."

She perused the grave. "We have more work before we uncover the body. Might be a couple hours before we can check. This mud doesn't make it any easier."

"That's okay." My voice caught in my throat. My vision blurred. "If you uncover the locket, her parents will want it after you finish processing it."

Blinking away tears, I did an about-face.

The sheriff touched my elbow. "I'm sorry for your loss, son. I know this is tough."

"You have no idea, Joe Bob. I have to inform her parents."

"You want me to do that? It's part of my job, son."

"I appreciate the offer, I do, but I have to do this."

I eyeballed my cellphone. Two bars. Enough to make a call. No, I couldn't do this over the phone. It had to be in person.

Carrie had clung to her sanity by believing in Emily's survival and the hope she would return safely. Her hold on reality had neared the end of its tether. How would this news affect her?

THIRTEEN

Gloria

M ister Blank raised his phone. "It's time for your progress report, Gloria. Let's see how well you dance now."

He placed a second phone on the TV tray and it played rock music from an internet website.

Gloria lay on the bed and stared at the ceiling of the room in which she had been held captive for twelve menstrual periods. She had found the message scratched on the wall by the previous captive in this room. That captive had been in the room for forty-six menstrual periods. Gloria had a vague idea how long it had been since her last progress report. Maybe two menstrual periods? It seemed like these weird progress reports happened about every two months.

"Come now, Gloria. Don't keep me waiting. You know how testy I get when you don't do what I say."

Next would come the threat. Mister Blank was *sooo* predictable.

His voice lost its jovial tone. "If you're not stripped in the next ten seconds, it will mean no food for two days."

Gloria sat up and lanced a deadly stare at Mister Blank. She didn't even know the monster's real name.

She stood without taking her eyes off him. She would show no fear; she never showed fear after those first few days. She confronted this monster without flinching. Holding his gaze gave her strength. She stripped off the white tee-shirt and dropped it on the bed. She stepped out of the white shorts and tossed them beside the shirt, all the while piercing her captor with a gaze that made her wish she was Medusa, with the power to turn him to stone.

Mister Blank had taken her clothes, her phone, and even her identity on that horrible night when she'd gone to a friend's house for dinner. When she returned to her car, a strong arm had wrapped around her neck and jerked her off her feet. A huge hand slapped a cloth over her nose and mouth. She'd taken a breath to scream and passed out.

When she woke, she was nude in a windowless room, lying on a narrow bed. The first thing she noticed was that her rings and bracelet were gone. She felt for the necklace her parents had given her last Christmas, but it too was missing. She touched her ears. Her earrings had been removed. She was as naked as the day she was born, and she felt as vulnerable as a newborn. All remnants of her past life had been ripped from her.

She had stood and walked to the door in the center of the far wall. She knocked on it, then pounded it with her fists as she screamed for help. The door seemed very solid, like her grandparents' oak dining room table. There had been no response.

She had moved to the other end of the room where one of the two doors led to a small bathroom. Fresh white bath and hand towels and a white washcloth hung on a rod. The stall shower had a new bar of soap and a bottle of unscented shampoo. The toilet paper holder held a fresh roll of toilet paper, still in its wrapper.

What was this? A nightmare variation of the Hotel California?

The other door led to a closet with a variety of funny costumes hung in it, plus a blue gingham dress. She put on the dress. It was too big for her, but at least she was no longer naked. She didn't feel as exposed, as vulnerable.

A small chest of drawers held a drawer of white tee-shirts and another of white shorts in various sizes. She opened the other two drawers, looking for underwear, but they were empty.

The room contained a mini-fridge/microwave combination like she planned to buy for her dorm room when she went to college. Food and water were inside.

An easy chair sat beside a wooden TV tray. A toothbrush still in the box sat on the tray beside a new tube of toothpaste and a bottle of mouthwash.

What version of hell was this?

Mister Blank's voice brought her back to the present. "It's time to dance, Gloria. Show me what you can do."

FOURTEEN

Carlos McCrary

I don't recall the drive from the Perkins Ranch to Austin, but I must have made it okay.

I braked at the curb a block from the house to wrap my head around this development. I hated to shatter Carrie's fantasy and confirm Frank's worst fears. How could I tell them without bringing them to their knees emotionally?

My experience had not prepared me for this.

Suck it up and do it, I thought.

Easing my foot off the brake, I idled the last block to their house.

Carrie's car sat alone in the driveway. Frank was a real estate broker who set his own hours.

Carrie gave me a house key when I first arrived, but I hadn't used it. I stood on the porch and debated whether to use the key or ring the doorbell. While I spun my mental wheels, the door opened.

"Oh, it's you, Chuck. I heard a car and peeked out the window."

She smiled, swung the door wide, and gestured me inside.

"You know, it's okay to let yourself in. That's why we gave you the key. I made a fresh batch of iced tea."

Faced by Aunt Carrie before me, I couldn't move. She jibber-jabbered, and I stood there like I'd grown roots on the porch.

Carrie noticed my expression and fell silent.

"You're crying."

Her voice grew louder.

"You're crying. You have news about Emily, don't you? I feel it in my soul. My horoscope said I would hear news from afar. She's dead, isn't she?"

I spread my hands in a noncommittal gesture.

"Let's get an iced tea and talk."

I led her to the kitchen, neither of us speaking.

One step at a time, I thought.

She handed me a tall, insulated plastic glass of iced tea. For once, she didn't fill the silence with jibber-jabber.

"Thanks," I said. "Why don't we sit at the table?"

She poured her tea and set two coasters on the table. "My horoscope said information would come at me so fast that it would be difficult to absorb. It said I don't need to tackle all this information today. Can this wait until Frank gets home?"

"It's important."

I considered her body language while she mentally prepared herself. At least she was sitting.

"I have news," I said. "It involves Emily."

Carrie pulled her shoulders back. "What news?"

"The Blanco County Sheriff called this morning."

She held my gaze. "Go on."

"Two boys went dove hunting in the boondocks and they found something."

I paused.

"The hurricane uncovered something buried in a creek bank in Blanco County."

"What— what did they find?"

I waited five seconds. "A body."

Carrie's eyes grew big as golf balls.

"Was it Emily?"

"The body was still buried. The CSI tech couldn't tell whether the vic was a man or a woman. They have to recover the body and remove the remains to the Travis County Medical Examiner's Office for forensic analysis."

"You were there?"

"The sheriff texted me the location and I met him there." I cleared my throat. "There's something else."

I waited. This would be the toughest hill for Carrie to climb.

"What else?"

"The person who buried the body draped a letter jacket over the victim before they filled the grave."

Carrie's lower lip trembled. "Emily wore her letter jacket the day she disappeared. A cold snap came through on St. Patrick's Day and she wore that jacket to school."

She gazed into the distance, seeing nothing but her own fears.

"She was proud of that jacket." She clasped her hands like she was praying. "Was it Emily's jacket?"

I inhaled a slow breath and nodded.

Carrie's head bobbed once. "We have to tell Frank."

She fished her phone from a pocket.

I raised my hand. "We don't know that the body is Emily."

Carrie jumped to her feet. "And Frank accuses me of not facing the truth. Are you out of your ever-loving mind? How can it *not* be Emily? She wore that jacket to school the day she disappeared. We have to tell Frank."

"I agree, but we shouldn't do this over the phone. The body was not *wearing* the jacket. The jacket had been draped over the body before it was buried. Shall I call Frank to come home early?"

She handed me her phone. "You call him."

I located his office number in her contact list.

"Frank, it's Chuck. Have you left work?"

"Just finishing. Why are you calling on Carrie's phone? Is she all right?"

"Yes, she's fine. I was about to call you and she handed me her phone."

"Do you need something from the store on the way home?"

"No, but you should come home now."

"Did something happen to Carrie?"

"Nothing happened to Carrie. No one is hurt. Just come home."

Frank was silent a second.

"You have word on Emily?"

"There's new evidence in the case. I need to talk to you and Carrie. Together."

"I'll be there in ten minutes."

He made it in eight. His tires squealed as he hit the driveway. I arrived at the front door as Frank rushed up the sidewalk.

He hesitated when he spotted me. "What happened?"

"Let's go to the kitchen. Carrie's there."

Frank yanked a chair from the breakfast table and sat where he could hold Carrie's hand.

"Okay. Tell us."

"The Blanco County Sheriff called a few hours ago."

I related my visit to the crime scene and the jacket that was found.

Frank squeezed Carrie's hand. "And you're sure it was Emily's jacket?"

"Her initials were embroidered underneath the collar."

Frank's shoulders sagged. He brought Carrie's hand to his face. The tears that had gathered in his eyes spilled over his cheeks. He brushed his lips across her knuckles. He kissed the back of her hand then rubbed his cheek against it. Her hand came away moist from his tears.

"Frank, the body hasn't been identified," I said. "It could be someone else."

Frank seemed far away mentally. His voice came whisper soft. "Who else could it be?"

"There are lots of ways someone else could have the jacket. Emily could have loaned it to someone, or someone might have stolen it from her locker. Hell, if Emily ran away instead of being kidnapped, she may have forgotten it in a restaurant booth. The jacket links the body to Emily, but it's not definitive evidence. Not until we have a positive ID on the body. Don't abandon hope yet," I said, "but prepare yourself."

"It's her," he moaned. "I feel it."

Carrie wrapped her free arm around Frank while he wept and moaned.

I had assumed this news would hit Carrie harder than Frank. Carrie had kept the faith even after Frank resigned himself to Emily's death years before. Confronted by the physical probability of Emily's fate, it was Carrie who comforted Frank.

Shows you how little I know about people's emotions.

As I sat motionless at the table, my aunt was strong while my macho uncle wilted and shriveled and aged before my eyes.

Frank squeezed a napkin and wiped his eyes. Releasing Carrie's hand, he blew his nose. He stuck the dirty napkin in his pocket and faced his wife. "We have phone calls to make."

"I can make those calls for you," I said.

Frank regarded me with nervous eyes.

"Thanks. I'll get our address book."

Carrie said, "People will ask about the funeral."

"Not yet they won't," I said. "The jacket means the body could be Emily's, but it's not one hundred percent certain until the Medical Examiner does a DNA test. I'll tell them it will be two weeks before we know."

"How soon can we have her body?"

"It will be a while. DNA tests require a few days, and they do forensic tests."

"Forensic tests?" Carrie said.

"Carrie, let's not discuss this. You and Frank don't need the details. Let the cops do their job. I'll call Detective Ortega first to brief him."

———

After I called Ortega, my next call was to Grandpa.

Grandpa drove over from George and Melissa's house. After tearful hugs and kisses all around, he drew me aside. "Let's go outside. Bring the address book."

He led me onto the back deck.

"Tell me everything that happened in Blanco County."

"Why? I'm the detective, not you. There's no call for you to listen to the gory details. It's bad enough for me to speak them."

"Son, it's not for *my* benefit; it's for *yours*. I'm an old man and I've faced lots of death, mainly in Vietnam. After that, I lost count of the friends and family I've buried. Believe me, part of grieving is to tell someone about your loss. You may not realize it, but you've had a loss—a big one. Tell me everything."

We sat at the picnic table and I related—no, *relived*—every minute from the instant I received Sheriff Bowie's phone call to when I arrived at the house to deliver the bad news. As I told Grandpa the story, I realized I did not observe the body, just the muddy jacket.

That insight made me feel better and worse simultaneously. Better, because a vision of Cousin Emily's decayed corpse would not corrupt my memories of her. Worse, because it revealed my reluctance to confront her skeletal remains.

I had shied away. Note to self: Confront the crime scene in all its gory detail; don't shy away again.

I had violated Rule Fifteen: *Never take anything for granted* because I also violated Rule Seventeen: *Never get personally involved in a case.* Breaking Rule Seventeen didn't bother me; I often take cases personally. Rule Seventeen is important though: Personal involvement creates bias in the investigator. That made me assume the body under the jacket was Emily. It might not be her.

Ninety-nine percent is not one hundred percent.

"Didn't you tell me this is a serial killer?" Grandpa said.

"Yes. The killer used her jacket to cover the body like a shroud. That indicates an emotional attachment or obsession with the victim. That's common among serial killers."

"I read that serial killers keep trophies from their victims, something to remember them by, like a souvenir."

"That's a myth," I said. "Most serial killers don't keep trophies. Trophies could link them to the crime. It's true that *some* killers collect trophies. Why do you ask?"

"What if Emily's kidnapper used her jacket to bury a different victim?"

"It doesn't matter if the body is not Emily. Emily's still dead."

"Probability is not certainty." Grandpa spoke the words like a mantra.

He took the address book. "I'll make these calls, son. Don't worry; I can handle it. I've faced as much, if not more, death than even you. I'll tell people that we don't know whether it's Emily. Most of these folks will want to talk about Emily, and they'll need someone to cry with over the phone. I'm good at that. You go catch the man who did this."

"Not today, Grandpa, not today. I'll split the calls with you. I'll get back on the case tomorrow. But not today."

We walked inside, his hand on my shoulder.

———

Detective Ortega texted me.

You'll be glad to know that Emily Crazinski's case was reassigned to Sergeant Nora Goodman in Homicide. She'll call you this afternoon.

Glad to know? Why would Ortega think I'd be glad the case was transferred? Maybe *he* was glad. He hadn't liked dealing with me anyway.

I texted back.

Did you confirm the Blanco County body is Emily?

My phone rang. It was Ortega.

"We don't have DNA results yet."

"If you don't know that Emily was murdered, why transfer the case to Homicide?"

"It wasn't my decision. The captain transferred it."

"Not that I'm complaining, but why? You're familiar with the case."

"Look, McCrary, you never liked dealing with me anyway, and I feel the same way about you. Missing Persons caught the case originally because Emily was sixteen years old, which made her a missing child. Missing children automatically come to us. We kept the case because we never learned different. Now that we have a body, it's a murder, regardless of who the victim is. Homicide handles murders. Plus, if Emily were alive, she'd be an adult, age twenty, nearly twenty-one."

"But you don't know that Emily was murdered. The DB may not be Emily."

"If the body you found in Blanco is not Emily, the fact that her jacket was buried with the body allows us to presume that Emily was kidnapped. Homicide handles kidnappings also."

"I didn't find the body. It was two boys hunting doves."

"Whatever."

Ortega disconnected without saying goodbye.

A few minutes later, Sergeant Nora Goodman called. "We haven't met, but Rod Ortega gave me your number when the case was assigned to me. We have DNA results on the body you found in Blanco County."

"I didn't find it. Two boys stumbled across the body while they were hunting."

"Whatever. The body is not Emily's. The DNA didn't match the sample swabs from her parents that you gave Ortega."

"Where are you?"

"At the ME's office."

I knew where that was. "I'll be there in twenty minutes."

"I'll get a coffee. Text me when you're close and I'll meet you in the autopsy suite."

———

Sergeant Goodman was a chunky, fortyish brunette gone prematurely gray. The chunky part came from the Kevlar vest she wore under her shirt. Her no-nonsense white sneakers were scuffed, but her khaki slacks had a knife-edge crease. Her black Austin Police knit shirt had the APD logo embroidered on the left chest. The shirt probably began life as a golf shirt in a factory in Chang Rai. Then a Thai woman making fifty cents an hour embroidered the logo on it. "Presto-Chango! You are an official United States police uniform."

Goodman's shield was clipped to her belt on the left. Her service weapon was clipped on the right. Not quite bookends, but she made the ensemble work.

We shook hands in the hallway outside the autopsy suite.

"Excuse the uniform, but I just came from a Career Day speech at a local high school. I usually wear plain clothes, but the Captain told me to wear my uniform."

"Looks good on you. Did you find a DNA match to anyone else?" I asked.

"Not yet. We'll access a couple more databases, but I'm not hopeful. I haven't observed the body yet. You want to come with me?"

"Like a trip to the dentist, but I will."

She held the door and followed me inside. Polite. I liked that.

"Dr. Sean Ryan, this is Carlos McCrary. He's a private investigator working with us on a missing persons case that may be a kidnapping."

Goodman told Ryan I was working with the Austin cops. Perhaps I wouldn't have to win her over like I tried to do with Ortega. I liked that too.

Ryan stripped off his surgical gloves and shook hands. "Pleased to meet you. You the guy who found the body in Blanco County?"

"No. Two boys who were dove hunting found it. Do I need a Vaseline mustache?"

"No. The body's been buried so long, there's not much smell."

"How long?"

"I can't pin it down because of the soil conditions and site drainage where it was buried. At least one year. Could have been ten years or more."

Ryan stepped to a wall of stainless-steel doors. He opened a door and slid out a shelf with the remains on it. I won't describe the body's appearance. Suffice it to say that it was decayed and disturbing, a grotesque mockery of a human being. This was no horror movie special effects; this was real. I have a strong stomach, but I swallowed hard.

The little skin that remained on the body was a creamy mocha color. Unless the ground had altered the skin's appearance, this wasn't Emily. A shaggy brown mass that looked like a mop head lay on the steel table near the skull.

"What's that thing beside the skull?"

"That's what's left of the victim's hair."

The lumpy heap looked like a tangled mass of brown string.

"We'll have to untangle it to be sure, but I think it's in dreadlocks."

"African-American?" I asked.

"Not necessarily. Dreadlocks are popular across racial lines, but the skin color indicates she was multi-racial. Doesn't mean much nowadays. Lots of people are multi-racial."

"How old was she?"

"We know from the degree of cranial-bone fusion and tooth wear that the victim was late teens or early twenties. The skull and pelvis tell us she was female. Approximately five-feet-nine-inches tall. That's plus or minus an inch. Based on her clothes, we estimate she weighed between 120 and 160 pounds."

"Cause of death?"

"Manual strangulation. We caught a break on the cause of death. Her hyoid bone was broken. We don't discover those broken very often. It's definitive evidence she was manually strangled."

I absorbed that fact. The images in my mind might be worse than the actual murder. "Sexual assault?"

"Too long dead to tell."

"Any dental work?"

"Yeah, excellent work. If we locate her dentist, we'll have a good ID. It's difficult to locate her dentist when we don't know who she was or where she lived. A chicken-or-egg problem."

I squared around to Goodman. "How did the killer get Emily's jacket?"

"If we have a serial killer, maybe he kept the jacket for a *token*, a souvenir. He could have used her jacket to bury a different victim."

"But we still don't know where Emily is buried," I said.

"Sometimes serial killers use the same area to bury their victims."

"We'd better take another look-see at the Perkins Ranch," I said.

"The body was found in Blanco County. This murder is their jurisdiction," Goodman said. "I just called to tell you the victim wasn't Emily."

"Ortega told me Emily's case was reassigned to you as a kidnapping. That's in Homicide's purview."

"Right."

"But this murder connects to Emily's kidnapping in Travis County."

"Let's see what the Blanco County authorities uncover. I'll liaise with them. Don't worry. I'll make sure nothing falls through the cracks."

"I'll call Sheriff Bowie," I said.

"Maybe he'll find more bodies on the Perkins Ranch."

"That's what I'm afraid of."

FIFTEEN

Mister Blank

Evita glared at the man she called Weirdo.

He always found that implacable glower unsettling, as if she was prepared to launch a surprise attack with some hidden weapon. No matter, proceed as normal. "Hello, Evita. It's time for your progress report."

"Can you at least play some decent music this time, Weirdo? Maybe something country. You haven't played country in a long time."

Of all his girls, Evita was the most uncooperative. At times, like now, she was even demanding. In all the years of his project, he had never encountered a girl like Evita. But despite her peculiarities, she was worth the extra trouble.

When he first captured her, he told her to call him Mister Blank, but she had adamantly refused. "As long as you insist on calling me Evita, I'll call you Weirdo. If you don't like it, screw you."

He had tried to starve her into submission. "Call me Mister Blank if you want me to feed you." Then he removed the food and water from her mini-fridge. Let her drink from the bathroom faucet. Serve her right.

Each day, he unlocked the door and offered to feed her if she called him "Mister Blank."

Her reaction had always been the same. "Screw you."

After four days without food, he tried one last time. "You ready to cooperate, Evita? Call me Mister Blank."

"Screw you, Weirdo. You can rape me and you can starve me to death, but that's all you can do. And when I die, who will you use for your weirdo sex games?"

He had considered that for some hours and concluded that Evita's sexual services, even given unwillingly, were worth her insubordination. They negotiated a compromise whereby she performed for him and his friend and he allowed her to call him Weirdo.

"How about some classic Reba McIntire?" he offered.

"Okay, Weirdo." She stood and stripped off her clothes.

Once again, her unadorned beauty astonished him. Over the years she had blossomed into a woman who was well worth any inconveniences.

Too bad she was about to expire.

SIXTEEN

Carlos McCrary

The FBI often steps in on serial killer cases. I suggested that to Sheriff Bowie over the phone.

"This ain't a serial killing yet," Bowie said, "not with just one victim."

"Sheriff, the FBI has ground-penetrating radar. You have those in Blanco County?"

Bowie laughed so loud that I lowered my phone's volume.

"Let's keep this case to ourselves, son. Me and you, let's poke around the Perkins Ranch on our own first, okay? If we don't find anything, maybe we'll call the feds, but I figure until we find a second body, the FBI fellows won't want the case. It's not like they've got nothing to do on other crimes."

"Joe Bob, between you and me, are you hogging the credit for solving the case? Do you have an opponent in the next election?"

"Son, I ain't had an opponent in the last eight years. I just don't want the feds to second guess me and shove me aside in my own county. You want in on this or not?"

"I want in."

"Meet me at my office tomorrow at nine a.m. Wear work clothes. Bring a denim jacket if you have one and heavy leather gloves. I'll provide the shovels."

Shovels? We'd need *shovels*?

A shudder ran down my spine when I realized how we would use the shovels.

————

That night, I pulled out my 112 missing persons files.

I had not sorted them by race. That was a philosophical choice. I believe that race doesn't—or shouldn't—matter. And, practically speaking, race is often indefinite. What am I? White or Latino? I am both, and a Medical Examiner could classify my body either way. It might even depend on whether the ME knew my name was Carlos. If I met this mixed-race victim socially alongside white parents or Latino parents, I would classify her white or Latino. If I met her beside black parents, I would call her African-American.

See what I mean? Race in America is as confused as it is irrelevant. If we must have a blank space for race, why can't we fill it with "human"?

I planned my first pass through the 112 files to screen for victims whose height was five-seven or taller. I disregarded weight. The longer the time between the kidnapping and the murder, the more difficult to predict the victim's weight at the time of death.

To make those examinations, I needed to examine photos of 112 missing girls. Each left behind a mystified, unhappy family. Having found one real victim—even one who might not be in my files—made the 112 losses more tangible somehow.

My vision blurred and I knew I was crying. I hadn't begun to review the files and I was already in tears. Tears for 112 families. Tears for Emily's parents. Tears for Emily. Tears for myself.

I carried the files to the kitchen and made coffee.

By one a.m. I had narrowed the field to three possibles: one from Burnet County and two from Travis County. Before I went to bed, I emailed the names and case numbers to the Burnet and Travis County sheriffs and sent a copy to Sheriff Bowie as a heads-up.

———

I met Sheriff Bowie at his office in Johnson City.

"Your email about the missing girls was in my inbox this morning. Thanks for the heads-up."

Bowie was old enough to be my father, but he seemed close to his Texas cowboy roots. I would bet he hiked and climbed and dug as well as I did. I followed him out to the Perkins Ranch, me in my Jeep Cherokee and Bowie in a silver Dodge Ram 3500 pickup the size of a tugboat.

October weather in Central Texas is funny. Four days earlier, it was swimming weather. Today was football weather, crisp and breezy. Even on Saturday, there wouldn't be anyone at the swimming hole.

After we curved onto Perkins Ranch Road, we didn't pass anyone else. We parked where we had four days earlier and scrabbled our way to the crime scene. The yellow tape hung between the trees, a relic left by CSIs. A loose end flapped in the breeze like a pennant.

The abandoned excavation was now just a hole in the ground. All evidence had been removed. The hole in the ground was akin to the hole Emily's disappearance had left in the lives of our entire family.

"If I was the killer," Bowie said, "I would bury my victims farther upstream. Less likely to get washed out on the higher ground. You search that side of the creek, and I'll search this one. We'll work our way upstream staying in the gully. Then you walk back on the mesa above and I'll take the pasture on my side. Holler if you notice anything."

Briars, wild grapevines, willows, and bushes choked the narrow gully. Where it widened, oaks and junipers and cottonwoods soared above the undergrowth. I was glad for the leather gloves. I soon wished I had taken the sheriff's advice and bought a denim jacket. Maybe even a leather one.

We beat our way up the gully for ten minutes and covered seventy-five grueling yards. The underbrush clawed and counter-attacked us with every grudging step. My back ached from clambering stooped over and we had barely begun. The steel garden spade I carried weighed heavier with each step I took. I repeatedly retrieved my hat from a host of spikey obstacles. Thorns ripped my shirt, and my arms and face oozed blood from a dozen nicks and scraps and scratches. And they itched. Boy, did they itch.

I wondered how Bowie was doing, then I observed him ahead, trudging onward like an armored vehicle. Or a minesweeper.

The next hundred yards was a wide creek bed with small side cascades falling from one rocky ledge to another. The creek arched around the mesa's base. A turkey across the creek gobbled at Bowie and spread his tail to notify the sheriff he was trespassing on the gobbler's territory.

The sheriff paused and waved at me.

"Lookie there, Chuck. You have gobblers in Port City?"

"Nope, but in the Everglades, we have deer like that one."

A deer drank from a pool fifty yards ahead.

I couldn't resist. I snapped a picture with my phone. It would be more scenic if the clouds parted to let the sun shine. And if we weren't hunting for an unmarked grave.

The rocky creek grew deeper. The gully narrowed and duck-and-cover brush and brambles clogged it again.

Finally, I reached a spot where I could stand upright. A breeze in the clearing chilled my chest through the sweaty shirt. Leaning the shovel against a bush, I fished a bottle of water from my backpack, and drank half. As I screwed the lid back on, I spotted an anomaly on the slope above.

A tributary runoff had cut a groove in the rocky face of the mesa. The channel trickled to the creek bed in a series of rivulets marked by tiny cascades, dry since it hadn't rained since Hurricane Stefano. The other runoffs I had noticed cut through the bank of the gully in a narrow trench I could step across. This one had a flat place halfway up like a landing in a flight of stairs.

From below, I noticed an earthen dam had plugged the watercourse and displaced the cascade to one side. That created a second gulch that side-stepped its fall to the creek. The second ravine was raw and ragged and smelled like freshly-exposed earth. The abandoned original channel was dry and overgrown with grass.

What had triggered the dirt plug halfway up the channel?

We had come hunting another grave. On one level, I hoped we found one. On another level, I hoped we wouldn't. Something about the dirt platform above my head seemed ominous. If this were a horror movie, this is where the spooky music would play.

I fought my way through the junipers jammed on the slope until I reached the mass of rock and mud. The smell of juniper and mud with a touch of manure filled the atmosphere. Ten yards above the channel, a small landslide had formed a dirt pile beneath the mesa's edge. The tailings of that dirt-fall blocked the channel.

Someone had dug near the edge of the mesa.

"Joe Bob," I called. "Can you hear me?"

A distant voice responded. "Yep. I hear you. You find something?"

"Yeah. I'll climb to the mesa and see what it is."

"I'm on my way."

I heard thrashing in the brush across the gully and I scrutinized the rocky slope to pick my first foothold.

On some level, I knew what I expected to find on top. Carrie said Emily weighed 120 pounds when she vanished. As I climbed, my backpack felt like it weighed 120 pounds.

God only knew what she weighed now. My eyes burned.

I kept climbing. I refused to shy from this grave, if that's what it was.

I hopped the gulch at the top and scaled the last step to the mesa. Scattered live oaks shared the mesa with junipers and mesquites. Rocky outcrops reared their heads above the scraggly wild grass that filled in between scattered prickly-pear cactus.

Five yards to my left a mound of dirt and rock and wild grass peeked nine inches above the mesa top—so slight I could miss it stuck under the branches of a giant prickly-pear cactus. The mound was plonked on the mesa's edge, a dinosaur-sized cow patty that dribbled over the side into the gully.

The mound was wide enough and long enough for a grave.

My heart climbed into my throat.

"Joe Bob," I croaked, feeling queasy.

I spoke again, louder. "Joe Bob, bring your shovel."

I heard the sheriff ram through the underbrush before I saw him.

He puffed his way up the slope and stood propped against his shovel while he caught his breath.

"Looks like a grave, doesn't it?"

"I made photos from all angles. What next? Call the Austin CSIs?"

"Nope. That's why we brought the shovels. It *looks* to be a grave, but we don't *know* it's a grave. Not yet anyways. Austin PD charges my department a fee to use their personnel or equipment. It ain't cheap, either. We don't call them until we know it's a crime scene."

"I never dug for a body before. How do we do it without destroying evidence?"

"There are two parts to it. First, we remove the mound so's we uncover the real grave. That's overburden, and removing it is the easy part."

"How do we do that?"

"I'll show you. It's more *scraping* than *digging*. Lookie here."

Bowie dropped to a knee and grasped his garden spade like a canoe paddle, one hand on the steel handle and the other on the oak shaft above the blade. He scraped a half-inch of loose dirt, pebbles, and grass from the center of the mound and dragged it to one side.

"See that? Tease it off a little at a time, like peeling a potato. We stop when we see something that shouldn't be there. Why don't you tackle that cactus and cut it out of our way? That's not delicate work. Best way is to stab the root two or three inches below the ground. You cut the root with the shovel blade, then roll that sucker away, slick as a wet catfish. Have at it, son."

I made three stabs with the spade before the prickly-pear toppled over. I tumbled it aside with the blade. Slick as a wet catfish.

Bowie stopped to catch his breath.

"Alrighty. You been watching me. You do the same as me from the other side. Scrape the mound down to original ground level. Be alert and stop if you notice anything that's not natural."

"Something the killer dropped, like a button or a glove."

"Basically, anything that ain't dirt, grass, or rock."

We scraped soil from opposite sides until we removed the overburden. I was right about Bowie: The man was a human backhoe. I was hard pressed to match him.

Bowie stood and stretched his arms and shoulders.

"Take a break. This next part is harder. I brought sandwiches. Peanut butter and jelly so's it wouldn't spoil without no refrigeration, although it's cold enough today that I needn't have worried."

"I'm hungry enough to eat it if it did spoil."

We each chugged a bottle of water and caught our breath. We perched on a limestone outcropping to eat the PB&J. The breeze evaporated the sweat from my shirt and cooled me off, but it didn't stop the itch.

Bowie stuffed the empty sandwich bags into his backpack.

"Time we got back to work."

We moved back to the site and Bowie dropped to his knees.

"See the soil in the middle? Dirt and not much dead grass mixed in it. But on the sides, the original grass ain't been disturbed. It was buried, but it's there, still rooted."

I scanned the area we had scraped clear. Tufts of dead grass formed the outer circle for a bullseye that matched the grassy prairie atop the mesa. The center made a darker oval, seven feet long and three feet wide. It felt ominous, like a hole into the center of the earth. In a movie, the scary music would get louder.

As I snapped pictures, my stomach churned while I contemplated what lay beneath the black dirt. I hoped I didn't lose my peanut butter and jelly.

"Has to be a grave, Sheriff. We call the Austin CSIs now?"

"Don't jump the gun, son. We haven't proven it's a crime scene yet. That's why the next part is harder."

He hefted the shovel.

"Next, we trench the undisturbed dirt on this side, next to the grave. We dig the old compacted dirt out, and the new dirt covering the body falls into the trench without us shoveling. We maybe loosen the dirt some, but we'll be real gentle. That way, we uncover what's in the grave and we don't disturb any evidence. Follow what I do and you start on the other side."

This was the creepiest feeling I had ever experienced. I was digging up a grave. Perhaps my cousin's grave. I swallowed hard and followed Bowie's example.

Another half hour and we unearthed it.

———

I set my boot on the shovel blade's top flange and leaned on it. The blade forced its way into the packed dirt. I leaned again and gained another three inches. Jerking back and thrusting the handle down, I levered the blade up and loosened another spadeful. I heaved the dirt and pebbles onto the waste pile.

I was getting good at this. At home in Port City I pumped iron alongside a former NFL defensive lineman, but I got sore from using my muscles in an unaccustomed way.

Sheriff Bowie displayed no sign of fatigue.

We dug the relief trench six feet long, two feet wide, and three feet deep. A cupful of dirt fell loose from the grave and dropped into the trench. I knelt and raked more grave dirt into the trench with gloved fingers.

The scary music would reach a crescendo.

There it was. A flash of plaid peeked from the dirt.

"Sheriff, that's fabric. Could be a shirt."

Bowie tossed his shovel aside. He knelt in the trench beside me. "Let me tease the dirt out of the way." He brushed the soil aside with his fingers and exposed more of the plaid cloth.

He lifted the cloth and grunted. Standing, he yanked his gloves off.

"There's a body under there. *Now* we have ourselves a crime scene. I'll call the Austin CSIs."

———

We ate the remaining sandwiches while we caught our breath.

Bowie and I walked the top of the mesa looking for more graves. A mound of overburden like the one we already found could be a grave. Alternatively, a body in a shallow grave might leave a depressed area where the body had decomposed.

We didn't find either a mound or a depression. That didn't mean there weren't more graves on or near the mesa. Our examination was cursory, and we were tired.

All day long, I had confronted the possibility we would locate Emily's grave. I submerged the notion into my subconscious. Anytime it fought its way to the surface, I suppressed it again. And again. And yet again.

After an hour we sat on a limestone shelf and awaited the Austin CSIs.

In the seventy minutes we waited for the technicians, I perused the gravesite. The whole time, I wished I was anyplace else. The prickly-pear cactus lay on its side ten yards away. The pile of overburden ringed the gravesite, the earthen fortification of a prehistoric stronghold. The waste heap Bowie and I had dug from the relief trench spilled off the overburden pile.

I heard the CSI van motor and their dust cloud billowed before they came into view. I looked south where the primitive road emerged from the prairie below.

The van climbed into sight and lurched across the mesa.

After I stood to greet the Austin investigators, I noticed the scrap of cloth waving in the breeze like a plaid flag over Emily's last resting place.

It was the same crew that processed the first grave four days before.

I gave them a greeting that I don't remember and stood aside while the sheriff briefed them. After he finished, I motioned him aside. "Joe Bob, I can't help with this; I'd just be in the way. I'll wait in the Jeep."

"Don't blame you, son. I'll call you if we learn anything you ought to know."

———

I tilted the Jeep's driver seat back, opened the windows halfway, and closed my eyes. I fell asleep—God knows I was plenty tired and sore.

The sound of Sheriff Bowie's boots sliding down the gravel trail woke me.

The sun had dropped toward the horizon, and the late afternoon wind was cold. I closed the windows, exited the Jeep, and met Bowie.

"Them CSIs uncovered enough of the body to know it's not Emily."

"You ID the body?"

"Nope, but Emily was blonde. This victim has long black hair."

My scoured arms creeped like spiders crawled on them. Could the body be Ling Cheng?

"That means we haven't located Emily's body. The search isn't over."

"We have a serial killer," Bowie said. "Now I call the FBI." Bowie clapped my shoulder. "We'll let them hunt for more bodies. They're real good at this. You go back to Austin."

"The first one was buried in the gully. We ought to finish searching the gully."

"Yeah, but me and you don't have to do it. The feds will locate any additional bodies, or a cadaver dog will. I'll tell old man Perkins he's gonna have company on the ranch the next few days. You can go on home if you like."

This time I was happy to share the news with my aunt and uncle over the phone. There was hope that Emily was alive. Faint hope, but real.

———

Thanks to daylight savings time, I reached the house while it was still light. Carrie and Frank were in the kitchen working on dinner.

Carrie wiped her hands on her apron and hugged me.

"My horoscope said I'd receive good news from an unexpected source today."

Frank mumbled under his breath, but he continued chopping onions.

"We don't know what happened to Emily," I said, "but we know the new grave isn't hers. With the second grave, we have a serial killer, and Sheriff Bowie is calling in the FBI."

Frank scraped the chopped onions into a frying pan.

"They gonna hunt for more graves there?"

"Yeah. Within a day or two, they'll blanket the Perkins Ranch with ground-penetrating radar and cadaver dogs. If there are more graves, they'll find them. This gives me a chance to take a couple days off. I'm returning to Port City until we have more leads. You all must be tired of me being underfoot every night."

"Don't be silly, Chuck. We're glad you're on the case. Aren't we, Frank?"

"Sure, sure."

"It's been two weeks since I've been home. I ought to show my face at the office. I'm flying out tomorrow morning."

"Have you heard anything from Terry?"

"No. My emails, voicemails and texts are like putting messages in bottles and throwing them into the ocean."

"What will you do about her?"

"Nothing. The ball is in her court. She knows I want to talk, but I can't force her to respond."

Carrie threw me a sad look. "I'll tell you what Frank keeps telling me: You need to move on with your life."

———

Sunday in Port City, I went fishing with Clint. Monday, I puttered around the office and checked my snail mail. Tuesday, I bought lunch for my new insurance company client and reviewed the case. That night I drove by Terry's apartment. Her car was there and I saw a light in her window. She hadn't responded to any of my messages so I drove home with my soul as decayed as the body in that first grave on the Perkins Ranch. Wednesday, I returned to Austin.

I was single again. Unattached. Available. Eligible. Alone.

Whoopee.

SEVENTEEN

D r. Sean Ryan, the Travis County Medical Examiner stood beside the body. Sergeant Nora Goodman and I stood across from him.

"The victim was late teens or early twenties. Female. Asian, most likely."

"Is that her natural hair color?"

"Yes. Straight black, not artificially colored or straightened. That usually means she was Asian or Native American. Combine that with the bone structure of the facial bones and the femurs, and I conclude she was Asian. She was five-foot-ten. Weighed around 150."

"Cause of death?" Goodman asked.

"Not enough left to tell. The hyoid bone was intact, but it's only broken in about twenty-five percent of strangulations. We found cable ties around the wrists and ankles. She was bound before she was killed. She didn't walk to the site, so the killer may have killed her elsewhere and carried her to the site."

"That would take a strong man, wouldn't it?" I asked.

"I'll leave that to you detectives to figure out. We didn't find any marks on the bones that would indicate a gunshot or a cutting instrument like a knife. Could be strangulation, but I couldn't swear to it."

"Time of death?"

"Like the first one, it's too vague to tell because of the conditions of burial. One to five years."

"Any dental work?"

"Nope. Perfect teeth, but slight marks on the molars indicate she wore braces when she was younger."

"I have a lead on her identity," I said.

Goodman pulled out a notebook. "That'll make it easier to locate the orthodontist. Who do you think she is?"

"Ling Cheng, a friend of Emily Crazinski."

"Spell her name."

I did.

I had downloaded Ling's graduation picture from the internet. I showed Goodman. "Notice the straight black hair."

"Send the photo to my phone," Goodman said.

I did. I considered the photo again. I compared it to the body. Something didn't compute. "The hair's wrong."

"How so?"

"In the graduation photo, her hair is shoulder length. The hair on the body is a foot longer."

I had a brainstorm. "The killer is not just a murderer. He's a kidnap-and-keep freak. Hair grows about six inches a year. If that body is Ling Cheng, he kept her captive at least two years before he killed her. That indicates the time of death was approximately one to two years ago."

I had another inspiration.

"That explains how Emily's jacket ended up in the grave. The killer kidnapped all three girls and held them captive an extended length of time. He had Emily's jacket two years later when he killed Ling."

"If this victim is Ling Cheng," Goodman said.

"That's easy to confirm once you contact Ling's orthodontist. Orthodontists make an impression of their patients' teeth before and after orthodontia. Shouldn't be difficult to locate him or her. Look for one whose office is close to Ling's home or school."

"That's gonna take manpower," Goodman said.

I grinned. "You mean *person*power, don't you?"

Goodman made a dismissive gesture. "Whatever. It requires *resources.*"

"Sometimes that's the job."

"We'll get right on it. You have Cheng's last known home address?"

"Yeah."

I gave it to her and she noted it.

"By the way, there was a car key buried with this latest body," Goodman said. "The corpse's finger was stuck through the key ring."

"Did you identify the car?"

She waggled a hand.

"It's an ignition key to a Toyota between model years 2004-2009."

"Is there a serial number on the key?"

"No. It's an after-market key, made someplace like a hardware store."

"Fingerprints?"

Goodman shook her head.

"Wiped clean."

"How about the first body the boys found in the creek bed? Did you ID it?"

The Medical Examiner spoke. "I was about to tell you. She's Francine Tinker, from Burnet."

While I was in Port City, the Burnet County Sheriff followed up my email and contacted the missing girl's parents. They had come to Austin with their daughter's dental records and the ME had identified her body two days before.

Francine had been a student at Burnet High School. She disappeared five years before in November. She met friends from Burnet High in Marble Falls for a movie. Her friends last saw her when they left the theatre. Francine was going shopping at Walmart. Cops found her car in the store's parking lot two days later. The store's security video revealed nothing.

I remembered Francine Tinker's file photo. She had short hair in the photo her parents gave the sheriff. When her body was found, her hair was eighteen inches long and in dreadlocks, although with dreadlocks the actual length was longer.

"Maybe her hair length tells us how long the killer held Francine before he murdered her," I said. "Do you have her parents' contact information, Doctor Ryan?"

He did, and I called the mother first, assuming she had paid more attention to her daughter's hairstyle than the father did. Okay, that's a gender stereotype of either parental roles or gender differences, but there you have it. I am not *woke*. There are differences between men and women. And thank goodness for them.

Francine's mother said her ID photo was four months old when they gave it to the Burnet County Sheriff, and her hair was two inches longer when she was kidnapped.

That gave us a rough timeline of three years between disappearance and murder. Three years in which she was captive. Did she do the dreadlocks herself, or did someone else do them?

Francine was buried twenty miles from where she disappeared. Ling Cheng—if that's who the Asian victim was—was buried over fifty miles from Austin.

Where was Emily buried?

I rang Sheriff Bowie. "Did the FBI find more bodies while I was in Port City?"

"Funny you should ask. I didn't call the FBI. Instead, I asked Texas Search and Rescue to send over a cadaver dog. I'm with them now, me and a couple deputies."

"Uncover anything?"

"I was about to call you. The dog smelled something. I called the Austin CSIs. They ain't here yet, but the dog handler says his dog is ninety-five percent accurate. You gonna come out?"

"You don't need me for that. I have other fish to fry. The Austin CSIs will process the body in Austin like the other ones?"

"Yeah."

"I'll wait and see what they say."

Friday morning, I crossed the street to interview Harry Nelson. Again.

I rapped on the door. Again.

Harry Nelson opened the front door until it bumped against the safety chain. "Yeah?"

I gave him my hundred-watt smile. "Mr. Nelson, I'm Chuck McCrary, Carrie and Frank's nephew. We've met, but you may not remember. May I come in?"

Nelson's bulky shoulders and well-developed pectoral muscles strained against his U. S. Army Ranger tee-shirt that revealed a Ranger death's-head tattoo on his arm. He squinted against the bright sunshine behind me. "I was just about to work out."

Nelson told the neighbors he was forty-four years old, but I knew different. His sandy-blond hair was streaked with gray, and he appeared older. His stubbled blond beard was gray and the crinkles on his face and neck confirmed the slackened skin on his muscular arms. Time stands still for no man. Not even a Ranger.

"I'd like to ask you a few questions." I cranked the smile to two hundred watts. "May I come in?"

"What questions?"

"About Emily."

"Emily? I don't understand."

"Emily Crazinski. She disappeared four years ago."

What was wrong with this guy? How could he not remember his neighbor's missing daughter?

"Oh, yeah. I forgot. It's been four years?"

"Yes, sir. May I come in?"

Nelson glanced over his shoulder. "The place is a mess. I didn't know Emily well. I saw her at the Bobcat basketball games and sometimes we'd see each other if we crossed paths jogging. I'd wave from the car if I noticed her outside when I drove into my garage."

The first time I interviewed him on his front porch he had worn a long-sleeved shirt. That's why I didn't remember the Ranger tattoo. He didn't invite me inside. I didn't push it because I didn't want to be rude. Oh, the folly of an inexperienced detective. That was before I learned Rule Fifteen:

Never take anything for granted and Rule Twelve: *People lie. If they don't lie, they can be mistaken.*

The older, wiser me got pushy. "We ought to talk. Can I come in?"

Nelson was as tall as I was and his bulk filled the space between the door and the jamb. I wondered whether I would be that buff in twenty-something years, even beneath the wrinkled skin.

Nelson's gaze zipped back and forth. "I don't know anything about Emily's disappearance. You and the cops both interviewed me before. I couldn't help you then and I can't help you now."

He stepped back and began to close the door.

Alarm bells clanged in my mind. I needed to get inside.

"Mr. Nelson, I want to ask about Carrie and Frank."

"What about them?" He rubbed his chin, which was covered in several days' stubble. "Hell, they're your family. You know them better than me."

"I live in Port City. It's fourteen hundred miles away. You live across the street, and you talked to them at Bobcat basketball games. Believe me, you know them better than I do. Can I come in?"

"The place is a mess."

"Mr. Nelson, I'm a bachelor too. Your place can't be any messier than mine. My condo looks like a band of baboons had a party there. I really need to talk to you. There are things I don't understand about my aunt and uncle and things concerning this neighborhood."

I spread my hands in supplication. "Give me a break, huh? Can we talk?" *Just you and me, ol' buddy.*

Nelson scanned me up and down. He shifted his weight from one foot to the other. "I guess it's all right. Okay. I need to change." Nelson disappeared and left me to stare through the gap in the door. The foyer behind was unlit.

I listened closely. Inside, a door opened. A draft carried a whiff of marijuana out the door. A toilet flushed. A door closed. Another door closed. Silence for two minutes.

Did Nelson intend to leave me on the porch forever? I half-expected to hear his car screech backwards out the driveway and speed off down the street. I've watched too many action movies.

Another door opened and Nelson reappeared in the foyer in a long-sleeved shirt. He had changed his gym shorts for blue jeans.

"I have to close the door to unhook the chain."

Nelson closed the door. The chain rattled. The door opened. "Come in."

Now that I was inside, the acrid odor of marijuana drifted from Nelson's clothes. Or maybe from the shag carpet.

I trailed him into a living/dining room from the 1980s. The house was outdated when he bought it and hadn't been updated since. Dog's breakfast shag carpet, a sparkly popcorn ceiling, a chain-swagged hanging lamp over a marble-topped end table, over-stuffed green Naugahyde furniture, Formica dining room table with six matching chairs and plastic seat covers.

A *Sports Illustrated* issue lay on an end table beside a recliner.

The walls were hung with Asian landscapes featuring traditional temples, peasants tending rice paddies on terraced mountains, and water buffaloes hauling wooden plows.

Were they souvenirs from his Ranger career? If he was stationed in Asia, the paintings could have come from places he visited on leave.

The sole modern piece in the room was an HDTV with a screen the size of a pool table. Sitting on the television cabinet, it barely fit beneath the eight-foot ceiling. An antediluvian combination DVD and VHS cassette player sat on the cabinet beside the HDTV's base.

Nelson claimed his house was a mess, but—aside from being two generations out of date—it was neat and tidy. What I expected from an Army Ranger. Why did he say the place was a mess? Why did he want to keep me from coming in? What was he hiding?

The vibes from Nelson felt like ants crawling on my skin; something was out of kilter with him. My gut told me he was hiding more than a marijuana habit.

Nelson stood like he wasn't sure what to do next. He wasn't used to visitors.

"Uh, sit anywhere, I guess. You want a beer or something?"

It was ten o'clock in the morning, but I could nurse a beer a half hour to stretch the interview.

I edged toward a chair but remained standing. "I never say no to a friendly beer. Thanks."

Nelson hesitated. "I'll be right back." He left, closing the door behind him.

I had less than a minute before he returned.

First, I slid out the television cabinet's left drawer. A rack of homemade DVD disks filled most of the drawer, all with black marker scribbles on them. I snagged one from the left side of the rack and another from the right end and stuck them in my pocket. I transferred the disk now on the right end to the empty slot on the left. At first glance, Nelson might not notice they were gone.

The right drawer held a rack of old-fashioned VHS cassettes, also with handmade labels. They were too big to steal. I photographed both drawers' contents, closed them, and stepped to the couch.

Next, I hoisted the couch cushions and chair cushions. Nothing but a quarter and a dime. I scurried to the China cabinet. Nothing in the drawers but old cloth napkins. I riffled the stack of napkins. Nothing was hidden underneath. I cracked the bottom cabinet doors and peeked inside. Old China place settings. I jerked open the buffet doors. Nothing but another stack of napkins and a handful of different colored tablecloths that hadn't been used since the twentieth century. Nothing was hidden between the tablecloths. A drawer in the buffet held classic silverware, tarnished tan from age. No one today used silverware and I doubted Nelson had bought it. Might have been a wedding present, or he inherited it from his parents.

I made it back to a chair just as Nelson opened the door and carried in two long-necks wedged between the fingers of one hand. "You want a glass?"

"No, I drink from the bottle." I took the beer. "Lone Star. My favorite. Can't buy it in Florida."

Nelson tilted his bottle and drank half in one pull. He held the bottle on the arm of his recliner. "So, what do you want to know?"

I wanted to know what else he was hiding besides a marijuana habit, but I couldn't say that. "How long have you lived in the neighborhood?"

Nelson's eyes slitted. "What's that have to do with the Crazinski family?"

"I want to get a feel for the neighborhood. Was Emily kidnapped or did she run away? Perhaps something happened in the neighborhood to make her want to disappear."

That was blue smoke and mirrors; what I wanted was an emotional scan on Nelson. I needed him to talk about almost any subject.

I tried a different tack. "Have any neighbors given you a hard time?"

"I don't understand."

"A feud, a disagreement, a dispute over something. Tension on the block?"

Nelson waved a hand. "Nothing I know of. People mind their own business. There's no wild parties to disturb the neighborhood or line the streets with parked cars that block driveways. Maybe an occasional Christmas party, but those people are pretty good about not blocking my driveway. People could keep their lawns neater, but overall, it's a pretty quiet place." He drained another two inches from his beer.

"Tell me about the Christmas parties."

"Nothing to tell. I go to one or two every year. Mostly, I see my neighbors when I'm jogging or if they have kids on a Bonham High sports team. Then I see them at the games. The Crazinskis and two or three other families on the block have—*had* kids on a sports team." He shook his head. "Too bad about Emily."

"Do you have kids, Mr. Nelson?"

"That's a personal question."

"Yes, it is. *Do* you have children?"

"Not that it's any of your business, but no, I don't. My wife and I tried for several years, but it didn't happen. It's a painful subject."

"Sorry."

No, I wasn't.

"It's unusual for an adult to attend a high school game unless he has a family member playing."

Nelson shrugged. "What can I say? I'm a sports fan." He tapped the *Sports Illustrated* on the end table. "You know how much they charge for Longhorn tickets? Assuming they're not sold out. High school season tickets are cheap, and it's an inexpensive way to enjoy live sports."

"I love that HDTV. It must be spectacular to watch the Super Bowl on that monster." I wagged my beer bottle in a mock toast to the television.

Nelson beamed. "Eighty-eight inches. I subscribe to all the NFL and NBA games. Yeah, that's my baby."

"I bet you could have a great Super Bowl party with that beauty as a centerpiece."

Nelson gestured with his beer bottle. "What does this have to do with Emily's disappearance?"

"I'd like to understand the dynamics of the neighborhood. Was there a reason Emily wanted to disappear? Did you notice any unusual behavior at her basketball games?"

"Not that I recall. Just…" He shook his head. "No, nothing really."

My mental alarm bells rang.

"What did you think about?"

"It's probably nothing."

"What's probably nothing?"

"I think the basketball coach is a lesbian. That's not illegal, is it?"

Harry Nelson

McCrary left and Harry Nelson drew in a long breath and let it out. His heart rate slowed.

Funny to feel his heart beat so fast. He wondered what his friend would say about McCrary's surprise visit after all these years. His friend always gave good advice. Sometimes the advice came in a dream, sometimes in a nightmare. But always good advice, and always in the middle of the night.

Nelson had never seen a guy nurse a beer as long as McCrary. And what was the deal with those questions that had nothing to do with Emily Crazinski? He should discuss that with his friend. McCrary acted like he knew something he could not possibly know. No, it couldn't be. There was no way McCrary knew *that*.

He would ask his friend's opinion.

Why did McCrary come poking around his house again after all this time? The PI was cool with him four years ago. Did he suspect something? How could he? What tipped him off? And why the hell had he let McCrary inside? He should have stonewalled him. That's what his friend would advise. It's not like McCrary could get a search warrant. He wasn't a cop.

Nelson ought to have insisted that they speak on the porch. McCrary would have had to agree. On the other hand, not letting him in would look suspicious. Surely his friend would agree he couldn't afford to appear suspicious.

Too late to worry. McCrary had been inside and Nelson couldn't rewind the clock.

Nelson picked up the empty bottles and surveyed the living room.

He heard his friend warn him. What had he overlooked?

Wait a minute. He left McCrary alone while he went to fetch their beers. His friend would say that detectives were professional snoops, wouldn't he?

One couch cushion was an inch out of line. Nelson kept a neat house, no matter what he told McCrary. He opened the China cabinet. His neatly stacked napkins lay askew. He jerked open the buffet drawers. Same thing.

That freakin' McCrary had riffled through the room while Nelson was in the kitchen. His friend would be disappointed when he told him. Well, he wouldn't tell his friend. He didn't have to tell him *everything*, did he?

Nelson's heart rate climbed again. His attention cut to the television cabinet. He stepped to the drawers and opened the first one.

Something was different in the rack of DVDs. He looked again to determine which disks were gone.

Uh-oh. The detective had rearranged the disks hoping Nelson wouldn't notice. Nelson heard his friend say, "He's on to something."

McCrary had stolen two of his pretties. What if he connected the dots?

Nelson wouldn't tell his friend about the missing disks. What his friend didn't know wouldn't hurt him. At least, it wouldn't *worry* him.

But McCrary had two disks. That was unacceptable. It was time to act.

Nelson booted his laptop.

In *The Art of War*, Sun Tzu said, "Know your enemy."

He opened a search engine.

EIGHTEEN

Carlos McCrary

I set a sack of *pasteles* on Goodman's desk. A midmorning snack is good on a working Saturday.

"The Crazinskis' neighbor across the street, Harry Nelson, smokes marijuana and keeps a child porn video collection."

Goodman waved a sweet roll under her nose and inhaled.

"If the other cops don't eat these, I'll take them home to my husband." She chewed a bite and smiled with satisfaction.

"In the history of the world, have pastries ever survived to the end of a shift in a police station?"

"You're right." She wrapped a pastry in a napkin and stuck it in a drawer. "You were saying?"

"Harry Nelson, the neighbor, smokes marijuana and keeps a child porn video collection."

"The marijuana is a minor offense at worst, and in Austin, it's more of a *so what*. No Austin jury will convict. Now the child porn, that's serious stuff. What evidence do you have on that?"

I related my interview with Nelson. I had put the DVDs in plastic sleeves to avoid further contamination of any fingerprints on them. I pulled them from my briefcase. "Look at these."

She slipped on evidence gloves and we played a few minutes from each disk as she skipped through the tracks.

Goodman ejected the second disk. "This isn't child porn. These are homemade porn videos starring amateurs, maybe girlfriends. The females are young, yes, but could be over eighteen. This crap is disgusting and amateurish, but it's not illegal. I can't take these to Child Abuse. They'd laugh at me."

"Don't the girls look like they're there unwillingly?"

"Where's the evidence? They are *actors*. You know there's a demand for crap like this. Nelson may be so weird that he gets his jollies from this kind of ...of...hell, I don't even know what to call these. If it were evidence, where were the videos made? There's nothing in there to identify the location. Not even a window."

She slipped the disks back in their plastic sleeves and handed them back. "You see this crap all over the internet. Unfortunately, this is nothing new."

"Nora, my gut says Nelson is as dirty as a mechanic's hand towel. I don't know what his gig is, but I intend to locate his ex-wife and ask why they split. If these DVDs are any indication, I'd bet a banquet to a biscuit that he's involved in something more serious than misdemeanor marijuana possession."

"I can't investigate a hunch. Come back when you have more."

———

Something Goodman said tickled my memory while I drove to Carrie and Frank's house. *Homemade*. Goodman said *homemade*. But in whose home?

I booted my laptop and examined Nelson's DVDs again. The first disk was labeled with a nearly-illegible scrawl that might have said, "Clara dryyy one mo." The word following "Clara" didn't have three consecutive "y" letters, of course. Each squiggle was different, but all resembled a "y." It didn't help that the writing was faded and worn from repeated handling.

The six video files on the disk featured the same Caucasian girl.

In the first video, the girl named Clara wore generic white shorts and a tee-shirt and stood motionless, ramrod straight, beside a single twin bed jammed against the left wall.

Two identical doors on the end wall stood open. The right door had a lavatory and toilet visible. The left door led to a closet. I saw empty shelves and a few clothing items hung on a rod.

The girl's head shifted like she was listening. She bowed and danced clumsily. I won't describe the things she did. I had observed raunchier gyrations in a Super Bowl halftime, but those dancers were smiling, skilled professionals on an international television broadcast. Clara was a lonely awkward amateur, forced to function for an audience of one pervert. It was disturbing to contemplate.

The moves were meant to be graceful and sexy. Instead, they were bizarre with her frightened expression and the absence of music. There was no sound to the video. That was strange also.

The girl stopped and walked to the far doors. The picture jiggled and she halted on command.

I supposed the cameraman said something and that made the camera jiggle.

She about-faced and stood motionless in front of the closet.

The picture stuttered again and her eyes widened. Clara trembled and said something.

The image jiggled like the cameraman had gestured.

The girl exhaled and peeled off the tee-shirt, then the shorts. She was nude underneath.

She stood at attention before the camera and blushed pink from head to foot.

The camera jiggled as the operator gave another command, and Clara cowered. She entered the closet and brought out a costume. She had difficulty putting it on because of the panel and sashes.

Her body language indicated that her unseen captor gave her instructions on how to don the unfamiliar garment. Through trial and error, she succeeded and stood at attention in a pink and yellow costume that seemed familiar.

I recalled the 2018 Winter Olympics in PyeongChang on television. Clara wore a traditional Korean *hanbok*.

Clara danced in the *hanbok*, then removed it and replaced it with a Japanese *kimono*. After dancing in the *kimono*, she changed to a Thai dress. I recognized the style from a Thai restaurant I patronized. Two more costumes I couldn't identify followed it, but they looked Asian.

The awkward dances and costume changes ended, and Clara reached in the closet and pulled out a blue gingham dress. She repeated the performance in the dress.

She may have been relieved to have normal American clothes on again, but she didn't smile.

The camera jumped again and Clara hung the gingham dress in the closet and repeated a similar dance to the one she'd already performed, but nude.

Detective Goodman said the videos were legal, but I doubted that. Of course, I'm the world's youngest dinosaur.

The second through sixth files were similar but Clara was different. I couldn't put my finger on the difference but it was there. Clara stripped off her white shorts and tee-shirt and danced in the different costumes from the closet, ending with the nude dance.

Viewing the fourth video, I figured out what was different about Clara: Her hair was longer in each subsequent video.

Six videos, six different time frames. Same unhappy Clara.

I accessed the file directory on the DVD and changed the column headings on the directory to display the date the videos were created. The kidnapper had recorded the videos at two-month intervals beginning thirteen years ago.

To me, the DVD screamed, "kidnap victim." To Goodman, it was amateur porn.

The second disk was labeled "Gloria" or "Glenda" followed by "one mo." This DVD was made in a room identical in design to the room in the first DVD, but the room was different—the bathroom and the closet were reversed. Were the rooms constructed at opposite ends in the same attic?

Gloria was a girl of mixed race with an Afro hairstyle. The six video files were similar to Clara's but Gloria didn't complain, refuse, or cower.

She gave the cameraman a glare so cold it would freeze a lava lake in its tracks. They were recorded at two-month intervals. Presumably the DVD of Gloria started one month after her capture and covered the first year of her captivity at months three, five, and so forth. Was she a current captive?

I examined the file directory. The videos dated from the last twelve months, the most recent made about a week earlier. Gloria was a current captive. But where? In Nelson's house? Carrie and Frank said Nelson took frequent trips out of town. If he was a kidnapper, was he holding Gloria someplace far away? That seemed more likely than holding a captive in the heart of Austin.

When I returned to Port City, I had given Grandpa the weekend off too. He drove back to Adams Creek to be with Grandma.

I called him. "Have you had enough home cooking with Grandma? You ready to come to Austin to help me again?"

"Anything to help Emily. When do you want me?"

"If you leave now, you'll get here by nine tonight."

"I have a better idea. If I leave after breakfast tomorrow, I'll be there by noon."

Oh yeah. Grandpa didn't like to drive at night.

———

Sunday morning, Uncle Frank invited me to attend Sunday School with him. Jerry O'Doul had mentioned me to him the previous Sunday when I flew back to Port City.

I attended Sunday school with Dad and Grandpa whenever I visited Adams Creek, and I hadn't spent as much time with Uncle Frank as I wanted, so I said yes.

"Grandpa is driving over from Adams Creek this morning. I'm meeting him for lunch, so we'll drive two cars."

O'Doul's lesson was on Saint Paul's first letter to the Corinthians. Paul said love was patient and kind. Terry hadn't been patient with me, but I hadn't been kind to her. It was a moot point unless she relented and contacted me. I hadn't heard from her since she stormed out of my condo over a month ago. *Hmm.* Maybe it wouldn't hurt to call Ruby Voight.

After Sunday School, I drove to Mount Bonnell and climbed to the top to contemplate Lake Austin and the Hill Country. I pondered Terry and Ruby Voight and Vicky Ramirez and all the women of the world that I had known and those I had yet to meet. Somewhere there was a woman I could build my own family with. I decided to contact Ruby that afternoon.

I was climbing down the rough trail when Grandpa called at 11:30.

"I'm twenty minutes out. What have Carrie and Frank planned for lunch?"

"They're still at church. They're under enough strain. Let's give them extra time without you and me underfoot. How about the Plum Blossom Chinese restaurant?"

"Sure, provided you let me use a knife and fork."

———

The Plum Blossom server wrote our orders and left.

"Okay, son, while there's nobody to hear us, what's my assignment?"

"I, uh…acquired two DVDs I want you to watch. They could be clues to what happened to Emily. I'd like your take on what we know from those videos."

"Did you show them to Ortega?"

"Ortega is no longer on the case. Now that they have a murder victim, it was assigned to Detective Nora Goodman in Homicide. She didn't view the whole thing, but she said they were worthless as evidence."

"Okay, I'll have a look," Grandpa said. "Where are they? Back at Carrie's?"

"Yes. There's one other thing. The videos are porn."

"Porn? You mean they're pornography?"

"Yes. I don't want Carrie or Frank to know I have the disks. If they saw the videos, they might think something like that happened to Emily. I figure you've been around enough to play the videos without damaging your delicate sensibilities. It's for a good cause."

Grandpa grinned. "Who would've guessed I'd watch porn for a good cause? Pastor Ken would have a conniption fit."

———

Grandpa sat at the desk in Carrie's guestroom in front of my laptop.

I closed the door and handed him a pair of evidence gloves. "Wear these when you handle the disks and hold them by the edges. I don't want any more fingerprints on them."

"Now I feel like a real detective." He pulled on the gloves and took the disks. "Why are you over there? You should watch with me."

"I played parts of them three times. I don't want to bias your observations. You make your own interpretations. Take notes. There's a yellow pad in the drawer. I'll make coffee. You want a cup?"

"Sure. One cream, no sugar, like yours."

I took my time making the coffee. After returning to the guestroom, I glanced at the laptop screen. Grandpa was on the fifth file on the second DVD, playing it at quadruple speed.

I set his coffee beside the notepad. He had filled a page with notes.

"Thanks, kiddo."

He sipped coffee without shifting his gaze from the screen. He wrote another note.

I sat in the reading chair while Grandpa viewed the final video, his attention focused like a laser. He paused the video to write another note, then resumed, this time at double speed.

After it finished, he paused the video app. "This is good information, son. We can use this."

"How so?"

"In the first place, the videos are homemade, like you said, made by a smartphone, not a video camera."

"What makes you say that?"

Grandpa referred to his notes. "In the second DVD, the third video starts out sideways. The kidnapper forgot to rotate his phone horizontal and began the video vertically, then flipped to horizontal. When he transferred it to the disk, he forgot to crop off the sideways part. The image wobbles too much to be a camera on a tripod. The kidnapper's an amateur using a smartphone."

"You call him the kidnapper, not the cameraman. Why's that?"

"I'm no cop like Ortega or what's-her-name—"

"Nora Goodman."

"Goodman. As a private citizen, I form opinions all the time without evidence or probable cause or legal gobbledygook. My gut tells me those girls were there against their will. Let me show you."

He cued the first video and fast-forwarded to Clara in front of the closet in the white outfit.

"Notice that she stops, then listens to the kidnapper. She doesn't like what she hears and she objects. Her body language says it as plain as if she held a picket sign. She says, 'No way, Jose' and the kidnapper yells at her. That's why the picture jumps around. She complies, but any fool can tell she's under duress."

"Goodman doesn't agree."

Grandpa paused the video. "Goodman is a cop, and cops follow certain rules to protect civil rights. That's the way it is for law enforcement. But you and I, we're private citizens on a mission. We don't follow cop rules. We use common sense."

Grandpa shook his head. "Sorry, son, I got sidetracked and climbed on a soapbox. Where was I?"

He played the video again. "Notice in the second video, Clara doesn't protest. She does what the kidnapper tells her. The bastard broke her spirit."

He restarted the video.

"The videos on both disks were recorded in similar rooms, possibly at opposite ends of an attic. The ceiling slopes down to the wall on each side like an attic room added under the roof. Same thing on the second DVD."

Grandpa paused the video and gestured at the screen. "The walls, slopes, and ceiling were drywalled, taped, and bedded, but not painted. The far wall has two identically sized doors. The right door opens to a bathroom. See the lavatory and toilet? The other door is a closet. See the empty shelves and the closet rod inside?"

"Yeah. The whole thing looks like an amateur built it but didn't finish. There's no baseboard. I figure the house is a story-and-a-half or a two-and-a-half story."

Grandpa raised a hand. "Half-stories are built with a window. It's been in the building code since God's dog was a puppy. I learned that when Grandma and I added a guest room in our attic twenty years ago. We added dormers and skylights. No, these rooms in the videos were built in an existing attic—a big one. And it was done with no building permit because there are no dormers, no skylights, and no windows."

"What if the kidnapper did have a half story and covered over the windows to keep the victims in the dark?"

"Damn it, son, you shot my theory down in flames. It might be a half story."

"How big is the attic?"

"Bear with me. Notice the floor. He slapped on old-fashioned gray porch paint. I count thirty-five boards across. They run the full length. Look at Clara's bare feet and compare her foot to the floorboards. I reckon them to be milled lumber sold as 1 × 6s but measuring 5-1/2 inches wide. That makes the room sixteen feet across."

He paused the picture.

"The side walls are five feet tall. The slanted part rises to the eight-foot ceiling."

"How did you figure it's eight feet?"

Grandpa held a one-foot ruler to the screen. "A standard drywall sheet measures four by eight. Notice the taping and bedding and you can spot where the builder cut the drywall under the slope to fit. Look on the side walls and see the seam parallel to the floor a foot below the slope. That makes the side walls five feet tall. From that, you can infer the ceiling is eight feet."

He held the ruler against the screen where the side wall met the end wall. "See that? Coincidentally, on this size screen image, it's five inches tall."

"How big is the house?"

"If it's a straight line, the attic is over sixty feet long."

"Did you consult a Ouija Board?"

"An adding machine. It ain't forensic science, Supercop."

"Okay. Enlighten me, O Great Home Remodeler."

He pointed at the screen. "We see a lavatory and toilet. The bathroom must be five feet deep for them to fit on that wall. And the bathtub,

175

which we can't see, has to be a sixty-inch standard tub at the sloped end."

"Not that it's important, but couldn't there be a stall shower back there?"

"It wouldn't fit under the slope. Must be a tub."

"Okay," I said, "allow five feet for the bathroom, and six inches for the external and internal wall, say, six feet. How long is the main part of the bedroom?"

Grandpa touched the ruler to the screen.

"Count the drywall sheets. There are 1-1/2 sheets in the picture. That's twelve feet. Plus, the camera man is farther from the far wall, say, ten feet. Allow a minimum six feet for the stairway, even a steep one."

Grandpa scribbled numbers on the yellow pad.

"Sixty-two feet minimum, unless the house is L-shaped, then each side may be as short as twenty-eight feet, with the access stairs at the corner of the L. How big is Harry Nelson's house?"

"Let's check. Let me use the desk."

We switched places.

"I'll log in to the Travis County Property Assessor's website...Search for 'Harry Nelson'...Select 'View Map'...And there's the footprint."

I zoomed the map until the legend indicated the 20' scale.

"Hand me the ruler." I laid the ruler against the scale. "Scale is 20' = 1"."

I measured Nelson's house. "It's 3-1/4", so 65'." I spun the screen toward Grandpa.

"Sixty-five feet is plenty long enough. We know the next place to search." Grandpa grinned. "Unless we're chasing the wrong wild goose."

He wagged the notepad. "Let's consider the labels. The first disk is labeled 'Clara dancing one mo.' I assume she had been captive one month."

"You think it says 'dancing'?"

"The handwriting's awful, but it says 'Clara dancing' plain as day. Your generation didn't learn cursive handwriting in grade school. Study it again."

He handed me the first disk. If you knew what you were looking for, it did say "dancing."

"Hand me the second disk."

Grandpa handed it over.

"The second disk is labeled 'Gloria one mo'," I said. "That indicates this is the first disk for Gloria."

"Nelson—assuming he is the kidnapper—Nelson videoed Clara after he had her one month," Grandpa said. "He videoed the first track on this disk after he had Gloria one month. He videos his captives at regular intervals, for what that observation is worth."

"Okay. Gloria's is the latest disk. It was on the far right. The empty slots are for future videos."

"Makes sense to me," Grandpa said. "You stole these from a DVD rack in a drawer. How many disks were in the rack total?"

"Give me the computer."

Grandpa unplugged the charging cord and handed the laptop to me.

I located the smartphone pictures I had transferred to the laptop, then zoomed in on the photo of an open cabinet drawer. "That drawer looks twenty-four inches wide with disks every half inch." I counted slots. "Forty DVDs in there and half a dozen empty slots."

Grandpa studied the laptop screen. "What's in the other drawer?"

"Old VHS cassettes. They were too big to stick in my pocket, so I didn't steal any."

"Were they labeled?"

"Let me check." I loaded the photo of the other drawer. "About twenty VHS tapes." I zoomed the image. I hadn't examined the photos before.

My heart jumped in my chest. The first seven cassettes were labeled "Alice" at dates from one month to three years, five months. The last thirteen were labeled "Betty" at intervals from one month to four years, three months.

Grandpa and I stared at each other.

"Holy shit," he said, "the SOB's been doing this a couple of decades. VHS cassettes phased out by 2005. DVDs came in in the late 1990s."

"1997 to be exact," I said, "but Nelson doesn't use a video camera for the DVDs. He uses a smartphone. He made the DVDs after 2005, when smartphones with video cameras became standard. He used a VHS video camera before that."

"Carrie told me Nelson divorced his wife sixteen years ago. If he's the kidnapper, he began kidnapping these girls after the divorce."

Grandpa flipped to a fresh page on the yellow pad and wrote something. He rotated the page and handed it to me.

Alice

Betty

Clara

D-Unknown

E-Unknown

F-Unknown

Gloria

"Notice the alphabetical order?" Grandpa asked. "I don't believe it's coincidence. One of those unknowns could be Emily."

Rule Seven: *There is no such thing as a coincidence—except when there is.*

I accessed the file directory on the Gloria disk. I rotated the laptop where Grandpa could watch.

"The Gloria videos are less than a year old," I said, "and the most recent one is a little over a week old."

"Gloria is a current captive," Grandpa said. "She could be in Nelson's attic. That poor girl is over there praying someone rescues her. What will you do about it?"

"We can't be sure. Nelson was out of town a week or so ago. I remember glancing at his house and the windows were dark."

"When exactly was that? Does it coincide with the date of the last video?"

I racked my brain. "Damn, I can't remember. The only way to search his place is to breech by force and jam him against a wall while I tear the place apart. That's a crime known as 'home invasion.' If we're wrong, I could lose my PI license and draw a long prison term. The case against Nelson is as shaky as a fifty-cent ladder."

"To the cops and the district attorney, sure. But to us…?"

"We're making progress, Grandpa. A couple days more and I take this to Goodman again. We need evidence for a search warrant."

Grandpa scoffed. "You and I aren't cops. We don't need probable cause. We have to search that house. Hell, we did with Drucker and you had less evidence than this. This lead is more solid than Drucker's undercover jerk-off at the city park."

"Oh, I'll look. I will, but remember Rule Thirteen: *Sometimes you're wrong.*"

"One thing certain," Grandpa said. "There's more to Harry Nelson than meets the eye. Daddy told me where you see one rat, there are fifty more hiding in the wall. We hedge our bets and pursue every lead. We work hard enough, we'll get lucky."

Grandpa clapped me on the shoulder. "Son, you need more help than I can give you. It's time to call Snoop."

"I know. I'll drop Snoop and Gunner on Nelson like a net over a rabid dog. There's work to do. A couple of weeks ago, I asked the county sheriffs about girls missing in the last ten years. I also asked for files on missing girls from ten years back to sixteen years. The good news is we have two videos of possible kidnap victims. Wade through those old files as soon as they get here."

"Why sixteen years?"

"Carrie said Nelson divorced sixteen years ago. If he is the kidnapper, he couldn't have done it with his wife living in the house."

"You think I'll locate a match to that Clara girl in the older files?" Grandpa asked.

"And the newer files ought to have one for the Gloria girl who's been missing a year."

Grandpa's eyes shined like spotlights.

"Unless you find Emily or the Gloria girl in Nelson's attic."

Harry Nelson

Nelson tilted his desk chair back and contemplated the ceiling. He chugged another few ounces of Lone Star and pondered what he had learned on the internet.

McCrary had been in the Special Forces. He figured he was hot stuff since he won the Bronze Star in Afghanistan. Well, he, Nelson, would have won a medal if he had seen action. It wasn't his fault the North Korean gooks couldn't start a decent war when Nelson served sixteen months in the Demilitarized Zone.

McCrary thought he was as tough as Nelson and twenty years younger to boot. Well, Nelson qualified as Expert with rifle and pistol. He could kill McCrary at over 200 yards with his M16A4 rifle. If that didn't work, Nelson had his old reliable Colt .45 service automatic. If push came to shove, the Colt would stop a charging rhinoceros—or a nosy detective.

He tipped his chair down and finished the article on his screen. He clicked the link and jumped to another newspaper account where McCrary rescued teenage girls who were kidnapped and held as sex slaves in Port City. Nelson whistled when he saw the picture of the girl McCrary saved. She looked like a sister to his own pretty trophy, Evita.

McCrary wasn't the type to give up. Nelson's gut felt funny.

He and his friend needed to visit the gun range and shoot a few clips to polish their skills. In case either of them came across McCrary at a convenient place…

NINETEEN

Carlos McCrary

"Ruby, this is Chuck McCrary. Is this a good time to talk?"
"I'm glad you called. How are you?"
"Better than I deserve to be. Is that offer for dinner still open?"
"How about tonight? Do you like lasagna?"
"I never met a meal I didn't like. I love all food without bias or favoritism."
"I'll text you my address. Attire is casual. *Very* casual. You know what 'very casual' means?"
"Not really."
"It means to bring a toothbrush."
Whoa, I did not see that coming, I thought. *When will I ever get used to twenty-first century women?*
"Got it. Note to self: Bring toothbrush. When should I arrive?"
Ruby paused. "It's 5:30 now. How about 7:00?"
"Seven works for me."
"Plan to eat around nine o'clock."
It looked like my foray into single status was starting off with a bang— pun intended.

I bought another box of *pasteles* on the way to Goodman's office. If I kept this up, she and I would be best buds. Her husband too.

She spied the box in my hand as I crossed to her desk.

"Why are you bringing *pasteles* again, Chuck? Attempting to bribe a law officer?"

"I hope so."

I slid the box toward her.

"I viewed those DVDs from Nelson's house again. I have a theory to bounce off you."

Goodman popped the lid and inhaled the sugary aroma.

"Did you notice something we missed last time?" She selected a pastry and pushed the box toward me.

"I uncovered additional information I didn't have last time."

"Okay, what is it?"

I booted my laptop and loaded the photos of the TV cabinet drawers. I zoomed the image of the second drawer and its VHS cassettes. "We have four girls' names in the videos. Alice, Betty, Clara, and Gloria. When we considered the Clara and Gloria videos, we couldn't determine a pattern from two names. Now that we know four names, there's a pattern. Clara and Gloria may not be the girls' real names. Nelson might name his captives in alphabetical order and there's a D, an E, and an F in between."

"Okay, assume it's Nelson who made the videos, why did he do that when he has the actual girls?"

"Hell, why kidnap teenage girls in the first place? The guy's nuts, of course. It depersonalizes his victims. He takes their identities and gives them new names. A domination game? I'm no shrink. I'm hunting for a pattern to figure this guy out. I think the alphabetical girls' names are a pattern."

I leaned back and munched on a pastry while Goodman ruminated.

"We analyzed the images in the attic room and calculated the attic was minimum sixty-two feet long or else an L-shape measuring at least thirty feet on a side."

"Okay. What's your point?"

"Nelson's house measures sixty-five feet long and his roof line reaches high enough to build those two rooms under it."

"Assume you're right. What do you expect me to do?"

"Aren't these videos worth a second glance? Their GPS metadata will tell us where they were made. If they were made in Nelson's house, that would be enough for a warrant in any state in the union."

"Not based on what I've seen so far. Maybe if one of the girls was clearly underage, but both girls have well-developed pubic hair and breasts. They don't look like minors. Or if we could identify one of them as a missing person. Other than that, I doubt we could get a warrant."

"Humor me? See if you can pull the metadata."

Video files made on certain devices contain coded data like the date and time recorded or edited, file size, software used, image resolution, and so forth. Modern smartphones code their files with GPS coordinates where the video was recorded unless the user turns off the GPS function or removes it from the file after it's recorded.

She gave me a funny look. "For the sake of the *pasteles*, I'll ask my IT guy."

Goodman snatched the phone and punched buttons. "Hey, Selma. Nora Goodman here. I have video files I want the metadata on...No, I mean now. The files belong to a member of the public and he can't stick around for an hour. Whatever you're working on, it will wait. I need you and your super-sleuth software. Please."

She grinned as she disconnected. "She'll be right in."

I glanced across the squad room. A thirty-something black woman glided across the floor like a swan crossing a mill pond, despite the briefcase slung over her shoulder. Collar-length wavy brown hair framed a face that was ordinary except for the eyes. Her eyes glinted with an intelligence visible from across the room.

She slid an empty chair from a vacant desk and rolled it to Goodman's desk. She gave me a warm smile with straight white teeth. "Detective Selma Carmichael."

We shook hands and I handed her a business card.

"Chuck McCrary. I'm the guy who owns the video files."

She glanced at my card and handed me one of hers.

"You live in Port City, Florida. Why are you working a case in Austin?"

"I have a personal interest in the case."

"Chuck's cousin Emily Crazinski disappeared," Goodman said. "Rod Ortega and Chuck both searched for her four years ago and couldn't find any clues. The case went cold as a coffin. Chuck reopened it and he's uncovered two DVDs."

"I believe the man who kidnapped my cousin made the videos."

"I'll see what I can learn. Where are they?"

I handed her the two disks. "I need to know everything about these videos, including where they were recorded."

I scooted the pastries toward her.

"Have a *pastel*," I said.

"Smells delicious, but I avoid sugar."

Carmichael removed a laptop and mouse from her briefcase, pulled on evidence gloves, and inserted the Clara disk. She opened an app and did magical stuff with the mouse and keyboard that I couldn't follow.

"No GPS coding. Files on this disk were made by a smartphone so old that GPS wasn't on the phone."

She spun the screen where I could see. "The files were made thirteen years ago. There are the exact dates and times." She pointed at the numbers on the screen. "The files were made between six p.m. and three a.m. Standard mp4 files. Resolution is not a high-end phone."

She inserted the Gloria disk and did her thing. "Okay, this disk was made by a newer smartphone with the GPS function, but the GPS codes were removed from the files before they were transferred to the disk. These were made in the last year. One just thirteen days ago."

I hid my disappointment. I needed the location where they were recorded.

She peered over from her screen. "You said your cousin's been gone four years, but one disk is much older than that and the other is less than a year old."

"There were more disks sandwiched between these two."

"And where was that *sandwich*?" She made air quotes.

I glanced at Goodman.

She answered Carmichael. "That's not important."

Carmichael gave me a look, then nodded. "Right. Anything else I can do?"

"Detective Carmichael," I said, "could you watch the videos and give me your professional and personal opinion about their content? The videos involve nudity but no sex. Detective Goodman and I watched them, but we disagree. I believe the videos show kidnap victims—two young women held against their will. Detective Goodman claims a good defense lawyer would say they are homemade videos with amateur actors and an amateur videographer. I want a third detective's opinion. Would you watch them and make notes of your observations? We three can discuss them tomorrow. Okay?"

Carmichael gave Goodman a *what-the-hell-is-this?* look.

"Chuck is working closely with me on this case. You want to help or not?"

"Of course. Let's meet here at eight tomorrow morning."

Carmichael slipped the disks into their protective sleeves and stuck them in her briefcase.

———

I waited near the bottom of the arrivals escalator at Austin Bergstrom International Airport.

Snoop spotted me from the top. He glanced back to ensure Gunner saw me. He waved and they joined the passengers descending to baggage claim. Gunnar Knutson rode a couple of steps behind him.

Before he retired, Raymond Snopolski had been a homicide detective on the Port City police force. Naturally, everyone called him Snoop. He could shoot a hole in a dime at thirty feet and give you a nickel in change, or spend two minutes at a crime scene and draw you a complete diagram from memory a year later.

After he retired, he obtained a PI license. He works for several attorneys and for me from time to time.

"Carrousel two," he said as he reached the bottom. "Gunner and I brought enough clothes for an indefinite stay."

"How many suitcases is that?"

"One each. Janet and I traveled around Europe for a month with one carry-on suitcase each. You plan what you need and pack right. How many bags did you bring?"

"Two."

"You too lazy to do laundry, bud?"

"Snoop," Erik Gunnar Knutson said, "why don't you give me your baggage claim ticket and I'll fetch our bags. Gotta protect the wise old man."

Knutson was my teammate in the Triple Seven Special Forces squad in Iraq and Afghanistan. Naturally, we nicknamed him Gunner. Shooting a good rifle, he hits a poker chip at 1,000 yards as easily as I do at fifty. He looked like Thor from the movie *Ragnarök*, but with shorter hair. Whenever we were together, women's heads swiveled to ogle me. Funny how that never happened when I was alone.

While we drove to their hotel, I briefed them on the case.

Grandpa waited, sipping coffee in the kitchenette. I had rented a two-bedroom suite after Snoop's wife Janet told me he snored louder than a buzz saw.

"Magnus, it's good to see you again," Snoop said. "Have you met Gunner Knutson?"

Snoop made the introductions, then sent Gunner to put their suitcases in the bedrooms.

"So, Magnus, you keeping Chuck's nose to the grindstone?"

"I help all I can. Here's the keyfob to the blue Jeep Cherokee parked out front. I rented it at the airport. I checked you all into this suite. Here's a keycard. Chuck and I each have keycards also. Just in case."

Snoop slipped the keyfob and keycard into his pocket.

"I see you ordered coffee, Magnus. Are those bagels?"

"I wanted you to feel at home. We Texans are more into *pasteles*. I ordered bagels and cream cheese for what our British friends call *afternoon tea*. Does Gunner like bagels?"

"Nobody doesn't like bagels, Magnus."

Gunner returned to the living room and fixed a bagel and coffee.

With Snoop and Gunner on board, this case would develop at warp speed.

I hoped.

———

Tuesday morning, I showed up at Detective Goodman's desk at eight o'clock.

"No *pasteles* today?" she asked.

"If I were the suspicious type, Nora, I'd think you loved me only for my pastries."

"With me happily married twenty-five years, I ain't interested in your looks. A girl's gotta stop and smell the pastries when she can. You want coffee?"

"I just finished breakfast. Where's Detective Carmichael?"

"She texted me. She's running late."

"Suppose she agrees that those two girls are kidnap victims. What do we do?"

"Nothing we can do," Goodman said. "Those disks are not valid evidence. We have nothing to say they belong to Harry Nelson. And you can't testify to anything since you stole them."

"If necessary, could we do the same as Ortega and I planned for Drucker's computer? I could swear that I took the disks from Nelson's house. They'll have his fingerprints on them, along with mine, of course. You could get a warrant from that."

"Yeah, maybe. If the contents of the disks indicate that a crime was committed, which I don't think they do."

She rolled her desk chair back. "Realistically, you have to do this on your own. We can't give you backup or police cover. Not officially. Violations of Nelson's civil rights and all that."

Selma Carmichael walked in the door. "Sorry I'm late, guys."

She took another chair. "I played those videos. Too many times." She handed the disks to me. "I agree, Chuck. Those girls were under duress. What do you make of both girls wearing costumes from four Asian countries?" She referred to a sheet of paper. "Korea, Japan, Thailand, and Cambodia."

"You recognized which countries they were?"

"Not at first. I researched it. The costumes appear authentic. Probably acquired in the countries they came from."

"The man who gave me the disks was stationed in Korea while he was in the U.S. Army. He could visit those countries on leave. He has landscapes from each of those countries hanging in his living room. And he's a pedophile attracted to teenage girls. Lots of child prostitution in Thailand and Cambodia."

Carmichael's face crunched into a frown.

"If I were a judge, I'd say the videos are evidence that the women were captives. Have you copied the disks?"

"Sure."

She slipped the disks into their plastic sleeves and swiveled her chair toward Goodman.

"If this were my case, I'd run these for fingerprints. I'd like to know who else has handled them."

Goodman accepted the disks. "I'll run these to the lab."

Carmichael said, "What now, Nora?"

Goodman shrugged. "Nothing more we can do unless we get some juicy fingerprints. The ball is in Chuck's court."

I didn't tell them I had Nelson under surveillance 24/7.

We were waiting for him to make another out-of-town trip.

———

Harry Nelson

Who were those two guys who arrived with McCrary? he thought.

They drove a Jeep the same model as McCrary's. Both Jeeps had rental car decals on their windshields. McCrary must have brought them from out of town. The younger man looked like a movie star and the older man looked like a cop. The older man seemed familiar.

They followed McCrary into the Crazinski house.

Nelson sat on a bar stool across the darkened bedroom from the window. The sunlight shown on the window screen. He had lowered the blinds and slit them to half-inch gaps. Nelson sat back ten feet and the stool gave him the angle to peer through binoculars at the Crazinski house. With the inside lights off, nobody could see him in his second-story room.

His friend would be proud. He would show his friend the observation post if he visited tonight.

Nothing happened for an hour, then someone moved behind one of the Crazinski windows. The light winked out. Why sit in the room in the dark? Were they watching his house like he was watching theirs?

His lips curved into something that might have been a smile. He was watching the watchers.

Earlier, Nelson had observed Carrie Crazinski doing laundry in that room.

The man who looked like a cop troubled him. Where had he seen that guy? Oh, yes, on a website where he researched McCrary.

Nelson returned to his office, woke his sleeping laptop, and booted his search history. There it was. The man was Raymond Snopolski, an operative McCrary hired as needed. He spent a half hour learning all he could about Snopolski. *Know your enemy.* Dammit, Snopolski was as dangerous as McCrary.

Nelson ruminated on the movie star who had arrived with Snopolski. There was nothing about him on any of the websites. Nelson remembered the way the movie star walked into the Crazinski house. Nelson knew men like that when he had been a Ranger. Men who moved like panthers stalking prey. The movie star had the look of a professional soldier. He was undoubtedly hazardous to Nelson's health also.

McCrary wouldn't call in a skilled detective like Snopolski or a professional soldier like the movie star unless he had set his sights on Nelson's love nest.

Nelson had played defense for fourteen years. For fourteen years, no one had noticed him hunkered down. Even McCrary had passed over him four years before.

But now McCrary was onto something.

It was time for Nelson to play offense. He must take McCrary out of the picture. With him gone, the two new men would go back to wherever they came from. McCrary was the leader; he was the head of the snake. Cut off the head and the body dies.

But McCrary's men were surveilling him. How could he surprise McCrary?

Nelson smiled. He had a friend…a *good* friend…a *close* friend…

TWENTY

Carlos McCrary

G randpa and I were back at the Plum Blossom while I posted Snoop and Gunner to follow Nelson if he left his house.

I had delegated Grandpa to locate Nelson's ex-wife. He spent Monday and most of Tuesday morning researching. He met me for lunch.

"Did you locate Harry Nelson's ex-wife?"

"Yeah, and it was like unraveling a sweater to follow the leads. I waited at the Texas Department of State Health Services when they opened yesterday morning. From there I visited the Travis County Clerk's office and the Austin Public Library. I drove to San Antonio late yesterday afternoon to visit the Bexar County Clerk's office first thing this morning."

"Why were you in San Antonio?"

"You gonna let me tell this or are you gonna interrupt my report?"

"Sorry. Pray continue."

"The ex-wife's name was Barbara Smith before she married Harry Nelson."

He slid a small notebook from his coat pocket. "I found their marriage license. They were married a little over three years and divorced sixteen years ago, like Carrie told you. It wasn't easy, but I found their no-fault divorce decree. She took back her maiden name as part of the divorce. The problem locating her was twofold: First, her new name was the same as her old name, Smith, and second, she had sixteen years after the divorce to move around and get lost. I guess that makes three problems since her first name was Barbara. If her name was Hermione or Isadora or Edwina, it would be easier. But no, her parents named her Barbara."

"You want a gold star on your homework?"

"You betcha. You ever locate a person with a common first name and a common last name, who had a sixteen-year head start?"

"That's what I do for a living."

"Smart ass." Grandpa grinned. "There were other complications, son. She remarried and changed her name again." He paused dramatically. "In San Antonio."

"And you tracked her down?"

"I did. It took eleven hours of research, which at my normal rate would cost you $11,000."

"It's a good thing I receive the family discount."

He flicked a note across the table. "Here are her particulars. Barbara Smith Lufton of Alamo Heights."

I glanced at the paper and stuffed it in my shirt pocket.

"Attaboy, Grandpa. You get the gold star. Lunch is on me."

"Lunch was gonna be on you anyhow, son. You're lucky I don't bill you for my expenses. You know how much it costs to park in downtown, now that these high-tech Californians and other Yankees moved here?"

"Californians aren't Yankees, Grandpa."

He waved my objection away. "A mere technicality. They're Yankees to me. And don't start me on how much a decent hotel costs in San Antonio."

"I intended to pay your expenses anyway, but I forgot to tell you." I handed him five hundred-dollar bills. "Let me know when you need more."

"You think I'll refuse the money on account of Emily is my granddaughter." He stuffed the bills in his pocket. "I'm on a fixed income, don't you know. I'll gladly accept the money."

―――――

After lunch, I called Barbara Lofton from my car. I explained who I was and that I wanted background on her ex-husband. I asked to meet her.

"How did you find me? I've lived in San Antonio the last twelve years."

"I'm a private investigator. Finding people is what I do. Can I meet you at a convenient time and place? I'm in Austin, but I'll be glad to drive to San Antonio."

"Why are you investigating Harry? Is he in trouble?"

"I'm not investigating Harry. I'm investigating the disappearance of Emily Crazinski, a teenager who lived across the street from Harry. She would have been about four years old when you lived there. May I talk to you? I'll meet you anywhere you say."

"Emily? I remember a cute little girl with blonde curls. A teenager when she disappeared? Is Harry involved in this girl's disappearance? Are you a cop?"

"No, ma'am. I'm a private investigator hired by the Crazinski family. I'm asking routine questions about the missing girl's neighbors, like Harry. Where would be convenient to meet you?"

"I haven't thought about Harry in sixteen years, Mister…What did you say your name was?"

"Carlos McCrary, but everybody calls me Chuck."

"Okay, Chuck. I haven't thought of Harry since the day I divorced him, and I don't plan to start now."

I gave it another shot. Sometimes the second effort works, like in football.

"Emily Crazinski was sixteen years old when she vanished. Her parents have gone through hell for four years. They're desperate to find her or learn her fate. Won't you give me a few minutes of your time? Any small thing you recall about Harry, or about your old house in Austin, or the neighborhood, or one of the neighbors. Sometimes I only realize something is important once I find it. For Emily's sake, for her parents' sake, can I have a few minutes with you?"

A long pause. I waited.

"Okay, ask your questions."

"Where can I meet you?"

"I won't meet you—not in person. There are so many weird people in the world that I'd be a fool to meet a stranger I just met on the phone. If you want to talk, this is your chance."

I hate to interview people over the phone. I can't observe the subject's eyes or analyze their body language or study their facial expressions. However, Barbara Lofton wouldn't give me a face-to-face.

"Okay. I noticed you were eighteen when you married Harry and he was thirty-four."

"How did you learn that," she asked, "and what business is it of yours?"

"Emily Crazinski was sixteen when she disappeared. She may have been the victim of someone with an unnatural interest in young girls."

I let the implication hang in the silence.

After a few seconds, Barbara Lofton cleared her throat.

"Harry and I met at a church social. He told me he was twenty-three. I was seventeen, and I was thrilled that an older man, a *mature* man, a *grown* man, was attracted to an unsophisticated high school senior like me. After I turned eighteen, we eloped. We were married two years before I discovered his real age. We planned to take a cruise, and we went to get passports. That's when I noticed his driver's license."

"Why did he lie to you?"

"It's funny you should ask. Harry never gave me a straight answer to that question. Now that you mention men attracted to young girls, I wonder about something else."

I waited for her to continue. When she didn't, I prompted her. "What did you wonder about?"

I heard a sigh over the phone.

"Harry…Harry lost interest in me around the time I turned twenty-one."

"Lost interest how?"

"He acted…he seemed to…not find me attractive anymore."

If this had been a video call, I would have seen her blush.

"Was there anything that prompted this change? Did you change your appearance? Did something unusual happen to either of you?"

"No, I…"

She lapsed into silence.

I gave her a minute to think. "Did you think of something?"

"It's nothing, really."

"Anything you recall might help Emily."

A longish pause. "One day Harry noticed I had a gray hair. He told me to pluck it out. One silly gray hair. Can you believe it?"

"That must have surprised you. What happened?"

"He was adamant. I told him my mother began to turn gray in her twenties, and she had beautiful salt-and-pepper hair. If I plucked every gray hair that came in, I'd wind up bald. I figured Harry would laugh, but he didn't."

"What happened?"

"He asked me to dye my hair. One solitary gray hair and he wanted me to color my hair. I refused."

"Ms. Lofton, I know this is difficult, and I appreciate your candor. When you say he lost interest...?" I left the question unfinished.

"If you must know, Harry didn't want sex anymore."

"I have an unusual question: Did Harry ever ask you to wear a white tee-shirt and white shorts and dance for him?"

The line was silent for a while.

"How...How did you know?"

"So, he did ask you to dance in a white tee-shirt and shorts?"

Her voice sounded whisper soft. "Yes."

"Thanks for telling me. That's useful, believe me. Changing the subject, what did Harry do for a living?"

"He didn't have a job. He managed his investments. He inherited a lot of money when his parents died."

"How did they die?"

"We never discussed it. They died before I met him."

"Does Harry have family? Siblings? Aunts or uncles?"

"He was an only child. He never mentioned any family."

"Was there a particular incident—a last straw—that prompted you to sue for divorce?"

Lofton paused a long time.

"Ms. Lofton, are you there?"

She cleared her throat. "I found something profoundly disturbing on his computer."

"What was it?"

"Pornographic videos."

With encouragement, she told me about the videos. They were worse than the ones I had stolen. Nelson was a pedophile. Could that be what cratered his marriage? What were the odds that two potential pedophiles surface in one investigation? Was Nelson connected to Drucker?

I repeated my phone number in case Lofton remembered anything else, thanked her, and ended the call.

———

I called Flamer.

I know, I know. People think "flamer" is derogatory slang for gays. *My* Flamer is my Internet-Guru-in-Chief. He contacted me when I first started McCrary Investigations. He emailed me out of the blue and offered to do my online research. His email address is *Flamer21* at one of the free email sites. He signs his emails *Flamer*. It's the only thing I know to call him; I can't call him "Hey, you."

It was two years before I met him face-to-face. To this day, I don't know his real name or where he lives. He's a private person.

"This is Flamer."

"I need an in-depth report on Harry Nelson." I spelled Nelson's name and recited his address.

"Austin, Texas? Why are you in Austin?"

I told him the whole story, including the videos I stole. Rule Six: *You never know what you'll need to know.* Background would give context and significance to an isolated datum that Flamer might otherwise skim over.

"That's tough, boss. I have a niece myself. How deep should I dive?"

"Go crazy. This guy's vibes freak me out. I haven't proven anything yet, but my gut tells me he's a thunder whacko. I think he's a pedophile, a kidnapper, and a serial killer. He hasn't worked for the last twenty years. Where did his money came from? He has an Army Ranger tattoo. Begin with his service record. Did he serve in Asia? Lots of child prostitutes available to soldiers."

"Gee whiz, Chuck. What a great idea: Begin with his service record. I would never have thought of that in a million years. What else should I do? Maybe Google him? Should I do that? How about running a criminal background check?"

"Okay, okay. I know you're the Sultan of Sarcasm. Sorry."

"Anything else you want to tell me?"

"Find a place he owns or has access to where he could keep two or three kidnapped women for several years. I know about the house where he lives. I think he owns or has access to another place. Find it."

"Wow. Anything else?"

"Nope."

He disconnected. No goodbye, no see-you-later, no hang loose. Flamer isn't much for social norms.

That evening, Flamer emailed a report with details from his deep dive into Harry Nelson's history. It was worse than I expected. I was glad Snoop and Gunner were watching for an opening.

Harry Nelson was born Harrison Arthur Nielson to a couple of thrifty Danish immigrants. His ex-wife was right; he was an only child. Nielson played fullback on the high school football team in the small town of Prospect, Montana but hadn't received an offer for a college scholarship.

I felt a twinge of sympathy. It was close to my personal story. I started at tight end on the state championship football team my senior year, but I wasn't fast enough to play Division One football.

Like me, Nielson enlisted in the U.S. Army after he graduated high school. Nielson tried out for the Rangers, whereas I was Special Forces. He qualified as Expert Marksman in pistol and rifle. He was stationed in Korea as the Cold War was winding down. Unlike me, he never saw combat. Unlike me, he was discharged for the good of the service after sixteen months' duty in Korea with an OTH discharge—other than honorable.

That meant he was involved in criminal activity that nobody could prove. Nielson was Trouble with a capital T.

He returned to Montana and married a local girl after a short courtship. Nielson's parents died in a house fire caused by a faulty gas heater. The

Montana police believed the fire was arson, but they couldn't prove it. Nielson collected the fire insurance, repaired the house, and sold it. He never bought monuments for his parents' graves. Did the omitted monuments indicate that Nelson had issues with his parents? If so, it might provide insight into his pathology, if I were interested in his pathology. I would leave that to his lawyer and shrink after I captured him.

It was interesting that Flamer had unearthed such an obscure piece of information. I would not have thought to check that. I wondered if Flamer had a personal experience along that line. Did someone close to him lie in an unmarked grave? The things I don't know about Flamer would fill a book.

Nielson and his young wife relocated to San Francisco where he took a security guard job. He and his wife bought matching million-dollar life insurance policies on each other.

Three years later, his wife was murdered in a mugging gone wrong as they returned from a night out to celebrate his wife's twenty-first birthday.

Neilson hadn't worked since.

He married twice more. First in Las Vegas to an eighteen-year-old showgirl and later in Chicago to a teenage waitress.

The showgirl was gunned down three weeks after her twenty-first birthday. She was a dancer at a casino on the strip, gunned down at five in the morning in a drive-by shooting as she walked to her car. The murder was unsolved and Nielson collected on his wife's two-million-dollar life insurance policy.

Flamer inserted a comment: "How many casino dancers have two-million-dollar insurance policies, boss? That should have been a clue to somebody. If the Vegas police had pursued that anomaly, how many subsequent murders would been prevented?"

It was pointless to speculate, so I just shook my head and moved on with his report.

In Chicago, Nelson changed his name to Harrison A. Nelson. His third wife, the Chicago waitress, was killed in a hit-and-run one month after her twenty-first birthday. The driver was never found.

Surprise, surprise, Nelson's wife had a two-million-dollar life insurance policy.

He relocated to Austin, dropped ten years from his age, and changed his name to Harry Nelson, no middle initial.

That is where he married his fourth wife, teenager Barbara Smith.

Three dead wives, three lucrative insurance policies. How did fourth wife Barbara Smith Nelson Lofton survive?

I called her.

"Ms. Lofton, Chuck McCrary again. One more question: Did Harry Nelson buy a life insurance policy on you?"

"Harry bought five-million-dollar policies on each of us after we married."

"What happened to the policies?"

"After I hired the divorce attorney, he told me to cancel the policy on my life immediately. I canceled it with a certified copy to Harry mailed from the attorney's office before I left. The attorney insisted."

"So, Harry knew the policy was canceled."

"The attorney was very forceful that I should do that before leaving his office."

"Your attorney saved your life."

"What the hell does that mean? Saved my life?"

"Are you sitting down? Are you at home?"

"Yes. I was watching TV with my husband."

"Here's what you need to know: Harry was born Harrison Arthur Nielson in Prospect, Montana. His parents died in a house fire and he sold the house and moved to California. He was married three times before he met you. All three wives died within weeks after their twenty-first birthdays, and all three had large life insurance policies with Harry as beneficiary."

"Ohmigod. Harry planned to murder me for the insurance money."

I heard another voice in the background.

"I'll tell you in a minute, honey. It's that detective I spoke with yesterday. He has more dirt on Harry. I'll put the phone on speaker."

A click and the background noise changed.

"Chuck, you're on speaker with my husband, Larry Lofton."

"Mr. Lofton, I'm sorry to meet you under these circumstances. I'm

Carlos McCrary, a private investigator looking into the disappearance of a sixteen-year-old girl."

"Barbara said something about Harry Nelson trying to murder her?"

"Harry's three previous wives died under suspicious circumstances soon after their twenty-first birthdays. They all had large life insurance policies payable to Harry Nelson. That's what Ms. Lofton referred to."

"Is my wife in danger? After fourteen years?"

"Mr. Lofton, I have no way to know if Harry has tried to find your wife since their divorce. The insurance policy was canceled, so he no longer has a monetary motive. Ms. Lofton was difficult to locate, and I'm a professional. However, there's no statute of limitations for murder. If Harry ever comes to trial, your wife could be a material witness against him."

"How do I protect my wife?"

"Give me your email address, and I'll send you my report on Harry. Give that to your local police and discuss your situation with them."

"Oh, Christ, this is bad news." Larry Lofton gave me his email address.

"I just forwarded the report. Let me know when you receive it. I'll hold."

I listened to the air conditioner hiss from Lofton's end of the line.

"Okay, I got it."

"Good. Is Ms. Lofton still there?"

"Yes, I'm here."

"Do you have blueprints or a floorplan of Harry's house in Austin?"

"No, I—wait, I videoed the contents for our insurance agent when we bought homeowners' insurance seventeen years ago. The agent said to video our contents for proof of loss in case we had an insurance claim, like a fire or tornado damage. The video should be on my hard drive. I seldom delete anything. Would that video help?"

"Yes, ma'am. Can you send it to my Dropbox?"

"Now that you mention it, I have a Dropbox account. The file name is *Austin Homeowners Contents*. I remember that." She gave me her Dropbox login info.

"Thanks. I'll download it after we finish. Good luck, Ms. Lofton. You have my number if you need me."

Nelson was undoubtedly a murderer, and could be a kidnapper. Why did he switch from murdering his wives to…what?

As I disconnected, I was chilled to realize that, regardless of whether Emily was alive, her twenty-first birthday was a few weeks away.

I made a mental note to calculate the approximate ages of the three bodies we had found already when they were killed, but I knew what I would find.

What was significant about a twenty-first birthday?

I had a deadline—Emily's birthday—and an increased sense of urgency.

Aunt Carrie's vision had come in the nick of time.

TWENTY-ONE

G randpa poured his second coffee and handed me the pot across the kitchen table. We had lingered after dinner when Carrie and Frank went to a movie.

"Is Gunner on duty?"

"It's Snoop. He's staring out Carrie's laundry room window like a cat waiting for the canary to fall asleep. Or we're the canary and Nelson's the cat. Gunner's waiting in his Jeep down the street to follow Nelson if he leaves."

"How long since Nelson made an out-of-town trip?"

"We started surveillance Monday night. Today's Wednesday. He's bound to leave soon. So far, every time he leaves the house, it's a local trip to the store and he's back in two hours. All trips were between eight a.m. and nine p.m.—times when I can't hit his house because the neighbors might see me and call the cops. When Nelson does leave town, I expect him to go in the middle of the night, so it's not obvious that he's gone."

"What will you do when he does leave?"

"Search his house like I did Drucker's."

Grandpa nodded. "Be tougher this time with Nelson's alarm system."

"I'll manage."

"Nelson is our prime suspect, but there are others," he said. "Tell me his every connection to Bonham High School."

I refilled my cup. My first had gone cold.

"First we have two victims," I said, "Emily and Ling Cheng."

"Was the second body identified as Ling?"

"Not yet. Detective Goodman is hunting for her orthodontist, but it's a safe bet it's Ling."

"Okay. Go on."

"We have two teachers, Desmond Drucker and Jerry O'Doul. Both had Emily and Ling as students. There's the guidance counselor, Eleanor Feinstein, and Harry Nelson, who is a regular at Bonham High School sporting events. He watched Emily and Ling play basketball."

"That's all the connections?"

"No. Kenny Hoar was sleeping with Emily and he attended Bonham, but I eliminated him as a suspect."

"Why?"

"Because of the videos I found in Nelson's house."

"Goodman could be right about the videos. They might be legal and have nothing to do with Emily. I wouldn't eliminate Hoar. Not yet."

"Okay. I'll keep him in mind if we come up empty after I ransack Nelson's house."

"So, Emily and Ling were students of Drucker and O'Doul. And Feinstein counseled Ling Cheng. You need creamer in your coffee?"

He slid the jar toward me.

"Did she counsel Emily?" he asked.

"No. Eleanor met Emily the way she meets all new students, but she didn't know her well. Emily was a sophomore and hadn't considered which college to attend. Besides, Carrie and Frank are Longhorns. It was a foregone conclusion that Emily would attend UT." I didn't mention Emily's plan to attend the University of Florida and join the Army.

I spooned coffee creamer into my cup and shoved the container across the table.

"Here's an aerial shot of the school and the parking lot I downloaded from the internet. This circle is where Emily's car was parked. This one is Drucker's English Lit classroom, and this one is—was, I mean—O'Doul's physics lab."

Grandpa stirred creamer into his coffee, took a sip, and nodded approval.

"What was Emily's last class on the day she disappeared?"

"Let me check her class schedule." I riffled through my files. "Here it is."

I scanned the page. "English Literature. Drucker taught her last class."

"We know the creep has an unnatural interest in young girls," Grandpa said.

"I combed his house. Emily wasn't there."

"That could mean that he did kidnap her," Grandpa said, "but he stashed her someplace else."

"You're right. I'll call Flamer."

Flamer answered on the second ring.

"What miracle do you need today, boss?"

"I want a deep dive on Desmond Drucker." I gave him Drucker's full name and address. "Include every piece of real estate he has access to. We're hunting for a house where he keeps a kidnap victim. Drucker teaches English Lit at James Bonham High School in Austin, Texas."

"What happened to your interest in Harry Nelson?"

"He's on our list. We're covering the bases."

"You're hoping for a miracle, boss."

"Hope is possible."

"For what it's worth, Chuck, I believe in miracles."

———

Before heading to bed, I called Ruby. She loved the flowers I had sent her and showed them to me on the video call. They still looked fresh. She gave me six brownie points for sending flowers. I explained that my case was gathering steam and I might not be able to see her again for a while. She said she understood and wished me good luck.

I said I could use all the luck I could find.

She told me the six brownie points bought me up to two weeks to call back. Then she blew me a kiss over the phone. You gotta appreciate a woman like that.

That night I dreamed about basketball. Girls' basketball. Specifically, Bonham Bobcats basketball.

In my dream, the team picture on Emily's bedroom wall came to life and a dozen girls emerged from the photo and materialized in the girls' gym at Bonham High School. The team warmed up in their home uniforms —white with red trim. A dozen basketballs sailed through the air as the coach ran the girls through their paces.

In my dream, another basketball flew out of nowhere and blindsided me in the head. That was impossible; I was observing the entire Bobcats team. In my dream, I looked to the other end of the court where the visitors' team drilled in their blue uniforms with white trim. One of their balls had gotten away and hit me.

Bam!

I woke with my ears ringing like I had been smacked in real life. I closed my eyes and recaptured the image. The other team. The other dozen girls. *When Harry Nelson attends a basketball game, he sees two sets of teenage girls to fantasize about.*

The average seventeen-year-old girl in America stands a smidgeon over five-foot-four. Emily was five-foot-eight. Ling Cheng stood five-ten. Francine Tinker was five-nine. Did Francine play basketball for Burnet High?

How many of the other hundred plus missing girls played basketball, and did their teams play Bonham High?

The clock on the nightstand indicated *3:10*. I wouldn't sleep anymore that night.

I carried the 112 files to the breakfast table and brewed a pot of strong coffee.

As I went through the files, I eliminated girls five-foot-four or less. Yes, I know that short girls play basketball, but I needed a manageable number to test my hypothesis. That left sixty-three files. From those files, I eliminated girls who had disappeared more than a year out of high school. Forty-two files remained.

I could manage forty-two phone calls. I would wait until the sheriff's offices opened for non-emergency calls. Eight a.m. sounded right.

I walked outside to fetch the Austin newspaper. I had finished the sports section when Carrie came in at 7:10.

"Why the files piled on the breakfast table? You discover another clue?"

I hadn't told Carrie my suspicion about Nelson. If she ran into him in the neighborhood, I didn't want her to act strangely. That could put him on his guard.

"I'm testing a theory that the kidnapper picked his victims from girls he watched play basketball at Bonham High School. This stack represents forty-two tall girls for me to research to determine whether they were on a basketball team that played the Bobcats."

"Harry Nelson comes to the Bobcat games. You think it's him, don't you?"

"*Uh-huh.*"

"Why? He's nice enough, though he does keep to himself."

"Nelson has an unnatural attraction to young girls."

"And you know this how?"

"I'm the world's greatest private eye. I find out things."

Carrie grinned. "Okay, be that way."

She poured herself a coffee. "Have you finished the local section? I want today's horoscopes."

Of course, she did. She checked horoscopes every day ending in Y. Clap-trap and fiddle-faddle.

Carrie thumbed through the newspaper. "Emily's horoscope says: *Volatile emotions may surface among members of your household today.*"

She gaped at me over the newspaper. "That means you'll learn something important today. Why else would our emotions get volatile?"

She returned her attention to the newspaper. "Your horoscope says: *Today should be a wonderful day. Your physical energy is good, and you should look and feel wonderful.* Sounds like a good day for investigating."

Carrie stopped to sip her coffee. "Let's read mine...Oh my God. It says: *Family members who live far away might plan a visit. A lot of phone calls or emails could be exchanged.*"

She jumped to her feet. "I have to tell Frank. Emily will contact me again." She clutched the newspaper and hurried from the room. Seconds later I heard them squabbling from the other side of the house. I couldn't make out what they said, but their tone of voice told me more than I wanted to know.

The *volatile emotions* in Emily's horoscope had emerged in my aunt and uncle's bedroom.

I wished eight o'clock would hurry.

———

At 8:01 I called the Burnet County Sheriff.

"Sheriff Wilton? This is Chuck McCrary."

"Hey, Chuck. I meant to call you. Nice catch on identifying Francine Tinker. Francine was good friends with my daughter and I know her folks. Naturally, they'd rather have found her alive, but…well, knowing is better than not knowing, right? Her parents said they were thankful to know what happened to her. She'd been missing for nine years, you know. It's not a happy ending, but at least, it's an *ending* and not a never-ending mystery. You did a hell of a job there, son."

"Thank you, Sheriff. One more question: Did Francine Tinker play basketball for Burnet High?"

"Don't think so, but she and my daughter played on the volleyball team."

Volleyball? Why didn't I think of that? It worked as well as basketball. In fact, adding other sports gave the killer a larger target population from which to choose his victims. How many missing girls had played high school soccer and lacrosse?

"Is Burnet High in the same athletic district as James Bonham High?"

"I don't think so. Why do you ask?"

"I believe the kidnapper picks his victims from girls who play sports with and against the Bonham High girls' teams. But if Burnet High is in another district, my theory doesn't work."

"How about the playoffs?" Wilton asked. "My wife and I drove to Austin to watch our granddaughter play Bonham in the playoffs."

———

I called Detective Goodman. "Nora, it's Chuck McCrary. Do you have results on the fingerprints on those two DVDs?"

"They came in this morning. The techs found yours, Nelson's, and one or maybe two more sets that aren't usable. There could be two accomplices or just one."

"So, nothing you can act on."

"I do have some good news though. We located Ling Cheng's orthodontist. He's bringing Ling's tooth impressions to the ME's office this afternoon."

"Good. Let's assume the ME confirms the second body is Ling Cheng."

"Okay. Go ahead."

"Francine Tinker played volleyball for Burnet High. Her team had a playoff game against Bonham High two weeks before she disappeared. The killer attended the game, spotted Francine, and selected her for his next victim."

"The first step in solving a serial killing is to discern a pattern. I think you've found one."

"Francine Tinker was the first victim to disappear. Emily disappeared four months later. Ling Cheng disappeared sometime between the following May and August."

"Correction, boy wonder: Francine was the first *known* murder victim. There might be a dozen more like those girls in the videos. God forbid."

———

Coach Esther Ledbetter came in the door and scanned the teachers' lounge. She was dressed in a Bonham High polo shirt with a basketball logo and white shorts and basketball shoes. She wore her whistle on a red and white lanyard. My football coach at Theodore Roosevelt High School wore his whistle everywhere. It must be a requirement for the coaches' union. I remembered Nelson's comment about the basketball coach's sexual orientation and wondered if Coach Ledbetter had a thing for young girls. I had nothing that tied her to Emily's disappearance, but I kept an open mind.

"Mr. McCrary? I'm Esther Ledbetter."

We shook hands, and I handed her a business card.

She set the card on the table. "Let me get a Diet Coke and I'll join you."

Ledbetter selected a can from the refrigerator and stuffed a dollar in the honor jar before sitting across from me. "What can I do for you?"

"Do you remember me?"

She looked puzzled. "You look familiar, but I don't..." She shrugged.

Mr. Fisher hadn't told her who I was. No matter.

"I'm Emily Crazinski's cousin. I interviewed you after Emily disappeared."

Ledbetter perused my card. "Now I remember."

"I'm taking a fresh look at the case."

"Have there been new developments?"

"It's better if we keep that to ourselves for now. You understand."

I don't know why detectives say that, since people never understand why we don't tip our hand. But they accept the fiction without question.

"Of course."

See what I mean?

"Do you have the basketball schedule from Emily's last season? And from the ten years before that?"

"They're in my office. Why do you ask?"

"Where do I get the old volleyball schedules?"

"The volleyball coach or the school office should have them. Why?"

"To find out when Bonham High played Burnet High in any girls' sport during the last sixteen years."

"Sixteen years? What happened sixteen years ago?"

"A serial killer may have been kidnapping female high school athletes who played for or against Bonham High for the last sixteen years."

Ledbetter's jaw dropped. "Oh Lord. That can't be good. Let's stop in the admin office on the way to my office."

We gathered copies of all girls' sports schedules from sixteen academic years prior.

Ledbetter's office was shoehorned into a closet-sized space off the hall between the girls' gym and the locker room.

She removed a stack of files from the visitor's chair and rolled it toward me. "Take a seat." She set the stack on a battleship-gray file cabinet and plopped in her desk chair. "Okay, what's the deal, Chuck?"

"I need the names of adults who regularly attend Bonham High girls' games. Adults who are not related to the players. I want to cover all girls' sports, but let's start with basketball. Do you have records or personal memories of non-family fans?"

"You think the killer may be attending our games?"

"It's something I need check out. What kind of non-family adult attends a girls' basketball game? And how do I get the names?"

"Most adults are parents or grandparents. But you said non-family members. Let's see...We have a few teachers who attend. They come if they have a student or two who plays on a team or if they played the sport when they were in school. Mr. Drucker, for example. He played basketball in high school. He attends most of our games. Of course, he's single. I don't think Desmond has much of a life."

I had seen a team photo on Drucker's bedroom wall. I hadn't paid attention to it. I made a mental note to review the photos I'd taken at Drucker's. I kept them in an encrypted file, since they were evidence in my breaking and entering expedition.

"How about season ticket holders?"

Ledbetter stepped to the file cabinet. She opened the third drawer. "I made a file somewhere...Here we go." She lifted a manila folder with Season Tickets on the tab and handed it to me.

"This lists the basketball season ticket holders for the last ten years— since we first sold season tickets."

I flipped the folder open and thumbed three sheets back. "That's it? There's fewer than twenty names on the list each year."

Ledbetter shrugged. "Girls' sports aren't as popular as boys' sports. That's why the administration encourages teachers to come to the games. It improves student morale for their teachers to support them. The administration gives the teachers a discount price."

I scanned the lists for all ten years. I recognized three names: Harry Nelson, Desmond Drucker, and Jerry O'Doul. The first two were on the list every year; O'Doul had dropped off three years ago.

O'Doul? O'Doul had retired from teaching three years before. Jerry O'Doul. *Hmm.*

———

Returning to my rented Jeep, I reviewed my notes from my first investigation. I consulted a copy of the Austin cops' map that marked where they had found Emily's car. Spot 793.

The ginormous student parking lot had over 800 spaces. The closest spots were reserved for seniors. Juniors with a B+ average had the next closest spots. The farthest spots were for the underclassmen on a first-come, first-served basis. Rank hath its privileges.

As a sophomore, Emily parked in the quarter of the student lot furthest from where I stood. Each morning, she would have crossed three-quarters of the student lot, bypassing the teachers' lot, to reach the main entrance. For security reasons, everyone entered the building through the main entrance.

My watch said *2:20.* School let out at 2:30. While I waited, I walked to the far side of the lot and contemplated the wall of the school facing me.

James Bonham High School is shaped like the letter H, if the H had three vertical lines instead of two. The two-story school has six wings, branching from the central spine, three on a side. Close to 2,000 students were enrolled.

A bell clanged in the distance. I glanced at my watch. *2:30.*

In seconds, students gushed from the exits in bunches of twos or threes or fours, shouting and waving. They high-fived and grinned, slapped backs and shook hands like they intended to arm wrestle as they zigzagged their way through the teachers' lot to the student lot.

I pictured Emily as she crossed the teachers' lot, then the student lot to reach her car. None of her classmates said they had seen her after school that day. Popular as she was, I couldn't conceive that she hadn't had a conversation with a friend after class. She always walked with a friend or two.

But not on St. Patrick's Day four years earlier.

On the day she disappeared, somewhere between her last class and her car, she must have stopped to talk to someone. Someone who told the police they didn't see her. Someone she knew. Was it a teacher or a student? A parent? A school administrator? Nobody saw her in the lot. She hadn't joined the other students' mad dash for freedom that day. She'd stayed behind, inside the school. Why?

As I pondered Emily's fate that day four years before, the pavement two yards from me cratered and dust flew in the air. A split-second later, the sound of the gunshot reached my ears. I juked sideways and ran at right angles to the direction of the gunshot. Someone wanted to kill me, and I had to lead them away from the students.

I doubted anyone else heard the shot over the noise of the car engines as they left the parking lot, but my ears are tuned to such things. Sound travels about a thousand feet per second. A rifle bullet fires between 2,000 and 3,500 feet per second. The instant the bullet hit the pavement I reflexively began counting *one-thousand-one*. I never finished the first *one-thousand*. The time between the shot hitting the pavement and the sound reaching me meant the shooter fired from more than two hundred feet. From that distance, he was shooting a rifle.

The shot came from somewhere on the steep hill across the street. Limestone strata stepped like giant shelves twenty feet high as they climbed two hundred feet from the street to the top. Houses clustered the ridge for a quarter of a mile to enjoy the view. Junipers and live oaks covering the hillside concealed the shooter.

Another bullet whizzed close enough to feel the shock wave. I saw what might have been a muzzle flash, or it could have been the sunlight glinting off a shiny leaf halfway up the slope. Either way, it was my best clue.

I carried a handgun. Not a chance against a rifle at that distance, even if I spotted the shooter. I needed to get closer.

Sprinting across the street toward the mesa, I dodged the after-school traffic as I ran. One thing was sure: The shooter was a lousy shot. His first bullet missed by six feet when I was a sitting duck.

Another bullet struck the windshield of a passing car where I had just cut to my left. *That is a muzzle flash near that juniper tree next to the twisted live oak. Juniper ten feet tall shaped like a Christmas tree*, I memorized. *Live oak with a fork in the trunk about seven feet up. One hundred feet above the street, about the fifth or sixth limestone shelf from the bottom. Got it.*

Cutting to the right, I angled toward the shooter as I lunged into the shrubbery at the base of the mesa and clambered up the slope. Glancing over my shoulder when I reached the first limestone shelf, I saw the car with the shattered windshield had pulled to the side of the road. Hopefully, the driver had not been hit.

Clawing upward, feet slipping on the stony soil, I grabbed branches to assist my mad rush toward the shooter.

He must have parked at the top, maybe in the city park on the ridge that provided a panoramic view. Then he climbed down so he could hide close enough to take a good shot at me. Now that he had failed and I was chasing him, he would be scrambling back to his car.

My mind raced as I scaled from one limestone shelf to the next.

How had he known I was at Bonham High School? He must have followed me. But from where? Where had I picked up the tail?

Nelson. Nelson was the source. We were watching Nelson, and Nelson must be watching us. He could surveil Carrie and Frank's house from a second-floor window and alert an accomplice lurking nearby when I left. The accomplice followed me to the school, then—figuring I would be inside for a while—parked at the top of the mesa and climbed down the slope to get closer to the school. He shot at me when I returned to the visitor's parking lot. The fact that I had walked to the student lot was a lucky break for him; it was closer to the mesa.

I angled toward the top of the mesa to cut him off before he could regain the park.

Five minutes passed like an hour as I pushed and struggled up the steep slope. He had a three-minute head start since he was already halfway to the top. Also, he had made the climb down and had at least a passing familiarity with the path back to his car. On the other hand, I had never climbed this mesa and I made several false starts and turn-backs as I snaked my way from shelf to shelf.

Still forty feet below the safety fence at the top of the mesa and twenty yards to east, I saw the shooter climbing with an M16 rifle slung across his back. He scrambled to the base of the park's limestone retaining wall. His dark green jacket silhouetted against the white stones as he ascended.

Jerking to a halt, I took a two-hand grip on my Glock. I shouted for him to halt, hoping he would look back and I could see his face.

The shooter never looked back as he clambered up the limestone face.

Damn, but he was fast. I held my breath. *Easy squeezy, nice and easy.* As he topped the wall and disappeared into the park, I got off two shots. The first bullet kicked up a limestone cloud where it hit. The second bullet tore a hole in his jacket in the middle of the back, but he never slowed. Either he was Superman or he wore a Kevlar vest under his jacket.

The guy was a lousy shot, but he had good equipment. Shooters who invest in good equipment are usually serious about their sport and they practice. But this shooter hadn't. *Hmm.* Why would an amateur shooter have professional equipment?

By the time I made it over the wall, he was gone. The park was deserted.

The guy had fired three shots. It took twenty minutes to find the Christmas tree juniper and the crooked live oak. I managed to find two brass casings. I didn't touch them, just photographed their positions with my phone so they would be easy for the Austin CSIs to locate again.

I called Detective Goodman. While I waited for her and the CSIs, I slid down the mesa and asked the driver of the car with the shattered windshield to wait for the cops. I figured the CSIs could find the slug somewhere in the car and use it and the brass to identify the weapon.

I decided not to tell the family about the attack. There was no reason to worry them; there was nothing they could do. Snoop, Gunner, and I would wear Kevlar vests from now until the case was solved. What would I say if Carrie or Frank noticed the vests? I would wait and see; maybe it wouldn't come up. Who was I kidding? Carrie would notice it in a heartbeat.

The attack proved I was closing in on the killer. Or he *believed* I was getting close. But close to whom? Nelson wasn't the shooter, because Snoop and Gunner had surveilled him 24/7 since the day after they arrived.

Either Nelson was not the kidnapper, or he had an accomplice. My money was on an accomplice.

TWENTY-TWO

The next morning, Ruby called at 9:30. "Are you all right, Chuck?"

"Yes, I'm fine. I take it that you got assigned the brass and the slug from the sniper attack?"

"It was waiting in my in-basket this morning. When I saw you were the target, I had to call you. After last Sunday night, I have a personal interest in the case, but don't tell Detective Goodman. I really enjoyed last Sunday. I needed to hear your voice and know that you were okay."

"Thanks, Ruby. That's sweet. The guy took three shots. They all missed. It was an M16."

"One of the most common rifles around. I'll put a rush on it." She paused. "Anything else you want to tell me?"

"Yeah. I just remembered that Desmond Drucker owns an M16. See if he has one registered to him. Also check Harry Nelson and Kenneth Hoar." I spelled the names and gave her their contact info."

"Okay, I've got that. Anything *else* you want to tell me?"

Sometimes, my own ignorance about women amazes me. Finally, I got the hint. I lowered my voice to what I hoped was a sexy purr. "Yes. I wanted to tell you that I had a great time last Sunday night too, and I plan to call you as soon as I can."

"Make it sooner rather than later, lover. I'll call you when I finish processing the evidence."

"That's okay. You can go through channels and report to Goodman."

"Oh, I will. I added you to my *personal* distribution list—*very* personal."

"Thanks, Ruby. For everything."

I disconnected. Time to get to work.

At last I had a kidnapping pattern to analyze.

The Bonham Bobcats played in an athletic district with six Austin schools of similar size. The killer had snatched two girls from Bonham and one girl from Burnet that we knew of. If he were careful, he wouldn't call attention to Travis County disappearances. He would focus on other counties.

I reviewed all 112 files for girls from other counties who played Bonham High in the post-season, including the short girls. I eliminated the Travis County files. That left forty-nine.

Nine years before, the Bonham Bobcats hosted the Burnet Lady Dawgs in the volleyball playoffs. Francine Tinker played in that game and disappeared two weeks later.

I studied the Bonham post-season schedule in girls' sports for the last sixteen years. Bonham made the playoffs in lacrosse eight years before and in volleyball nine and six years earlier, but not in basketball or soccer. The Bobcats played schools in Elgin in Bastrop County and Corsicana in Navarro County, as well as ones in Burnet and Fredericksburg. I had not visited the sheriffs of Bastrop or Navarro counties because they weren't in the Hill Country.

I called the Bastrop County Sheriff and introduced myself. "Sheriff, I'm investigating a serial killing with Detective Nora Goodman of the Austin Homicide Division. Have any female students from Elgin High School disappeared in the last seventeen years?"

"Who did you say this was?"

I repeated myself and told the sheriff why I was interested in the disappearances.

"You think this kidnapper holds these girls captive for an extended time before he kills them?"

"Yes, sir, some victims for three or more years. We believe the pattern involves female athletes who played against James Bonham High School in Austin. Can you check?"

"Don't have to check; I know. We're a small town. We don't have many unexplained disappearances. This one happened five or six years ago. I don't recall the details, but she was a high school student. You want me to check whether she played sports and send you and Detective Goodman a copy of the file?"

"That would be great, Sheriff." I gave him my and Goodman's contact information.

Next, I called the Navarro County Sheriff. She wasn't in, but a deputy reviewed their files. They had no suspicious, unresolved disappearances of female high school athletes during the last seventeen years.

———

Friday afternoon late, the Bastrop County Sheriff's file on Helena Washoe arrived in my email. Washoe played on Elgin High School's lacrosse team. Eight years before, the team traveled to Austin to play Bonham. Ten days later, she disappeared from her driveway at 11:30 p.m., coming home from visiting a friend.

Did Helena Washoe drive a Toyota between model years 2004-2009? I scoured the file. The missing girl's 2005 Toyota Camry was left in the driveway at the family home. Helena's car keys disappeared with her.

I called Detective Goodman.

"Nora, this is Chuck McCrary. Was the ME able to identify the Asian girl's body from Ling Cheng's tooth impressions?"

"Yes. It's Ling Cheng. Any more activity from the mysterious shooter?"

"So far, no one's shot at me today, if that's what you mean, but I'm wearing a vest anyway. Do you have results on the brass casings or the slug?"

"Not yet. I'll call you when I learn something. There are thousands of M16s in Travis County. We're checking, of course, but I'd bet the weapon isn't in our database. We must be close to something or he wouldn't risk trying to kill you."

"That's what I figured. There's another development: You remember the car key the killer left with Ling's body? I may know where it came from." I told her what I knew about Helena Washoe. "I asked the Bastrop County Sheriff to email the file to you."

"Thanks, Chuck. I'll get the key from evidence and show it to the Helena's family. With luck, they'll recognize it."

"If they do, it means Helena Washoe's body is somewhere waiting to be found."

"Unless she's alive somewhere, also waiting to be found."

"After eight years? That would make her twenty-five years old now. I don't think so. If he's Nelson, he doesn't like women over twenty-one."

———

Grandpa squeezed a dollop of barbecue sauce onto his plate, sliced off a bite of brisket, and swirled it in the sauce. He stuck the brisket bite in his mouth and chewed a while.

I attacked my dry-rubbed ribs in silence.

"You're quiet today, son."

"I'm eating."

"I figured maybe you were quiet because somebody wants to kill you."

"I don't understand."

"Don't bullshit a bullshitter, son. When did you start wearing a Kevlar vest?" he said as he sliced his brisket.

"You just can't beat Texas barbecue."

"That doesn't answer my question, son."

There was no point denying it. "Yesterday. Thursday afternoon I went to Bonham High to check out the student lot where Emily parked her car. I was observing how the students act after school lets out. I was over to one side, minding my own business, and a sniper fired two shots at me from the mesa across the street. There were dozens of students there. He could have killed one of them with a ricochet or a bad shot."

"That's when you started wearing the vest."

"Yeah. Snoop and Gunner too."

"When were you going to tell your old grandpa about it?"

I smiled. "Next February 29th."

"That's more than two years from now."

"I didn't want to worry you; there's nothing you can do about it."

"How about Carrie and Frank? They'll notice you wearing the vest."

"I'll tell them that Snoop insisted that he, Gunner, and I wear vests as standard procedure."

"You think she'll buy it?"

I shrugged. "Either they buy it or they'll worry needlessly. You could back me up. Say that you agree it's a good idea."

Grandpa sniffed. "It's worth a try I guess."

"Thanks."

"You have those older missing person files from the county sheriffs?"

I was grateful that Grandpa changed the subject. "Not yet, but since we learned about Helena Washoe in Bastrop County, I expanded our search to the counties of every school Bonham High played in girls' sports in the last sixteen years."

"That's gotta be a potful of missing persons."

"Ninety-seven more. The good news is Nora Goodman's team will gather the files for us. They have the resources. She'll have them in her office Monday. Goodman is driving to Elgin today to interview Helena Washoe's parents. We hope they'll recognize the car key buried with Ling Cheng's body. Goodman will bring copies of the Bastrop County files back with her."

"If we're lucky," Grandpa said, "one of those files has a picture of Clara or Gloria."

"If that's the case, it ought to be enough for a warrant for Nelson's house."

"Nelson hasn't left town?"

"No. That worries me."

"Why?"

"Carrie said his house used to be dark at night when he left town, but Snoop noticed a pattern of lights that switch on and off in several rooms at night. Nelson must have put them on a timer to make people think he's home when he's not."

"Big deal. Grandma and I have kept our living room lights on a timer for years. Not a good idea for your house to appear deserted, even when you're home."

"But Nelson didn't do that light thing before I interviewed him a week ago."

Grandpa looked worried. "Maybe he knows you suspect him."

"I hope not. That would introduce a wild card."

"This isn't a poker game, son."

"Isn't it?"

Harry Nelson

This was serious. McCrary, Snopolski and the freakin' movie star had alternated surveillance on Nelson for five days. Whenever he left the house, one of them followed, dogging his steps from a distance.

Despite taking Ambien, he hadn't slept since he spotted the surveillance. He knew that the scheme he had played for fifteen years hung by a thread. That thread was unraveling.

To make matters worse, his friend who came to him in the night had not shown since the failed sniper attack. Where was his friend? McCrary must have freaked him out when he returned fire. What could you expect; his friend was not a veteran. Now his friend wouldn't even visit him. How could Nelson get his rifle and Kevlar vest back? He hesitated to call again; the cops could be tapping his phone.

The Ambien had made him drowsy and headachy. He didn't know whether he could handle the pressure of another night without his friend to talk to.

His chest felt tight. He couldn't take a deep breath. His lungs felt half filled with cotton. Had the Ambien done that? Or was he losing his mind?

He had been so careful, so meticulous for fifteen years. How did McCrary catch on? It was those freakin' DVDs. His friend warned him they were dangerous, but...but...the videos were such *fun* to play.

Watching them, he relived his best days over the last fifteen years. Success after success after success…Seven straight successes.

The whole system was crumbling. *He* was cratering too. Or was it the Ambien? He felt nervous and confused. He wished he could talk to his friend. Nelson suppressed a sob. This was the last straw; he couldn't stay at home. Home was no longer safe. That's what his friend would say if he were here. His friend would say, "You know where to go. That's why we made contingency plans."

It was time to load the minivan.

"Yes," he imagined his friend saying, "That's why we have Plan B."

He climbed the stairs to fetch Evita and Gloria.

He wished he could see McCrary's face when he found the girls' bedrooms in the attic.

Emily Crazinski

Emily had endured prison for fifty-nine menstrual periods, first in what she called Cage One, and later in Cage Two. She never knew what day it was, what time it was, not even what year it was anymore. She tracked time by counting menstrual cycles—the one certainty in her existence since her world had gyrated sideways and her universe shrank to one room. That one stable occurrence kept her sane. That and knowing that her parents were looking for her and would never stop.

Nelson jerked Emily from the beat-up easy chair where she was dozing. He spun her around and bound her hands behind her with plastic cable ties. Tearing off a strip of duct tape, he sealed her mouth shut. He herded her out of Cage Two, down the stairs, through the kitchen, and out the back door.

It was nighttime as he hustled her down the walk and into the garage. It was a small victory to learn it was nighttime. Hooray!

Every time Nelson entered her room, she watched for an opportunity to strike back. One time she had removed a wooden slat from her bed and hidden behind the door, waiting to club him into unconsciousness. He had told her through the door that he would not bring her food or water until he could see her standing at the far end of the cage. That's when she first noticed the peephole in the door. For the next fifty-nine periods, Nelson had never slipped, never shown weakness.

Nelson threw her into the rear of a minivan and secured her ankles with cable ties also.

Emily was astonished to bump against another woman dressed like she was in white tee-shirt and shorts. The stranger was similarly trussed, her mouth taped shut.

The other woman gaped at Emily, brown eyes round with surprise.

Emily knew she was not the first woman imprisoned in either Cage One or Cage Two. The rooms were not new, and she smelled the femaleness left by the previous prisoners on the mattress and the costumes in both closets. She figured Nelson was a serial kidnapper.

Regarding the other woman in the dome light, she wondered whether this brown-eyed woman had replaced her in Cage One after Nelson transferred Emily to Cage Two. Did he move Emily to make room for Brown Eyes? What happened to the victim who was in Cage Two before Emily? Perhaps the whole setup was a revolving door of one kidnap victim after another. If so, what happened to the victims who were rotated out?

The question had ominous implications.

Nelson opened the driver's door.

Emily struggled upright and gawked at the dashboard. The digital clock glowed *12:10* in green. Another victory: She knew the time for the first time in fifty-nine menstrual cycles.

TWENTY-THREE

Carlos McCrary

My cellphone jolted me from a sound sleep at 1:15 a.m. Fumbling the sheet back, I snatched my phone off the nightstand. Gunner's picture lit the screen. "What's up, Gunner?"

"Nelson left his house at 12:15 a.m. with his headlights off. Snoop called and I picked him up a block away. I've followed him for an hour."

"Why didn't you call earlier?"

"I waited to make sure he truly left town. He's on Highway 290 headed west, approaching Johnson City. If he U-turned, he'd need an hour to drive to his house and I could call to warn you. He's out of town, but there's a problem."

"What?"

"There's so little traffic this time of night I'm afraid he'll spot the tail. I dropped back a half-mile. If he takes a two-lane road, he'll spot me unless I drop back so far that I can't keep him in sight."

"Good job, Gunner. Too bad he parks his van in the garage. Otherwise, I would have stuck a GPS tracker on it. We play the hand we're dealt. Stay on him, but do *not* let him make you. If you must drop him, drop him. He's already suspicious and we can't let him know we're following. We need to find where he goes when he leaves home."

My heart rate climbed and the adrenaline flow swelled in my veins. *Showtime!*

———

I had studied Barbara Lofton's video from seventeen years before to prepare for this incursion. Her video had no images of the attic. I had memorized the house layout, but I hadn't determined the attic access. It was one of three places. Best case was a stairway hidden behind a door. Second best was a folding stairway that lowered from the ceiling. Worst case was an access panel in a closet ceiling.

If Nelson held prisoners in his attic, he went there regularly. The odds were good he had built a stairway.

Two days before, Nelson had gone grocery shopping. Gunner tailed him to insure he didn't return home unexpectedly. Snoop used that opportunity to case the house from the outside, including the backyard. Alarm sirens were mounted below the second-floor eaves on opposite sides of the house. Nelson had no outside security cameras, but every downstairs window was alarmed. I had noticed an alarm control panel beside Nelson's front door when I interviewed him.

The control panel was not on the video Nelson's ex-wife had sent me. He must have added the alarm system since the divorce. There would be another control panel in the rear beside the door from the kitchen to the garage.

Snoop had observed no alarm sensors on the second-floor windows, so I elected to breach on the second floor. Nelson's garage connected to the kitchen via a breezeway. An eight-foot wooden privacy fence stretched from the house to the garage, hiding the kitchen door and breezeway. Perfect to hustle a kidnapped teenager from the garage to the house with no witnesses.

The breezeway roof butted against the house below two windows on the second floor. I knew from Barbara Lofton's video that the windows opened into a game room. It had contained a new pool table, which she made a point to record from all sides while she said to the camera, "We bought this for $4,499." No telling what Nelson used the room for sixteen years later.

Nelson was insufficiently paranoid when he installed his alarms. He figured a burglar wouldn't have the balls to climb on his garage roof, or else he didn't think of it.

I saw a motion sensor in Nelson's living room when I drank that beer with him. I hoped he hadn't installed any on the second floor.

I muted my phone and lugged my duffel out the kitchen door. No point in waking anyone until I knew something definite. I snatched a folding ladder from my Jeep and glanced down the block. The nearest streetlights rose thirty yards one way and twenty yards the other. All I saw were dark houses and three cars sleeping in the driveways. All I heard were the breeze and the rustle of leaves.

Everything was a go.

Hooking the ladder over my shoulder, I gripped the duffel in my right hand and trotted across the street and up Nelson's driveway. My biggest fear was being spotted by someone walking a dog.

To prepare for the incursion, I had applied WD-40 liberally to the ladder hinges. The ladder unfolded without squeaking, but as I extended the steps, the latch pins snapped into place with a sound like an eight-year-old banging a stick on a trash can.

Maybe I was overly sensitive.

I hoisted the ladder to the roof edge and the thump against the gutter sounded like someone dropped a cymbal.

After I gained the roof, I boosted the ladder over the privacy fence and leaned it against the breezeway behind the house. No cop patrol on the street would see it slanting against Nelson's garage.

I held my breath and listened—ten seconds. All quiet.

The venetian blinds were closed on both windows. I removed the window screen and set it on the roof. It began to slide down the slope. I scooted it to the edge of the roof to rest against the rain gutter.

I clamped an eight-inch suction cup lifter to the pane and ran my glass cutter around it. A tap on the etched line and the cut piece came loose with a muted *tic*. I set the glass circle and suction cup on the roof against the gutter, beside the screen. Avoiding the razor-sharp cut, I felt inside and flipped open the window latch. The venetian blinds rustled at my touch.

Sliding the window open, I shoved the blinds away from the window and levered myself inside. I hauled my duffel in after me and eased the blinds back in place.

Ten seconds of listening, and I heard the susurrus of an empty house and the beat of my heart. I felt it in my soul: This B&E would not be a dud like Drucker's house.

Pulling a head strap mount for a light and GoPro camera from the duffel, I switched both on and aimed the light at the corners of the room. No motion detectors. I had caught a break.

The pool table sat in the same place. It had telltale streaks in the felt where the balls had been racked over the years. Carrie said Nelson had no visitors, and we hadn't observed any in the days we surveilled him. Whom did he play, if anyone? Solitaire pool?

I pivoted a slow 360 degrees. I would examine the video file later, at my leisure.

The central hall had a pull-down stairway hatch in the ceiling. The hole where the rope should hang was empty. The hatch was nailed shut.

Nelson had done that to prevent an escape from the attic. The blood coursed through my ears in a steady beat. Emily was so close, I could practically hear her voice. Where did Nelson hide the new entrance to the attic?

Quickly, I combed the second-floor rooms and closets. Nelson had converted a bedroom to a home gym with serious iron-pumping equipment that looked well-used. If he and I butted heads, I wouldn't underestimate him. I pushed on, hunting for the captive girls' personal effects. Nothing. Either Nelson hid his souvenirs on the first floor, or he kept them in another place, perhaps at the place Gunner was following him to.

I opened the closet in the middle bedroom on the second floor and discovered the new door hidden inside the closet. I tapped the door. It was solid oak, an exterior-grade door. A top-of-the-line deadbolt locked it. Nelson's do-it-yourself cell door.

Bingo! My hard work was about to pay off.

"Easy boy," I heard Grandpa say. "Don't skin the bear before it's been shot."

I regulated my breathing and my heart slowed and the adrenaline eased.

I banged on the door with the butt of my Glock. Three shorts, three longs, three shorts—*S-O-S*. I listened ten seconds. If Carrie or the new girl in the videos was there, she might hear me, even through soundproofing. Perhaps someone would shout or stomp on the floor.

I rapped again. Listened ten seconds. Nothing. I slipped the lockpick and tension wrench from my shirt pocket. Two minutes later I heard the last *click*, twisted the tension wrench, and opened the door.

Behind the door, a light switch was fastened to a stud on the right. I flipped on the stairway light. The open studs and raw wood revealed the innards of two closets that Nelson had cannibalized to conceal the staircase.

Mounting the steps three at a time, I rushed to the landing. Doors on either side teased me. Which one first?

I rapped an *S-O-S* on the right-hand door and pressed my ear to the oak. Nothing. I tried it again on the door on the left, then started work with the lockpick. In less than a minute, I slammed the door open.

"Emily, it's me, Chuck. I've come to take you home."

Harry Nelson

Nelson's gaze flitted to the rearview mirror. *That freakin' Jeep is still there, a quarter-mile back.* McCrary's crew thought they were so damned smart, following him to the grocery store and the volleyball game. They thought he didn't know they were there, but he had recognized them several days ago. He was too smart for McCrary.

He always parked in a busy public place to discourage attempts to attach a GPS tracker to his minivan, but McCrary's minions might get lucky. He couldn't afford that. Each time he returned to his garage, he examined underneath the van in case McCrary's team had succeeded in tagging him.

He wondered who was following him—Snopolski or the movie star.

Not McCrary. McCrary would break into his *home*, his *castle*. That bastard PI had the temerity to invade his privacy. Men had been killed for less.

It made no difference who followed him. He knew what to do. Plan B.

Nelson pushed down Loop 1 through downtown Austin, the cruise control set exactly on the speed limit. He couldn't afford a traffic stop. Not with two bound and gagged women in the back.

At 2:30 a.m. the traffic was sparse on the freeway. It was easy enough to spot the tail even with the bastard hanging well back; every other vehicle was passing him.

Nelson crossed the Barton Creek Greenbelt. He dropped into a lane that exited for U.S. Highway 290 west. The miles passed and other vehicles dropped off. It became easier to watch the tail.

He felt the rumble strip and jerked the wheel. A rush of adrenaline coursed through him as sweat popped out on his face. More sweat trickled down his ribs. He had eyeballed the rearview too long, drifted onto the shoulder, and nearly grazed a traffic sign.

Easy, easy. Keep it together. Follow Plan B.

He passed the exit to State Highway 71, which he normally took. No, stay on 290 until you lose the tail, he reminded himself.

Forty-five minutes later, he reached Johnson City and veered north on U.S. Highway 281 toward Marble Falls.

The only lights in the rearview mirror were from the vehicle tailing him. The lights dropped farther back as Nelson crossed the bridge over the Pedernales River, a mile north of Johnson City. He slowed to fifty-five. The tail dropped back so far it disappeared when he cruised over a small rise in the highway.

A mile farther he read the sign, Ranch Road 1323.

The tail lagged far behind him, the two headlights merging into a single point of light.

Nelson slipped into the left turn lane and slowed to a walking pace. He rolled onto Ranch Road 1323 West and paused on a paved turnaround area near the intersection. The headlights grew closer and became two again. Regardless of who it was, he had trapped the tail. The Jeep continued straight on Highway 281, and Nelson smiled to himself.

The Jeep disappeared over the next rise and Nelson powered west on

1323. His arms felt heavy. This indirect route took two hours longer than his regular route, but it was worth losing two hours' sleep to arrive unnoticed and untraceable.

Carlos McCrary

Calling Emily's name, I slammed the door open to reveal a space as dark as a cavern. My headlight beam lit the room I had seen on the DVD. The doors at the other end were closed. I couldn't tell which was the bathroom and which the closet. This might be the Clara room or the Gloria one.

It didn't matter anymore. The room was dark.

And empty.

Push on, I told myself. Emily is in the other room.

Wheeling about, I rushed to the other door. My heart climbed into my throat. I couldn't breathe.

I felt for the deadbolt with my lockpick. The lock should have surrendered. My fingers didn't cooperate.

Slow down, fellow, I told myself. You need a steady hand to pick a lock. Move too fast and you have to start over. Emily's there. She's behind that door. Take your time and spring her from this prison.

Click.

I shoved the door open. The second room loomed dark and empty. Like my heart.

Emily wasn't there either.

It was hard to stand, so I leaned on the wall. I felt for a light switch and with numb fingers I flipped on the light. At the far end, the right-hand door was open. That was the bathroom. This was—had been—Clara's room.

Pushing off the wall, I lurched to the center of the room.

Okay, fellow. You're a professional. Rule Seventeen: *Never get personally involved in a case.*

That would be laughable if this case weren't so serious. And so personal.

I knew with one hundred percent certainty that Nelson was *a* kidnapper. These two rooms and the videos proved that like a slam dunk.

But what about Emily?

I was ninety-nine percent certain that Nelson was *the* kidnapper—the one who abducted Emily. The good news was she had almost certainly been held in one of these rooms. Maybe she left a message. A sign. A clue.

The room contained the single bed from the videos. Outside the smartphone's field of vision sat a tattered easy chair and a college-dorm-sized combination mini-fridge and microwave. The mini-fridge contained food that had not spoiled and three frozen dinners in a tiny freezer compartment. Four bottles of water chilled inside. A dirty plate, fork, and knife sat on an old-fashioned TV tray from the 1950s. The tray seemed familiar. I nudged the leftover food. It was soft. If it had been abandoned more than a few hours, it would be dry and hard.

Whoever was captive here had left recently. Nelson took her when he rabbited. I was *that* close but I had missed them.

I had *missed* them. If I had listened to Grandpa and forced my way into Nelson's house, Emily would be free now as well as the other girl.

From what I observed, I figured Nelson had gone for good. Flamer had not discovered any other property where he could hold captives. If Gunner dropped the tail, we had nowhere to re-acquire Nelson.

I called Gunner.

"Stay on Nelson. I don't care if he spots you. He's onto us and he's done a bunk. I think the girls are with him. We can't afford to lose him."

"Too late, Chuck. I dropped off when he turned on Ranch Road 1323 fifteen minutes ago."

"Get back there. Find him."

My gut clenched like a fist. No, nothing I could do about that. Keep pushing.

I yanked the cushion off the easy chair. Nothing. I flipped the chair over and combed the underside. Nothing.

The cheap pressed-wood chest held women's white tee-shirts in sizes small and medium and women's white shorts in sizes 8, 10, and 12. No underwear and no personal items belonging to the captives.

Nelson had stripped his victims of clothes, jewelry, and phones. He must keep those tokens or souvenirs elsewhere in the house.

I examined the costumes in the closet. They were the ones in the videos. There were no notes in the pockets. I found one loose button in the gingham dress. The closet shelves were empty.

The bathroom cabinet had six used toothbrushes in the top drawer and two tubes of toothpaste still in the boxes.

The toothbrushes could contain DNA. I stuck them in an evidence bag. I didn't worry about chain of evidence. Nora Goodman would work with me unofficially after she saw my GoPro video. Or not. But I could analyze DNA with a private lab if I went it alone.

Feminine hygiene products of sundry types filled another drawer. A manicure set was in the last drawer. Extra toilet paper was under the lavatory.

The medicine cabinet held a tube of toothpaste and a half-bottle of mouthwash. I stuck the toothpaste and mouthwash in another evidence bag. There might be saliva residue on the bottleneck and fingerprints on the bottle and the toothpaste tube.

I stripped the bed. Nothing in the bedlinens. I flipped over the mattress. Nothing.

I rotated another slow 360. What had I missed?

The feeling that I'd overlooked a clue weighed heavily.

If Emily left a message, it would be somewhere Nelson couldn't see it. Otherwise, he would have erased it, painted over it, or otherwise obliterated it. If he had done that, I was screwed anyway, so I assumed she created a message that Nelson hadn't found, but someone like me could.

Where was the message?

Surveying the room again, I noticed a peephole in the door I had entered. I peered through it. The view was all wrong. Nelson had installed it backwards. He could stand outside and see a wide-angle view into the room.

That made sense. I hadn't seen chains or other restraints, and he had to ensure his captive didn't wait behind the door holding the TV tray like a club. He wouldn't open the door until he confirmed the girl was at the far side of the room.

Okay, how did Emily leave a message? She had nothing to write with. Toothpaste and mouthwash and food scraps wouldn't do.

My attention fixed on the TV tray and the knife and fork. A fork has sharp tines. Tines that could carve a message.

What could you carve with a fork? Drywall.

I scoured the room. The walls were unmarked.

My gaze fell on the open closet door.

I stepped into the closet and closed the door. It was pitch dark inside. I flipped my headlight on.

My heart leaped when I saw it.

Emily had carved her message in the drywall above the closet door: Emily Crazinski a/k/a Evita and her birthday and the date she disappeared.

Below her name was a single word—PERIODS, followed by forty-six tally marks.

Nelson held Emily captive in that room for forty-six menstrual cycles, say, four weeks each, three-and-a-half years, plus or minus.

To the right of Emily's message was another: Felicity Taylor a/k/a Gloria and two dates, one seventeen years ago, the other was October 23rd, one year ago. Twelve tally marks followed the dates. Felicity must have replaced Emily in the cell. She was the one who abandoned the dirty plate and leftover food.

I returned to the first room, and repeated the search with similar results. The captive or captives had no personal items.

Emily had left a message there too. She had carved her name and the phony name Nelson gave her and her birthday in the same spot above the closet door. This time PERIODS had thirteen tally marks, say one more year.

Why did Nelson relocate Emily and Felicity Taylor? Did he feel me closing in on him?

I hoped I would have the chance to ask him. Just the two of us. Alone.

I had proof Nelson kidnapped two women. Proof that wouldn't stand up in court unless the police found it in a lawful manner.

How could I get the cops to search Nelson's house legally without a warrant? I couldn't tell the cops about my illegal burglary.

The solution came to me.

My phone alarm warned me I had been in the house two hours.

I flipped off the lights and walked down the stairs. Moving to the main stairway, I knelt and peeked into the ground floor hall. As I expected, there were motion detectors.

I couldn't hit the first floor without triggering the alarm.

That was good. If I triggered Nelson's alarm system after I left, the system would call the cops and they could enter his house with no search warrant.

I climbed back to the first attic room and put back the toothbrushes, toothpaste, and mouthwash bottle. Let the cops find them.

But where had Nelson fled?

Harry Nelson

Nelson checked the rearview. Nothing behind, nothing ahead. Ranch Road 1323 stretched empty for miles.

He glanced back. Evita and Gloria were asleep.

Curving off the road, he stopped on the grass and popped the van's door. Groggy from sleep deprivation, he was still cocky enough to grin as he stood on the center stripe and relieved himself.

Piss on you too, McCrary.

Carlos McCrary

I retraced my steps to the game room, flicked off the headlight, and squeezed out the window. I stuck the cut-out glass circle in place with duct tape.

I wedged the window screen in its slot, boosted the ladder over to the driveway, and descended from the roof.

Pausing at the bottom, I listened. A car motored closer. I laid the ladder flat and stood in the shadows. I held my breath as the vehicle rolled down the street.

I had worn dark clothes and hidden in the shadows. I was okay. Still, it was butt-pucker time.

The car paused at Nelson's driveway. Country music drifted from its open windows. A newspaper sailed from the car's window and landed on the driveway. Another sailed from the opposite side onto Carrie and

Frank's front lawn. The car drove on. The country music faded in the distance.

I breathed again. My watch said *4:49*.

I folded the ladder, grasped my duffel, and sprinted down the driveway, across the street, and into the shadows behind my Jeep.

Snoop materialized at my elbow like a ghost.

"Well?"

"We struck gold. Emily had been there and another girl, but the bastard moved them in his van. Have you heard from Gunner?"

"He told me you called. He drove that country road thirty miles to the next highway. No sign of Nelson. Gunner is on his way back."

We had no clue where Nelson had gone with the women.

———

I approached Nelson's front door with my lockpick and torsion wrench. Thirty seconds with the lock and I felt the *click-click* as pins fell into place. After twisting the deadbolt open, I pressed the latch, and opened the door. The alarm's *beep-beep-beep* warning sounded from the control panel.

In forty-five seconds, all hell would break loose. The sirens would scream loud enough to wake the whole neighborhood. Sirens alone often scare off thieves before the police arrive.

Forty-five seconds passed and the sirens stayed silent.

Maybe they had a sixty-second delay, not forty-five.

Fifteen seconds passed.

Nothing.

The *beep-beep-beep* stopped. The alarm panel had reset.

Any second, the alarm company would call the phone number they had on file and ask Nelson his code word. Every alarm system I knew worked that way. Nelson wouldn't answer the phone, and they would call the cops. The cops would send a patrol car.

Simple.

I waited on the porch near the open front door and listened for Nelson's phone to ring inside.

Nothing.

If he told the alarm company he was leaving town, they could call the cops without the confirming telephone call.

I figured three minutes tops before the cops came.

Five minutes later, Snoop and I wondered where the cops were.

"Why didn't Nelson's alarm company call him?" I said.

"Did he let his contract lapse?"

"I'll call the emergency number."

"Travis Security Systems, what is your emergency?"

"This is Carlos McCrary. I'm Harry Nelson's neighbor. His front door is wide open and his alarm is beeping inside. I believe a burglar is in his house."

"What is the street address?"

I gave it to her.

"Mr. Nelson's contract with us expired last year. We no longer monitor his alarm system. I suggest you call 9-1-1." She disconnected.

I called 9-1-1.

"This is Carlos McCrary. I'm Harry Nelson's neighbor." I gave the dispatcher the address. "His front door is open, but he doesn't answer the doorbell. I'm afraid something bad happened like a heart attack or a stroke. Would you send a patrol car to see whether he's okay?"

In less than ten minutes, two uniformed patrol officers arrived in a black-and-white.

"You the guy called for the welfare check?"

I introduced myself and handed the older cop my business card.

"I'm working with Homicide Detective Nora Goodman on a serial murder and kidnapping case in which the man who owns this house is a person of interest. Harry Nelson might have taken his own life, or you may find kidnap or murder victims inside. Either way, I know Detective Goodman would appreciate you making a thorough search for Mr. Nelson. A *very* thorough search, wearing gloves so you don't taint any evidence that might be in plain sight."

Ten minutes later, they walked out. The younger cop stood in the door at parade rest, a sentry. The older cop walked over to me.

"We found a crime scene inside. I called the Crime Scene Unit. My partner and I will secure the scene until the techs arrive. You say the homeowner is Nora Goodman's POI?"

"Yes, sir."

"I'll call her."

I listened to his part of the conversation.

"Detective Goodman, this is Sergeant Will Chasen…Yeah, I know it's early…Thing is, we made a welfare check on a guy named Harry Nelson after a neighbor saw his front door open…Yeah, he wasn't inside, but we saw evidence in plain sight that he had held two people captive. The neighbor who saw the door open is a PI named Carlos McCrary…Yeah, he said he's working the Nelson case with you…You want to talk to him?"

He handed me his phone.

"Nora, the uniforms checking Nelson's welfare check saw evidence of kidnapping in plain sight. I saw Nelson last night, so he hasn't been gone long. You should visit the crime scene and issue a BOLO. Maybe we can catch him with the two girls."

"I was asleep. I'll need a half hour to get there. You sure a BOLO is justified?"

"Last I knew, Nelson was driving to the Hill Country with two girls captive in his red Honda Odyssey." I gave her the license number. "Issue an Amber Alert in Burnet, Blanco, and Llano Counties, as well as Travis and Williamson. Can you do that from home before you leave?"

"Can't do the Amber Alert; Emily is over seventeen."

"The other girl he kidnapped is Felicity Taylor. She is seventeen. She disappeared October 23rd last year. Find a missing person report on her. Use your resources, get her picture, include it and Emily's pictures in the Amber Alert. I'll alert the news media soon as we finish."

"Good. I'll issue the alert. Will you be at Nelson's in a half hour?"

"Yes. I'm staying at my aunt and uncle's house across the street. I need a shower and a pot of coffee, but I'll meet you at Nelson's in half an hour."

"Do you have Harry Nelson's picture?"

"No, but I know where to get one."

TWENTY-FOUR

The letdown after my invasion of Nelson's house left me with the shakes and drenched in sweat as my body purged the adrenaline from my bloodstream. My bones felt tired and sore as I trudged to the house.

Snoop walked with me. "You smell like a locker room after a football game, bud. Shower and change clothes while I make coffee. You gonna wake your aunt and uncle?"

"If I do, Carrie will talk my ear off and I won't get my shower. You wake them, but wait until I'm in the bathroom. Tell them everything we know."

———

Fifty minutes later, coffee in hand, Goodman, Snoop, and I convened our council of war around the dining room table. I ran clips from the GoPro video on my laptop and fast-forwarded through the insignificant segments. Carrie and Frank pulled up chairs behind us and watched over my shoulder.

I fast-forwarded to the scene where I found Emily's and Felicity's messages.

"Nora, what did you find on Felicity Taylor?"

"Junior at Llano High School. Played on the volleyball team. Disappeared two weeks after playing at Bonham High. I included her picture in the Amber Alert and distributed it to the news media. You mentioned over the phone that you could get a photo of Nelson."

I leaned toward my aunt and uncle.

"Carrie, can you and Frank ask your friends whether they have videos of Bonham High girls' sports games that might have a shot of the stands?"

"Sure," said Frank. "What do you have in mind?"

"Their videos might contain a shot of Harry Nelson in the stands. One of you take the videos to the Austin Police and watch with the cops to identify Nelson."

"I'll do that," Carrie said. "I'll make the calls in the kitchen so I won't disturb you."

"Thanks. Frank, go to Sunday school and church. Tell everyone: Emily is alive."

"I'll ask the preacher to announce it from the pulpit. We'll ask the whole church to pray for her and Felicity Taylor."

"That's good. Tell everyone to keep their eyes open for Harry Nelson and his red Honda Odyssey, in case he comes back to Austin."

"I'm sure they'll see the Amber Alert," Frank said.

"Some people block Amber Alerts or don't pay attention to them. Ask your whole church to post and repost on social media."

"Good idea," Goodman said. "Right now, Nelson could be a ghost. We don't have a picture to broadcast on the TV news. Carrie, after you collect the videos, bring them to the station and I'll watch them with you."

"I'll do that."

"Aunt Carrie, Nelson told me he attended neighborhood Christmas parties. While you collect videos, maybe a neighbor has a picture from their party with Nelson in it."

"I'll make those calls."

"Before you go," I said, "do you know how long Emily's period was?"

"Twenty-nine days."

"That means she'd been in that house since she disappeared. She and Felicity were above my head the whole time I interviewed Nelson. I could have walked upstairs and found that staircase anytime, and I didn't do it."

Carrie patted my hand. "There was no way you could know, Chuck. If you hadn't broken in tonight, we would *never* have known."

"But we lost him, and we lost the girls. *I* lost them."

I finished my millionth cup of coffee. Outside the sun rose and a fresh new Sunday commenced, full of promise. All over the world, people go to church to pray for salvation, solace, and succor. Emily didn't know it was Sunday, but I knew she was praying for salvation.

I hoped I hadn't blown my chance to rescue her and Felicity.

Harry Nelson

Nelson fought to stay awake. He curved onto a narrow eastbound road that had no center stripe. The rising sun assaulted his vision like a searchlight. He hoisted a hand to shield his vision and his minivan drifted into the other lane.

A westbound pickup honked and swerved into the ditch. The driver waved a fist through his open window and screamed a curse.

Nelson seized the wheel in a death grip and wrestled the Honda back into his own lane. The adrenaline rush banished the exhaustion for a minute.

He was glad the sun had risen. It was hard enough to find Plan B in the daylight; it would be next to impossible at night. He lowered the sun visor and sat straighter to elevate his eyes into the shade. That was better. He could see. No more close calls.

He drove east until he reached a deer fence and followed it for a half mile. Yes, he recognized it. Ahead, a gravel driveway jutted to a tall steel gate. Glancing in the rearview mirror, he slowed. He bumped off the road onto the driveway and coasted to the rusty gate.

Peeking over his shoulder, he observed Evita and Gloria in the back asleep. At least, they weren't moving.

He reached in his glove box for the remote and the gate swung open with a raspy groan.

Easing off the brake, Nelson rolled the van past the end of the gravel.

The driveway morphed into a rocky road bulldozed across the countryside. He paused to ensure the gate closed behind him, then fed the van enough gas to bump along the rock trail.

He shuddered from exhaustion. *It won't be long now*, he thought. The track snaked upslope through the sparse junipers, mesquite, and scrub oaks. The minivan bucked its way along the trail. The jostling made him need to urinate again.

I hope the girls haven't peed on my carpet.

———

Emily Crazinski

Emily spent the trip's first hour rolling around the back as she felt in the dark for a weapon, a tool, anything useful. The back was as barren as an empty box. *Someday Weirdo will slip up*, she thought, *but not yet.*

Then came the longest night of her life, bouncing, swaying, juddering over railroad tracks. Exhausted, she fell into a fitful sleep.

Sometime in the night, the highway noise changed and she awakened. The van changed direction and slowed.

Emily squirmed her fingers into position where she could tug the tape off the brown-eyed woman's mouth. Brown Eyes returned the favor and they leaned their heads together.

"My name is Emily Crazinski," she whispered. "I've been a prisoner for fifty-nine menstrual periods."

"I saw your message in the closet. That was a great idea. I never would have thought of it. I'm Felicity Taylor, captive for twelve periods. I carved a message too."

"How long is your period?"

"Thirty days, give or take."

"When were you kidnapped?"

"October 23rd."

Emily made a quick mental calculation.

"It's October again."

"Who cares what the date is?"

"It's good to know. Why is Nelson moving us?"

"Is that his name? He told me to call him Mister Blank."

"He tried that crap with me too, but I told him I'd call him Weirdo instead. His name is Harry Nelson, and he lives across the street from me. We've been caged in his attic, and we're not the first girls he's kept in those cages. Did he tell you why he's moving us?"

"He didn't say. What happened to the other girls?"

"Whatever happened to them, it can't be good. I hope we don't find out the hard way."

The van stopped. Emily heard the *tick-tick-tick* of the turn indicator. She felt a sharp curve and the tires crunched across gravel. Another stop and Emily heard the glove box open. Seconds later the minivan accelerated again.

The sun had risen. She wriggled to a sitting position and gyrated to where she faced front. The dashboard clock said *7:43*.

"Hey, Weirdo," Emily shouted. "We need to pee. It's been over eight hours since we used the bathroom. If you don't want us to pee on your carpet, find us a toilet. Fast."

Emily winked.

Felicity winked back.

Nelson twisted his head toward the rear.

"Clever of you to remove the tape. You can shout your heads off out here in the sticks. No one lives for miles around."

"We still need to pee, Weirdo."

"Hold it in a few more minutes, Evita. There's a creek the other side of this hill."

Emily leaned her lips to Felicity's ear. "He won't call me Emily, so I won't call him Mister Blank. Weirdo calls me Evita."

Felicity whispered back, "He calls me Gloria, but I just call him Mister Blank."

"Start calling him Weirdo. We've got to stick together. You've met the other one, the tall one, right? I call him Nutso. It drives him up the wall." She grinned. "He pretends it doesn't bother him, but I know better."

Emily memorized landmarks. She would need them to find her way out.

The van followed the track over the rise and dipped to the valley beyond. A shallow stream dribbled at the bottom, reduced to puddles and a trickle in the absence of recent rain. The rocky trail crossed the watercourse at a natural ford and tracked up the other side to disappear over the next hill. Emily scanned the creek banks. No sign of human habitation.

The van nosed to the rock-strewn creek bed and Nelson parked. He tapped an overhead button and the rear hatch beeped open. Leaving the driver door ajar, he walked to the creek, urinated, then moved to the rear of the Honda.

"One at a time. Who needs to go the most?"

Emily twisted to the open hatch.

"Felicity first. I can wait another minute, but don't waste time."

Nelson dragged Felicity to the rear bumper by her ankle. Cable ties tightened around each ankle and a third tie through the other two ties made links in a chain.

Nelson tugged until her feet hung over the bumper. He jammed the razor-sharp blade of a carton cutter under the center link and ripped upward. The tie flew out the rear hatch.

"Okay, Gloria. Go pee in the creek."

Felicity scooted from the van and screeched. "Damn, there's burrs in the weeds. I can't walk."

Emily hadn't considered their shoeless condition. If she got loose, she couldn't outrun Nelson. She would have to disable him. But how? The carton cutter could slit his throat with one swift motion, but could she force herself to kill him?

"Nothing I can do about the stickers," Nelson said. "Blame Mother Nature. Careful where you step."

Felicity turned her back.

"Cut my hands loose and I'll pick the stickers out."

Felicity's wrists were shackled like her ankles. Nelson cut the center tie and retracted the blade.

"Like I said, yell your head off if you want. There's not another human for miles."

Felicity perched on the bumper and plucked the stickers from her feet.

Nelson closed the hatch, seized her arm, and led her to the creek. She winced and groaned with each step.

Looking through the windshield, Emily studied every motion. If he didn't put the cutter back in his pocket, maybe she could snatch it when it was her turn to pee.

Nelson released Felicity's elbow and she waded up to her ankles. The creek bank was strewn with rocks.

Hmm.

If Emily grabbed a fist-sized rock while his attention was distracted, she could knock him unconscious. Maybe she couldn't slash his throat, but she could sure as hell give him a concussion.

Felicity dropped her shorts around her knees and squatted over the water.

When she was done, Nelson removed another cable tie from a pocket and bound her hands behind her.

He thumbed the remote and the rear hatch opened again. He stuffed Felicity into the back, found another cable tie, and shackled her ankles.

He reached for Emily's ankle. "You're next, Evita."

Emily scooted to the rear without assistance.

Nelson cut her ankles loose, and Emily stepped onto a bare spot on the ground. She presented her wrists to her captor.

She felt the quick pressure on her wrists and heard the blade *snick* through the cable tie. If she had shoes…She recalled Grandpa saying, "Almost don't fill a bowl. Focus on what you *have*, not what you *lack*."

What did she have? Rocks in the creek. Actually, *one* rock would do.

She picked her way through the weeds to the rocky path.

Nelson grasped her elbow as she walked. He held the closed cutter in his other hand.

She eyed the creek. A fist-sized rock lay beneath the surface, a suitable size for her small hand. It even had a prong on one end. "Focus on what you *have*," Grandpa said.

Nelson released her arm as she stepped into the water.

She felt his gaze focused on her ass. He was eyeballing her tookus, not the water. Nevertheless, she stutter-stepped to disturb the pool's surface.

Neither she nor Nelson could see the deadly rock on the bottom, but she knew it was there, waiting for her.

She stopped beside the rock and squared around to face him. "I can't pee if you watch, Weirdo. Turn your back."

Nelson laughed.

Emily glowered at him. "Turn around or I'll bite your damned dick off."

Emily held his gaze with a look that would ignite dead grass.

Nelson's face clouded. He rotated 180 degrees.

Emily reached to the bottom, felt the rock with her fingers, and waded toward Nelson. She gripped the rock so she could strike with the point and waded closer.

"I don't hear anything, Evita. Maybe you didn't need to go after all."

"It takes a while to get started. Don't turn around or I swear to God I'll bite your dick off.

Emily swung the rock with every shred of her strength. Nelson wheeled at that instant. The rock grated across his temple as she gouged a bloody trench across his forehead.

She hoisted the stone to strike again.

Nelson shrieked and ducked and jerked his hands to his head. The carton cutter flew into the creek.

Emily pounded the back of his left hand with the bloody point.

Nelson clenched her wrist in an iron fist and shook the bloody bludgeon loose.

She tried to knee him in the balls, but he jerked his hip and caught the blow on his thigh.

He punched her in the mouth with his other hand, the one she had smashed with the rock. He shrieked from the pain as he hit her.

She felt like an eighteen-wheeler had slammed her. Her face went numb. Her vision faded to red. The world wheeled around her. She fell to the rocky bank and lay still. Her bladder released.

Harry Nelson

Nelson waded into the creek and washed his head and his hand. His palms and the water were streaked blood red. He fingered the gouge across his forehead. Damn, it burned like fiery coals. Nelson needed stitches and he was miles from the nearest hospital. To top it off, he didn't dare leave the girls alone until he secured them in the house. That would take time he could not afford.

Evita lay on the stones, her legs in the water. She was breathing, but she wasn't going anywhere. Not for a while.

Nelson stumbled to the minivan and fell into the driver's seat. He twisted the rearview mirror to examine his forehead in the dome light. It looked even worse than it felt. He didn't have a first aid kit. Perhaps there was one in the house. He had no alternative but to push ahead.

Plan B.

He stared at Evita lying in front of the minivan. He ought to drive right across her. Crush her to a bloody pulp like she did his forehead and his hand. He should abandon her as fodder for coyotes and buzzards. She deserved that after the way she double-crossed him. The way she betrayed his trust.

But what would his friend say? She's not twenty-one yet. She's still ripe, not over-ripe. Not yet. Don't be premature. She's good for a few more weeks, until her expiration date. That's what his friend would say.

Besides, his friend had a thing for Evita. He had invested time—months even—teaching her what he liked. She was a seasoned performer for his friend.

He consulted his cellphone. One signal bar and that disappeared while he watched. *No service*, he thought. *That's the disadvantage of cellphones in the wilderness.*

As Nelson sat in the driver's seat, his forehead improved from a fiery coal to a needle-sharp stab. He ransacked the glove compartment and found a bottle of pain relievers. His left hand screamed in protest as he twisted off the cap. He snatched a bottle of water from the door pocket and twisted the top open with his teeth. He swallowed three.

He would survive. That's what Rangers did; they survived and triumphed. That freaking McCrary couldn't stop him. Snopolski couldn't stop him. The movie star couldn't stop him. And that little bitch who attacked him with a river rock surely couldn't stop him either.

He stumbled back to where Evita lay half in the water. He drew a deep breath. That felt better. Okay, he would save the bitch, no matter how badly she had treated him. He threw Evita over his shoulder and carried her to the van. Tossing her inside, he shackled her wrists and ankles.

He cranked the engine, slipped into low gear, and splashed across the creek, powering uphill and into the next valley.

The rocky trail dropped to a meadow of buffalo grass, wildflowers, live oaks, and cactus. Among the oaks, a large wooden ranch house sat nestled beside a creek.

Plan B.

Twin ruts sketched a primitive driveway across the buffalo grass and around the house to a weather-beaten barn in the rear.

Ten feet from the barn door, Nelson jerked the minivan to a stop.

He regarded his image in the mirror. It could have been a Halloween mask. The puffy wound flashed shades of red and yellow. Something blue bubbled inside the wound. Bloody trails marked his cheeks and traced the sides of his nose and the creases at the edge of his mouth. The bleeding had slowed to an ooze, but he had nothing to blot his face. There was a towel in the house.

Evita groaned. He supposed that was good. He had hit her harder than he intended, but it was instinct. He might have fractured her facial bones and jammed them into her sinuses. That would kill her as surely as a bullet to the brain, but not as fast. Instead, it appeared that a bloodied lip and ugly bruises were her only damage. They would heal.

Bruises always heal, he told himself. Even the bruises parents cause their children. It's just that some injuries take years to avenge. You wait until you're grown, then burn their house while they sleep. Why hadn't those bruises healed?

He popped the rear hatch and inspected the bindings on the girls. They were secure. Good.

He relocked the minivan and hobbled to the back porch. The key was hidden in its assigned place.

As he flipped on the lights in the kitchen, he thanked FDR for electrifying rural America in the 1930s. Opening the breaker box in the utility room off the kitchen, he flipped on the water heater and the well pump. The water heater hissed, and the pump wound up to speed outside.

He opened the kitchen faucets, and they sputtered rusty water then ran clean. He did the same for the lavatory and shower in the bathroom. He flushed the toilet.

The combination den/dining room was dusty but looked like he remembered. So did the living room on the other side of the stairway.

So far Plan B was working like a charm.

He climbed the creaky stairs to the second floor. He inspected the bedrooms, one in each corner of the house. The manacles in the two back bedrooms were coiled like sleeping snakes near the eyebolts cemented into the hearths. The two front bedrooms had the king-sized beds he and his friend had brought to the ranch years before. All was well.

He bled the air and rusty water from the bath fixtures upstairs before returning downstairs.

Rummaging through the kitchen drawers, he found scissors to cut the cable ties. He returned to the minivan and opened the rear hatch.

Evita's eyes fluttered, and she squealed when she saw his face.

"Hello, girly. Yes, you did that to me. Are you happy to face the result? I could have killed you, you know, but I let you live. Your punishment shall be no food for three days. Can you walk?"

Evita felt her swollen lip. She flexed her arms and legs.

"I think so."

He leaned inside and his wound burned like fire. He groaned while he clipped the cable tie between Emily's ankles.

"Okay. Let's go."

Nelson caught her elbow and led her up the back steps, through the kitchen, and upstairs to the left rear bedroom.

"This is your new home. Sit in that chair."

"Why?"

Nelson sighed.

"You're already going hungry for three days, Evita. Do you want an additional punishment?"

She peered around the room, then sat on the chair.

Nelson fastened the manacle to her ankle and cut her wrists free.

"That's a portable toilet. A case of water is on the shelves, along with food. I'm heading to an ER to get stitches. I expect to be back before dark. You'd better eat while you can. I'll remove the food when I return."

"What if you're killed in an automobile accident? We would starve to death."

"Why would I care? I'd be dead."

He left and locked the door behind him.

Nelson returned to the minivan and escorted Gloria to the right rear bedroom and locked her manacle. He showed her the portable toilet, the case of water, and a box of dried, non-perishable food.

"I need medical attention. I'll be back tonight."

"What if something happens to you while you're gone?"

"Then you'll die," he jeered. "You should pray for my safe return. Yeah, that's it. Pray for me." He laughed as he locked the door.

Nelson considered his shocking visage in the bathroom mirror and debated whether to wash off the dried blood. If he looked like an ax-murderer in a Grade B horror movie, he might see a doctor quicker. On the other hand, someone would remember an appearance like that. He imagined the nurse telling her boyfriend, "Boy, you should have seen the freak we treated in the ER today." He didn't want to be any more memorable than necessary.

Wetting a towel with warm water, he blotted his face as clean as he could. Contemplating his handiwork, he decided he looked pitiful enough to be served promptly, but not so bad he would be unforgettable.

He nodded to himself then regretted it; the wound throbbed like a mallet had smacked his forehead.

He switched off the downstairs lights, locked the kitchen door, and pocketed the key. Backing the minivan in an arc, he shifted into low gear, and jammed his way up the rocky trail.

His cellphone signaled a text. He must have driven close enough to the highway to receive a signal.

Braking at the low-water crossing, Nelson read the text.

There is an Amber Alert for you and Evita and

Gloria. They don't have your picture, but they have your vehicle and license plate.

Crap. He ought to hole up and heal, but his wounded forehead and hand demanded medical care. The bones in his hand might even be broken. He needed those stitches sooner rather than later and an X-ray to see if his hand was broken. It was no comfort to think that if the cops had his picture, no one would recognize him the way he looked. His red Honda Odyssey was another thing entirely. Belatedly, he wished he had bought a less conspicuous color.

Awkwardly using one hand, he plugged the charger into his phone and splashed across the creek.

He stopped at the steel gate and consulted his GPS. The nearest hospital was in Burnet, fifteen miles away, nineteen minutes. The Amber Alert was issued for Travis County for sure. But that freakin' McCrary or one of his minions followed him into Blanco County and watched him turn toward Gillespie County on Ranch Road 1323. He assumed they would issue the Amber Alert in Blanco and Gillespie Counties too. He had captured Gloria in Llano County, so they would include it.

Maybe they didn't issue the Amber Alert for Burnet County, but Burnet County adjoined Travis, Blanco, and Llano Counties. No, he couldn't chance someone spotting him. He would have to move farther away from Austin for treatment.

Twisting the mirror, he examined his wound. The edges oozed yellow pus. He felt nauseous contemplating it in the mirror.

He used his GPS to locate a hospital in Lampasas. There was one thirty miles away, thirty-six minutes via U.S. Highway 183. He'd never kidnapped a girl in Lampasas County. Maybe it was clear.

He told the GPS to guide him to the Lampasas Community Hospital.

Thumbing the remote to open the gate, he made a phone call.

TWENTY-FIVE

Emily Crazinski

After Nelson left, Emily stretched the manacle chain to its limit. She couldn't reach the bedroom door. Emily had hoped to talk to Felicity again. That was not going to happen.

That was okay. Nelson would be gone for hours. She had time. Her heart swelled at the possibility she could do something positive for the first time in nearly five years.

Okay, time to act on her main objective—escape. Her leg shackle was fastened to the long chain with a padlock. A second padlock secured the chain's other end to the eyebolt. She couldn't break the fetter with her own strength.

The weakest point was the eyebolt. She must break the eyebolt loose from the hearth. Easy to say, but everything is easy to say.

She knelt at the hearth and scrutinized the eyebolt.

Weirdo or maybe Nutso had drilled a hole into the stone hearth. Then he hammered a cylindrical metal anchor into the hole and screwed the eyebolt into the anchor. Friction held the eyebolt in the anchor, and friction kept the anchor in the stone.

Okay, simple enough. She either unscrewed the eyebolt or jerked the anchor loose from the hearth.

With pliers, she could stick the handle through the hole and use the pliers for leverage to unscrew the bolt. A screwdriver would work too. Grandpa Magnus always joked, "If we had some bread, we could have a ham sandwich, if we had some ham." Emily had neither pliers nor screwdriver.

The padlock had a two-inch shackle and a one-inch body. Three inches of leverage. Not as good as pliers, but it might be enough. Emily grasped the lock and twisted until her hands bruised. It felt like shoving against a parked bulldozer.

What other options did she have? If she couldn't unscrew it, she had to knock it loose.

With a hammer, she could bang the eyebolt on one side, then the other until the vibrations worked the bolt or the anchor loose. It didn't matter which one. But she had no hammer. Okay, what else could she use to hit the eyebolt?

Her gaze fell on the twin-sized bed.

She dragged the mattress onto the floor, then the box springs. Six wooden slats between the bedrails supported the box springs. Yes, the metal bedrails. She could attack the eyebolt with a metal rail. The rails were heavier than the 1 × 4 slats and harder to handle.

She would try a wooden slat first. It was lighter than the metal rail, but she could swing it faster. She had intended to use the wooden slat in Cage One to club Nelson. Why not use it as a hammer? She recalled from Mr. O'Doul's physics class that force equals mass times speed, or something like that. Talk about irony. Anyhow, she could swing the wood faster to compensate for its lighter weight.

Yes, that ought to work. It was worth a try.

She gripped the slat at the end and stood above the eyebolt like it was a golf ball on a tee. She swung the board hard as she could and missed.

Emily laughed. She missed the first time she'd swung at a golf ball when she was a kid too.

She swung again and smashed the eyebolt at right angles to its axis. The soft pine bounced off the bolt, an ugly notch gouged in its side.

Flipping the board over, she slammed the bolt from the opposite direction. First from the left, then from the right, she swung the board at the steel bolt until the blows shredded the end of the slat.

She reversed the board and swung the other end. Over and over until the sweat soaked her tee-shirt and her hair dripped on the floor.

She sat in a chair to catch her breath.

After her heart rate slowed to normal, she examined the eyebolt and anchor.

Was there any change? Had she made any progress on the anchor? If she had loosened the eyebolt in the anchor, she could use the padlock for leverage to unscrew the bolt.

Emily strained with the padlock again, pushing against the eyebolt.

It didn't work.

Tears dribbled down her cheeks in a stream of frustration. Her first chance to escape in like forever. The first time she had options, and it didn't work. *It didn't work!*

Grandpa Magnus's words came to her. "Nothing in the world takes the place of persistence. My mother, your great-grandmother, God rest her soul, always told me to keep on keeping on."

She could swing a bedrail.

Emily stepped to the bed. The bedrails were affixed to the headboard and footboard by slots at each end. She yanked the bedrail and it released from the footboard slot. It had been fastened by two hooked tabs clipped onto two rods embedded in the headboard.

Two hooked tabs. Hooks small enough to fit the hole in the eyebolt.

She unhooked the bedrail's other end and stuck the hook in the eyebolt. She jammed the bedrail against the bolt and rotated it a half turn. The bedrail hit the fireplace on the other side. She unhooked the rail, rotated it 180 degrees, and twisted the bolt again, over and over. Steady as the tides and relentless as gravity, Emily focused on unscrewing the eyebolt from the anchor.

In five minutes, it came loose.

She was free. She had been a captive, a prisoner, a slave, for more than four years. Now, she felt free.

"*Whoo.* Now *that's* what I'm talking about." She gave herself a mental high-five.

The twelve-foot chain remained fastened to her ankle. She draped the chain around her neck and across her left arm so she could walk without dragging it across the floor.

Emily twisted the door knob. Locked. Damn, she wasn't free quite yet.

———

Carrie Crazinski

Carrie hauled an old-fashioned address book from her kitchen drawer. She knew which neighbor would have Nelson's picture.

"Sherry, Carrie Crazinski. I have good news. Emily is alive...No, she's not home yet, but we know who kidnapped her. It was Harry Nelson...I know. I've known him for years and never suspected either...I need a favor. You snap pictures at your parties. Did you take photos of Harry at your Christmas party?

"We need a picture for the television people to show on the news. Do you have a picture of Harry you could email?

"You do? Great. Yes, send it now.

"Next favor, did your videos of Bonham volleyball games show Harry in the stands?

"Don't worry about it. Someone else will have a video. See you soon."

Carrie brewed a cup of tea while she waited for Sherry's email. Where was that stupid email? Didn't Sherry know time was precious? Finally...there.

She opened the attachment and zoomed the picture. Not great but it was the best she had so far. She cropped it so only Harry's face showed and forwarded it to Goodman's email and made more phone calls. Two more friends had videos of Bonham High girls' basketball games. She located two more photos of Harry and emailed them to Goodman. She arranged to collect two more sets of game videos from another mother and a father.

She ran the thumb drives to the Austin Police HQ and watched them with Detective Goodman.

Emily Crazinski

Emily considered the locked door knob. *Okay, another obstacle to overcome. One battle at a time.*

She walked to the window and gazed down. The drop from the second floor was too high to risk jumping barefoot. Besides, she wouldn't leave Felicity behind.

Okay, how do you break a sturdy, oak, six-panel door? The century-old wood would be hard as steel.

She dropped the chain to the floor and hefted the bedrail. Holding it like a battering ram, she lunged at the panel next to the doorknob.

Clunk.

Bouncing off the door, she tripped over the chain, dropped the bedrail, and skidded on her butt across the floor.

Yes! The door panel was cracked. *If I can crack it, I can break it,* she thought. *It's merely a matter of persistence.*

Levering herself to her feet, she retrieved the bedrail, and ran at the door again.

Clunk.

The crack grew bigger. *This is going to work.*

Another run and the bedrail crashed through the door panel.

Emily jerked the bedrail from side to side like a pry bar, back and forth, splitting the puncture wider. She reached through the hole and unlocked the door from the other side.

Yes, by God. I'm free.

She rearranged her chain so she could walk and limped to Felicity's door. Unlocking the door, she peered inside.

Felicity lay on her bed, her face in the pillow.

"Felicity, wake up. It's me, Emily. I'm free."

Felicity's head stirred.

"How did you get loose?"

"I'll show you. Let's get your mattress and box springs off."

Fifteen minutes later, Felicity draped her chain around her neck and over her arm like Emily.

"What now?" Felicity said.

"We run like hell."

Their chains clunking on the steps behind them, the two women limped down the stairs.

Felicity stopped in the kitchen and stared at her feet.

"We don't have shoes. The ground is covered in rocks, burrs, and cactus. We're barefoot, for God's sake. We can't walk away. The nearest town must be twenty miles."

Emily gripped Felicity's arm. "Do you like living like a caged animal and having freaks use you for a sex toy?"

Felicity lowered her gaze and shook her head. "Sorry."

"Then we walk out. A barefoot hike through the woods is better than being a slave to these vermin."

Emily released Felicity's arm. "Let's get the hell out of here."

Felicity pointed at the refrigerator. "We'd better take water."

Emily found grocery bags in the pantry and filled two bags with bottles of water. She handed a bag to Felicity.

"I need a weapon," Emily said, "in case Weirdo comes back before we get to the highway."

Emily opened kitchen drawers until she found a set of cooking knives.

"I'll take the French chef's knife. You need a knife too."

Felicity studied the selection. "I'll take a steak knife. It's easier to handle."

"Let's roll." Emily led the way out the kitchen door.

Emily knew they were in trouble when she took the second stride on the buffalo grass at the bottom of the kitchen steps.

"Ouch!" Her feet felt like she'd stepped on a bed of thumb tacks. Standing statue-still, she studied the rustic pasture around their feet. She had known the walk would be difficult, but she hadn't anticipated facing an obstacle course of burrs, thorns, and cactus.

The picturesque meadow stretched into the trees until it was lost from view in the vegetation. Analyzing the pastoral scene, the devil was in the details. Dried twigs and fallen branches as sharp as broken pottery littered the ground under each tree. Husks of dead cactus pods with two-inch needles lay partially hidden in the tall grass. Stickers and nettles sprinkled the sunlit spaces with tiny booby traps of shrapnel.

Even with the sun overhead, the cool breeze raised goosebumps on her arms and legs. The autumn night would be cold wearing only a tee-shirt and shorts. She retreated to sit on the steps and examined her feet. Her soles oozed droplets of blood. *Two freaking steps*, she thought. *I took two freaking steps, and my feet are ruined.*

Felicity remained on the porch.

"What can we do? We'll never make it across this minefield barefoot."

Emily extracted the stickers and thorns and wiped the blood spots off her soles.

"Maybe Weirdo or Nutso left extra shoes upstairs. And clothes—we need clothes too. It's cool right now; tonight will be colder. We need extra layers of clothes."

With her feet injured, Emily limped more climbing the stairs than she had descending them. Dragging the chain behind her as she mounted the steps, she felt like a zombie from a horror movie. She could hear Grandpa Magnus urging her onward. Keep on keeping on.

A chifforobe in the first bedroom held an assortment of men's clothing, including a man's coat and a pair of sneakers. "I wear a size ten," Emily said. "If I put on a couple pair of these socks, I should walk okay in these. Look for shoes in the other bedroom, and put on extra clothes to stay warm tonight."

Emily hobbled to the bathroom, sat on the edge of the tub, and washed the blood off her feet. Returning to the bedroom, she discovered a pair of khaki Bermuda shorts in a drawer.

"Felicity," she shouted toward the other bedroom, "look for some pants too."

She had to thread the entire chain and manacle through the leg to put them on, but she managed. By the time she had put on the sneakers, an extra man's shirt, and the coat, Felicity met her in the hall.

"These hiking boots I found are bigger than those sneakers. I wear a size eight shoe. I can't walk in them very well even with three pair of socks. Your size-ten feet would work better. Will you swap with me?"

"Sure."

Emily and Felicity finished dressing and caught a glimpse of themselves in a full-length mirror hung in the hall.

Emily wore a Bonham Bobcats baseball hat, an extra-large man's jacket that hung to her thighs, Bermuda shorts that hung to her calves, and size thirteen hiking boots. She had knotted a man's belt around her waist and shoved the French chef's knife in it, leaving both hands free.

Felicity wore a Stetson, a plaid flannel man's shirt, a pair of blue jeans with the pants cuffed up several times, and bright orange sneakers.

The girls stared at each other and laughed.

"Aren't we a sight?" Emily said. She wrapped the chain around her shoulders like a stole and posed like a fashion model. She made a funny face at Felicity.

"Too bad we can't take a selfie."

"Hey, Tyra Banks," Felicity answered, "*America's Next Top Model* is right here."

They guffawed until the tears flowed.

"Sorry I didn't think about the belt," Felicity said. "I saw one in the other bedroom. I'll do that too. I'll meet you downstairs."

"Before we go down, fill your pockets with trail mix and snacks from our rooms. We don't know how long it will be before we can eat again."

———

Harry Nelson

Nelson coasted into the drive-in lane. He hadn't eaten in sixteen hours. The blood loss didn't help either.

"I'll have a Big Mac, large fries with extra catsup, and a large chocolate shake."

"That'll be $9.24. Please drive to the window."

He flopped the sun visor across the driver's window so he couldn't see the cashier's face and the cashier couldn't see his.

Parking under a tree at the rear of the lot, he gobbled the food clumsily with one hand, dribbling sauce on his shirt. McDonald's Wi-Fi gave him internet access to get his story details straight. He gulped four painkillers, then headed to the hospital.

The red pylon for the emergency room towered next to the curb on Highway 183. The ER parking lot was too visible from the highway in case the Amber Alert had included Lampasas. He glided to the back lot and sandwiched his Odyssey between a pickup truck and a white minivan in the third row.

He hobbled around the building to the ER entrance. The glass doors sucked open as he approached. A gray-haired black nurse sat behind the reception counter at a computer station. Her nametag read Lakeshia Alexander, RN.

"Nurse Alexander? Can you help me?"

Lakeshia Alexander saw his forehead and gave him a concerned expression.

"Of course, we will. What's your name?"

"Harrison Arthur. I live in Tamasa."

"Where?"

"Tamasa. It's a small town northwest of here. I was hiking near the Colorado Bend and I tripped and hit my head on the rocks. I may have broken my hand too. It hurts awful bad."

The nurse tapped on the keyboard.

"May I see your driver's license, Mr. Arthur?"

Nelson felt his back pocket.

"Oh crap. I lost my wallet in the creek. My insurance card was in it too. Oh Christ, I hurt. Can you treat me anyway?"

"Of course, Mr. Arthur. What's your address?"

"421 Fifth Street in Tamasa. I moved here a month ago from Montana."

Alexander tapped the keyboard again.

"What's your phone number?"

Should he make up a number or give his real one? His number wasn't listed, but the cops get the newest technology to find people. He couldn't claim his phone had fallen in the creek because it was clipped on his belt in plain sight. He should have stashed it in the car with his wallet. Too late. Water under the bridge.

He recited his phone number and she tapped it into the computer.

"What's your date of birth?"

He rattled off the lie that cut ten years off his age. He was so used to the lie, he didn't think to invent a birthday.

Nurse Alexander gestured to the waiting area.

"Have a seat. If you need to use the restroom, take your phone and we'll call when the doctor can see you. It'll be real soon. There's not much wait on Sunday morning." She smiled. "We already finished treating the Saturday night bar fights." She winked.

Nelson sat far from the three other people in the lobby. He didn't talk to anyone and he didn't want anyone to remember him.

Five minutes later, an orderly rolled a wheelchair over.

"Harrison Arthur?"

He stood. "Yes."

After asking his birth date, the orderly wheeled him to the treatment area.

In ten minutes, a doctor examined him.

"I don't believe you have a concussion, but I ordered a CT scan to be safe. We'll also get an X-ray of your hand."

"Can you stitch my wound first?"

"I'll do that now."

She gave him a local anesthetic, cleaned the wound, and stitched it. After applying an antiseptic, she bandaged it.

"Will you have someone to change the bandage?"

"No. I live alone."

"It helps that you can see the wound in the mirror. We'll send you home with extra bandages. Take it easy the next three or four days and you'll be fine. In a couple of months, come back and one of our plastic surgeons will tidy up your scar."

The same orderly arrived with a wheelchair.

"I'll escort you to the CT scan and X-ray. Date of birth?"

"You asked me that twenty minutes ago."

The orderly shrugged. "Hospital policy. We ask all patients their date of birth every time we do anything. That ensures we treat the right patient. It's for your protection."

An hour later, Nelson was discharged. He tottered to the Odyssey. The other minivan still sat beside his, but a sedan had replaced the pickup.

His hand wasn't broken, just badly bruised. He flexed his fingers. They felt funny with the compression bandage around his palm.

His stomach growled. The Big Mac, fries, and shake were long digested. The clock on the dashboard said *2:30*. Maybe he could find a barbecue place before he left town.

His phone signaled another text:

They have your picture. You are on all TV stations. Even the cable news. They broadcast a picture of your Honda.

Damn. Time to change plans, he thought. *Plan C?*

He slapped the Honda in gear and set off for the ranch house. He would make do with the food at the ranch.

Nelson held his breath as a car slipped in behind him on the street. His fire-engine red Odyssey was a red cape waving at a bull. He needed an alternate route to the ranch, a road that avoided Highway 183.

Most restaurants had Wi-Fi. He spotted one and parked in back under a giant oak. He booted his tablet, signed on to the open network, and accessed a map website for an alternate route.

He picked a two-lane county road headed in the ranch's direction. He scrolled the satellite image to the county line. There it was. The Lampasas County road crossed the Burnet County line and changed numbers, still heading toward the ranch.

When he input the address into the GPS, it kept rerouting him to a major highway. He spent another five minutes copying the directions onto a notepad.

Switching the GPS to map mode, he rolled from the parking lot. He saw Lampasas in his rearview mirror and breathed easier.

It had taken him forty minutes to drive to Lampasas Community Hospital. He needed two hours to drive the county roads back to the ranch.

He didn't rest easy until he passed the steel gate and bounced far enough along the trail to be out of sight from the road.

He drew a deep breath. Not being able to drive the Honda made him a virtual prisoner at the ranch. He couldn't drive to a grocery store or an ATM. If his wound became infected, he couldn't visit a doctor. No matter, that's what friends are for.

He had a friend…a *good* friend…a *close* friend…

———

Emily Crazinski

Emily felt a small thrill noting the time on the battery-powered clock in the den. It said *12:30.* Knowing the time was a novelty after almost five years with no calendar and no clocks.

Weren't they a sight? Two young women dressed in mismatched men's castoffs, carrying plastic grocery bags in each hand filled with water and snacks, and with knives stuck in their cinched-up belts like Peter Pan's lost boys out to attack Captain Hook's pirates. Oh, and don't forget the twelve-foot chains draped around their necks.

Standing on the front porch, Emily asked, "Which way? I was unconscious the last part of our drive here."

"I was lying on the floor in the back. I didn't see anything," Felicity answered. "Sorry."

Emily peered at the angle of the sun's shadow. "That way is north. This rocky track is probably what we drove in on. Let's follow it. It's got to reach a road."

"Unless we take it the wrong direction and wind up at a dead end in the woods."

Emily frowned. She would have put her hands on her hips if they weren't occupied holding her rations.

"If you have a better idea, let's hear it."

"Sorry."

Felicity seemed to be sorry for a lot of things. Emily hoped she could count on her in a pinch. She was only seventeen. *Merely a child*, Emily thought and smiled. *I must be the leader.*

They scrambled along the rocky trace, snaking their way up and down two ranges of hills, stopping whenever they needed to catch their breath. The snacks in their pockets were depleted. They still had some in the plastic bags.

From the angle of the sun, Emily guessed they had been underway for three hours when they came to a boulder ideal for sitting. "Let's take a break and have a snack. One bottle of water and one snack. We should ration because we don't know how far we have to go to find civilization."

"Okay." Felicity opened a package of peanut butter crackers to go with her water.

"We're out of shape," Emily said. "Not much exercise in those prison cages."

"Sex and the occasional dance performance. That won't keep anyone in shape."

Emily twisted the cap off a water bottle and opened a bag of trail mix. "I was in good shape when I played basketball at James Bonham High School about a million years ago." She drank half the bottle at one *glug*.

"I played volleyball for Llano High. We had a match with Bonham a couple of weeks before I was captured. We won three sets to one. Sorry."

"Our basketball team was always better than our volleyball team. Hey, it's only a game."

Emily gave Felicity a high five.

They finished their break and trudged up the rocky path. The clouds thickened and the breeze became chilly. They crested a hill and Emily paused to survey the land ahead of them. "There's a creek down there. That could be the one we stopped to pee in. What do you think?"

"I wasn't paying attention at the time. I'm sorry"

I wish you'd stop being so sorry all the time, Emily thought.

"It's not important. Let's roll. Time's a-wastin'. It'll be dark in two hours."

A few minutes later, Emily paused again. "Yeah, this is where I hit Weirdo Nelson with the rock. See? That's the rock I hit him with."

"How do we cross the creek?"

"On those stepping stones over there." Emily pointed, then led the way. *Can't you figure out anything by yourself?* But she was only a child.

By now they were each down to one plastic bag that held the remaining water and snacks.

"I'm getting tired," Felicity said. "Let's stop and rest."

"Can't stop now. We're nearly there.'

They struggled up the next hill.

"I think this is the last hill before the highway," Emily said.

"You mean we're close to the road?"

"Yeah. Once we're there, we can flag down a car and get help."

They trudged upward with renewed vigor.

"Hallelujah," said Emily when they reached the hilltop. "That's the highway in the distance. I can just make out the gate we came in."

They picked their way down the hill, stumbling on the rocks. At the bottom the trail smoothed, and they walked easier toward the gate.

"I'm worried," Felicity said. "The whole time we've been coming down that hill, not a single car has come down that road. What if we get there and no one comes along?"

"Then we turn westward and walk toward the setting sun until it gets dark. We stop for the night and continue in the morning. Whatever we do, we don't give up. Never give up, never give in. *Never.*"

Wow, Emily thought, *where did all that emotion come from?*

Thirty yards from the gate, Felicity paused. "I hear a car coming. Quick, we have to get over that fence and flag them down before we miss them." She dropped her plastic bag and trotted across the prairie.

Emily dropped her bag and followed, glad that Felicity was showing initiative.

They jolted to a stop at the gate as the vehicle roared into view.

"Quick. Over the gate. Hurry!" Emily shouted.

They clambered over the gate as a white Chevy Suburban pushed closer, the hum of its engine growing louder.

Emily yanked off her hat, jumped up and down, and waved at the Suburban. Felicity waved her Stetson and shouted, "Stop. Help us."

The engine quieted as the Suburban slowed.

"It's going to stop," Emily said. "We made it."

"Thank God," Felicity said.

They stepped into the road, big grins on their faces, as the Suburban coasted to a halt a few yards away.

The SUV clicked into park and the driver's door opened.

Emily rushed toward the driver then pulled up as the man exited the vehicle.

"Well, well, if it isn't Evita and Gloria. What are you two girls doing so far from home? And you're not wearing your tee-shirts and shorts either."

Emily slid the French chef's knife from her belt and brandished it.

"Leave us alone, Nutso. Turn that car around and drive away. I'll kill you if you come any closer. We're never going back. Never."

The driver pulled a revolver from his coat pocket and leveled it on Emily's heart.

"Evita, didn't anybody ever tell you not to take a knife to a gunfight?"

TWENTY-SIX

Nora Goodman

D etective Goodman inserted the first thumb drive into her computer and copied it to the central network file for the Emily Crazinski case. She handed the drive to Carrie Crazinski. "You can have this back. Pull your chair over. Watch my monitor while I copy the other two drives."

Goodman copied the other two and returned them to Carrie. She played the video. "Give me commentary about what we're seeing."

The detective played the video at double speed through the warm-ups and the first part of the game. During a timeout, the camera panned to a shot of the stands. Goodman rewound and played it regular speed. "Let me know when you spot Nelson."

"There's Sherry Martinez and Ted. That's Jake Klinefelter. He's Tosca's father. Never misses a game. That's Kenny Hoar. He's the one who got Sandy Lynch pregnant while he was dating Emily."

Carrie made a face. "He made Sandy get an abortion. I don't know what the world is coming to with all this promiscuous sex and abortions."

Goodman realized she had told Carrie to make commentary. Now she regretted it.

"There's Barb and Jim Narita," Carrie continued. "Their daughter,

Kiko, plays middle blocker. She received a scholarship to the University of Houston."

"Carrie, you don't have to name everyone in the stands. I'm interested in Nelson."

"Okay. I'll shut up."

They watched awhile, then Goodman sped up the video. She rewound when a new audience image filled the screen.

Carrie pointed at the screen. "There's Harry. Pause that. That's him behind the visitors' bench." She huffed. "That's odd."

"What's odd?"

"Well, first that Harry is sitting behind the visiting team's bench, but also that he's sitting with Jerry O'Doul and Desmond Drucker."

"Why is that odd?"

"Jerry O'Doul and his mother Jerusha attend our church. When was this video made?"

Goodman tapped her keyboard. "Three years ago."

"That explains it. Jerusha is wheelchair-bound. Jerry cares for her 24/7 except when he brings Jerusha to church on Sunday. He quit teaching at the high school three years ago to care for her fulltime, the poor woman. This game must have been played about the time he quit teaching school. I still don't see why he and Harry and Drucker are sitting behind the visitors' bench."

Goodman played the next video. "This game was played last year." She paused the video. "Is that Jerry O'Doul and Desmond Drucker sitting with Harry Nelson again?"

Carrie frowned. "You say this was last year?"

"Yes, it was. Carrie, if this video was made after O'Doul quit teaching to care for his mother 24/7, who's tending to her while he's at the basketball game?"

Carrie grimaced. "I don't understand this. Jerry is a fine Christian gentleman. He teaches my husband Frank's Sunday School class. It's not like Jerry to neglect Jerusha."

Lakeshia Alexander

Lakeshia Alexander brewed a pot of tea before cooking dinner. Her husband Morris was watching football on television. "Morris, how much time left in the game?"

"About a minute. Start dinner anytime, sweet cheeks."

"I'm in the mood for pizza."

"Okay by me."

"When the game's over, I want to watch my news." Lakeshia had set their DVR to record the local news at five o'clock and the national news at five-thirty every day.

She phoned in a pizza order to be delivered and relaxed in her favorite chair in the den. Minutes later, Morris picked up a book and handed his wife the remote. "Game's over, sweet cheeks."

She played the local news while he read his book.

"The Austin Police Department is asking for the public's help to locate a missing teenager and a young woman.

"The teenager is Felicity Taylor, age seventeen, last seen October 23 of last year in Llano, Texas. The young woman is Emily Crazinski, age twenty, last seen over four years ago in Austin, Texas.

"Both young women are alleged to have been kidnapped by Harry Nelson, age forty-four, of Austin, Texas. Nelson is a person of interest in two other kidnappings and two murders. If you see Harry Nelson, do not try to apprehend him. He is armed and dangerous.

"Both women were seen with Nelson last night in Nelson's red Honda Odyssey in Blanco or Gillespie County."

A stock picture of a red Honda Odyssey and a graphic of a Texas license plate flashed on the screen.

"An Amber Alert has been issued for Felicity Taylor. Austin police believe that Nelson has the two women with him somewhere in Central Texas.

"Felicity Taylor is five-feet-eight-inches tall with black hair and brown eyes. Emily Crazinski is five-feet-nine-inches with blonde hair and blue eyes.

"Anyone with information about any of these three people is asked to contact the Austin Police Department at the number on your screen."

All three faces displayed on the TV screen. Lakeshia yelped and paused the program. "Morris, that man, the kidnapper, he came to my Emergency Department today."

Morris looked up from the book. "That guy? Harry Nelson?"

"Yes, but he said his name was Harrison Arthur. He claimed he lived in Tamasa, but he mispronounced it. I remember thinking that was strange—him living there and not knowing how to pronounce the name of his town." She pointed at the television. "It's him. I remember his cleft chin."

"Don't just sit there, sweet cheeks, call the Austin police. Their number is on the screen."

Carlos McCrary

Detective Nora Goodman's name and number displayed on my phone.

"This is Chuck."

"We got a hit on the television news stories. Someone spotted Nelson in Lampasas around noon today."

"How reliable is the report?"

"An ER nurse at Lampasas Community Hospital admitted him to their emergency department for a wound to his forehead. I talked to her. She's dead certain it was him. Recognized his cleft chin. I'm on my way to Lampasas. Want to come?"

"We'll need two vehicles. I'll meet you there. In fact, I'll bring Snoop and Gunner."

————

Snoop and Gunner came in one Jeep. I drove the other in case we split up. We wheeled into the hospital visitors' lot and met at the reception desk.

An orderly led Snoop, Gunner, and me to the hospital's security office.

When we arrived, Detective Goodman was at the video monitors with a man in casual clothes and a woman in a pants suit.

Goodman gestured us over.

"Chuck McCrary, this is the hospital administrator Rhonda Rollins and Lampasas Police Sergeant Horace Wilcox."

Rollins seemed close to retirement age.

"I came from home," she said, "after Sergeant Wilcox called."

We did introductions all around.

Wilcox was a bald, middle-aged black man wearing a plaid shirt and dark gray slacks. "Detective Goodman called me from Austin and I did preliminary work while she drove up. She filled me in on you and your colleagues. Y'all look over our shoulders."

Wilcox squared around to the monitors. "This is our first picture of Nelson at the hospital. This image is the back lot. Notice the time stamp at 12:02 p.m. when he exits the red Honda Odyssey."

Wilcox paused the image and zoomed in. "That's the license plate from the Amber Alert. The birthday he gave the hospital also agrees with the Texas driver's license for Harry Nelson. He didn't park in the spots reserved for the ER."

"Those spots are visible from Highway 183," Goodman said. "He was hiding from the Amber Alert."

"That makes sense," Wilcox said. "Even in the back he didn't take the closest spot. He parked between two other vehicles to make his Honda less noticeable."

Wilcox switched to a different view. "Here he walks into the ER at 12:06." He flicked to a different image. "That's Nurse Alexander. She logged Nelson into the hospital's system at 12:09. She recognized him on the news when she arrived home after her shift."

"Lakeshia Alexander registered the man as Harrison Arthur, 421 Fifth Street in Tamasa," said Rollins. "That's a small town a little north of here. It doesn't have a hospital."

"Harry Nelson was born Harrison Arthur Nielson. Did you research the address in Tamasa?" I asked.

"It was a vacant lot," Goodman said.

"Did Nurse Alexander get his phone number?"

"Good point," Rollins said. "I'll check." She transferred to a computer at the next desk and worked the keyboard. "It's an Austin area code." She recited the number.

I wrote it down. "Nora, if that's a real number and we call it, Nelson will spot the caller ID and know we have his number. He'll dump the phone or yank the battery. If he doesn't know we have the number, maybe we can track it. You can ping the phone. Maybe Nelson slipped up and gave us his real cell number."

"I can ping his phone at the police station," Wilcox said as he swiveled to face us. "We'll go there after we finish here. The doctor told me he made seventeen stitches to close a bad laceration on Nelson's forehead. Nelson claimed he was hiking near the Colorado River and slipped crossing a creek and hit his head on a rock. Doc said his wound is consistent with his story. He also suffered a badly bruised left hand."

He referred to the security monitors. "Here's another shot after they treated him." An orderly wheeled Nelson toward the camera. A large bandage covered his forehead, and his left hand was swathed in a compression bandage. Wilcox played a different monitor. "This is Nelson leaving at 2:25."

He swung back toward me. "That's all the useful video at the hospital. We traced him on traffic cams. He drove into town on Highway 183 from the south and left the same way. Anything else you folks need to ask Ms. Rollins before we go to the station?"

"I think we're good," Goodman said. "Ms. Rollins, thanks for your help, and please tell Nurse Alexander again how much we appreciate her call."

I tossed Snoop the keyfob to my Jeep. "I'll ride with Sergeant Wilcox." Snoop, Gunner, and Goodman followed Wilcox's unmarked car while he drove us to the police station.

My phone rang and displayed Carrie's picture. I sent it to voice mail. I didn't have time for a half hour of jibber-jabber.

"Sergeant, can you get a warrant this time of night to ping Nelson's phone?"

"I'll call Justice of the Peace Tomás Avila at home. I've known Tommy all my life. When I tell him why we want this Nelson feller, he'll come to the station or we can go to his home."

He gazed at the clock on the dashboard. "Tommy's kind of an early-to-bed, early-to-rise sort of fellow. He won't be too fond of us calling after ten o'clock at night, but he'll do it."

Wilcox called the JP and explained what he wanted and why. They were still talking as we arrived at the police station. Wilcox parked, but made no move to exit the car.

"You sure that's okay, Tommy? You're the man. Okay, I'll see you tomorrow." He disconnected, snatched a Stetson hat from the seat beside him, and popped the police cruiser's door.

"Tommy's already in bed. He gave a verbal okay and said to go ahead. I'll visit his office tomorrow and we'll do the paperwork."

"Is that legal?"

Wilcox grinned. "It's legal if Tommy and I say it's legal."

He hopped from the cruiser and jammed on his cowboy hat.

"Yippee-ki-yay, cowboy. Let's catch a bad guy."

In the station, Wilcox led us to his dispatcher who was seated at a desk by the police radio. "This is Helen Corcoran. She'll ping Nelson's number."

Goodman recited the number.

Corcoran tapped her keyboard.

"First thing I can tell you," she said, "is it's a real number. I'll track it the last twenty-four hours."

She called up a cellphone tower map on the monitor.

"This guy has traveled all over the place. You want me to print the *wheres and whens*, Sergeant?"

"Yes, please, Helen."

In two minutes, she handed us a list with each tower's location and the times Nelson's phone pinged it.

Wilcox led us to a Central Texas wall map in the bullpen. Using an erasable marker, he drew an X on the map for each cell tower Nelson's phone pinged.

"That feller drove the long way 'round from Austin, didn't he?"

"I can explain that," Gunner said. "I tailed him from Austin last night, but we didn't know that he had the girls in his car, and we didn't know he knew about the tail. He took that roundabout route to shake the tail."

Gunner tapped the map.

"Here, north of Johnson City, past the Pedernales River. That's where I lost him. He pinged this tower near Round Mountain after he turned west on Ranch Road 1323 and I dropped the tail. We were afraid he would learn we were on to him. Nelson stayed on 1323 until he dropped off the cell grid here, then he drove through the back country to Texas Highway 71. That's where the Horseshoe Bay tower picked him up again. He stayed on the main highways and reached Bertram at 5:51 a.m."

Gunner considered the wall map. He consulted the printout. "Nelson dropped off the grid again at 6:00 a.m. after he left Bertram. He didn't come back on until 9:58 a.m. at Briggs when he hit Highway 183. He stayed on the grid until he left it at Briggs again at 3:30 this afternoon."

I stuck two red post-it dots on the map. "That's four hours off the grid. That's when he dumped the girls. We'll find the girls in the boondocks somewhere between Bertram and Briggs."

Goodman stared at the map. "That's hundreds of square miles of back country. If we can't track his phone's GPS, we're out of luck."

"We're due for a little luck, Nora," I said.

"Helen, will you please access the phone's GPS and call log?"

"You'll man the dispatch desk?"

Wilcox made an elaborate bow. "Be my pleasure."

Corcoran walked into another room and closed the door. Wilcox replaced her at the radio. "We bought this super-special equipment to track the GPS on cellphones, but our contract with the manufacturer includes a confidentiality clause. We keep the hardware out of sight. It doesn't take long. You folks want coffee?"

Aunt Carrie called again. Answering the phone would require an hour-long conversation on what I had been doing. I sent it to voicemail.

"If this works, we're in for another long night," I said. "Better make it strong."

By the time the coffee brewed, Corcoran exited the other room wearing a grin big as Texas. "We got the SOB."

She handed Wilcox a sheet of paper. "These are his last GPS

coordinates before the phone went off the grid again. Nelson made one phone call at 9:59 this morning. I wrote the number on there. It's the 512 area code. That's Austin."

"Who does the number belong to?" Wilcox asked.

Corcoran frowned. "It's a burner. No GPS. It received the call from Nelson at 9:59 in north Austin, then was powered off. It's been dark ever since."

Wilcox carried the paper to the wall map. He consulted the paper and followed the latitude and longitude markers on the map to where they crossed north of Bertram. He marked another X on the spot and circled it.

"Nora, you should fill to-go cups for you and your teammates." He handed the GPS coordinates and 512 phone number to Goodman.

Goodman turned to Snoop, Gunner, and me. "You fellows ready to help me catch the bad guy?"

I grinned. "Yippee-ki-yay."

———

I rode with Goodman.

Aunt Carrie called again. This time I replied with a text.

Cannot talk until tomorrow. We are on Nelson's trail. Timing is crucial. Say a prayer and go to bed. I'll call tomorrow. Love, Chuck.

"Is that your Aunt Carrie who keeps calling?"

"Yeah. She's the master of fiddle-faddle. Ask a five-cent question and she'll give you a five-dollar speech. I love her like crazy, but…" I waggled my hand.

"I have an uncle like that, especially when he's had a few beers."

We drove in silence for a while. Snoop and Gunner followed in the Jeeps, our small convoy advancing to the battle.

Gunner and I rode to battle in a Hummer convoy in Afghanistan a decade before and half a world away. Now we rode to battle again, this time in Jeep Cherokees.

Our destination was a point on the earth's surface denoted by latitude and longitude coordinates, not a street address. The GPS would lead us to the nearest point on the roads in its database and then instruct us to "Navigate off road." Goodman's GPS led us to a narrow country road with no center stripe. The screen displayed the destination far off the road in a blank area. If there was a road to it, it wasn't on the map.

"I'll keep rolling until we reach a right angle to the target," Goodman said. "That gets us the closest we can from this road."

"Every house has a private road to it, even if the GPS doesn't know it. There's a deer fence. Let's follow it awhile."

Goodman let the car idle to walking speed.

"This is as close as we get, Chuck. We'll climb the fence and continue on foot." She braked to a stop.

"We haven't passed a gate in this deer fence," I said. "Keep rolling. There must be a gate. Watch for a mailbox. It should be near the driveway."

Goodman rolled ahead. "Might as well."

We reached the gate three hundred yards farther. Goodman curved into the gravel driveway and crunched to a stop at the steel gate. Snoop and Gunner halted the Jeeps behind us.

"An electric gate," Goodman said. "Any suggestions?"

"Hit the high beams." The headlights flooded the steel gate with light.

"Wait here." I popped the door and stepped to the gate. A cotter pin held the hinge pin in place, not a padlock. An amateur installation. I withdrew the cotter pin, slipped the hinge pin out, and swung the gate open. Slick as a wet catfish.

Goodman led the convoy through.

I closed the gate and returned to the car. "The GPS says we have another half mile as the crow flies, but it's farther when we zigzag across those hills. In the police station before we left Lampasas, I memorized a satellite view on the internet. We ought to leave your sedan and continue in our Jeeps."

"Does the road get rougher?" Goodman asked.

"Yes, but the real problem is the creek over the next hill. The road passes through a low-water crossing. And there's another range of hills between the creek and the ranch house."

Goodman stopped on the grass. "Good idea. Let's transfer."

Goodman accompanied me in the first Jeep. Snoop and Gunner drove the second. We forded the creek and powered uphill with parking lights on. I stopped below the top so we could gear up.

Goodman adjusted her armored vest. "Chuck, you were in the army. I'm more of a city cop. How do you suggest we approach this?"

"Gunner and I have Special Forces training in stealthy approach. I suggest that we take the lead. You and Snoop follow twenty yards behind and watch what we do."

She glanced at Snoop. "Are you a veteran too?"

"Nope. I thought about it, but decided to be a cop instead."

"You and I will bring up the rear." She waved me ahead. "Okay. You and Gunner take the point."

I faced Gunner. "Remember the last time you and I geared up together?"

Gunner's grin flared in the dim lights from the Jeeps. "The Triple Seven. We hit Ghar Mesar in Afghanistan. This time we won't face a dozen Taliban waiting in ambush."

"Just one Ranger, qualified as Expert Marksman in pistol and rifle, who knows the territory. It won't be easy."

Gunner grinned. "It never is."

It was 2:30 in the dark, cool October morning under a cloudy sky.

That summer in Afghanistan it had been 90 degrees at midnight. The sweat evaporated in the dry air as fast as it formed and left my skin gritty, sticky, and crusty. Tonight, the Texas breeze felt cool and silky. A good omen, if I believed in omens.

"I have two thermal monoculars. I'll use one and Snoop will use the other. No conversation unless I break the silence, agreed?"

Nods all around.

I led our assault team toward the hilltop, Gunner at my side. Like old times, but with no Taliban. This time we challenged one scumbag, but he was a veteran Army Ranger. The tricky part was to capture him before he grabbed Emily or Felicity for a hostage. As a serial killer, Nelson had nothing to lose.

We struggled up the rocky trail. In Afghanistan my team infiltrated through apricot orchards. In the Hill Country we advanced through a wilderness strewn with rocks big as golf balls and softballs. There was a risk of noise from walking across the stones, but the oak thickets around us concealed cactus and mesquite that could rip our legs to bloody strips. Better to risk dislodging the rocks.

We topped the hill and followed the rocky trail around a curve. A deer flashed on the monocular and scampered away through the woods. The ranch house peeked through the trees ahead, its outline a ghostly orange that reflected more heat than the countryside.

I stopped and dropped, motioning the others to hit the dirt while I surveyed the field. At 2:45 a.m. I didn't expect to see movement, but I followed Rule Fifteen: *Never take anything for granted.*

My rules have kept me alive so far.

The house's heat signature indicated heat generated inside. I hoped it was two girls and one sleeping scumbag named Harry Nelson. Stoves, water heaters, a television or two—all radiated additional heat. The total was tiny, but the thermal monoculars responded to slight variations in temperature.

I didn't spot the Honda Odyssey, but it might be behind the house. The satellite view showed a small outbuilding behind the house—a garage or a barn.

We waited three minutes, then advanced down the slope. I halted where the meadow flattened out between us and the house fifty yards away.

"Snoop, take cover behind that giant oak twenty yards from the corner of the house. Watch the front and the right side from there in case Nelson runs out the front door or jumps out a window. Nora, you and Gunner go left. Stay thirty yards away. There should be another oak over there big enough to hide behind.

"Nora, I suggest you drop off at ninety degrees to Snoop and watch if anyone comes out a door or window on that side or in the front. You won't have a thermal imager, but I may switch the lights on before Nelson runs.

"Gunner, you continue around and meet me in the rear. You and I will infiltrate from the back. There's an outbuilding; we'll check it first."

Curving ninety degrees, I sneaked across the grass until the Honda and the outbuilding came into view. I dropped to the ground again to observe. Burrs and needles stabbed the palms of my hands, and I jumped up. Okay, so I had better now crawl anywhere. Without the monocular, the house looked dark as the inside of a Hill Country cavern. Through the thermal imager I made out the outline, windows, and door.

I circled until I spotted Gunner approaching from the other side. I motioned him over.

"No doors on that side, boss. Just the front and back. But the house sets low enough that someone could jump out a window like you said."

We crept to the Honda, and I laid my hand on the hood. Cool as the October night, so I figured Nelson had been inside for hours.

The outbuilding was a barn, not a garage. The thermal image showed it as cold as the trees. I moved to a broken window on the side and peeked in. No heat sources. It was clear.

"Gunner, stay here and cover me. I'll pick the lock, then wave you over after I open the door."

"Hooah, boss."

The wooden back porch had five steps. Not to risk a creaky step, I edged to the side and slid under the porch rail. If Nelson heard me, he could shoot through the wooden wall. I stayed low and quiet. I picked the lock instead of hunting for a hidden key. I had hit Drucker's house in daylight when I knew he wasn't home. This porch was pitch black and Nelson could be inside listening in the quiet night,

The kitchen door had six glass panes. I peered through them with my thermal imager. Nothing visible. I felt the keyhole with my fingertips. I knew my lockpick set by feel. It felt clumsy unlocking the door in the dark, but I managed.

As soon as I motioned Gunner over and stepped inside, I knew something was wrong.

TWENTY-SEVEN

Houses have an atmosphere whether they're occupied or vacant. Maybe it's a sensory thing or a mystical vibration in the universe, but most times I know whether someone is in there or if a building sits empty. Perhaps I smell the humans so faintly that I'm not aware of it or maybe I hear someone breathe. Or their heart beat. I don't know how I knew it, but I did. The instant I stepped into the kitchen, even before I hit the light switch, I knew the old ranch house was empty.

I flipped the light switch back and forth. The power was off.

We were too late. The girls had vanished again and so had Nelson. I felt as though I stood on the platform of a train station watching the last caboose of the day chug away.

"Nelson doesn't intend to come back anytime soon. He cut the power at the breaker box. Find the box, Gunner. We need lights."

I switched on my headlight.

Rule Fifteen: *Never take anything for granted.* We would search the house, but we wouldn't find anyone. With luck, we might find a clue to where Nelson took the girls.

"Gunner, after you find the lights, call Snoop and Nora in. I'm going up."

I dashed up the stairs three steps at a time to the central hallway. A bathroom stood with its door open. I stuck my head in. Empty. The door on the left rear had a hole bashed in one panel. I shoved it open. The bedroom behind it was sparsely furnished and the bed was strewn across the room.

I swung my headlight in an arc.

A homemade manacle lay on the floor. One end of the chain was padlocked to an eyebolt. Shiny metal filings in the screw threads flashed in the beam. There was a matching anchor embedded in a hole in the hearth. Metal filings littered the stone around the hole.

Who unscrewed it and how?

The bed was disassembled and one bedrail lay bent and battered. Had Emily rammed the bedrail into the door? Was that how she broke the door?

I examined the doorknob. It was installed with the lock on the outside, not the inside. Designed to lock someone in, not to keep people out.

I stepped into the closet and scanned the inside walls with my headlight. Emily had scratched her name and birthdate inside the closet and a short message: We escaped.

You go, girl, I thought. My mood soared.

I pivoted to the bed and noticed blood on the pillow. Fresh blood.

The hallway lights came on. Gunner had located the breaker box.

Snoop hurried in. "They're gone, bud."

"They escaped. Emily left a message in the closet. She also left blood on the pillow. That worries me, but at least they escaped. Let's check the other room."

The bedroom across the hall locked from the outside too. That bed was disassembled also and the bedrail and homemade manacle lay abandoned.

"Emily unscrewed her manacle from the hearth, then battered the door open. She unlocked Felicity's door from the outside and unscrewed her eyebolt also," I said. "They hid in the woods somewhere."

"Or they walked toward the highway," Snoop said.

"Why didn't we pass them as we came in?"

"They didn't know who we were. Maybe they hid in the woods."

Something didn't fit that scenario. I studied the homemade manacle.

"The leg iron is unlocked. How did Emily unlock the leg iron? If she had the key to the leg iron, she wouldn't need to unscrew the eyebolt from the fireplace. That makes no sense."

Snoop headed toward the door.

"Regardless, we have to comb the woods."

———

The four of us spent two hours shouting Emily's and Felicity's names and honking the horns on our vehicles. We walked a hundred-yard radius by flashlight and uncovered no trace of the girls.

"Snoop, I just remembered: The girls in Nelson's dance videos were barefoot."

"Yeah. So?"

"When I breached the attic rooms in Nelson's house, I didn't see any shoes."

"Oh geez. I see what you mean: The girls are barefoot."

"This ground is covered with cactus, rocks, and burrs. They couldn't walk far or they would shred their feet."

"Then where are they?"

"Maybe they were recaptured."

We gathered beside the back porch.

"How the hell did Nelson leave?" I asked the group. "Where did the other vehicle come from?"

"He could have kept another vehicle here," Snoop said, "like a four-wheel drive to use around the ranch."

"Whatever he used," Gunner said, "he didn't call anyone from here. No cell service."

"He has an accomplice," Goodman said. "That's the call he made to the 512 number. The accomplice came and took Nelson away."

"And the girls," I said.

Another idea came to me.

"Who owns this place? Flamer didn't uncover any property in Nelson's name other than his Austin house."

"Let's check the mailbox on our way out," Snoop said.

"Good idea. Never mind that it's eighteen different federal crimes to look in someone's mailbox."

"Yeah, never mind that," Snoop said.

"Let's leave this like we found it, folks," I said. "It's possible Nelson could come back and not know we were here."

We stopped at the mailbox beside the driveway. It was empty. I had committed eighteen different federal crimes for nothing.

———

Goodman left for home.

I hadn't slept in over twenty-four hours and it was worse for Snoop and Gunner. I felt so tired I could fall asleep hanging from a mesquite tree. And we needed to drive two Jeeps back to Austin in one piece, not to mention ourselves. We bounced our way to the ranch gate where I had a cellphone signal. My phone said Austin was a ninety-minute drive, while the nearest hotel was in Burnet, seventeen miles away. Good enough.

I pulled through the gate and parked a few yards off the highway.

Gunner rolled to a rest behind me as I exited the Jeep. He rolled down the window as I approached. Leaning into the window, I said, "We'll leave my Jeep here and the three of us will prop my eyes open long enough to drive to a hotel in Burnet in your Jeep. Gunner, you and Snoop have had a longer day than I have so I'll drive. We'll retrieve my Jeep tomorrow—or later today since it's already tomorrow."

Snoop laughed. "I'm so tired that what you said almost makes sense." He sat in back and fell asleep before I goosed the Cherokee to highway speed. Gunner and I told Special Forces stories on the way to Burnet to keep me awake.

I woke in a king-sized hotel bed nine hours later and didn't recall checking in. I had last talked to Carrie and Frank at eight o'clock the night before when I told them I was driving to Lampasas. After that I was too busy, then too tired, to talk.

Ruby had left me a voicemail. "Harry Nelson, Desmond Drucker, and Kenneth Hoar all have M16s registered to them. None of the weapons have been used in a crime so they aren't in our database. Also, I couldn't find a match to the brass or the slug that hit that car in any other database. The good news is that I heard scuttlebutt that Goodman got a lead on Nelson last weekend. I can hardly wait until you close this case and we can celebrate. Good luck."

I called Aunt Carrie and spent the next hour giving her and Frank a meticulous narrative of the previous night's events.

———

When I returned to Carrie and Frank's house, it was five-thirty Monday afternoon.

Carrie hugged me so tightly I had a hard time breathing. "You came so *close*. You're my hero, Chuck. I know you'll bring our girl back safe and sound."

She waved her newspaper. "Your horoscope says: *The proper way to make an assessment is to gather facts then form an opinion. Do this today and you'll be rewarded. Keep in mind that most people do the opposite. They form an opinion first, then search for confirming facts.*

"My horoscope says: *There's a marvelous structure behind the things you experience today. To be curious about what makes it so is to touch your potential for genius. Curiosity is its own reward.*" She smiled serenely. "Everything will be all right."

I wished I felt that confident. "I hope so, Aunt Carrie. Now, I need to do some research."

"That's good, Chuck. Gather facts, then form an opinion like your horoscope says."

Clap-trap and fiddle-faddle, but I smiled before I went into the guest room.

I fired up my laptop and searched the Burnet County Central Appraisal District website to learn who owned the ranch where Nelson had fled with the girls. Title belonged to J. J. Blankenship. The tax bills went to a post office box in suburban Austin.

Scouring the internet for J. J. Blankenship, I discovered a Josiah Joseph Blankenship, born 1896, died 1969. He owned a ranch in Burnet County and founded Blankenship Bank and Trust in Burnet in 1933, after President Roosevelt's bank holiday. That fit the name on the ranch's title so it must be the same man. A Burnet County history website credited Blankenship with financing local farmers through the Great Depression with most farms and ranches intact. After Blankenship died in 1969, the bank was acquired by a larger bank and the Blankenship name disappeared.

This was a head-scratcher. Blankenship died in 1969, and he still owned the ranch more than fifty years later?

I called Detective Goodman and told her what I had learned. "Can you get a warrant to reveal who the post office box belongs to? The owner of the box must have a connection to Nelson."

"Getting a warrant for a post office box involves the federal government. It's easier to herd squirrels through a dog pound. I'll start the process, but you'll be old and gray before we have the warrant. Isn't there another way to locate the ranch owner?"

"I have one or two ideas, yeah. What chaps my ass is that Nelson still has those two girls. I'm mad at myself for not having Gunner stay on his tail Saturday night."

I called Grandpa. "You up for Chinese?"

"The Plum Blossom in twenty minutes?"

"You're on." I beat him there.

I wasn't hungry, but I knew I should eat. I had slept until after three o'clock that afternoon and my internal clock acted like I was in China instead of a Chinese restaurant. I considered ordering a glass of wine but passed. I would have a bourbon and Coke before bedtime. That would help sync my body clock to Texas.

Grandpa walked in and scanned the room. He smiled as he spied me and hurried over. "Soon as we order, I want a blow-by-blow of what went down yesterday."

"Of course."

A server materialized and took our order.

I used most of the meal to tell Grandpa all that had happened since we ate barbecue for dinner Saturday night.

As I finished, the server brought the bill. I handed him a credit card and waited for him to leave. "Grandpa, I need you to drive to Burnet tomorrow and learn everything about that ranch and about J. J. Blankenship. The initials may stand for Josiah Joseph. Learn the identity of the current beneficial owner of the ranch." I filled him in on what I knew about

Blankenship. "Visit the bank and talk to the oldest employee. They might know somebody who knew somebody. Search for a Burnet County Historical Society or a Genealogical Society. In some counties they're the same organization but look for both. Learn who Blankenship's heirs were. His will could be filed in the County Clerk's office."

"I'll drive there first thing in the morning."

I mixed a bourbon and Coke at ten and was asleep by ten-thirty.

TWENTY-EIGHT

I sent Snoop and Gunner to stake out the post office box where the Blankenship ranch tax bills were mailed, but I didn't expect results. The Burnet County Tax Collector mailed tax bills for the year in the middle of October. That was two weeks ago. Whoever owned the post office box might not check it until next year.

But what else could I do? Rule Sixteen: *Sometimes you have to do something, even if it's wrong. At least you'll know you tried.*

While Snoop and Gunner loitered outside a post office, I drove to Burnet County to scour the Blankenship ranch by day. If that didn't yield results, I would interview the owners of the adjoining ranches.

The ranch's mailbox held two pieces of mail. One was a coupon for a discount oil change at a tire and auto store in Burnet. It was addressed to *J. J. Blankenship or current resident.* The other was a campaign flyer for a candidate for the Burnet County Commissioners Court addressed to *Occupant.*

I stuck the pieces back in the box. That mail had arrived in the last two days, so the post office wasn't holding the mail. Someone collected the mail often enough to keep the box from getting full.

Had Nelson fetched the mail on Sunday? If there were an accomplice, perhaps he had picked up the mail.

My small invasion team was so intent on rescuing Emily and Felicity that we hadn't considered other evidence like mail when we were at the ranch house. I would make a thorough search this time.

I slipped out the hinge pin to open the gate and bumped my way along the rocky trail.

I had returned to search for clues where Nelson had taken the girls or how he left the ranch. Had he kept a second vehicle there? The alternative was that an accomplice had come to the ranch and given Nelson a lift.

Cresting the final row of hills, I observed the ranch house in daylight for the first time. The answers to all my questions gobsmacked me in a blinding flash of the obvious. The big house, the valley, the four chimneys, the ancient oak trees—the view from where I stopped.

The scene was identical to the painting in Jerry O'Doul's house. I had stopped on the exact spot the artist had stood to paint the picture.

Jerry O'Doul, short for Jeremiah. Jerusha O'Doul. Josiah Joseph Blankenship. They all began with a J. Jerusha's married name was O'Doul, of course. Her maiden name must be Blankenship.

I attempted to call Flamer. No signal. I didn't need another clue. I knew the answer. Jerry O'Doul was Harry Nelson's accomplice.

Slamming the Jeep ahead to the next clearing, I jerked a K-turn and dashed back toward the highway, gauging the phone's signal strength while I bounded and bounced along the rocky trail. I crested the hills closest to the highway and had two bars of signal, enough to text. I texted Flamer:

Do a deep dive on Jeremiah "Jerry" O'Doul, former physics teacher at James Bonham High School and his mother Jerusha O'Doul. Find connections to Josiah Joseph Blankenship (1896-1969), aka J. J. Blankenship, Burnet County, TX, possibly Jerusha's father.

I thrust closer to the highway until I had three signal bars. I called Snoop on the Bluetooth and used both hands to keep the Jeep on track.

"I just saw the Blankenship ranch house in the daylight. Jerry O'Doul has a painting of that house in his home."

"You think O'Doul is the accomplice?"

"Do ducks swim barefoot? I just hope he's the *only* accomplice. There could be others in this sicko club for hunters of teenage girls. Desmond Drucker has a weird fascination with young females also, and all three scumbags overlap at Bonham High School."

"You want Gunner and me to abandon the post office box?"

"Yeah, we don't need the owner anymore. It's O'Doul, either mother or son. You and Gunner stake out O'Doul's house. Emily and Felicity may be inside. Harry Nelson could be there. Tell me everyone who comes and goes. Anyone who comes out—and I mean *anyone*—could hide one or both girls in the trunk. You follow them. Call Frank for extra manpower. Grandpa too in case you need him. Cover every escape from the house, front, back, and both ends of the alley. I'm driving back from the ranch. I'll be there in ninety minutes. I'll call Nora Goodman to see whether she has enough for a warrant."

I disconnected and called Goodman. "Nora, Chuck McCrary. You were right about Nelson. He has an accomplice."

"What did you learn?"

"Yesterday I combed the Burnet County tax records for the ranch where Nelson had the girls." I told her about the registered owner J. J. Blankenship and the ranch house painting at O'Doul's home.

"Jerry O'Doul's mother Jerusha may have inherited the Blankenship ranch. She's the right age to be Blankenship's daughter and everyone's name begins with J. Is that enough for a warrant for O'Doul's house?"

"We need proof that O'Doul is the ranch's beneficial owner. Prove that, and the messages Emily left in both closets justify a search warrant for O'Doul's house in Austin."

"Is Emily's latest message admissible evidence? We didn't have a warrant when we hit the ranch."

"We had a warrant to track his phone. The phone was where we thought it was. We're good on that. If necessary, we claim exigent circumstances. I'm pretty sure a judge will allow it. Nelson is a person of interest in kidnapping, sexual slavery, and several murders. Get proof that O'Doul owns or controls the ranch house, and I'll get the warrant."

"My researcher is running an extensive background check on mother and son. I'll have information in two hours."

I didn't stop to close the gate. I powered onto the highway and screeched toward Austin like a bat flying out of a campfire.

———

Flamer struck gold.

His call reached me at the Liberty Hill city limits where I would jump onto Highway 183.

Jerusha O'Doul was born Jerusha Jedidah Blankenship. She was J. J. Blankenship's only child. Perhaps she never changed the ranch's title since she could sign her name J. J. Blankenship. Whatever the reason, Jerry O'Doul had Jerusha's unlimited power of attorney, which gave him control of the ranch.

I gave Goodman's email address and phone number to Flamer. "Give me ten minutes to call her, then email her the info, then call her to answer any questions. Good job, Flamer."

Flamer being Flamer, he disconnected without a word.

I lane-hopped through Liberty Hill, slewing around slower vehicles and leaving a trail of honking, cursing drivers. Sorry folks, this is an emergency.

I called Goodman with the news.

"Good work," she said. "I can get the warrant. I'll send two black-and-whites to pen Nelson and O'Doul in the O'Doul house until I bring the warrant. Two hours tops."

Two hours wouldn't do. Bad things can happen in two hours. Nelson or O'Doul could murder Emily or Felicity and then commit suicide. Or they could split the girls and each take one and run. Or barricade themselves and hold the girls hostage. Or...or...or...

My mind wanted to race away with horrible scenarios of alternate futures. I focused on driving, but Rule Sixteen popped into my head, unbidden. *Sometimes you have to do something, even if it's wrong. At least you'll know you tried.*

According to the GPS, I had a forty-five-minute drive to O'Doul's house, all but the last mile of it slogging on Highway 183 or Loop 1. From experience I knew that traffic conditions on those two highways were as unpredictable as rolling dice. I would be lucky to make it in an hour.

I jumped onto 183 and slammed the accelerator to the firewall just as my phone rang. "Yeah, Snoop."

"They're making a run for it, Chuck. Two cars and they split up—"

Snoop was talking so fast his words ran together. "Slow down, Snoop. I can't understand you."

"They're making a run for it, both of them, in separate cars. They must have spotted the black-and-whites when the cops pulled up in front of O'Doul's house and they panicked."

"Both of them?"

"Yeah. They split up."

"O'Doul must have abandoned his mother. I'll tell Goodman to bring someone to care for the old lady. You're following the runners?"

"More chasing than following since they know I'm behind them. Nelson drove a blue Dodge Caravan out the rear to the alley. O'Doul drove a white Chevy Suburban down the driveway and cut across the front lawn to bypass the black-and-whites blocking the street. The black-and-whites jammed the street so tight they couldn't move and I couldn't drive around them to chase O'Doul. He shook us off."

"So…we have no one chasing O'Doul?"

"That's right. We're chasing Nelson though. O'Doul's driveway opens in back to an alley that runs the whole block behind the house. I stationed Gunner at one end of it and Frank at the other, while I covered the front exit on the street. Nelson managed to get around Frank and took off. Gunner's chasing Nelson, but he's a couple of blocks behind. I'm trying to catch them."

"Are the girls with them?"

"I saw at least one person in the back seat of O'Doul's Suburban. I'd bet it was one girl. They would split the girls for each one to have a hostage. That's what I would do if I were them."

"What about Uncle Frank?"

"He served his purpose in the alley, so I sent him home. He's an amateur and could do more harm than good if he joined the chase."

"How about Grandpa?"

"He hadn't made it to O'Doul's house yet when they split. I'll call Magnus and tell him to go home."

"No, I'll call him. You're busy chasing through traffic. Any idea where they're running to?"

"Don't know. Wait, there's Nelson ahead. He's climbing on Loop 1, heading north. Maybe he's running to the ranch."

"He would if he doesn't know we were there. He still thinks the ranch is safe. Tell you what: I'll turn back to the ranch. I'll beat him by an hour. Get here soon as you can and bring the cavalry."

"Be careful, bud; there's two of them."

"At least two. Let's hope there's not three or four."

I called Goodman. "Nora, both O'Doul and Nelson bolted from O'Doul's house. I can't guarantee it, but I think they're heading back to the ranch. They may not realize that we know about it. They left O'Doul's mother home alone. She has dementia and is confined to a wheelchair. You'll need EMTs for her when you execute the search warrant."

"I'll have Rod Ortega execute the warrant. I'll meet you at the Blankenship ranch."

Angling off the highway, I rolled twenty yards and skidded to a stop, mushrooming a dust cloud. I closed the gate and reinserted the hinge pin. Nelson would find the gate as it was when he and O'Doul left two days ago with Emily and Felicity.

Nelson should arrive in an hour, maybe forty-five minutes. After I crossed the first row of hills, my cellphone would be useless. I called Snoop as I splashed through the creek. "I'm at the ranch. What's your status?"

"I nearly caught Nelson and Gunner, but Nelson is blasting up 183, dodging commuters like he's driving NASCAR instead of a minivan. I called Gunner and told him to stop lane-hopping and let Nelson think he lost us. Goodman called me. She told the Highway Patrol to set a roadblock in Leander."

I jounced my way up the first hill. "The ranch has been in O'Doul's family for generations. He was driving here before they built Highway 183. He knows this country like the back of his hand and we have to assume he taught Nelson the alternate routes. Nelson will drop off the highway and take to the back roads before he hits Leander."

"I agree, but we have to try. Pray he'll be stupid and stay on the highway."

Pausing on the hilltop, I asked, "Have you heard from the black-and-whites chasing O'Doul's SUV?"

"Nothing. He got away clean. Goodman issued another Amber Alert. She called ahead to the Burnet County Sheriff. He'll post a watcher in Bertram in an unmarked car and set a roadblock on both ends of the road to the ranch. Should be blocked within the hour."

"By which time, Nelson could have driven through. Burnet to Bertram is a slower route to the ranch. I assume they're coming here. Nelson will arrive forty minutes earlier. Anything else to tell me before I'm out of cell range?"

"Good luck, bud. I'll see you when I get there."

I gunned the Jeep down the hillside. Halting at the barn, I dragged the door open and parked the Jeep inside. I snatched my duffel from the back. As I jammed the barn door closed, it scuffed a jagged scar across the buffalo grass.

I smoothed the grass with my feet as best I could. The grass damage wasn't obvious. In another hour, the shadows would track across the meadow. Nelson and O'Doul had no reason to notice the streaks in the grass, even if they parked in back. If they entered through the front door, they wouldn't pass the barn.

It was easier to pick the lock on the kitchen door in the daylight. I scanned the kitchen to ensure it looked the way I had found it.

Walking through the great room, I could tell that Goodman, Snoop, and Gunner had been there. I rearranged the furniture cushions and slid the dining room chairs under the table.

A walk-through of the front bedrooms confirmed that all was in order, awaiting O'Doul and Nelson. They would never get that far after they arrived. If they did, it would be over my dead body.

Felicity had been held in the right rear bedroom for the few hours before Nelson moved the girls again. I hadn't looked in the closet before. I looked now. She had not left a message like Emily's. Perhaps she hadn't found a tool to carve the wall.

I set Emily's room back the way I found it. Reflecting on the blood-spotted pillow again, I felt a weird sensation in my throat; I couldn't swallow. The manacles dropped so casually on the floor made real the conditions that Emily had braved for more than four years.

Killing was too good for Nelson and O'Doul. I hoped they would surrender so they would spend decades in prison to contemplate their moral failings.

Time to set the ambush.

Ideally, I would wait for Nelson in the bedroom behind the door. When he stepped into the room, his back would be to the door and I would whack him with my blackjack. However, I didn't know which girl was with him or which room he would enter first.

Instead, I waited by the window at the front of the hallway above the stairwell. I checked the angle of the hall mirror. No, he wouldn't see me until it was too late.

In my mind, I rescued Emily first. She was virtually my sister, nearly as close as my real little sister Margarita.

Nelson would climb the stairs with his back to me. Probably would not carry a gun in his hand. He outweighed Emily by a hundred pounds and was trained in hand-to-hand combat. He would herd her up the stairs while he followed. She would recall which room she had been in two days before and she'd curve that direction. When Nelson neared the top of the stairs, I would rush him and knock him unconscious with the blackjack.

At least that was the plan. Special Forces commander, Captain Hank Ramirez said, "No battle plan survives contact with the enemy."

I spent an hour at the window, waiting for Nelson's Caravan to bounce down the trail. The blue minivan would peek through the trees as it descended the hill. I would step back from the window into the shadows and wait—the patient spider prepared for the fly.

My pre-mission adrenaline pulsed as I got my game face on.

I would hear his key rattle in the lock. Louder if he used the front door, but I would hear the kitchen door also. It was quiet in the country;

the only sound was a pair of mockingbirds. I imagined the door would open and I would hear voices as Nelson told Emily where to go and what to do.

It was never Felicity in my mind. It was Emily with Nelson, followed by Felicity with O'Doul.

I would crouch in the hall corner. Nelson couldn't see me from the first floor. As he climbed behind Emily, I would creep cat-like along the rail until Nelson reached the top step.

Bam! with the blackjack. Nelson would hit the floor like the sack of shit he was.

I imagined Emily would spot me and scream for joy. She would want to run to me, but I would motion her back while I searched Nelson for weapons. I would secure his wrists with plastic ties. Then Emily would rush to me with joyful tears. I would hug her tight and tell her that her long nightmare was over.

That's how *Carlos McCrary–Superhero* took down Nelson in my imagination.

I ran that mental scenario in variations. In one scene Emily spun at the top of the steps and shoved Nelson down the stairs. He fell and broke his neck. That was a good one.

Another alternative had Nelson with Felicity instead of Emily. Felicity pivoted right instead of left. I still bashed Nelson unconscious, but Felicity didn't run toward me because she didn't know who I was. I would tell her I was Emily's cousin and she would smile.

I enjoyed my daydreams until I realized another half-hour had passed and Nelson hadn't arrived. The sun would set in thirty minutes. Shadows of oak trees enfolded the clearing in dusk.

I didn't think the Burnet County Sheriff's roadblocks and observers would catch O'Doul or Nelson. The Hill Country is honeycombed with county roads, ranch roads, private roads, and rudimentary trails scraped across the fields by road graders. Anyone in a high-clearance vehicle can drive almost anywhere if they know the territory.

I expected Nelson and O'Doul to drive back roads to reach the ranch unseen. Perhaps that was why they were taking so much longer than I expected.

With no lights, the hallway was murky. I could hardly make out the bathroom door at the rear of the house.

Nelson would flip on the electricity when he arrived. He would switch on the hall light from the bottom of the stairs. With him at the light switch and me in the corner, there was no way he would see me.

Another hour passed, and I used the upstairs toilet. The tank couldn't refill until the water came on, so it had one flush in it.

Where were they? Had I guessed wrong about the kidnappers returning to the ranch? Where else could they go?

Then I heard an engine—a big engine from a Chevy Suburban, not a small engine from a Dodge Caravan. I peered out the window. It was getting dark but there were no headlights. The engine sound came from behind the house. Hurrying down the hall, I peeked from the bathroom window as a headlight beam swung across the glass.

O'Doul drove the Suburban in from the rear. He had taken a different trail from the backside of the ranch. One I didn't know about and didn't think to search for.

Hopefully, I hadn't made a fatal mistake. Snoop says each mistake is a learning experience. Make enough mistakes and you get smarter and smarter, unless one of your mistakes kills you.

The Suburban's engine sounded like a tank in the quiet countryside. When it seemed like it couldn't grow louder, it stopped.

Snoop, Gunner, Detective Goodman, and the Burnet County deputies had staked out the other highway, and the bad guy bypassed them. Would Nelson drive the Caravan in from the rear also? What if there was another low-water crossing on the rear entrance?

In the dead cellphone area, there was no way to contact reinforcements, and I had no bugle to sound *Charge!*

Returned to the front of the house, I awaited O'Doul. My plan would still work, but I would target O'Doul instead of Nelson. Same-same.

The back door clicked open and man-sized footsteps sounded crossing the kitchen. O'Doul's voice carried up the stairwell. "Flip on the breakers. I'll get the girls."

If O'Doul didn't have a girl with him, who was he talking to?

"Bring my box of DVDs," Nelson said. "We'll have 'Tuesday Night at the Movies' later."

Nelson and O'Doul had met somewhere and arrived together. That tipped the odds the wrong way.

The captain's words echoed: *No battle plan survives contact with the enemy.*

Forget the blackjack. This called for my Glock 19.

TWENTY-NINE

The *thunk-thunk-thunk* of breakers flipping on broke the silence. The well pump outside whirled up to speed. The toilet tank whistled while it filled.

A light from downstairs bathed the upstairs hall in reflected light.

A troop of footsteps stamped on the back porch. They echoed through the kitchen and grew louder.

Showtime!

"Chop chop, Gloria," O'Doul said. "Your suite awaits you upstairs. We'll fix dinner and call you both soon. The four of us will have a nice party after we eat."

"You too, Evita," Nelson said. "Up the stairs."

The back of a brunette's head came into view as she climbed the steps. I recognized her Afro hairstyle. She had to be the one known as Gloria. Felicity Taylor was the girl I had seen on the Gloria DVD.

O'Doul's hand prodded her ahead by squeezing her buttocks.

The sight of that grasping, controlling, domineering grip lanced through my mind, a bolt of black lightning. It symbolized the years of captivity and depravity these two men had inflicted on more young women than I could count.

Keep calm and control your breath, I reminded myself.

Emily trailed three steps behind O'Doul, and Nelson had not come into view.

Felicity reached the top of the stairs.

I crabbed sideways along the hall, my pistol held in a two-hand grip.

Felicity saw me in the hall mirror and screamed.

Shock and awe.

I shouted as loud as I could. "Police. Freeze, O'Doul. You're under arrest. Felicity, hide in your bedroom until this is over."

O'Doul's hand fumbled at his waist. I spotted the pistol as he seized it and drew.

I punched two slugs into his chest. He fell against the banister and slid headfirst down the steps. I shot him in the throat. He wouldn't rise from the dead behind me.

Felicity screamed again and froze with her hands over her mouth.

On the steps, Nelson's hand snaked into view like a striking serpent and seized Emily's wrist. He jerked her backwards out of sight.

Felicity blocked the stairs, screaming like a banshee.

I prodded her aside and bolted downstairs.

"Stay here," I shouted over my shoulder. "I'll be back."

O'Doul's body sprawled as a barricade from the wall to the banister and blocked half the steps. If I leapt over, I would bash my head on the edge of the stairwell.

I trod on O'Doul's thighs, then his stomach. The unsteady footing felt like standing on a pillow on a trampoline. In my peripheral vision, I saw Nelson throw Emily across his shoulder and bolt across the den.

I made a final step on O'Doul's chest, and reached the bottom.

I whirled with my Glock lowered but ready.

Nelson had disappeared.

With Emily.

———

Harry Nelson

Nelson careened through the kitchen, off balance from the struggling woman thrown over his shoulder. He slowed near the back door and kicked it open. Bolting across the porch, he descended the steps two at a time.

I knew it. I knew it, he thought. *That freakin' McCrary has had me in his sights for days.*

The Suburban and the Honda glowed in the twilight a few tantalizing steps away, but O'Doul had the keys to the Suburban and Nelson had left the Honda keys in the ranch house two days before. No way he could go inside for either key. He would have to make it to the Dodge Caravan they had left a half mile behind the house when he met up with O'Doul. It was difficult carrying a struggling woman on his back, but it was that or die. *Or prison,* he thought. *No, never prison.*

Emily squirmed and beat on his back. He shook her violently. "Do I have to knock you unconscious, Evita? Or will you be calm for me?"

Emily jerked and twisted. "Screw you, Weirdo. Let me go. The police are here. You're a dead man if you don't give up."

"That wasn't the police; that was your stupid cousin. Look around. Where are the cop cars? McCrary is alone. The police always come with backup."

Nelson tightened his grip on the struggling woman and trotted down the rocky trail.

His head wound throbbed with each step. Stumbling in the twilight, he slowed to a fast walk. If he fell, he might drop this wild woman. He couldn't let her to escape; she was his only leverage. He had to be more careful. He would have to hike to the Caravan to make his escape. A half mile to freedom.

Carlos McCrary

I stampeded across the kitchen, down the steps, and into the back meadow. It was nearly full dark. A three-quarter moon halfway to its zenith shown through a hole in the clouds. I shot three holes in the Suburban's grill and three more in the Honda's. Stepping toward the rear, I fired off holes in a front and a back tire on the passenger side of each vehicle. Nelson couldn't circle back and escape that way. In the twilight I made out tire tracks across the buffalo grass from the Suburban.

I dashed back inside, dragged O'Doul's body off the steps, and hurdled up the stairs. I flipped on the light in Emily's room and reached in my duffel.

After strapping on a headlight, I stuffed a thermal monocular in my pocket. The thermal imager to follow them through the woods; the headlight for me to carry Emily to the house after I captured Nelson and immobilized him. I stuck cable ties in my pocket.

I ejected the Glock's magazine and replaced it with a full one. Nineteen bullets for Nelson if I needed them, but I preferred the SOB to experience a lifetime in prison. I knew the kind of treatment child molesters received from other prisoners.

Felicity peeked around the doorjamb as I paused on the top step.

I must have presented a fearsome sight: headlight strapped across my forehead, armored vest, and pistol in one hand. Not to mention the combat boots.

"It's okay, Felicity. I'm Emily's cousin Chuck McCrary. I'm a private investigator, and I'm here to rescue you. Don't worry; I do this for a living."

I smiled. Warmly, I hoped. "The Austin police are on their way. Stay here and you'll be safe. Okay?"

She bobbed her head.

Descending the stairs, I skipped two steps slippery with blood.

I sprinted out the kitchen door and leapt off the porch. "Emily! Where are you?"

Emily Crazinski

As he ran, Nelson jostled Emily so bad it was hard to catch her breath. With each step, her weight pounded on her diaphragm.

From the distance she heard Chuck's voice. "Emily! Where are you?"

She braced her hands on Nelson's belt, lifted her torso, and yelled, "I'm here, Chuck. He has a gun."

Nelson slapped her on the butt with his gun like a disobedient child.

Screw you, Weirdo. She smiled to herself. Served him right.

Nelson picked up the pace until he was jogging. Emily's teeth rattled until she clamped them shut.

Nelson wedged his way up the trail, crested a small hill, and jolted down the other side.

Chuck's voice carried again. "Where are you?" He sounded closer.

She braced her hands against Nelson's belt like before. He felt the movement and jammed to a stop. He flipped Emily off his shoulder as she began to shout. He clamped his hand over her mouth.

Carlos McCrary

Emily's voice floated through the woods from the back trail. "I'm here, Chuck. He has a gun."

Nelson must have stashed the Dodge Caravan along that rough track and ridden in with O'Doul.

I had to catch him before he escaped in the Caravan. Trotting, I followed the rough trace up a hill and down the other side.

With no shoes, Emily couldn't walk, let alone run across the rough countryside. Nelson had to carry her across his shoulder. That would slow him down. His head and his left hand were injured. I had a feeling Emily had something to do with that. Thank God for small favors.

Viewing the trail through the monocular, I pushed ahead. Yes, a faint trace of shapes in motion twisted through the trees, rocks, and cactus. Sixty yards later, I paused and hollered again. "Where are you?"

Another scream was throttled as it started, and I ran toward the sound. The rock-strewn path curved forty-five degrees right. I danced across the backcountry.

A hundred yards later, I halted and hollered again. "Nelson, I'm coming for you. You're mine, you sorry bastard."

A commotion emanated from the wilderness.

Nelson screamed, "You bitch!"

I scanned the forest through the monocular. A coyote's eyes glowed like phantom headlights in the distance. Two deer bolted and a larger light splotch flared in the woods. It could be a cow, but it might be Nelson and Emily.

I ran faster.

Nelson knew I would follow the trail. He would abandon it in his attempt to elude me. A hundred yards farther I paused to scan a 180-degree arc.

There it was. He had left the trail and angled downhill.

The light glowed brighter. I hoped it wasn't a cow.

Emily Crazinski

"Nelson, I'm coming for you. You're mine, you sorry bastard."

Chuck sounded closer. He was following the trail and gaining ground. It wouldn't be long now, Emily thought.

Nelson set Emily on the ground to catch his breath. He held her wrist in a steel grip.

"Your only chance is to let me go, Weirdo. If you don't, Chuck will kill you."

"I'm not afraid to die, Evita. I prefer death to prison."

Weirdo doesn't even see the irony, she thought. *He's afraid of prison, yet he's imprisoned me and others for years. Calling him "Weirdo" doesn't say the half of it.*

Emily lowered her head and jerked on his arm. She sank her teeth into the heel of his wounded hand and shook it like a wolf killing prey.

He screamed and hit her with his free hand. "You bitch."

He threw her over his shoulder and headed downhill.

Carlos McCrary

Yes, the light marker was them.

Shifting into stealth mode, I flowed through the woods, silent as a fog. My Special Forces jungle warfare training had saved my life in a gunfight with a handful of Serbian mobsters in the Florida Everglades. In the Everglades, I hadn't needed to worry about anyone but me. In this Hill Country wilderness, I had to consider Emily as I edged closer to the light source. Thirty yards. Twenty.

The monocular's ghostly image revealed Nelson facing ninety degrees to my right. He couldn't see me in the scattered moonlight as I crouched among the trees. To him, I was just another juniper shrub.

The light smudge expanded and resolved into two people. Nelson's head showed above Emily's, his chin next to her ear. He had set her on her feet and wrapped his left arm like a python around her neck. He didn't need his injured hand to hold her. His other hand jammed a Colt .45 against her temple. If he pulled the trigger, there wouldn't be much left of her head.

If it were daylight, I would take the shot. I would assume a two-hand Weaver stance, align the white dot on the Glock's front sight with the slot in the rear sight, and punch a slug through Nelson's right ear. I had done it before in hostage situations, but those were in better conditions. One was indoors, but the light was good. This was nighttime. Mottled moonlight struggled through the branches. Not good enough.

Sighting through the monocular, I identified the target. Thermal images appear fuzzy; it's the nature of the equipment. Impossible to make a tight shot. Aiming and shooting from a one-hand grip is chancy under the best conditions. A miss by millimeters would kill Emily.

No way.

Maybe sweet reason's voice would persuade him. "Harry, it's over. If you surrender and cooperate, you avoid the death penalty. Help them locate the other bodies. The District Attorney will let you live if you testify against O'Doul and Drucker."

I didn't know whether Drucker was involved. My bluff was a shot at the buzzer from mid-court. Maybe Nelson would incriminate Drucker.

"O'Doul's dead," Nelson replied, turning toward my voice. "I watched him fall. And Drucker refused to get involved with Jerry and me. He likes to look, but he's afraid to touch. The man has no balls."

Nelson rolled his head from side to side, struggling to pick me out from the dark forest shapes.

When he turned away, I shifted sideways.

"Even so, you don't have to die today. Enough people have died, Harry. Enough death for a dozen lifetimes. Drop your weapon and let Emily go."

Edging left, I crept across the slope, silent as the moonlight that filtered through the forest canopy.

"Her name is Evita. No, McCrary, just let me get to the Dodge, and I'll release Evita after I get there."

I traversed the slope like a tiger creeping through the jungle. As I closed with the target, I stuck the thermal imager in my pocket. I needed both hands for the final blitz.

"How about it, McCrary? I give you Evita and you give me a head start in the Caravan. Five minutes is all I ask. Five minutes."

I angled across the hillside behind Nelson. My eyes had dilated and Nelson's bulk glimmered like a ghost in the thin moonlight that dappled through the trees.

"McCrary? You get what you want; I get what I want. Hell, Evita gets what she wants. Everybody wins."

Holstering the Glock, I slid my Ka-Bar knife from its sheath. While I inched toward Nelson, I transferred the razor-sharp weapon to my left hand. I assumed he was wearing a Kevlar vest.

"McCrary, are you there?"

I edged close enough to grab his gun hand.

A twig snapped.

Nelson twirled, jerking Emily with him.

I lunged and clamped my hand on his wrist like a bench vise. Emily's life depended on me forcing his gun barrel away from her.

Nelson released Emily and clenched my wrist with his left hand. His grip didn't feel injured to me.

"Run, Emily," I shouted.

Nelson forced the strength of both arms against my one. Bad odds. In the darkness, I felt the gun curve toward me.

I punched the knife at his shadowy form aiming below the waist to get under the vest.

Nelson swiveled his hips and the blade glanced off his belt. He jerked his gun hand free and swung the barrel in my direction.

I thrust the knife again and hit the vest. The third time I jammed lower and harder. Skin and muscle yielded as I rammed the blade to the hilt. I twisted it ninety degrees and ripped the steel sideways. The fabric of his pants did not slow the slice of my blade through his intestines.

Nelson grunted and released my hand as he clutched his abdomen. In the moonlight the blood bubbling from his lips appeared black.

His knees crumpled like the air had escaped from a balloon. He collapsed in a heap and tumbled a half twist down the slope.

I flipped on the headlight and located his gun. I searched him for more weapons and found a knife strapped to his shin. I felt for a pulse, but I knew he was dead.

Emily's nightmare was over.

THIRTY

"Chuck? Is that you?" Emily peeked from behind a cedar tree.

"In the flesh. Your parents and I have been searching for you. Sorry I took so long."

"My feet are cut. I stepped on the rocks when I ran away."

I jumped to her side.

Emily wrapped her arms around my neck and crushed me with a hug so fierce I had trouble breathing. She sobbed and shivered, but it wasn't from the cool night air. We stood there in the wilderness while the clouds scudded across the moon. I held her gently and patted her shoulder until she finished bawling.

She loosened her grip on my neck and sniffed. "Do you have a Kleenex?"

"In my pocket."

She sniffed again. "Good." She released my neck. "Better give me two."

I did and she blew her nose.

"Hand me the used one. I'll stick it in my pocket."

"*Eww.* I wouldn't do that to you. That's gross." She blew her nose again.

"No trash cans out here." I stuck out my hand. "Give."

She did.

"I have more if you need them."

Emily stared at me. "What's that thing on your head?"

"It's a headlamp." I turned it on. "This will light our way back to the house."

"Where are Mom and Dad?"

"At home waiting for you to call and tell them you're safe."

"Let's call now."

"We're in the Burnet County boondocks. No cellphone signal. We'll go back to the house and drive to the highway. Then we'll call. I sometimes doubted you were alive, but Aunt Carrie never lost faith that we'd find you."

"I'm barefoot. You'll need to carry me piggy-back like you did when I was little."

I squatted down and repeated familiar words from years ago. "All aboard the McCrary Express."

As I picked my way back to the house, Emily kept shivering.

"Why am I shaking so bad, Chuck? It's not that cold."

"Adrenaline. Relief. Exhaustion," I answered. "Take your pick. It happens to me too. It's an after-action effect. Just remember that you're safe now. You're safe, and I'll have you home before dawn. You can sleep in your own bed. Your parents left your room just as it was. They had faith you would come home."

She laid her head on the back of my shoulder. By the time we reached the meadow behind the barn, my shoulder was damp from her tears.

I heard engines in the distance. "That's the cavalry."

"Who?"

"An Austin police detective, Nora Goodman, who was assigned your case. Also, two operatives I brought from Port City and some Burnet County deputies. It will take them a few minutes to get here. That road is rough going. They waited at the south entrance to the ranch. Nelson and O'Doul fooled us when they came in from the north."

I climbed the porch steps so she could stand on her bare feet. I handed her more tissues. "Blow your nose. You can wash your face in the kitchen."

Emily grabbed my hand as we climbed the steps. She didn't release it until she stood at the sink.

After she washed her face and hands, I handed her a towel.

"Ask Felicity to come out to the back porch. Tell her it's over and she's safe too. I'll meet Detective Goodman and the others."

As I trotted around the house to the main trail, Snoop's Jeep reached the bottom of the slope. Goodman's unmarked car followed, trailed by two patrol cars from the Burnet County Sheriff's office. No sirens but their red and blue lights flashed.

Snoop lowered the window. "Nelson and O'Doul never showed. Gunner and I figured we should search the house since we're already here. Nora Goodman and the deputies are behind me. What happened?"

"The girls are safe. Nelson and O'Doul are dead."

"How did we miss them? Did they get here first?"

"No. They came in the back way."

"What back way?"

I shrugged. "I'll tell everybody at once. Let's gather near the back porch. The entire house is a crime scene."

———

Detective Goodman drove Felicity Taylor straight home to Llano to reunite the frightened girl with her family ASAP. Goodman told me she would return the next day to take Felicity's statement. "Tonight should be for homecoming; tomorrow for tidying up loose ends," was the way she put it.

Good idea.

The Burnet County deputies agreed to secure the ranch house until the Austin CSIs arrived. Burnet County used the Austin Police Crime Lab like Blanco County did. Small world.

Emily sat at the top of the porch steps with her arms around her knees, still shivering. She had managed to find a pair of men's shoes upstairs that she could wear.

I draped my jacket over her shoulders. "If you'll wait here, Emily, I'll get our transportation."

Walking to the barn to retrieve my Jeep, I remembered Nelson and

O'Doul had blocked the door with their SUV. When I shot out its radiator and tires, I trapped my Jeep inside. No biggie. The next day the CSI techs would tow the Suburban and the Honda. Then I would send Snoop and Gunner to fetch my Jeep.

That was okay. Snoop's Cherokee had room. Emily piled in back with me. Gunner drove while Snoop rode shotgun. As soon as we located a cell signal, I called Carrie and Frank's landline. When it began to ring, I put the phone on speaker and handed it to Emily.

Carrie answered. "Chuck, is there any word on Emily?"

"Mom?"

"Emily, is that you?"

Both her parents burst into tears. I felt misty-eyed myself.

Emily and her parents talked the whole way back.

The next day all my aunts, uncles, cousins, in-laws, etc. arrived at Carrie and Frank's house—and Emily's home again—for a huge reception and "Welcome Home" party.

Emily forced a smile and a hug for everyone, but I could tell her heart wasn't in it. She seemed overwhelmed by all the people and noise. Understandable; she had been in isolation for four years except for her two captors.

I stayed close to her side but in the background for the first hour. When anyone called me a hero, I gave them my best *Aw-shucks* attitude and reminded them that Emily was the real hero.

After the receiving line thinned, I ducked out. It was Emily's party, not mine.

O'Doul's house was encircled with familiar yellow crime scene tape. Sergeant Will Chasen was on duty to keep the public out.

"Carlos McCrary, right? You're the guy who started this whole thing with the welfare check at Harry Nelson's house."

"Call me Chuck."

We shook hands.

"Is Detective Ortega inside? I'd like to talk to him."

Chasen thumbed his radio. "Detective? Chuck McCrary is here."

He listened then disconnected. "Ortega's upstairs. Put on booties on the front porch. They're collecting evidence."

Ortega was in the master bedroom. "How's Emily?"

"She seemed overwhelmed by all the family that showed up to her welcome home party. Some of Uncle Frank's side of the family flew all the way from Denver."

"I've seen that reaction before from long-term missing persons victims. She'll need a lot of therapy."

"A lot of therapy" sounded like a long time. Some guys from the Triple Seven still battled post-traumatic stress disorder years after they returned stateside.

Ortega thumbed over his shoulder. "We found an M16 in that closet that was fired recently and not cleaned. I'd bet it's the one that fired those three shots at you." He gestured at the wooden shelves against the bedroom wall. "O'Doul kept a video collection like Nelson. We've watched a couple but they were made in different rooms than Nelson's videos. O'Doul recorded them himself in his own attic."

He pointed at the ceiling. "We found two rooms for captives up there. The CSIs don't think the rooms have been used for years. You remember the extra sets of fingerprints we found on those two DVDs you gave Detective Goodman?"

"Yeah. She said they weren't usable."

"We managed to identify them. The unknown prints were Jerry O'Doul's and Desmond Drucker's."

"Nelson must have loaned the disks to them," I said.

"Watching these videos, we suspect O'Doul and Nelson swapped captives like trading cards until a few years ago. We don't know what Drucker's involvement is yet, but we intend to find out."

"Why did O'Doul and Nelson stop swapping girls?"

"Maybe it was too difficult to make the switches without the neighbors noticing? Maybe Drucker had something to do with it. Who knows? We're still investigating."

"Where is O'Doul's mother?"

"Three women from the church picked her up," Ortega said. "A judge appointed an attorney from Mrs. O'Doul's church as her guardian *ad litem* until Jerry O'Doul's estate settles. The poor old lady doesn't have any other family."

"The church will be her family. Fortunately, there's enough money in Jerusha's and Jerry's estates to care for her indefinitely."

———

Ruby Voight answered my call on the first ring. "Your two weeks aren't up yet. You get three more brownie points for calling me early. You now have enough brownie points to redeem for a backrub. The TV news said you rescued your cousin and another other."

"Yeah. Why don't I tell you all about it over dinner? What's your favorite place to celebrate?"

"Bernard's American Bistro. Give me twenty minutes to put my face on again. Order me a Pinot Grigio if you beat me there."

I did beat her there and her Pinot Grigio arrived about a minute before she did.

She lifted the goblet. "What shall we drink to?"

I raised my mug of Lone Star. "To Emily's freedom after four years gone."

We clinked and sipped.

Ruby set her glass down, gave me an expression I couldn't read, and grabbed my hand. "You don't realize it, cowboy, but Emily isn't free yet. She might never be."

First Ortega and now Ruby. Finding Emily and bringing her home wasn't enough. Emily had a long road to travel. "Ortega said something similar."

"This isn't about just the captivity, although that's bad enough. It's about rape and domination and humiliation. Emily's body is free, but part of her mind is still captive. Every time she sees Nelson's house across the street, she'll relive the terror. Every time one of her friends starts to say something and then stops—afraid to offend her—she'll wonder what they were thinking. Every time a man asks her for a date, she'll wonder if he knows. And if he does know, does he intend to rape her too?"

I didn't know what to say to that so I just squeezed her hand.

"It's every woman's secret fear, but it actually happened to Emily—not just once, but repeatedly over more than four years. It's not easy coming back from just one rape. I can hardly imagine what it would be like for it go on and on for years on end. And at the hands of more than one rapist."

Ruby's eyes stared somewhere over my shoulder, but I don't think she was seeing anything in the restaurant. Her focus seemed far away.

I squeezed her hand again.

She switched her focus to me. "You may have guessed the rest. I was raped three years ago."

"I'm so sorry."

"After rape counseling and a couple of years of therapy, I'm about ninety percent okay now."

She sipped her wine. "And—as you know—I can enjoy a normal sexual relationship with a man once more."

I lifted my mug in a toast. "And I'm very glad about that."

When we finished our dessert, Ruby pushed her empty plate aside. "You didn't ask what happened to the rapist."

"I didn't want to pry."

"He's in Huntsville, serving twenty years to life. My therapist said that testifying against him in court was part of my healing process. She was right. It felt like getting back at the bastard. I pointed right at him in the courtroom and said, 'That's the son of a bitch right there.'" She grinned.

"I'm glad to hear that."

"Of course, Emily won't have the opportunity to testify, but there's nothing to be done about that."

"Neither man would surrender."

"I know. I read the transcript of your statement to the police."

She picked up her purse. "Let's continue the celebration at my place."

"Maybe I can redeem my brownie points for that backrub."

"As long as it's followed by a front rub."

———

The CSIs found all of Nelson's DVDs and VHS cassettes in the ranch house. Using both kidnappers' videos, Goodman and Ortega identified the other four missing girls, plus four more that O'Doul had imprisoned in his attic. It took two weeks, but they located the graves for all five of

Nelson's murder victims and all four of O'Doul's victims on the Perkins Ranch.

Jerry O'Doul had graduated from Burnet High School, and he knew the swimming hole on the Perkins Ranch from his school days. That's why he and Nelson buried the girls there. The Perkins family never had a clue that the isolated mesa was a dumping sight for murdered girls who never survived their twenty-first birthdays.

As far as I know, Ling Cheng's parents were never heard from again. The People's Paradise has no "due process" or "Freedom of Information Act." Carrie and Frank paid for her funeral. The entire student body and parents from Bonham High came to her memorial service. The Bonham Bobcats girls' basketball team announced they would wear the Chinese characters for Ling Cheng's name on their jerseys the next season to honor her.

Desmond Drucker's fingerprints matched the extra set on Nelson's DVDs. He was charged as an accessory to kidnapping. The search warrant for his house and computer found child pornography on his computer, and he pled guilty to both crimes. He was killed by inmates in prison, but that was over a year later.

Nelson died with no will. The attorney appointed to handle his estate located four cousins in Denmark. They sold the house.

Life would never be the same for the Crazinskis, but we had the biggest Thanksgiving crowd the family had ever put together in Adams Creek, and again the next day in Austin.

THIRTY-ONE

M y cellphone played *The Eyes of Texas*. It was the week before Christmas in Port City. Actually, it was the week before Christmas everywhere, but I was back home in Port City so that was my point of reference.

I answered as a video call. "Merry Christmas, Aunt Carrie."

She wore the big gold earrings Emily had given her for her birthday two weeks after the rescue. "How are things in sunny South Florida, nephew?"

"Fine, Aunt Carrie. It's eighty degrees outside and partly cloudy on Port City Beach. I'll show you." Swiveling my chair, I aimed my phone outside. "See the sailboats on Seeti Bay? And here..." I swung toward the ocean. "A beautiful day at the beach."

"It's thirty degrees and sleeting in Austin."

"That's why I live in Florida."

"It's nine o'clock in Florida. Why haven't you left for work?"

"I'm working from home today. And it's eleven o'clock. We're an hour ahead of Texas—not one hour behind."

Carrie made a dismissive gesture. "These time zone thingies always confuse me."

Time zones and other things, I thought.

"Eleven o'clock is worse. Why aren't you at your office, or else stalking some unfortunate woman's wayward husband with a telescopic camera?"

"I told you I'm working at home today. How is Emily? I've been meaning to call her, but I'm still catching up on my work from when I was in Austin."

Carrie twisted her mouth like she was tasting something bitter. "A lot has happened since Thanksgiving—none of it good."

"What happened?"

"Every time Emily sees Harry Nelson's house across the street, it dredges up bad memories and she starts to cry. We put our house on the market. We're moving to Round Rock."

"You think that will help?"

"Her therapist says a change in environment will help her heal."

"How's the therapy going?"

Carrie waggled her hand. "She's getting better, but it's slow."

"What about school?" I asked.

"She enrolled in Bonham High, but she dropped out. She's four years older than the other students and all her friends have graduated. Plus, she's a distraction in every class because the whole school knows her history. The Monday after Thanksgiving, she refused to go back."

"What about private tutoring?"

"That's what we're doing. Her tutor says she's so smart that she'll be ready to take the GED by this summer."

"Does she plan to start college next fall?"

Carrie's eyes twinkled. "That's the one thing that's gone right since Thanksgiving. Can you keep a secret?"

"Of course."

"You should act surprised when Emily tells you. Can you act surprised?"

"I believe so, Aunt Carrie."

"Emily told Frank and me that she wants to attend the University of Florida just like you did. Her therapist says it will be good for her to go someplace where nothing will remind her of the kidnapping. She intends to study criminal justice and become a cop. She wants to tell you herself at Christmas. You're coming to Adams Creek for Christmas, right?"

"I wouldn't miss it. It'll be great to see Emily again—and you and Frank, of course."

"Are you bringing that girlfriend you mentioned, Terry Something-or-other?"

"Kovacs. Her last name is Kovacs."

"Is she Polish or Hungarian or something?"

"She was born in Georgia. That is the American state of Georgia, not the *Republic* of Georgia in eastern Europe."

"There's a republic in Europe named after Georgia?"

Like I said, for a smart woman, Aunt Carrie gets confused, God love her.

"It's not important, Aunt Carrie. I'm not bringing Terry. We broke up."

"That might be a blessing in disguise. I don't want you tricked into marriage by a foreigner who pretends to love you until she becomes an American citizen, then divorces you."

"Terry is as American as you and Uncle Frank, but yes I am unattached again."

I didn't tell Carrie that Ruby planned to visit me in Florida before Christmas. Carrie would jibber-jabber about it all over town. I had even given Ruby her own ringtone on my phone, *The Yellow Rose of Texas*.

"You deserve a girl who loves you for the fine, brave young man that your parents raised. You should get married. Your parents want more grandchildren, you know."

Aunt Carrie never knew how to end a conversation. It was up to me.

"Yes, ma'am. Well, thanks for calling, and I look forward to seeing you and Frank and Emily at Christmas. Merry Christmas, Aunt Carrie."

"Merry Christmas, Chuck."

The end

DEBT OF HONOR
CARLOS MCCRARY PI, BOOK 9

I composed a text to Snoop and Angie:

Going in ten seconds.

I paused with my finger on the send button. The last dim light seeping from the lateral hallway went dark, and I sent the text.

The soft squeak of Pete's rubber soles on the tile floor grew louder. A scrape as he grazed a picture leaning against the wall. "Oh, shit," Pete said. The picture frame crashed to the floor and echoed in the corridor.

There went our stealth and surprise.

"Maybe they didn't hear the crash," Pete said.

I twisted the doorknob. "Too late now; we're committed."

Throwing the door open, I met three Chinese running down the aisle, guns drawn. The leader aimed his pistol. The two behind him fired without stopping.

A slug slammed my vest over my belly button, slowing my rush into the warehouse and knocking the breath from my lungs. It felt like I'd been kicked in the gut.

I couldn't return fire accurately because I didn't know where Gunner was. The punch to my gut didn't help either. I fired twice, aiming high enough not to hit anyone, good guy or bad guy. I pivoted and stumbled at a right angle down a side aisle, gasping for air. I slinked along the aisle, struggling to stand upright.

About the time I caught my breath, I reached the second side aisle, and two shots rang out. A bullet clanged on the shelf near my head and flashed a shower of sparks. I whirled and fired a three-shot burst. The shooter screamed, fell, and rolled out of sight.

I broke into a trot toward the far end of the aisle. A Chinese soldier leaped into view and fired a pistol. I returned fire. Two of the three rounds riddled his chest. I knelt to feel his pulse. Dead.

The warehouse echoed with shouts in Chinese and small arms fire.

I reached the rear of the warehouse. Amongst a scattering of tables and chairs, Gunner lay on the concrete, tied to an overturned chair. He was either dead or unconscious or playing possum. I hoped he was playing possum.

Another denim-jacketed shooter and a man in a black suit stood on either side, trying to haul Gunner's chair upright. Two hundred pounds of dead weight is hard to lift using one hand to hold a gun.

I aimed at the denim-clad gunman. One through the chest, and he fell backward, firing wildly.

The black-suited man shoved his pistol against Gunner's temple.

Black Suit and I stared at each other while the gunfire around us slowed, then stopped.

Hank rounded the far rack of shelves with his arm around the neck of another Chinese soldier. "I killed one, and this one surrendered."

Black Suit switched his focus to Hank Rodriguez, then back to me. Probably couldn't decide which of us was the bigger threat. "Stop where you are, or I will kill him," he shouted in good English.

Tank Tyler dragged another man in a gray suit around a corner. The man was limping from a bleeding leg wound. "There's another dead one at the back end of this aisle," Tank said.

Pete returned. "I shot a man dressed like that dead one," he said, pointing.

"Stop where you are," Black Suit repeated, "or this one is a dead man."

I motioned Tank, Hank, and Pete to stay where they were. "You guys stop, but keep that one covered."

I walked toward the man in the black suit. "What's your name?"

"You stop. I will kill him."

"I believe you." I stopped fifteen feet away. "That won't be necessary. I'm Chuck McCrary. What do I call you?"

Black Suit jammed his pistol into Gunner's throat.

I lifted my hand in a peaceful gesture. "Nobody else needs to die today. There's been enough killing for one day."

Black Suit gawked from one of us to another, calculating his chances of dodging our bullets. He arrived at the identical conclusion I did: He was thoroughly screwed. He placed his pistol on the floor and stepped away. "My name is Kang. I am a Chinese diplomat, with a diplomatic passport in my jacket pocket."

I glanced at Gunner's motionless body. A fist squeezed my heart. Best case, he was unconscious. Worst case, he was dead.

Kang straightened himself taller and smirked. "I have diplomatic immunity. You must allow me to call the Chinese Embassy. This is the law in the United States."

I stepped closer to Hang and smashed his smirk with the barrel of my rifle, knocking him further from Gunner.

"Too bad, Kang," I said. "I don't care about your diplomatic passport. We're not cops. We're private. And this isn't business; it's personal."

———

Available in Paperback and eBook from Your Favorite Bookstore or Online Retailer

ABOUT THE AUTHOR

Dallas Gorham's books combine murder, mystery, and general mayhem with a touch of humor—all done with a PG-13 rating. His Carlos McCrary, Private Investigator, Mystery Thriller Series can be read and enjoyed in any order.

Dallas writes in the mystery, thriller, and suspense genres. (Take your pick: His novels have all three elements) His stories will get your heart pounding and leave you wanting more. He writes to hit hard, have a good time, and leave as few grammar errors as possible (or is it "grammatical errors"? Hmm.)

In his previous life, Dallas worked as a shoe salesman, grocery store sacker, florist deliverer, auditor, management consultant, association executive, accountant, radio announcer, and a paid assassin for the Florida Board of Cosmetology. (He is lying about one of those jobs.) If you ask him about it, he will deny ever having worked as an auditor.

Dallas is a sixth-generation Texan and a proud Texas Longhorn, having earned a Bachelor of Business Administration at the University of Texas at Austin. He graduated in the top three-quarters of his class, maybe. He has also been known to lie about his class ranking.

Dallas, the writer, and his wife moved to Florida years ago to escape Dallas, the city, winters (Brrrr. Way too cold) and summers (Whew. Way too hot). Like his fictional hero, Chuck McCrary, he lives in Florida in a waterfront home where he and his wife watch the sunset over the lake most days. He is a member of Mystery Writers of America and the Florida Writers Association.

Dallas is frequent (but bad) golfer. He plays about once a week because that is all the abuse he can stand. One of his goals in life is to find more golf balls than he loses. He also is an accomplished liar (is this true?) and defender of down-trodden palm trees.

Dallas is married to his one-and-only wife who treats him far better than he deserves. They have two grown sons, of whom they are inordinately proud. They also have seven grandchildren who are the smartest, most handsome, and most beautiful grandchildren in the known universe. He and his wife spend waaaay too much money on their love of travel. They have visited all 50 states and over 90 foreign countries, the most recent of which was Indonesia, where their cruise ship stopped at Kuala Lumpur.

Dallas writes an occasional blog post at http://dallasgorham.com/blog that is sometimes funny, but not nearly as funny as he thinks.

If you have too much time on your hands, you can follow him at the following social media links:

<u>www.DallasGorham.com</u>

facebook.com/DallasGorham

twitter.com/DallasGorham